To Mikeie

Thank you so much for all of your support. I hope you enjoy Dashiel's story.

DOTZEMASTER: PHANTASM CREED

DOIZEMASTER
PHANTASM CREED

TONY M. QUINTANA

Crystal Carriage
PUBLISHING

First edition 2021
Tony M. Quintana asserts the moral right to be identified as the author of this work.

Cover artwork and design by Jeff Brown Graphics
Interior design by Liz Schreiter

Library of Congress Control Number: 2021910787
ISBN 978-1-7369340-0-5 (hardcover)
ISBN 978-1-7369340-1-2 (paperback)
ISBN 978-1-7369340-2-9 (ebook)

crystalcarriagepublishing.com

Crystal Carriage
PUBLISHING

TO MY PARENTS:

For all of their support and love. For raising me to believe that family is forever, dreams are beautiful, and hard work and a positive mind-set are key to making them come true.

Empire of Zaphyrelia

Goizza

Picarta

VICEROYALTY OF ARBERICE

Tadeos

Barcelle

Minka

Kerganium Mines

Myrtalo

CARMINE KINGDOM

Carbakiel

Nymphe

Azahar Forest

Azahar

Merchiant

CHAPTER I

FORBIDDEN DAYDREAM

Each morning, Azahar awoke with the rays of the sun, beautified through the barrier that bordered the town. The sunlight skimmed over the crystal waters of the lake, traversed the wooded paths among the tall, robust trees, and awakened the colors in everything it touched. The light of dawn finished its gentle sweep by resting upon the roofs of the centuries-old Azahar houses.

As it did every morning, the sunshine illuminated the windows of the parlor within one such house. The light danced impishly and landed on the face of a young man.

Dashiel panted as his sweaty fingers grappled with the copper doorknob that had guarded his father's den for countless years. It had become as green as the moss growing in the windowsills. Dashiel's frequent handling was to blame for such change.

The sweet aroma of sycamore filled his nostrils, bringing back memories: A sycamore door with a greening knob, illuminated by the morning light. A sickly child, whose parents had recently left for work, dragging his feet to the doorway of a forbidden room. Frightened by the possibility of his illness turning to death and haunted by the emptiness of his home, he found relief at the mere touch of the doorknob. He did not beg for more days as much as he did for a companion.

Dashiel did not see the door as a barrier to a forbidden room but as a charm. It guarded the Ermitage patriarch's study, which served as the resting place of objects that told his father's glorious but silent past. He had only been inside once or twice, but the items remained inside his mind. An outdated, shredded Zaphyrolean flag hung from a silver hanger, medals and ribbons shone through a thin layer of dust, and two dulled machetes awaited their owner inside a Chinese vase.

Dashiel wanted to know more about his father's past and the objects related to it, especially his most precious possession, a baton that hung above the fireplace, his trusty weapon from his time in the imperial army. Deep down, Dashiel knew it would never happen.

He closed his eyes. "Another day," he murmured, taking a big breath and releasing the doorknob.

He turned his sights to the cuckoo clock next to the door, which read ten after eight. He blinked out of his stupor. He was late for work.

Trying to fit an apple inside the tiny pocket of his vest, Dashiel opened the front door, allowing the sounds of Stamen Plaza and its people to seep into his house.

He glowered at his neighbors, who were well into the morning routine: leaving for work, kissing their spouses and children goodbye, selling, buying, and cleaning. The same old things they had done for years, waiting for a younger generation to take over and repeat the cycle.

Dashiel jumped down the steps and rushed onto a forest trail.

The safest way to traverse the forest in Azahar was by taking the paths that connected the town's four zones. Like all the others, the path that Dashiel took to work was lined on both sides with seemingly endless iron torches and numerous fenku trees. Centuries before, the generous Gailfaur had given the fenku to Azahar as a gift for the townspeople's faithfulness. The species was best known for the way each tree wove together its branches with other fenku to create a roof during intense weather. Because of their noble nature and mystical abilities, the fenku were considered sacred, and cutting them down was a severely punished crime. The Azahar had developed an intimate connection with the fenku, just as they had with the creatures of the forest.

Given the mild weather, only a few fenku intertwined their branches that morning. The others bloomed with flowers and fruit. The silky fenku leaves shone brightly in the sunlight, as if they were sewn with thousands of diamonds. For the most part, Dashiel had gotten used to everything in his daily life. Everything except the beauty of this sight, which inspired him. When he contemplated the palette that painted the forest, Dashiel sometimes wondered if the colors beyond Azahar were the same.

Dashiel arrived at the town's library, where he worked as an assistant.

He'd been assigned his job on his sixteenth birthday. Everyone in Azahar received a duty that contributed to the greater good of the community. Dashiel's mother taught at the school in Azahar. His father was the custodian priest, the person in charge of looking after Gailfaur and serving as an interpreter between the Azahar and their mythical caretaker. His work proved to be of vital importance.

Dashiel opened the door with caution so its bell would not give him away.

"There you are, you inefficient foozler!" a screechy voice greeted him. The musty walls rumbled, and dust fell off the ancient bookcases.

Old Timothy Astor, the owner of the library, was a disagreeable man in every single way possible. Bitter and ill-tempered, he lived a life of solitude, always perched on his tall, mahogany desk. Some rumors said that he was over two hundred years old. To tell the truth, they may have had a point. At times he seemed like a walking corpse, much more so than a typical man who was beyond retirement age.

"Good morning, Mr. Astor," Dashiel said with a nervous voice, putting a coarse working apron on.

"Shut your mouth and start on your chores!" Astor pointed at him with his trusty quill, his prune-like fingers twitching.

"Yes, sir." Dashiel picked a broom up off the creaky floor.

The broom was the only thing Dashiel liked in that place. When the owner was not around, the broom would become a bloodied sword or mystical staff.

"Sweep, dust, listen, and then get out," Old Astor growled. "And don't you dare touch my books."

Dashiel started on his tedious chores, while the repulsive man worked on his latest book, sitting high on his desk like a gargoyle.

They worked in silence for hours. Given the absence of any kind of sound, Dashiel could not help but daydream. It was a risky thing to do because Old Astor hated when Dashiel didn't pay attention to his commands. In the past, Dashiel's reverie had led to several whacks from the old man's cane. But, as usual, Dashiel was quite bored and could not help but zone out.

Daylight drained into dusk, and as soon as the hoarse words "Ermitage, scram!" rumbled from the direction of Old Astor's high desk, Dashiel took off his apron, hung it on a rusty hook, and scampered away from the library and its owner as quickly as he could.

His walk home took him past the lake, its water pink as a peach in the dying rays of the sun. In contrast, the trees surrounding the lake remained as green as ever, quivering in the spring breeze.

Dashiel arrived at the usual spot, close to the lakeshore, where his friends Grimley Deguiser and Donner Calla tossed pebbles into the lake.

"Took Old Astor long enough to let me go tonight," Dashiel said, sitting down next to his friends.

"It's all right," Grimley said, tossing another stone. "I still got some time before I have to leave."

The exhausted fishermen had already retired to their homes. Nobody was there except for the three friends and a herd of wild jukkes, Azahar's aquatic deer, who roamed the upper part of the lake.

Dashiel's attention shifted from his friends' conversation to the cry of the waterfalls that spilled into the seemingly bottomless lake. They were yet another reflection of Azahar's tranquility. Soft and lazy, the crystalline liquid traveled all the way from a spring in Gailfaur's sacred terrains to the rocky lake basin. It was the deity's gift to humans.

No one in Azahar knew how the spring had come to be or how its water traveled to the lake from the other side of the forest. Visiting Gailfaur's terrains, the haven for the deity and its creatures, was strictly prohibited. Dashiel and his friends had tried to sneak their way to the land, like every child had at a young age, but it was impossible. Neither the law nor the forest itself allowed it.

"I've got a surprise!" Grimley said, rifling through a burlap sack. He took out various wooden weapons. "I made these for us. We will train with them!"

"Train? For what?" Donner asked.

Dashiel looked at Donner, a confidence crossing his freckled features. "You've heard the stories. Outside is dangerous. We need to learn how to fight."

Donner leaned back onto the ground and put his arms behind his head, groaning.

"Not again."

Grimley stood up, now holding a lance that he'd made by combining three pieces of wood. "Dashiel Ermitage, I challenge you. Use as many weapons as you want. You don't stand a chance against me."

"Want to bet?" Dashiel sprung to his feet. "Bring it on!"

Dashiel looked at the ground, rummaging through Grimley's mountain of wooden weapons. There were all sorts of options, ranging from a slingshot to a mallet. While Dashiel was choosing his weapon, something caught his eye. A simple stick. Simple, but somehow gripping.

Dashiel shook off the odd sensation, grabbing an oak sword instead. He and Grimley readied themselves and took opposing positions, brandishing their weapons and waiting for Donner to reluctantly call a start to the duel. When it arrived, both boys leapt toward each other. Dashiel repeatedly swung the sword at his friend, but Grimley dodged each thrust with ease.

"Come on, Dashiel!" Grimley shouted. "Is that all you got?"

After toying with Dashiel for a while, Grimley disarmed him with his lance. Dashiel had to admit that his friend's gift for single combat was impressive. Without hesitation, Dashiel picked up the slingshot and a few pebbles from the ground. The second wave began.

Dashiel shot at Grimley, but his friend easily dodged the few rocks that came anywhere close to him. Grimley seemed to be invincible, no matter whether Dashiel used the wooden daggers, the mallet, or the second lance. He let Dashiel take his best shot and then disarmed him, showing off more of his skills each time. The mountain of wooden weapons had dwindled to the simple wooden stick that Dashiel had noticed earlier. Dashiel picked it up and pointed it at his friend. He stood in his defensive crouch, waiting for Grimley to attack.

"OK, that's it," Grimley said, throwing the spear to the ground. "I win."

"Not true," Dashiel said. "I can still beat you."

Unable to control himself, Grimley laughed. "You'll never beat me. And you'll definitely never beat me with a lousy stick."

Dashiel said nothing, waving the stick from one side to the other, imagining that he was fighting off a ferocious beast. Dashiel liked to train, but it was frustrating training against Grimley. His friend would always beat him—not just in combat but in pretty much everything else, too. Whether it was racing, swimming, school, or talking to girls, Grimley always came out on top, though Dashiel always kept trying.

"Maybe," he murmured, imagining Grimley's expression after a defeat. He tossed the stick into the pile of weapons that had failed to beat his friend during the duel. Grimley and Dashiel both sat next to Donner, who had observed their duel with casual interest. Dashiel silently began drawing something in the humid dirt with his finger, letting his imagination wander. He closed his eyes, breathing in the fresh smell of the soil.

"One day you'll be stronger, Dashiel," Grimley said, snapping Dashiel out of his reverie. "Both of us will be. And when that day comes, we will leave Azahar. We'll have real adventures, not fake ones like the tales in your book."

Dashiel thought of the book on his nightstand. It was old, and its weathered spine barely held its pages together. During most of his childhood, a disease had left him bedridden. Dashiel spent years confined and lonely in his house with only the characters of his book to keep him company. Those same heroes had inspired Dashiel and Grimley to have adventures.

A breeze created ripples on the surface of the lake, which now appeared a dull shade of orange. Fawn jukkes played and splashed in the water while running circles around their carefree mothers. Dashiel barely registered Grimley and Donner's conversation—something about Danille Larkspur, the prettiest girl in town. That particular topic of conversation usually would have piqued Dashiel's interest, as all Azahar boys were crazy for her, but his mind was elsewhere.

"We'll leave Azahar," Dashiel said faintly, sparking the previous conversation back to life. "One day."

Donner stretched his legs. "How would you leave? No one can leave the forest. Or even enter it." He huffed. "Thank goodness!"

"We'll find a way," Dashiel said.

"And we'll do it together," Grimley added, projecting a confidence that would inspire even the most skeptical person.

Dashiel leaned back on the ground, which was damp thanks to Azahar's springtime dew. The sun had set, and the sky had begun to fill with blinking lights. His mind wandered again, this time picturing the stick. Simple, broken, and incomplete as it may have been, Dashiel could not stop thinking about the underdog weapon.

"Did you guys hear about the sightings?" Grimley asked, his dark eyes sparkling with excitement. "A few lumberjacks saw imperialists at the outskirts of the forest."

Both Dashiel and Donner sat up straight. Donner wrapped his arms around his legs and buried half his face in his knees, while Dashiel, grin on his face, crawled closer. Grimley always knew everything that was going on inside and outside of Azahar. He had great knowledge of the empire and everything that revolved around it. Such insight was a rarity in Azahar. Ever since the town became isolated from the rest of the land, the forest's council had discouraged any talk about the empire because it thought the news would upset the town's frail equilibrium.

And, Dashiel thought, they wanted to discourage wanderlust. He and Grimley were not the only ones who wished to leave the forest.

To avoid unwanted problems, the townspeople were also prohibited from going to the edge of the barrier. The only citizens allowed at the edge were lumberjacks and botanists, who harvested the driest trees that grew there and planted saplings, respectively. Before he'd turned sixteen, Dashiel had wanted to be a lumberjack, to go to the edge of the barrier and catch a glimpse of the exterior.

"Are you serious?" Dashiel asked.

"Dead serious. And not only soldiers, but Ochre Brigadiers too," Grimley said, unable to hide his enthusiasm.

"You're always going on about the empire," said Donner, clenching his hands together.

"I swear it's true." Grimley patted his knees with both hands, eyes bulging.

"How would you know?" Dashiel gave his friend an inquisitive look.

"When I heard about them, I went to the edge, and I saw them with my own eyes."

"Do tell. How were they?" Dashiel's heart thundered with excitement.

Grimley stood up. "They're as tall as a tree and as big as a rhino. They're not fast, but they make up for it with elephant strength."

He mimicked the movements of the enemies.

"Their shiny bodies are blinding, and they have ghostly eyes and expressionless faces." Grimley took out his gold-studded pistol, which he'd received during his heirloom ceremony, and aimed it at one of the jukkes. "They wield cannon rifles that shoot bull's-eyes every time and enormous swords with the destructive power of a hundred fires." Grimley put his pistol away. "Their hands can lift a man and split him in half."

"Let's change the subject," Donner said, trying to conceal his fear and annoyance. "You guys shouldn't yearn for the Outerland's danger. Gailfaur could hear you and punish all of us by lifting the barrier."

Grimley seemed to realize that he had gone too far with his story and took a seat next to his frightened friend. "Don't worry, Donner. Gailfaur would never let harm come to us. But we need to be prepared if we want to survive out there."

"We're all safe." Dashiel patted Donner on the back. He frowned. "We're all trapped here . . ."

The three friends enjoyed the rest of the evening, sitting beside the lake until night covered the forest and the moon's rays took the place of the sun's.

Back at home, Dashiel called for his parents, but neither answered. The only sounds came from his father's study. His father was raising his voice as if he were in some kind of argument. Elias and Emily were no strangers to marital quarrels, because of their contrasting personalities, but they would never argue in the study.

Dashiel approached the study as other voices joined his father's, muffled behind the door. Holding his breath, he pressed his ear against the wood. Great was his surprise when the door slowly opened with a screech.

The glow of the fireplace illuminated the room, its books and Egadrisean knickknacks strewn all over the place. The fire's glow illuminated the gilded baton his father had hung on the wall, the possession he prized above all others.

The voices stopped.

His father sat at his desk, brows as arched as a bow, eyes as wide as the summer sky, and lips tighter than a knot. Next to Elias stood Dashiel's mother. There were two unfamiliar people in the corner. The man was big and muscular, with dark, tanned skin—a rather intimidating fellow. The woman standing next to the mountain of muscle was tall and slender, with a nose as long as a woodpecker's perch.

"Why, hello, honey!" Emily said, finally breaking the silence. As usual, her light brown hair was styled into two intricate pigtails, and her glasses were stained with the ink she had used to grade her students' homework. Her eyes moved toward her husband, who breathed with abnormal heaviness.

"Good evening, Son," Elias said coldly.

Elias had never been an affectionate type of father. He was distant and quiet, though Dashiel tried not to judge him for it. He knew the burden that his father carried on his shoulders. All Dashiel wanted was to make his father proud, but it seemed like an impossible task at times.

"Good evening, Papa, Mama," Dashiel said.

Elias stood from his chair. "Dashiel, let me introduce to you some good friends of mine." He stretched his arm toward the strangers in the corner. "This is Charlotte Malanks and Rupert Golk."

"It's a pleasure to finally meet Elias's son," said the long-nosed woman, grabbing Dashiel's hand. A faint smell of peach syrup flowed from her mouth.

"*Mil pleeser, lettei mer*," said the enormous man, smiling and displaying his sharp yellow teeth.

Dashiel did not fully understand what he had said but assumed that it meant "nice to meet you." Dashiel inclined his head.

Elias turned his attention to the small fireplace. Dashiel startled at the sight of a third stranger. The young man leaned against the fireplace, partially hidden in the shadows. His ebony hair shone like silk, sitting perfectly above his exquisite facial features.

"And this right here is Sylvain Aurante," said Elias, taking a seat.

The young man at the fireplace didn't do anything at first. He stood there with his eyes closed and his arms crossed, as if he were in some kind of trance. After a long moment, Sylvain opened his eyes, revealing irises the color of emeralds. When Dashiel met his gaze, time slowed and all sounds subsided. Dashiel's heart raced, and Sylvain's eyes glistened.

Neither of them said a word. Sylvain broke eye contact and inclined his head. He then closed his eyes and returned to his meditative state.

Dashiel inclined his head, returning the greeting though Sylvain would no longer see it.

"Well, Son, we were in the middle of something, so if you may," said Elias with a serious expression on his face.

"Of course," Dashiel said, his downcast eyes spilling, disappointed at having to leave.

"Good night, Eli," Emily said. Her words—and the nickname— soothed Dashiel's mood.

Dashiel inclined his head once more to say goodbye to his new acquaintances. He left the study and closed the door behind him. When he reached the stairs, the mumbling began once again.

Tired from the day, Dashiel immediately lay down on his bed. For a moment, he was tempted to read a bit of his book, but exhaustion got the best of him. The only thing he could do before inevitably falling asleep was think about his day: his boring job, his practice with Grimley, and the terrible Ochre Brigadiers.

He then thought about his parents' friends downstairs. They were interesting, yet odd, especially Sylvain. Dashiel couldn't recall the last time he'd met someone new—it had been years because everyone in Azahar knew one another. The questions brewing behind his eyes would remain unanswered. Knowing his father, inquiries about the visitors would be far from welcome. The soothing chirp of crickets lulled him to sleep and disintegrated all ideas.

CHAPTER 2

PIERCING URGE

The breezy spring days passed by rather quickly, and the end of the month was fast approaching. Dashiel spent yet another day sweeping the creaky hallways in Astor's library. The dust seemed endless in that old place. Just when he thought he had cleaned it all, he would return the next day to a layer of dust and spiderwebs.

Today, the old man sat in his customary position at his elevated desk, reviewing pages from a tall pile of papers and pasting them into an old book. His crooked, crusty cane hung on a perch next to him, ready to either hurt the library assistant or help the old man walk.

For some reason, Dashiel didn't feel the need to zone out that morning. He had things on his mind that could surely help him reach his typical pensive state, but he did not feel like it. For the first time since he'd started this job, he didn't mind his tedious activities. He focused on getting rid of the obnoxious sea of dust ahead of him.

Not long after Dashiel began dusting, Grimley crashed through the library's door, throwing the dull, peaceful environment into chaos. Dust particles flew from the unreachable parts of the shelves and fell all over the place like snow. The perfectly aligned pile of papers sitting on the old man's desk fell to the floor. Astor frowned and screeched like an old owl.

"What is the meaning of this?" Astor fisted the table with his long, bony fingers. His voice echoed off the library's ancient wooden walls.

"Dashiel, something's happened," Grimley said, impassioned and out of breath. "You've got to see it."

"My assistant has no business with you," Astor said. "Now, get out this very instant!"

The old man stood up and began stacking the few papers that had remained on top of his desk.

"Ermitage! Clean up this mess."

"Yes, Mr. Astor." Dashiel looked back at his boss, who grumbled and cursed. He turned to Grimley and in a low voice asked, "What's going on?"

"No time to explain. Come with me," Grimley said.

"You know I can't leave," whispered Dashiel.

"Meet me at the edge," Grimley whispered before running full speed back through the library doors.

"Ermitage!" Astor screeched without pulling his attention from the mess. He arranged the fallen papers, completely engrossed in the task.

Dashiel placed the broom next to the doorframe with the utmost silence and tiptoed out of the small building. As he put more distance between himself and the library, he knew he would regret what he was doing. But going to the edge was worth it.

Grimley ran faster than a deer, but Dashiel managed to catch up with him as he headed south along the town's footpaths. At first, the paths were clear, with no one in sight. But as they got closer to the edge, more and more citizens began to appear, all going in the same direction.

The edge had as many trees as the rest of Azahar, but the landscape changed drastically at the barrier. Beyond its bounds, there were fewer trees, and the paths that used to connect Azahar with the rest of the country rose from the mossy, leaf-strewn ground. For Dashiel, the land beyond the barrier was breathtaking. The fields and the hills extended for miles, meeting the sky at the horizon.

The barrier's edge became crowded with other Azahar, most of them lumberjacks, all murmuring about whatever had happened there.

"Don't touch it!" a man yelled from the crowd.

Dashiel could not believe his eyes when he followed the man's gaze to a green crack, seemingly in midair, right where the barrier was supposed to be. Right next to it, the worn blade of a colossal sword rested half buried in the ground. The weapon glowed a dull red, and smoke helixed skyward off it.

The crack in the barrier discharged green sparks as it slowly welded itself back together. Everything within a five-foot radius of the sword had been burnt to a crisp, and some of the trees around it had been damaged or even splintered. Dashiel looked around to see if there was anything else going on, but the only thing that drew his attention was Sylvain Aurante standing in the middle of the crowd, staring directly at the crack in the barrier. In the days since Dashiel had met Sylvain and his companions, he'd seen the mysterious young man walking freely through town as if he were a local. An indescribable feeling traveled his body every time their eyes met.

"Dashiel," Grimley called, interrupting the brief reverie. "No one saw who did this. It must have happened in the middle of the night."

"A sword as destructive as a hundred fires," Dashiel murmured to Grimley. He turned to his friend. "Do you think it's them?"

"If it is true, Azahar is in serious trouble." For the first time in a long time, Grimley seemed worried.

In the middle of the tumult, three Olivine Berets arrived, wielding silver lances and wearing their green uniforms, berets, and armor. Everyone moved aside, allowing them access to the barrier.

Being an Olivine Beret—or an Azahar guard—was one of the most difficult jobs to attain. Only a chosen few were worthy of wearing the uniform. On rare occasions, some Azahar youths who demonstrated potential were offered a choice between the guard and another job.

This was the case with Grimley, who'd been allowed to choose between becoming an Azahar guard or a torch keeper. Although Grimley's choice had seemed obvious—the guard was highly regarded and respected—he'd decided to become a torch keeper without hesitation. Dashiel couldn't understand why Grimley had turned down the chance to become an Olivine Beret.

One of the guards waded into the crowd and stopped in front of the sword.

"Mayor Lilac and the council have called an emergency meeting in front of the Council House," the man said in a strong and clear voice. "You are also hereby informed that the edge of the forest is a restricted area for everyone, without exception, until further notice." The other guardsmen took up positions beside the sword and shepherded everyone deeper into the woods.

"Let's go," Grimley said, returning to the path.

Dashiel took another look around, searching for Sylvain, but he was gone.

With a sigh, he turned back to the path. Above, the leaves fluttered in the wind. The breeze carried nine luciums toward the accident. The nymph spirits inhabited the sacred terrains and served Gailfaur, assisting the centaur deity by taking care of his barrier and creatures. They commonly roamed around, but the presence of so many of them together meant that the damage had been significant. The guards had left with the townspeople, leaving the luciums to do their job.

Dashiel took one last look at the barrier. The sword had turned grayer, but it still gave off overwhelming heat. Without a backward glance, he joined Grimley on the path to the Council House.

Unlike the other plazas, Pistil Plaza—or the main plaza—was the largest, contained the most important buildings, and was always bustling with people going about their daily business. There, at the foot of the Council House's staircase, everyone waited for the mayor and the council members. A palpable anxious energy spread in the air. The murmuring crowd fell into a hush the instant the mayor came out of the building. The council followed closely behind.

Dashiel and Grimley met up with Donner, who still had his shepherd's hook on him. "Why do you think they want us here?" Donner asked.

"The barrier has been damaged," Dashiel answered. Donner gasped, launching into a question that cut short when the mayor's voice boomed through the plaza.

"My dear people," the mayor said. The crowd filled with an anticipatory silence. "I fear that I have bad news to share with you. Yesterday, two imperial enemies managed to enter the forest." The murmuring grew among the frightened townspeople. "No one has seen the intruders, and we thought it was a false alarm, but there have been some incidents that have confirmed our fears."

The crowd began to whip itself into a frenzy.

"How is this possible?" a man behind Dashiel shouted.

"Is it true that the barrier was pierced?" demanded a merchant woman.

"Who would do something like that?" another man asked.

The mayor raised his hands, an attempt to stem the chaos and fear that had set in among the people. "We aren't sure how it happened. The enemies were able to penetrate the barrier late at night, and we fear that they might be what the Outerland calls Ochre Brigadiers."

"How did you let this happen?" demanded a miner, visibly exasperated.

"Is Gailfaur in danger?" another woman asked.

A lone man stepped out of the crowd and ascended the stairs. He was tall and well built, his hair and beard were scruffy, and he wore a white tunic and an olivine sash embroidered with runes, the characteristic garments of the deity's custodian and Olivine Beret mentor. Dashiel's father, Elias Ermitage, stood before the people.

"His Sereneship, Gailfaur, is in perfect health. He has told me personally," Elias said. "He has, in effect, felt the presence of unwanted visitors." Elias stood his ground on the steps as the crowd continued to grow louder. "We need to remain faithful. Both the council and Gailfaur are doing everything they can to protect us."

The matriarch of the merchants—who was Donner's mother—moved to the mayor's side. "While this incident is under further investigation, the council has decided to implement a few precautionary measures." She took out a piece of paper and read a prepared statement. "Everyone below the age of fifteen is to remain inside their houses until further notice. This means that school and other activities will be suspended."

Dashiel closed his eyes and inhaled deeply with relief. He would rather die than be trapped inside his house again.

"Hopefully this won't be necessary, but if the situation worsens, there might be a need to form a hunting party," she said.

People's murmurs grew louder. Grimley elbowed Dashiel with a smile on his face.

Donner's mother raised her voice over the buzz of the crowd. "Please know that the council has come to the conclusion that volunteers under eighteen will not be accepted. They are to finish their daily obligations during daylight hours and then return home."

Several youths shouted complaints about how unfair the rule was, Grimley among them.

"Complain all you want, but the decision is final. Anyone who breaks these rules shall be severely sanctioned by the council," said the mayor, temporarily putting an end to the grumbling. "Please comply with the new regulations and be cautious. I promise you that the intruders will be caught and dealt with soon enough. You may go now."

As the crowd began to disperse, Elias walked across the square toward Dashiel.

"You heard the rules?" he asked with his habitual cold tone.

"Yes, sir," Dashiel answered, looking directly into his father's gray eyes.

"Follow them." Elias broke eye contact, gaze settling on the forest. He walked past Dashiel and disappeared behind the tree line.

Grimley clasped both hands to Dashiel's shoulders and shook him.

"Eli, this is our chance," his friend said, as confident as ever. His eyes were full of fire. "Forget about the hunting party. Let's go find those stupid Brigadiers on our own. We'll be heroes! If we stop them, the council might allow us to visit the Outerland."

"You heard the council, Grim," Dashiel replied. "You heard my *father*. They'll punish us."

"Maybe, maybe not." Grimley snorted. "This is what we've been waiting for. This is what we've always wanted. This is *everything* we talk about. Now's our chance to have an adventure together. A real, live adventure."

"You're right," Dashiel said. "We've always wanted an opportunity to prove ourselves worthy and leave. But this is different. We're not ready. How are we going to fight against their weapons? With wooden swords?"

"I have my pistol, and you . . ." Grimley wrapped a hand around his chin and drummed his thumb against his bottom lip.

"What?" Dashiel said sternly. "A lousy stick?"

"You could use your father's baton."

Dashiel scoffed. "You know I can't take that. If I stole it, my father would skin me alive."

"I can't believe this," Grimley said, a bite to his words. "We might not ever get a chance like this again. And we're not even brave enough to take it?" He shook his head, letting go of Dashiel. "If you aren't cut out for this, I'll do it by myself."

"You can't do this," Dashiel said. "Those Brigadiers will chop your head off in a second."

"I'm stronger than those idiots." Grimley pointed his trembling finger at Dashiel. "Just like I'm stronger than you."

"Grimley, you can't. That's suicide. Please don't."

"If both of us went, it wouldn't be." Grimley was starting to deflate slightly.

"For our friendship," Dashiel said, seriousness in his eyes, "promise me you won't do it."

Grimley tried to dissuade him with his stare, but Dashiel did not change his mind.

"Fine." Grimley stomped away without saying another word.

Relief flooded Dashiel; his friend wouldn't expose himself to such danger. For all of Grimley's bluster and talent, the two of them didn't stand a chance against a single Ochre Brigadier. Dashiel's relief was short lived as he felt a familiar whack on the back of his head.

"Playtime's over, Ermitage," Astor snarled. He grabbed Dashiel's shirt collar and pulled the boy to within inches of his face. "If you ever desert your duties like that again, you'll wish you'd never been born, understood? Back to work!"

Astor grabbed Dashiel by the ear and pulled him all the way back to the library, refusing to let go. Dashiel shrieked in pain during the entire trip. He felt like Astor was going to tear his ear off, but the old man was too angry to listen to reason.

CHAPTER 3

THE BATON
AND
THE FLUTE

The following days brought plenty of uncertainty and fear to Azahar. Accidents had increased alarmingly, including damaged property, injured civilians, and even the death of a local fisherman. Everyone was certain of who was responsible. The Brigadiers were striking, though they left no trace.

After the fisherman died at the hands of the soldiers, the mayor called for an emergency hunting party, and most of the adults in Azahar agreed to join. Several times they tried to find the Brigadiers, but all attempts ended in failure. Fearing more deaths, the council reduced working hours for the entire town. Everyone finished their duties by midday and returned home immediately.

On one particular day, Astor did not allow Dashiel to leave by curfew, punishing him for deserting his duty when Grimley came to get him. When the old man finally dismissed Dashiel, the sunset had already rendered the treetops a dull orange and the torch keepers had already lit the torches.

He began his walk through the solitary paths, letting his mind unwind as the torches kept him warm and cozy. The fenku leaves glistened like stars. The night sounds of the forest blended into a symphony. The sisyphus wolves howled, the jukkes splashed in the nearby river, and the lion-tailed elves and gnomes, though hidden, played their instruments to the moon.

A scream rang out, shattering the tranquility of Dashiel's walk. The woods rang with another scream, and then another. The sound became stronger and clearer. It was Donner.

"Help! Somebody! *Please!*" His friend's alarmed voice echoed through the trees.

A shiver ran down Dashiel's spine, quickly followed by an intense burst of adrenaline. Without a second thought, Dashiel took off into the woods, weaving between the trees, homing in on Donner's screams.

Dashiel found his friend lying on the mossy, leafy ground. A fenku had fallen on Donner, trapping his leg.

"Here you are!" Dashiel ran to his friend. "How did this happen?"

"Dashiel, thank Providence you came," Donner cried, voice laced with pain. He tried to wiggle his way out from under the tree, to no avail. "They were huge! They were dreadful!"

"Who?" Without pausing, Dashiel crouched and attempted to lift the trunk. It rose a couple of inches, but it was too heavy. Dashiel let go of the tree, which dropped onto Donner's leg again. He let out a piercing shriek.

"Sorry!" Dashiel said, standing up and trying to remain calm. "We need to get you out of here."

"Hurry up! I can't feel my leg." Tears ran down Donner's cheeks.

"On the count of three, I'll lift the tree," Dashiel said, crouching once more beside the heavy trunk. "When I say *three*, do everything you can to move out from under it. Got it?"

Donner nodded.

"One . . . two . . . *three!*" Dashiel summoned all his strength to lift the tree a bit higher than he had before. Using his arms, Donner crawled out from beneath the tree, and just in time. The trunk slipped from Dashiel's grasp.

"Let's get you to my house," Dashiel said, inspecting Donner's right leg. It looked severely wounded, spilling blood all over the place. "My mother will know how to treat you." He put his friend's arm around his neck and slowly lifted him up from the dirt.

"Careful!" Donner wailed, trying to stand on his left leg, which had only suffered a few scratches. Together they hobbled toward the plaza. "What happened?" Dashiel asked. "Who did this to you?"

"I met up with Grimley right after he finished lighting the torches. One minute we were alone, and the next we were face-to-face with them."

"Who are you talking about? The imperialists?"

Donner was fading fast, on the edge of passing out. He grew heavier in Dashiel's arms, no longer able to walk. His eyes fluttered closed, and he struggled to speak above a whisper. "The . . . Ochre . . . Brigadiers."

Dashiel had feared this answer. "And Grimley? Where is he?"

He shook his friend. There was no answer.

"Donner, please. Donner! Where's Grimley?"

It was no use. Donner had fainted.

Dashiel needed to get his friend home as soon as possible. Using all his strength, he adjusted his grip on Donner and dragged him along the paths.

Stamen Plaza was deserted and dark when they arrived. Dashiel yelled for help, but nobody answered, for everyone must have been asleep by that time. The only source of light came from the Ermitage house. Dashiel hurried, gathering his strength to carry his friend through the vegetable patch in front of the house. He struggled through the front door, finding some of the candles lit. But nobody was home.

He gently lowered his friend to the floor and began cleaning his face with a dusty rag that he always kept in his pocket.

"Donner. Wake up!" he called, but his friend remained motionless on the ground. Dashiel looked at the wound, which continued to spill blood over the floor.

He hurried to the kitchen, wet some rags, and placed them in a bowl. Adrenaline raced through his body. His heart shook as if it were going to burst out of his chest. He needed to keep calm. If he did not, there would be grave consequences for Donner.

When Dashiel was little, his mother taught him how to treat some wounds. No one had ever shown him how to cure a wound this severe, but he had to try. He flung open the kitchen cupboard, which was full of jars that housed a variety of liquids and solids. Dashiel read each label as fast as he could until he found the one he was looking for: sisyphus wolf saliva. Without hesitation, Dashiel grabbed the jar, opened it, and spilled its contents onto the pile of wet rags.

The murky and viscous saliva had little pieces of decaying meat in it. Dashiel's stomach turned at the sight of it, but sisyphus wolf saliva had extraordinary healing properties, and it was the best chance they had. Dashiel grabbed the rags and returned to his friend.

Struck by the severity of the task ahead, Dashiel took one last shot at finding some help. He poked his head out the front door. "Anyone! Someone's hurt!"

Like last time he'd cried for help, there was no response.

With no hope of finding help, Dashiel knelt beside his friend. He spread out the rags, covering the deep wound on Donner's leg. The cloths turned red as they absorbed the blood. He could feel its warmth as he applied pressure to the wound.

"Who asked for help?" a voice rang from outside. A single light brightened as it approached the house. "Who?"

"Me! Ermitage! Come here, quickly!" Dashiel covered his friend's knee with another rag.

"What happened?" asked a hoarse, elderly voice as the light neared the door. A woman crossed the threshold. As she surveyed the scene, she mumbled, "Oh my."

Dashiel did not look up from his friend's wound. He recognized the voice. It belonged to Ramilda Begonia, his next-door neighbor and the wife of the lumberjack patriarch.

"Thank you for coming," Dashiel said, beads of cold sweat sliding down his back. "The Ochre Brigadiers threw a tree on top of him. His leg is in bad shape."

Ramilda placed the oil lamp she was carrying on the table next to the door and crouched next to Dashiel. The woman looked like a ghost, wearing a white robe over a white nightgown, her gray hair loose. Her face, normally a warm copper, was almost as pale as her clothing.

She took a moment to analyze the oozing wound. "It's fractured."

"Fractured? Are you sure?" Dashiel asked.

"Young Ermitage, my husband's had this exact injury about a hundred times. You really think I don't know what I'm talking about?" She huffed. "We'll need something to stop the bleeding. A tourniquet will do."

Dashiel grabbed the sleeve of his shirt and ripped it off. He kept tearing until he had a large bandage made of coarse beige fabric.

"Good thinking," Ramilda said, taking the fabric. She looped it around Donner's thigh and fastened it tightly. "This should stop the constant hemorrhaging."

"Where is everyone?" Dashiel asked, wiping the sweat from his brow with his bare arm. For the first time in almost an hour, he took a deep breath. His neighbor's oil lamp let off an ambrosial smell, which preyed on his nose.

"A couple of hours ago, those metal brutes brought down a whole building," Ramilda said, getting to her feet with difficulty. "The council assembled another hunting party to stop them once and for all."

She looked down at Donner's motionless body. "We need to wake him up. Smelling salts might do the trick. I'll be right back. You stay here." The woman grabbed her lamp and hurried next door.

Moments after Ramilda left, Donner began to regain consciousness. Amid groans, he opened his eyes.

"Where . . . am I?" he asked, trying to sit up. Once more, Dashiel crouched next to his friend.

"My house," he said. "Don't move." Dashiel held a glass of water to his friend's lips, and Donner drank from it with difficulty.

"Is Grimley back too?" asked Donner, water dripping from his pale lips.

"Not yet. What happened?"

"I met up with Grimley in the woods on our way home. All of a sudden, two huge shadows cornered us," Donner said, grimacing. "We ran and hid, but they found me. One of them pulled an entire tree out of the ground. He swung it at me and hit me, and I went flying. Then he dropped it on me."

Dashiel moved a bit closer to his friend. "And Grimley? What happened with him?"

"He found me under the tree. He tried to help, but he couldn't move it. I thought we were done for, but for some reason, the Brigadiers ignored us and left." Donner rubbed his forehead. "Grimley took out his pistol and followed them deeper into the woods. They went north. Probably heading for Gailfaur's terrain. They're slow, but if they get there, the town is in trouble."

Donner tried to move his injured leg but couldn't manage it. His face was slicked with sweat, yet he shivered as if half frozen.

"I think they want to assassinate Gailfaur, and . . ."

"Without him, there's no barrier," Dashiel finished. It was clear what he needed to do. A burst of adrenaline coursed through his veins. "I'm going to go look for Grimley."

"Please don't," Donner begged. "You don't understand. The Brigadiers are bloodthirsty. They like making their victims suffer. The one who hit me with the tree was loving it."

"I'm not planning on fighting them," Dashiel said, getting to his feet. "I'm just going to find Grimley and bring him back."

He scoured the Ermitage residence for anything that he could use as a weapon. He searched the kitchen first, eventually grabbing a dull bread knife out of a drawer.

"Not a chance," Donner said as Dashiel stuck the knife into the pocket of his vest and headed toward the exit.

"I know, but there isn't anything—" An idea struck Dashiel. He knew what he could use to defend himself in the forest.

He ran to his father's study. The room was off-limits when his father wasn't home, but desperate times called for desperate measures. The flame in the fireplace flickered weakly, projecting a dim light. Directly above the fireplace sat a pair of glass hooks, and upon them hung a gold-and-silver baton with eagles on both its tips, their wings twisting into the baton's central grip. His father's precious and mysterious weapon, Orphée. All Dashiel knew about it was that his father had wielded it when he was a soldier many years ago.

Orphée had hung above Elias's fireplace ever since Dashiel could remember, proud and bright, never disturbed by its owner. Elias had categorically forbidden his son from touching the things in his study—above all, the baton. A lump grew in his throat at the mere notion of taking his father's most prized possession, but he had to do it. Otherwise Grimley would die.

Dashiel inched toward the baton. Though he was in a hurry to save Grimley, his feet would not allow him to move any faster. When he was finally face-to-face with Orphée, he grabbed the weapon. Dashiel's sweaty palms slid along its runic, metallic surface. After a deep breath, he removed the baton from its hooks. It was much lighter than it appeared, its colorful sheen gleaming in the dim glow cast by the fireplace.

Weapon in hand, Dashiel hurried toward the door. But another idea had him freezing in place. If he bumped into the Brigadiers, how would he let the hunting party know where the enemies were?

There was only one instrument in Azahar capable of making itself heard miles away, and it resided at the Ermitage house: Gailfaur's Flute, which Elias kept under lock and key.

"I've got a weapon," Dashiel called to Donner as he left the study and bounded up the stairs.

Donner sat up, grimacing in pain. He blinked in disbelief when his eyes locked on Orphée. "You're taking your father's baton? If the Brigadiers and wolves don't kill you, he definitely will!"

Dashiel entered his parents' bedroom and went straight for Elias's dresser, where his father kept the pan flute's case hidden. Using the kitchen knife that he had tucked into his vest pocket minutes earlier, Dashiel pried the lockbox open. There, on a bed of crushed velvet, sat Gailfaur's Flute, sparkling in the moonlight. For the Ermitage family, Gailfaur's Flute was Azahar's greatest treasure. Dashiel had always wondered if the flute was the family heirloom he would receive at his heirloom ceremony.

Made from marble and precious gems, it was the only instrument capable of summoning Azahar's deity, if properly played. Elias was the only man who knew how to use it, but surely it could help Dashiel alert the rest of the town to the Brigadiers' location. As prepared as he'd ever be to fight off two imperial enemies, Dashiel descended the staircase.

"This is insane, what you're about to do," Donner said. "I can't convince you not to go, can I?"

"No. I'll bring our friend back," Dashiel said, glancing at the forbidden tools he held in each hand. "Mrs. Begonia will be back soon. Don't go anywhere." He began to fill an old lamp with oil.

"Very funny . . ." Donner retorted, glancing at his destroyed, saliva-embalmed leg. "Good luck, Dashiel."

Dashiel left the safety of his home and hurried into the woods, lantern and baton in hand and flute hanging around his neck. Looking back, he saw Ramilda Begonia entering the Ermitage residence. A short-lived relief took over. Donner was in good hands. He would be fine. As he moved through the woods, Dashiel hoped that he and Grimley would be equally safe by the end of the night.

CHAPTER 4

THE AGONY OF A MOONLIT STROLL

Dashiel returned to the spot in the woods where he had found Donner. The toppled, bloodstained tree confirmed the location.

Night had fallen, and the forest seemed more ominous than ever. Still, Dashiel stood tall. He'd never given in to fear before. None of the Azahar had ever worried about an attack. The luciums, under Gailfaur's command, kept peace between humans, animals, and plants.

And yet the Brigadiers were here. Dashiel looked around at the carnage and the forest, and for a quick moment, he wished that someone from the town would show up and stop him. He searched for a light from the hunting party—any light—in the distance. The woods were dark, and he was alone.

Dashiel scoured the forest floor, hoping to find footprints or traces that would lead him in the right direction. Unfortunately, when the tree had fallen, it had strewn its silky leaves across the ground, covering everything like green snow.

A tremor beneath one of the leaf piles caught Dashiel off guard. He wouldn't normally fear the woods at night, but the situation made him feel uneasy. Dashiel peered closer and recognized what had startled him: a dying fenku branch, writhing on the ground, reaching for its fellow fenku for the last time. The Brigadiers hadn't stopped at attacking the people. They'd also killed the gentle trees that protected the Azahar like their children. Moved by this pitiful sight, Dashiel knelt in front of the fenku and placed his hand on the splintered trunk.

His hands moved up and down the warm surface until his fingers came across what he was looking for: fenku sap. The rainbow-colored fluid was sacred. It could only be used for two purposes: to crystallize and gift to Gailfaur or to ease the suffering of a dying fenku.

With sap running down the edges of his fingers, Dashiel drew a straight line on the bark. When he was done, Dashiel placed his hand on the branch as it expired.

"I'm so sorry," he murmured, his stomach turning hard as a rock. He had to keep going.

More determined than ever, Dashiel resumed his search for traces of Grimley or the Brigadiers. To his surprise, their trail appeared before him. The dying branch had cleared aside the leaves and laid bare a set of enormous footprints, which confirmed that the Ochre Brigadiers were headed north.

He followed the tracks until he came across the path to the lake. The trail of footprints split in two. One path veered toward the lake. The other led into the heart of the forest, which hid Gailfaur's clearing, the entrance to the sacred terrains. Dashiel walked until he reached the lake. Under the light of the full moon, it gave off an eerie vibe, almost as if wraiths had replaced the water or lurked beneath its surface. He moved along the trail, which continued all the way to the shore before drowning in the ghostly waters. If the Brigadiers were clever enough to walk in the shallow water to avoid leaving footprints, they were much smarter—and even more dangerous—than the Azahar had initially believed. It was no wonder the hunting party couldn't find them.

"Grimley!" Dashiel called, swinging his lantern from side to side. "Grimley!"

He tried again but received no response. Dashiel returned to the place where the trail of footprints forked. Discarding the possibility that the Brigadiers and his friend roamed the lake, he turned his eyes to the set of prints that led directly into the heart of the forest. Dashiel followed the footprints, unprepared for what lay ahead. The northern part of the woods was the densest and the darkest. Hundreds of fenku, their branches entwined, prevented all light from seeping in. This darkness served as the hallowed ground's first line of defense.

As Dashiel made his way deeper into the forest, the moonglow dissipated, leaving the oil lantern as his sole source of light. Pursuing the Brigadiers' tracks was impossible—the footprints blended with the dirt, grass, leaves, and branches—so Dashiel was forced to follow the path instead.

The silence in this particular part of the forest made Dashiel even more nervous. He thought once about turning back, but he couldn't. Grimley needed him.

The fenku grasped for him with their branches, undoubtedly trying to keep him away from their master's grounds. Dashiel moved quickly, evading their twisted claws. He was on edge, jumping at the slightest sound. It all seemed so hopeless: He had no idea how to use the baton or Gailfaur's Flute. If he couldn't figure it out, he would likely die.

A piercing scream broke the heavy silence, commanding all of Dashiel's attention. A chill ran down his back. The same scream pierced his eardrums yet again. This time, Dashiel recognized its owner: Grimley.

He couldn't see more than a few feet ahead, but Dashiel ran through the dense foliage, trying to home in on his friend's voice. He ran with no sense of direction, frequently bumping into trees. Relying on his lantern, Dashiel burst through a narrow gap in the fenku, finding himself in a dark, open space. Gailfaur's clearing. He took a few cautious paces forward, stepping on a golden pistol, which had shattered into pieces on the ground.

It was Grimley's family heirloom. He must have been near.

Grimley's screams—and all other sounds—were absent from the clearing. With a trembling hand, Dashiel steeled himself and swung his lantern to the right, illuminating the trees at the edge of the clearing. Still nothing. He swung his lantern to the left. To his surprise, the lantern illuminated his friend, standing right in front of him, pale as milk.

"Dashiel! What are you doing here?" Grimley whispered, eyes wide with concern.

"Where are they?" Dashiel whispered back. "Where did the Brigadiers go?"

"Dashiel, you must go back." Grimley pushed his friend back from whence he came. "I was wrong; they're too strong. They could hurt you."

Dashiel swung his lantern from one side to the other. "Where are they?"

"You've got to leave." Grimley kept on pushing.

"Where?!"

Grimley pointed to the other side of the clearing.

"Right there . . ."

A pair of deep purple eyes appeared in the darkness, and the ground began to tremble. Whatever was hiding in the woods made a huge racket as it approached Dashiel and Grimley.

"Dashiel, let's head back!" Grimley yelled, but Dashiel could not move.

He gazed at the creature, fear and wonder in his eyes. A giant metallic monster slowly stepped out of the shadows and into the glow cast by his lantern. Its uniform, made of ochre-colored chain mail, reflected the scant light. Its face was a somber mask, with a pair of lifeless purple eyes peering out from behind a helmet. The machinery operating within its chest creaked and clacked. Startled at the sight, Dashiel dropped his lantern, which died with a timid hiss as it hit the ground. Everything became dark.

Dashiel reached for the flute around his neck and blew into it. A euphonious sound shook the woods. In response, the fenku unwound themselves from one another. Moonlight illuminated the clearing.

Dashiel, his friend, and the Ochre Brigadier, enormous and ghastly, came into full view. Dashiel grabbed Orphée with both hands.

"Grimley, run," Dashiel commanded, holding the baton defensively.

"Don't bother," Grimley said, picking up the two broken halves of his pistol. "You don't stand a chance. Believe me. I tried."

"The others must have heard the flute. We must keep the Brigadier from entering the sacred terrains," Dashiel said.

Razor-sharp blades grew from the Brigadier's arms, and it swung them at Dashiel and Grimley. Both boys managed to dodge the blows, slowly walking backward into the woods.

Turning its sights on Grimley, the Brigadier attacked again. Agile as ever, Grimley dodged the blade. It lodged itself in the trunk of a fenku with a deafening thump.

"Forget this! Let's go!" Grimley yelped, turning and fleeing.

Dashiel was about to follow him, but before he could move, Grimley flew back across the clearing, hitting a rock on the other side. A second Brigadier, with the same emotionless purple eyes, emerged from the shadows. It had come to help its comrade finish the job.

"Grimley!" Dashiel rushed to his side. The rock had knocked him out, but Dashiel could still feel his friend's heart beating. How long would he last with the baton? If Dashiel didn't do something, and quick, he and Grimley would die.

This was his moment. He stood up and held his baton in a defensive position, waiting for his foes to do their worst.

The first Brigadier managed to liberate its metal arm from the tree, which split in two and crashed to the ground. The second soldier, in a casual display of strength, picked the tree up off the ground, wielding it like a weapon. Both walked slowly toward the pair of boys. Dashiel's knees buckled.

The second Brigadier stopped a short distance from the boys, preparing itself for attack. As Dashiel faced his final moments, regret pierced his heart. He had failed to save Grimley and protect Azahar.

A distant chirping sound sliced through the air. A silver arrow with a chain attached whistled past at great speed, landing in the trunk of the tree that the Brigadier held up.

"Now, Rupert!" a voice yelled from afar. The chain tensed as someone pulled from the other end, tugging the tree forward. The Brigadier lost its balance and fell to the ground, followed by the tree, which landed on top of it with a metallic crash.

Three people emerged from the woods into the clearing. Dashiel immediately recognized them. They were the three oddballs he had met weeks earlier in his father's study.

The largest of the three, Rupert, crossed the clearing until he stood next to Dashiel and Grimley. The others positioned themselves in front of the Brigadier, Charlotte with a musket and Sylvain with a silver crossbow. With a single hand, Rupert picked Grimley up and slung him over his shoulder as if he were a sack of flour.

"Charlotte, go northeast. Alert others of position," he called, in stilted speech that said he wasn't quite fluent in Garatei, the continent's main language.

"Got it." Charlotte reentered the darkest part of the woods.

"Sylvain."

"Commander?" Sylvain didn't take his eyes off his enormous adversary.

"I take *lettei mer* to safety," Rupert said, moving stealthily around the Brigadier. "Distract. Others be here soon, *brootha*."

"Understood."

Rupert bounded through the trees, Grimley in tow. In the clearing, only Sylvain, Dashiel, and their two adversaries remained. The fallen Brigadier began to squirm, trying to rid itself of the tree. Its partner took two large steps forward, drawing a massive sword—the same kind of sword that had pierced the barrier days before.

"You should leave, Dashiel," Sylvain said, continuing to stare down the Brigadiers with his brow furrowed, eyes narrowed, and crossbow drawn. "Your friend needs you. Please . . . be careful."

Dashiel was still processing what had just happened. A minute earlier, he was on the brink of death. The next, this group of his father's acquaintances had arrived to save him. It was the right moment to escape if he wanted to survive the night.

He fled the clearing, running as fast as he could. In the distance, Rupert moved swiftly through the dark with Grimley bouncing against his shoulder. Dashiel only needed to follow him to return to town.

A booming metallic sound rang out behind him. The Brigadier had finally rid itself of the heavy tree, and now it was two on one. Dashiel's head told him to leave all behind and go back to safety, but an inexplicable feeling pulled him toward the clearing. Maybe he'd never save Azahar, and maybe he'd never be as skillful or as strong as his friend. But even if it cost him everything, Dashiel Ermitage would never let his fears convince him to abandon someone in the face of danger.

The Ochre Brigadiers began their attack against Sylvain, swinging their big arms and sword. Sylvain skillfully avoided each attack. When he saw the opportunity, Sylvain shot his crossbow, aiming for the Brigadiers' joints. The arrows could not damage the enemies, but when shot at the tubed joints, they could temporarily slow them down. But these two adversaries were more than a single arbalist could take on.

One Brigadier managed to knock Sylvain off his feet with a single swipe of its arm. Standing over him, the soldier lifted the enormous sword as high as it could, ready to finish him off. A single strike from the sword would crush Sylvain to smithereens. Mercilessly, the sword began its lethal descent. Sylvain closed his eyes. And Dashiel made his move.

A high-pitched twang dissolved all other sound in the clearing. Dashiel had blocked the attack. Sylvain's exhausted panting and the clinking of the Brigadier's clockwork innards were the first two sounds to return.

The imperial machine swung its sword once more, but again Dashiel stopped it with his father's baton. The Brigadier's partner joined the attack, but Dashiel, with surprising agility, moved the baton from hand to hand, blocking strike after strike. The enormous strength of the blows paled in comparison to his defense. He had no idea what was happening. Perhaps this was the power of Orphée?

"I didn't know you could do that!" Sylvain said, astonished, as he got to his feet.

"Me neither!" Dashiel replied, incredulous.

"Let me teach you something," Sylvain stood up.

"What?"

"Hit that baton against the ground three times."

As instructed, Dashiel tapped his baton against the forest floor. To his surprise, one end of the baton became increasingly heavy. In a matter of seconds, it was difficult to hold the staff with one hand.

"Wow! It feels like a hammer," Dashiel said, trying not to drop the baton.

"And it hits like one too. Try it." Sylvain shot at the Brigadiers, gaining their attention. He ran to the other side of the clearing. The Brigadiers swiveled their heads, following his progress. "I'll distract them."

Dragging his heavy weapon along the ground, Dashiel slowly approached from the rear. Sylvain shot his arrows while dodging various attacks from the enemies. Dashiel positioned himself behind one of them. Using both hands, he lifted the baton and slammed it into the Brigadier's back. The strike plunged into its metallic torso, creating a sound like the ringing of a bell. The furious Brigadier turned and swiped at Dashiel.

He dropped Orphée into the grass and flowers as he dodged the attack. "What now?"

"I said I'd distract them." Sylvain glanced at the large fenku branches that lay on the forest floor. "But I just thought of something better."

He ran to the tree, quickly gathering the elastic branches. "I need you to be the one to distract them for a while. And grab the baton and bring it over here."

"I can't. It's too heavy now."

"Yes, you can." Sylvain sat down next to the pile of branches. "It's our only chance."

Running to the other side of the clearing, Dashiel managed to avoid two wild swings from the Brigadiers. His father's weapon still lay among the flowers in the middle of the clearing. It was too heavy to grab quickly, and he certainly couldn't race away from an attack with its weight in his hands. Dashiel dodged a few more swipes from the Brigadiers while Sylvain wove the fenku branches into a long vine.

"Whenever you're ready, Dashiel!" Sylvain looped one end of the vine around a tree, cinching it tightly with a clove hitch. He ran the other end to the opposite side of the clearing and did the same. The line was taut but flexible as rubber.

"Dashiel, the baton!" Sylvain yelled, pulling back the vine. It was now or never for the two of them.

Jolted by the command, Dashiel jumped into action, running toward the weapon. Using all his strength, he grabbed the baton. To his surprise, it wasn't as heavy as before. With difficulty, he ran past the two Brigadiers, making his way to the vine. With each step, the baton became a little lighter. The Brigadiers turned as Dashiel sprinted past, then walked single file toward their two victims.

"Now what?" Dashiel panted, skidding to a stop next to Sylvain with Orphée in hand.

"Hit the baton three more times and give it to me," Sylvain said, pulling the vine back, tensing it as much as possible.

"Will you be able to lift it?"

"Yes, if we do it quickly."

Dashiel lifted the baton and tapped it against the ground three times. Grunting beneath the weight, he brought Orphée to his partner. Sylvain grabbed the weapon with his free hand, using it to pull back the vine and creating a massive slingshot. The two Brigadiers were meters away, getting alarmingly close now.

"Shoot! Now!" Dashiel yelled, seeing how close the enemies were.

"A little bit more," Sylvain said, gritting his teeth and stretching the vine with all his might. The baton started to fall to the ground, getting heavier by the moment.

"NOW!"

Sylvain let the vine go, and the release of its tension shot the baton like a bullet. With such speed, strength, and weight, the projectile perforated the Brigadier in front, burning a clean hole in its armor and continuing its flight to the other side of the clearing. The giant soldier fell backward and lost its grip on its sword, which lodged in the second Brigadier. Hot, yellowish liquid gushed from their pierced metallic tubes, splashing all over the forest floor. Having fallen to the ground, the young men watched the two Brigadiers topple, landing among the leaves with a definitive thud. Their bodies continued to spout the yellow substance, which soon covered the entire clearing.

It was over. Dashiel and Sylvain were victorious.

Dashiel quickly stood up, unable to believe his eyes.

"That was grand!" Dashiel squealed with joy, adrenaline still pumping. "Don't you think?" He offered a hand to Sylvain to help him up. Sylvain regarded his gesture with a serious expression, the same one he'd worn the day they met.

"Yes, it was." Sylvain's solemn facade dissolved for a brief moment, and he smiled. He took Dashiel's hand and pulled himself up. "You should go get the baton."

"Right."

Splashing in the liquid, Dashiel looked all around until he found Orphée embedded in the same rock that had knocked out Grimley. Dashiel grabbed the baton with both hands and, with great difficulty, extracted it from the rock.

Returning to Sylvain, Dashiel felt the same strange feeling blooming inside him that he'd felt the first time he'd locked eyes with Sylvain.

He looked at the Brigadiers lying on the forest floor. It was clear that Sylvain and Dashiel had managed to incapacitate the soldiers but not kill them. Both were staring directly at him, their metallic faces still devoid of emotion. Dashiel shuddered as he gazed into those dull, purple eyes. Yet after all they had done, he still could not resent them.

"'Beware those whose entire existence is devoid of purpose,'" Sylvain recited, collecting his crossbow, "'for they steal innocent lives to get a glimpse of what they lack.'"

Dashiel stared at him blankly. "What?" Something in those words seemed awfully familiar to him. He did not know why.

"Nothing." Sylvain shook his head.

As they left the clearing, the adrenaline began to wear off. Dashiel felt the pain of the hits he had taken and an intense throbbing in his palm. He took a look. At some point during the battle, he must have cut his hand, and now it was bleeding.

Sylvain noticed Dashiel's grimace and slowed his pace. "Are you all right?"

Dashiel closed his hand and moved it out of Sylvain's sight. "Nothing. Just a scratch."

"If you say so." Sylvain rotated his shoulder in place. "Let's call it a night."

They followed the path back to town, leaving the fallen Brigadiers behind.

CHAPTER 5

NO GOOD DEED
GOES UNPUNISHED

ashiel had been sitting outside the tribunal room for hours. The mayor had convened the patriarchs and matriarchs at the Azahar Council House for a meeting of vital importance. As Dashiel sat on a bench outside the room, muffled voices filtered through the closed cherrywood door. He didn't have the slightest idea what was going on inside. He only knew that Grimley was in there. Time had seemingly passed quickly after he and Sylvain defeated the two Ochre Brigadiers.

Dashiel closed his eyes and tried to remember everything that had happened since.

Right after leaving Gailfaur's clearing, Sylvain and Dashiel came across the hunting party. At first, no one believed the pair had finished off the invaders. But once the party saw the metal carnage and hot yellow liquid for themselves, they couldn't deny it. Awestruck, everyone gathered around the two young men, asking endless questions about the fight. Dashiel's father appeared among the multitude of townspeople, giving his son a disapproving look.

Dashiel nervously walked toward his father with the objects he had taken from his house, leaving Sylvain to answer the townsfolk's questions. He stood in front of his father, waiting for him to say something. Instead, Elias wordlessly took the baton and flute, both covered in the yellow substance, and headed for home.

Dashiel followed. He thought about explaining himself, but he knew his father would not listen. He had gone way too far this time.

Elias walked ahead of him, straight and silent as an oak tree. Dashiel still believed that what he had done was the right thing, but the idea of letting his father down haunted him. Halfway down the trail, he had a sudden recollection from his sickly days, a memory of his father reading to him before bedtime. Back then, Elias had seemed warmer and happier. Back then, they could talk to each other. That had all changed, about the time Dashiel's health improved.

The pair arrived back in town around midnight. Dashiel's mother anxiously waited for them.

"Dashiel Elliott Ermitage!" she yelled when she caught the first glimpse of him. She ran to him and hugged him. "Don't you ever do something like that again!" Her grip was so tight that it nearly asphyxiated him.

Dashiel tried to talk to his father. He wanted to explain himself, but his father had already gone to his study, shutting the door behind him.

Later that night, a loud knock on the door awoke the Ermitage household. When Emily opened the door, a man wearing the green uniform of an Azahar guard stood before them.

"The illustrious mayor has convened an urgent hearing. The patriarch of protection and matriarch of education are requested to attend."

Dashiel, awakened by the hard knocking, slowly descended the stairs. The guard saw him and quickly resumed his proclamation. "The presence of young Dashiel Ermitage is also required. By Mayor Lilac's order, I am to escort him."

His mother looked over her shoulder, where his father was emerging from his study for the first time since they'd arrived home. Both of them conversed with the guard. Their words became distant. The memories blurred in his mind, becoming harder to recall, until everything went dark.

A noise from inside the tribunal room snapped Dashiel out of his reverie. He blinked at his surroundings, all of which made him uncomfortable. The cold, mossy stone walls. The dying candles that gave off a dim light that hurt his eyes. His socks were still drenched in the yellow liquid that had gushed from the Ochre Brigadiers. As much as he tried, he couldn't find a comfortable position on the rickety bench. The cut on his hand throbbed underneath the bandage he'd applied before arriving.

No longer able to bear his curiosity or his uncomfortable seat, Dashiel stood and listened at the door. He tried to concentrate on what the council was discussing, but the old and warped door distorted their voices. He knew that he and Grimley were there to be reprimanded. The council had sworn to punish anyone who disobeyed the curfew rules. Nevertheless, his friends were safe, and the Ochre Brigadiers were no longer a menace to the people he loved. Whatever the punishment was, Dashiel had no choice but to accept it.

The voices ceased for a moment, and the door opened, causing Dashiel to spring back to his seat on the bench. Out walked Grimley, looking sick and dragging his feet. He took a seat beside Dashiel.

"What did they tell you?"

Grimley didn't say a word. His face was apple red, and his lips trembled. Dashiel put his hand on his friend's shoulder.

"Don't touch me!" Grimley shook off Dashiel's hand. "Leave me alone."

"What's the matter?" Dashiel was confused by his friend's reaction. "What did they—"

Before he could say anything else, the door opened to reveal Elias.

"Ermitage," Elias called sternly. "Enter."

Dashiel was concerned about his friend, but as he entered the dimly lit room, his mind went blank and his heartbeat quickened.

"You can go home now," Elias told Grimley in a cold voice, following Dashiel into the room.

Elias closed the door behind Dashiel, darkening the room even more. All the council members were there. Nine of them, sitting next to the mayor and observing Dashiel from above as he took a seat in front of them. The dim candlelight rendered their features almost macabre, but Dashiel could still recognize some of the faces.

"Council is in session!" The mayor called everyone to order, not bothering to look at Dashiel. "We are here to question young Ermitage about the actions that have taken place this same night."

He squinted at a piece of paper in front of him. "Young Ermitage, is it true that you disobeyed Azahar's rule number eighty-three by going in search of the imperial enemies, better known as Ochre Brigadiers?"

Dashiel looked up. "Yes, but I did it to—"

"Silence!" The patriarch of the miners cut him off with a sharp shout. He calmed his tone and said, "Just answer yes or no."

"Yes, sir."

He picked up a quill and scribbled something on the same piece of paper. He then raised his wrinkled eyes. "Is it true that you deliberately disobeyed Azahar's rule number twenty-five by wielding an unauthorized weapon in the form of a baton?"

"Yes, sir."

The mayor continued. "Is it true that you not only stole from an Azahar council member but also took one of the items most important for the town's survival, Gailfaur's Flute, without permission?"

"Yes," Dashiel answered quietly. He wanted to explain himself better, but it was no use. Every question and answer seemed to dig his grave a little bit deeper.

"Is it true that you used the flute, knowing the only person allowed to use it is the patriarch of protection?"

He turned to his father, who stared at him with an expressionless face. For a moment, Dashiel wondered if his father felt ashamed of him.

"Yes," Dashiel replied once more, "but if you allowed me to explain—"

"Silence!" Elias Ermitage's voice thundered.

Dashiel stopped speaking and looked down at his shoes, noticing their wear and tear.

"I've finished with my line of questioning," the mayor said. "If anyone else wants to ask a question or add information, now is the time."

The old man leaned against an arm of his chair. The council members whispered to each other.

"Is it true that you saved young Calla's life in the woods?" Donner's mother asked.

"Yes," Dashiel answered, allowing himself a little giggle.

Donner's mother gave him a tender look. "Thank you," she mouthed, obviously trying not to give herself away. With her question, she had tried to help his case.

"If I may add," the lumberjack patriarch spoke, stroking his long, white beard. "A trustworthy source of mine told me that young Ermitage also took young Calla to safety and tended his wounds. Is that true, Ermitage?"

"Yes, sir," Dashiel said.

"What's more, I was told that he was quick and effective in carrying out the treatment," the lumberjack added, looking at the mayor.

The council members began to whisper among themselves once more.

"Is it true that you intended to find young Deguiser and bring him back to safety?" Dashiel's mother asked.

"That's irrelevant," another patriarch snapped, his voice ringing out in the chamber. Dressed in the finest Azahar silk, Grimley's father stood out from the other members of the council. "I'd like to remind the matriarch of education that we judge actions, not whimsical intentions." He turned to the mayor. "The matriarch is trying to validate the erroneous actions of her own son."

Dashiel's father turned in his chair to face Omilier Deguiser. "You want actions?" he said, breaking his silence. "Actions you shall get."

Elias turned to Dashiel with confidence in his eyes. "Is it true that you and young Aurante defeated two lethal imperial assassins all by yourselves and, by doing so, protected all of Azahar's inhabitants, including the Deguiser family?"

"Yes, sir," Dashiel answered with pride, relieved that, in an odd way, his father was defending him.

"What insolence! How dare you ridicule me in such a manner?" Deguiser's nostrils flared.

"I've heard enough!" the mayor said, sitting up straight in his chair. Everyone fell silent. "In accordance with his actions, both bad and good, I've arrived at a verdict. For breaking Azahar rule number eighty-three, Azahar rule number twenty-five, and Azahar rule number thirty-eight, his heirloom ceremony shall be moved from his seventeenth birthday to his nineteenth. The heirloom ceremony is a privilege one must earn, not a right."

He looked down his nose at Dashiel.

"Consider yourself lucky that's all you got, young man." The mayor stood from his seat. "Case closed."

The council members began to leave the room. In a matter of seconds, most of the council had exited the building. Dashiel stood next to the chair he'd sat in moments earlier, waiting for his parents to come talk to him.

Then something caught his attention. In a corner of the room, Mr. Deguiser was arguing with the mayor. They both kept to a mutter at first, but Deguiser's voice steadily rose with his anger. The argument became more and more tense, until Deguiser stormed out of the room. Dashiel was certain that the argument had something to do with the punishment Grimley had received.

Emily walked over to her son and embraced him tightly. "Whatever they say, I'm proud of you, Eli."

"You were lucky," Elias said, slapping Dashiel on the back of his head. "Never—listen to me—*never* steal from me again, understood?"

"Yes, sir," Dashiel said, bowing his head.

Dashiel wasn't happy about waiting two more years to receive his family heirloom, but a wave of relief washed over him. He'd avoided a stricter punishment and had helped the town. For a moment, he imagined himself as one of the heroes in his book.

The Ermitage family abandoned the council's chamber. As they passed the bench in the corridor, Dashiel thought of Grimley and his odd reaction after his hearing. He frowned, recalling his friend's distress.

"What is it, honey?" Emily's asked.

"Grimley wasn't himself when he got out." Dashiel looked at his parents. "What was Grimley's punishment?"

Elias's expression commanded Emily not to say a word, but she did not obey. "Unfortunately, something much worse than yours, dear."

"Why?" he asked.

"Because even if Grimley's intentions were good, it was proven that he accidentally led the Brigadiers to the sacred terrains," she said.

"What?" Dashiel snapped. "He was trying to stop them."

"His actions were reckless," she added. "It also didn't help that no one interceded for him during his hearing, as some of the council members did for you. I would have, but I didn't have anything to say."

"That's enough, Emily," Elias said, moving toward the exit. "We're not allowed to disclose anything about other people's hearings. Let's end this discussion now."

But Dashiel didn't want to end the discussion. He wanted to help his friend, and he felt a small sense of hope. "Maybe if I speak to the mayor, he'll change his mind about whatever punishment Grimley was given."

Elias turned around, frowning. "No," he said with a commanding voice. "We're going home. Immediately."

Dashiel didn't say another word, following his parents out the door. A great concern for his friend reigned inside his mind. Grimley's father was strict with him. He had always striven to polish his son into the perfect heir to the family's fortune. Surely he would punish him even further. But Dashiel couldn't help feeling like his friend didn't deserve that. Grimley was only trying to help, after all.

No matter Grimley's punishment, Dashiel couldn't do anything at that moment. He could only wait until the next day to console his friend.

CHAPTER 6

A BITTERSWEET OPPORTUNITY

After a long walk from the main plaza, the Ermitage family arrived home. As he walked through the door, Dashiel thought of Donner, who had lain motionless on the entryway floor only hours ago. Everything had happened so quickly that the night seemed like a dream, but the bloodstains on the floor quickly dispelled that notion. He hoped Donner's family was attending to him.

Drained of adrenaline, Dashiel fell victim to a new kind of exhaustion. He wanted to head upstairs to his room and sleep as much as he could until he had to go to work the next morning. He was halfway up the stairs when his father's voice called out from the ground floor.

"Dashiel, to the study."

Dashiel rubbed his eyes, sighed, and shuffled toward the study. Elias waited for him outside the open door, holding Orphée—now cleansed of the yellow liquid—in his hand. The first thing he did when he entered was gently hang Orphée on its hooks. The fireplace was roaring, its light reflecting off the metallic, intricate, ornamented surface of the baton.

"What's going on, Papa?"

"Sit down, Son." Elias's voice sounded noticeably tired. He took his usual seat behind his desk.

Dashiel sat, staring intently at his father. Elias laced his fingers together, setting his elbows on the desk.

"Dashiel, what do you know about what goes on beyond the forest?"

The question caught Dashiel off guard. Talking about the empire had always been prohibited in the Ermitage household and frowned upon throughout Azahar.

"So? What do you know about the Outerland?" Elias insisted.

Dashiel considered the best way to respond. He knew more about the empire than he wanted to admit, and he had learned it all from Grimley. He did not want to get his friend into more trouble. But when he saw his father's piercing eyes, he didn't see any option other than honesty.

"I know that the Empire of Zaphyrelia is a place feared by the whole world." Dashiel stared down, not daring to say more.

"That's true." Elias's uncharacteristic calm unsettled Dashiel. Why wasn't his father bothered by his knowledge?

The glowing firewood screeched inside the fireplace. In the quiet that followed, Elias asked, "What else do you know?"

"I . . . know that Abelon Asedia, the emperor, is the reason the empire is so feared."

"Right again. I wonder where you got your information." Elias gave his son an inquisitive look. "Why is Abelon Asedia so feared?"

Of all Dashiel knew about the empire, he was most familiar with the horrible tales of Abelon Asedia. "Asedia stole the throne years ago when he assassinated the legitimate ruling family. He acquired the ability to steal and use souls to animate Ochre Brigadiers. He's also tortured and killed innocent people."

Dashiel stopped talking, realizing that he had revealed the extent of his disobedience.

"Right once more, Son."

Dashiel looked nervously at his father, whose expression had not changed.

"But we don't have to worry," Dashiel said, exhaustion written all over his face. "For years, Asedia tried to conquer Azahar, but Gailfaur's barrier stopped him. He left us alone."

"The barrier did indeed protect us," Elias said, unlacing his fingers.

"The barrier will always protect us." Dashiel leaned back, a twinkle of confidence in his eyes.

Elias's eyes turned glassy as he pursed his lips together. "That's where you're wrong."

"What?" Dashiel sat up straight in his seat, his throat turning dry.

The fire in the ancient fireplace flickered, and the shadows began a macabre dance. They played over Elias's face, lending an ominous overtone to his next statement. "The barrier won't last much longer. Gailfaur has become weaker with time, and I'm afraid that Asedia's forces have finally figured out how to penetrate the barrier."

"You're worried about the two Brigadiers? They're junk now; they won't be able to harm anyone."

"The Ochre Brigadiers possess great strength, yes, but they lack autonomy. There's always an Asedian soldier commanding two or three of them. In all likelihood, that soldier is probably still hiding in the woods or on his way to the capital to report back to his superiors."

"That can't be." Dashiel rose from his chair like a spring. "We should go look for him. If we find him—"

"You're not going anywhere. Take a seat!" Elias gestured to the chair. "Don't get yourself into any more trouble. The council has been informed of the situation. They've assigned the Azahar guard to hunt for the intruder. Hopefully a human will be easier to track."

His mind elsewhere, Dashiel let himself drop back into his seat. "There's nothing we can do?"

"There is one thing. Come in," he said, raising his voice to reach the study's open door. He stood, waiting for the summoned guest.

Exhausted, Dashiel didn't turn to see who arrived. A pair of footsteps crossed the room and rounded the desk. Two familiar faces came into view: a big man with bulging eyes and a woman with an oddly long nose. Rupert Golk and Charlotte Malanks stood beside Elias.

"Dashiel, you've already met Rupert and Charlotte."

Dashiel nodded, not knowing what to say.

"Good to see in one piece, *mer*," the large man said with his strange accent, flashing an infectious smile.

"Dashiel, I need you to pay close attention to my words." Elias took a seat. "What I'm about to tell you is of the utmost importance. Your actions this evening were in the wrong, without a doubt. For that reason, you were punished."

"I understand," Dashiel said, sinking into his chair.

"However, your actions were also brave, and your intentions were noble. They showed an extraordinary sense of comradeship."

Dashiel sat up straighter, not sure what was happening yet intrigued by the shift in his father's tone.

"Your actions also qualified you for a unique opportunity."

"Unique opportunity?"

"Rupert and Charlotte both belong to an elite order that has secretly expanded throughout the empire. They call themselves the Cobalt Phantasms."

Dashiel couldn't have responded even if he wanted to. He did his best to take in what his father was saying.

"The mission of the Cobalt Phantasms is to ease the suffering caused by Asedia and his court. Whether fighting, researching, or aiding those in need, they have managed to maintain their work in secret for all these years. They travel far and wide throughout the continent of Egadrise. In the eyes of the government, their actions are indeed illegal. But they're morally necessary, for Zaphyrelia endures so many hardships."

"So, are you a rebel group?" Dashiel asked, his eyes illuminating. "Some kind of resistance?"

"Oh, no!" Charlotte took a step forward. "Rebellions, uprisings, and all remnants of resistance died in Zaphyrelia years ago."

"Right! Time Asedia claimer the throne and turner the *lettei* Belecrose into monster," Rupert interrupted, speaking in his strange way.

Charlotte gave Rupert an annoyed look before turning back to Dashiel, disregarding her partner's incomprehensible response.

"We can't offer a permanent change, but we can improve the quality of life of the empire's citizens. You cannot fathom the pain and suffering there is outside these woods. There are so many ways we can help, so we need the right people on our side."

"Dashiel, what they want to tell you is that you've been chosen to start training to become a Cobalt Phantasm," Elias said. "This is an enormous opportunity, and it comes with enormous responsibility. You've never trained for anything like this before, but Rupert and Charlotte think you would be a decent fit."

"It would be great if you accepted the offer." Charlotte leaned in, her nose a few inches away from Dashiel's. "Just think about it. We've been blessed in so many ways. Accepting is almost an obligation."

"You right for challenge, mer," Rupert said, winking.

"Me?" Dashiel's tired brain had trouble processing this new information.

"Yes, you. Your abilities are most needed in these times," Charlotte said.

"It would be an honor." Dashiel's eyes sparkled, but even amid his happiness, he could not help but recall what had happened with his friend at the Council House. "If I was chosen, Grimley must have been selected as well."

Charlotte and Rupert exchanged puzzled glances.

"Dashiel." Charlotte clasped her hands and lifted them to her lips before continuing. "Only you were chosen to join the order. No one else."

"But Grimley is prepared for something like this, even more than . . ." Dashiel banished a bitter thought. "Believe me, Grimley would also be a great asset to your order."

"I'm sorry, Dashiel. The decision is final. This opportunity is meant only for you." Charlotte held his gaze. "Do you accept it?"

With a single "yes," Dashiel could realize his dream of leaving the forest and living adventures like the ones he'd read about. He would finally escape the tedious life he had sought to leave behind. But something in the very fiber of his being kept that word stuck to his vocal cords. By taking this opportunity, he would be breaking the promise he and Grimley had made years ago. A promise that had solidified their friendship. The two friends would only leave the forest together.

"The offer sounds incredible, but there must have been a mistake. I'm not what you are looking for."

"Of course you are," Charlotte said. "You've proven yourself tonight."

"*Mer* got potential. Don't waste," Rupert added.

Charlotte nodded. "Your friend might be good, but you . . . I am sure you will be able to do extraordinary things."

Dashiel pondered their words. They thought he had potential. They saw the Brigadiers' defeat as a clear sign of his strength and wit. But they didn't know the truth. Defeating the Brigadiers had been possible only because of Sylvain, his father's baton, and a great deal of luck.

In his mind, he heard his own voice calling him a fraud and a liar. The voice echoed as it became stronger.

"I'm sorry. Count me out," Dashiel said. "I'm grateful that you came here, but I can't."

"You cannot be serious," Charlotte said, dismay written on her face. "Can we do anything that might change your mind?"

"You would only waste your time," he said, avoiding eye contact.

An uncomfortable silence filled the room. Charlotte and Rupert glanced at Dashiel's father, silently begging him to say something, anything. When Elias failed to speak, Rupert approached Dashiel. A massive hand landed on his shoulder.

"*Mil* apprentice begin journey after twilight day after tomorrow. You got until then to join apprentice." He and Charlotte walked toward the exit.

"If your response is yes, your father will tell you when and where to find us," Charlotte added. Then she and Rupert left the Ermitage house.

"What in the world?" Dashiel murmured. He had no idea what to think. His energy was drained, and his thoughts were tangled. He wanted so badly to be a Cobalt Phantasm, but it didn't feel right.

His father stood up from his desk and blew out the candles.

"Now, off to bed. It's been a long night for you," Elias said, grabbing a bucket full of ashes from a corner of the room. "You have things to think about."

He emptied the ash in the fireplace, and the fire and its light were extinguished.

CHAPTER 7

SECRET UPON SECRET

The next day, a sheer mist covered the whole forest. Sunlight shone through, giving the mist an orange tinge as it moved gently through the air. It was as if twilight and dawn had combined to delight the Azahar that morning, but it was all lost on Dashiel, who had too much on his mind to enjoy his surroundings.

His world felt different, yet inside the library, it seemed as if nothing at all had happened. Neither he nor Astor spoke a single word about the incident from the day before. Somehow he managed to complete his chores efficiently. And all the while, he thought about the offer from the Cobalt Phantasms. He thought about how much he wanted to join them. He thought about how joining them would hurt his friend. How he would hurt the noble cause of the order by inevitably failing. How he would hurt himself by not being honest.

He had to resolve this internal conflict fast. Otherwise, his mind would explode.

Because the curfew had not been lifted yet, Dashiel finished his work by midday. He went to Donner's house, but the family didn't allow him to see his friend, who was still recovering from the day before. Dashiel decided to visit Grimley. The urge to tell his best friend about what had happened manipulated his body like a puppet.

He arrived at Grimley's home, the biggest in the main plaza. He knocked until his knuckles hurt, but no one answered the door. He sat for hours on the porch steps, but no one appeared.

Finally, one of the household maids arrived. At first, she was reluctant to confess her master's whereabouts, but she gave in at Dashiel's insistence. Grimley had been sent to work his family's mines, she said, for that was what the council had decided.

Dashiel became sick when he learned the truth about his friend. He now understood Grimley's reaction after his hearing. He had lost the privilege of being a torch keeper. He had been sent away to a duty that he surely detested. He had likely been sent underground for some time, like all rookie miners.

Dashiel walked back home silently, lost in thought.

Instead of going inside, he climbed up to the rooftop, watching the sky until the stars twinkled into existence. He had done this ever since he could remember. Gazing at the night sky usually comforted him when he felt sad or upset. Tonight, Dashiel felt as if he were being torn apart. His ardent desire to leave the forest was counteracted by the promise he had once made to Grimley. His ardent desire to become as great as the heroes he had read about was counteracted by his lack of strength and skill. Leaving his friend behind would betray the trust between them. Declining this opportunity would crush the only chance he might get to fulfill his dream.

"When you were a kid, you would come up here when you were upset." Dashiel startled at the sound of his mother's voice. So deep in his thoughts, he hadn't heard her approach.

"I came here to think."

Emily took a seat next to him.

The night wind blew, grabbing leaves from the trees and dispersing them throughout the plaza. Now that the imperialist menace was gone, houses were lit past nightfall, and smoke emanated from their chimneys. The plumes were an opaque white because the Azahar used firewood from halban trees, whose insides were the same color as the smoke. Halban grew faster than other trees, so cutting them down did not harm the forest.

"About the opportunity . . ." she said with a soothing tone.

"I have to be honest. If not with them, then with myself. I didn't want to fight the Brigadiers back there." Dashiel giggled in spite of himself. "I was afraid. There was even a moment when I thought about turning back."

"You were hesitant to fight two enormous brutes. That's okay. We all would be. That doesn't mean you're a coward." Emily put an arm around Dashiel's shoulder, her shawl's tassels swinging in the air. Pride filled in her every word. "Bravery isn't the absence of fear. Bravery is acting even when you are scared to death. What matters is that you risked your life to find a friend when you thought he was in danger, and you went back to Sylvain when he most needed it."

"I don't know about that," Dashiel said.

Emily clenched her jaw, a sign of slight annoyance. "For Providence's sake! You managed to take down not only one but two of the most feared beings on the continent."

"The baton is the one responsible, and that makes me feel like a fraud. I don't deserve the honor of joining them," Dashiel said, burying his head in his knees. "Grimley would be a better Cobalt Phantasm than me."

"Listen well, Son." Elias heaved himself up the tree that climbed the house's side. "I'm too old for this," he mumbled as he struggled to situate himself next to Emily. "The baton doesn't grant ability or strength, but it can show the wielder his true potential, and that's what it did. It reflected what you are truly capable of."

"Grimley is indeed strong and clever," Emily said. "But maybe strength and cleverness aren't what the Phantasms are looking for right now." She straightened her glasses. "You set yourself apart with something else."

"What is that?" Dashiel asked.

"Your heart," his parents answered simultaneously.

"My heart?" Dashiel scoffed, leaning back. "Thanks, but clichés won't change my mind."

"You're wrong again," Elias interrupted. "You know nothing."

"Kindness and courage have become as important as anything in these times. They hold great power," Emily said. "Why not pick you, when you have enough of both to share with the whole town?"

"Breaking a promise," Dashiel said, "would be awfully kind of me."

"What promise?" Emily asked, confused.

"When Grimley and I were children, we promised to leave Azahar together. To live adventures and become stronger."

His parents exchanged baffled looks. He knew what they were thinking: under different circumstances, this plan would have been unacceptable.

"Dashiel."

He turned to his father, who was looking him straight in the eyes.

"You'd be a fool if you didn't do it. Are you a fool?" he said evenly. "Besides, you know Grimley. He would never forgive you if you didn't do it."

"I'm not a fool," Dashiel answered, his thoughts swirling. "And I guess you're right. He wouldn't."

Emily nodded at Elias. "We love you, honey, and we'll love you the same, whatever you decide." She rubbed her hand up and down Dashiel's arm.

Dashiel gazed at the brightest star and thought hard. Maybe his parents were right. Maybe he would dishonor his best friend by not taking this opportunity. Maybe the only way of growing and becoming stronger was to take the offer. Maybe he did deserve it. Mentally, he assembled and reassembled all the things that he had done, heard, and seen until a thought took hold in his mind.

"You're right," he said. "I'll do it. I don't know what it'll be like, but I can still try my best."

Emily put her hand on her son's cheek. "That's my boy."

"How are you going to explain my absence?" he asked.

"We'll say that you began your training as a custodian," Elias said. "It is a requirement to live in seclusion in the sacred terrains for some time. Enough time for you to complete your training."

"Wait. If I leave tomorrow, I won't get a chance to say goodbye to Donner and Grimley. Who's going to talk to Old Astor?"

"We'll talk to them about your absence," Emily said. "So you won't have to worry about that."

"Dashiel, one more thing. It is better that you don't say anything about your disease," Elias said as a sparkle of fireflies whirled through the air.

"Why not?"

"The Cobalt Phantasms don't recruit people who have or have had severe diseases," Elias answered. "If they find out, they'll most likely send you back."

"How am I going to hide it?" He studied his bandaged hand. "I can barely hide it here, where I'm safe."

"You must be extremely cautious," Elias said. "Don't tell anyone about it."

"I'm not sure if I can do that."

Elias took a big breath. "If you really think you can't keep the secret to yourself, I advise you to trust Sylvain Aurante with this matter. Only Sylvain."

"Sylvain?" Dashiel asked, confused.

"I've known Sylvain for some time," Elias said. "He can be trusted. I'm certain that he will help you keep your secret."

Everything was now set in place.

"I . . . I believe I'm ready," Dashiel said, finally smiling. "When exactly do I leave?"

"Tomorrow—twilight. I'll take you to the meeting point," Elias said as he stood up gingerly. "You must prepare yourself."

Returning to his room, Dashiel found a clean shirt and a pair of pants that his mother had recently mended. After putting them on, he grabbed a bag and filled it with various belongings. He moved quickly throughout his room, grabbing and packing things that he thought he'd need on his journey. What he was about to do was, without a doubt, crazy. But he'd made his decision, and he couldn't turn back now.

When he had finished packing, Dashiel sat on his bed, dropping his bag on the floor beside him. He opened his nightstand drawer and took out a small book, the ancient spine barely holding its wrinkled pages together. It was the book that had dared him to dream for so many years. Soon, he would prove himself as worthy as the grand heroes in the story. He opened his bag and buried the book beneath piles of clothes and other belongings.

He was ready.

CHAPTER 8

THE CUSTODIAN'S LEGACY

When the light had faded from the plaza, Elias and Dashiel left their house. Dashiel carried his bag on his back, and Elias wore Gailfaur's Flute around his neck and carried an old lantern in his hand. They moved with the utmost silence, eyes scanning the area to make sure there was no one in sight.

Dashiel closed the door to his house. His hand lingered on the knob as he said a silent goodbye. *I shall return to you soon, but I will not be the same. That is a promise.*

Instead of making for the trails, which were patrolled by the Azahar guard, they went straight into the moonlit woods. Dashiel followed his father for a long time, until the forest opened into a clearing. The sparse canopy of leaves allowed the moonlight to seep in. Indistinct sounds echoed from afar, maybe the howling of a lonely sisyphus wolf, the music that lion-tailed elves played with their steel pans, or the luciums' melodious laughter as they jumped from tree to tree.

"Just a moment, Son," Elias said. "I must do something before we continue."

Something materialized from the folds of his custodian tunic. Dashiel could barely see the object through the darkness, but his eyes flashed with recognition as it crossed into the lantern's light. Elias's baton, his prized weapon.

"Orphée?" Dashiel flinched.

"Let me tell you a story, Son. The baton's story," he began. "This is the rarest kind of weapon in the world. Inside, it carries the might of twelve different weapons. Thousands have sought to obtain one throughout the years. Made of kerganium, these ancient batons were said to have been forged by gods. These weapons were called doizemants."

"Doizemants?" Dashiel repeated. "Why name it Orphée when you could call it Doizemant? I think that's a better name."

Elias shook his head. "There is a reason. Years ago, back before you were born, this doizemant belonged to a powerful warrior. His name was Agatus Orphée, my mentor."

Dashiel's eyes widened. He listened with careful attention. His father's life was a complete mystery. Elias never spoke of the time before he became Gailfaur's custodian.

"Orphée came from a long line of warriors, but a cruel twist of destiny had taken away his family, disrupting the line forever. That is when we met. I was young, maybe around your age, but had the burning desire to be stronger." He chuckled. "Maybe you got that from me, kid.

"He needed an apprentice, and I a teacher. We needed each other, even if he didn't want to admit it. At first, he refused, but I kept asking until he agreed. He was bitter and stubborn, but we worked together quite nicely. I grew stronger, and so did our friendship."

Elias's nostalgic expression was brand new. His eye sparkled, something Dashiel hadn't seen for the longest time.

As if breaking from a trance, Elias frowned. "Then Orphée got ill with age and passed away. On his deathbed, he summoned me once. He took my hand and said, 'The most important lesson, you shall not learn from me but from the doizemant. It does not matter if others consider you insignificant. Inside, you have the power to move mountain and ocean as long as you nourish who your heart wants you to be. Act with kindness and responsibility to protect those around you.

Give your body to those who are good-natured and your heart to those who are impossible to reach.'" Elias took Dashiel's hand and placed the baton into it.

Confused over his strange behavior, Dashiel gazed at his father.

Elias closed his eyes. "He then said, right before passing away, 'Doizemant that holds the power I seek no more, I am grateful for your serviceThin space between ' and " The doizemant began to emit a bright light. "'I present to you the being you are to accept as your equal. Abandon our form, and be born again to serve your new master.'"

Numerous colorful lights floated down from the baton, disappearing before they reached the mossy ground. It emitted whispering voices and a warm sensation that expanded throughout Dashiel's body. Peace engulfed him, as if he were dreaming. The weapon shortened in length, its eagle adornments melting away. Silver leaves and golden rays sprouted on each of the baton's tips, forming stars. The leaves stretched downward, interlacing over the golden surface, forming the grip.

The light slowly faded away.

"What happened to it?" Dashiel asked, worried. "Did I do something to it?"

"No. The doizemant's physical form reflects its master's ability level."

"Master? Does that mean . . .?"

"Yes. It is now yours," Elias said, faintly smiling.

His father's prized weapon was now his. Dashiel's hands trembled. For a moment, a lump in his throat prevented him from talking. "But this is your greatest pride."

"Son, my greatest pride is you." Elias put his hand on Dashiel's shoulder. "I don't say it as often as I should, but you are."

Dashiel wrapped his father in a tight hug. "I'll guard it with my life."

"All right." Elias pushed him away gently. "I know you will."

As they separated, Elias ran his hand over the baton. "It's a fickle and whimsical weapon, and it's full of secrets. You will grow together, and it will be incumbent on you to discover all the secrets it holds."

"Mine," Dashiel said, looking at the baton with a heart full of joy. His mind exploded with the possibilities that it offered. It would be perfect for his journey. He didn't mind the simple form that it had taken. He kind of preferred it this way. The baton was him, and he was the baton. "Thank you, Papa."

"And now you can name it however you want," Elias said, his voice harmonizing with an owl's hoot.

"Orphée," Dashiel said without a thought. "I understand now why you named it after your mentor. You wanted to keep his memory and final lesson alive. I want to do that too."

He swung Orphée through the air.

"Besides, I'm no good with names."

"Very well, Son," Elias said. "Now, off to the meeting point. Your mother must be waiting for us."

They continued their walk across the darkened woods, passing hundreds of fenku and halban trees, navigating around herds of sleeping jukkes, and hiding from the Azahar guards. One mistake, and Dashiel's journey would end before it began.

They finally stopped in a place that Dashiel recognized: the spot at the edge where the Brigadiers had entered. The crack, though smaller than before, still floated in midair. The sword, now cold as ice, was still jammed into the earth.

"Why is the crack still there, Papa?" Dashiel asked.

"The luciums and fenku healed the flora and the burns on the ground, but they couldn't heal the barrier, not completely," Elias said coldly.

"Gailfaur is growing weak," Dashiel said, remembering his father's words. "The luciums and fenku get their powers from Gailfaur."

"Yes, indeed," Elias said, moving onward.

A few meters from the crack, a wagon, a horse, and four people awaited. Emily's eyes sparkled. "You're here."

Dashiel followed Elias toward the group. Rupert and Charlotte were there, as expected, standing next to a hooded individual who was petting the horse while holding its reins. His parents had already prepared him: Neither Rupert nor Charlotte would be joining him. Rupert's apprentice would ensure his training. It seemed the hooded figure would be his travel companion.

Inching a little closer, Dashiel recognized the man as Sylvain Aurante. He removed his hood, revealing green eyes that shone like emeralds and ebony hair that rustled in the breeze.

"We knew you come, *mer*," Rupert said, extending his hand to shake. "Hope you ready."

"I am," Dashiel said, shaking the enormous, hairy hand. "I'll do my best."

"That's how we talk, Dashiel," Charlotte said encouragingly. "Oh, you have no idea how happy I am that you will become one of us."

Rupert took Dashiel's bag and tossed it into the cart.

"Dashiel," Emily said. "We have something to give you that we think can help you during your travels."

She took a bag made of coarse gray fabric out of her pocket. The shuffling caused the contents of the bag to clink together. Dashiel opened the pouch to find a handful of coins, Zaphyrolean Imperial Crests.

"Your father and I have been saving it for years," she said, handing him the bag. "Use it in moderation and only when you need it."

"Thanks, Mama," Dashiel said.

She glanced at Elias, seemingly waiting for him to do something.

"Oh, right." His father reached into the folds of his cape and pulled out a wooden case. "Take it. It's for Orphée," he said, matter-of-factly, extending the case to Dashiel. No remnant of the emotion he had expressed earlier remained.

Dashiel's fingers clasped the smooth wood. He put the doizemant inside and carefully placed the case in the cart. A faint, skunky smell wafted from the cart's splintered planks.

"One more thing," Elias said, approaching Dashiel and handing him a yellow envelope tied with hemp string. Someone had written *Roderigo B. Regallette* in a neat hand. "I want you to give this to

Roderigo Regallette, and only to Roderigo Regallette. I'm sure you two will cross paths."

"Got it." Dashiel stowed the letter in one of his vest pockets. "And will you please try to advocate for Grimley?"

"You know we can't promise anything," Elias said, seemingly annoyed by the request.

"We will most definitely try, honey," Emily said. She started to tear up. "Promise me you'll take care of yourself."

"I promise, Mama," he said. "I still can't believe I'm doing this."

Dashiel hugged his parents.

"One final thing. I want you to remember this." Emily took his bandaged hand. "Do not feel ashamed of fear, for fear is as real as the reflection of a mirror. Beware of actions motivated by fear, for they are as real as the palm of your hand."

Emily turned his hand, revealing his palm.

"I will." Dashiel left his parents and hopped up onto the cart next to Sylvain.

"Listen to me, both of you," Charlotte said. "Use the paths that I've marked for you on your map. They will keep you off the imperial roads as much as possible."

Rupert took two small ochre booklets out of his pocket.

"Imperial identifications. Them handy, you move free in Zaphyrolean territory. Cost an eye. No lose them."

"Dashiel," Charlotte called, "your training begins the moment you leave Azahar. Do what your companion says, and you'll be fine. Whatever you might need, he will assist you."

Elias lifted the flute from around his neck and held it in front of his mouth. "I will open a passage in the barrier using the existing fissure. It will not last long. The luciums might come and try to close it."

"Ready, Dashiel?" Sylvain asked.

Dashiel's heart palpitated. His eyes fixed on the Outerland beyond the barrier.

"Ready."

Elias blew the flute, but there was no sound. And yet the crack began to open, sending green sparks flying. When the fissure was big enough for the wagon to pass through, Sylvain urged his horse into trot.

"Remember, don't tell anyone outside of the order where you are from. The identifications have all the information you might need," Charlotte said, walking alongside the wagon. "And most important, your real names are the most valuable things you will have out there. Don't trust anyone with them."

"May Providence be with you," the three adults said in unison.

As Dashiel waved at his parents, something beyond them caught his eye. Luciums were floating gracefully toward the edge. And deeper in the woods, a figure stared at him. The unexpected spectator was made of pure light and glowed brighter than the stars. Tall as some of the trees, the half-human, half-horse creature observed his departure. It was a centaur, and not just any centaur. It was Gailfaur, the forest deity, in all his glory.

Dashiel couldn't believe his eyes. He had never seen Gailfaur before. He realized it was a sign from Providence. He was doing the right thing, and he was going to be fine. Gailfaur gave him strength, the final push into his journey. There was no turning back, and at this point, he did not wish to do so.

The cart moved through the passage. Dashiel's heart beat wildly. Despite his frequent daydreaming, he'd never imagined that he would leave the forest in such a way. As the cart carried them through the hole, Dashiel felt like he was seeing everything for the first time. Every tree, every rock, and even the sky seemed to have a different color, sound, and aroma.

Maybe . . . he thought, a little green spark landing on his hand. *No,* he corrected himself. *It's possible, and it is happening.* When he opened his hand, the spark flew away with the breeze.

CHAPTER 9

BLOOD-BORNE COMPLICITY

The long-forgotten road that used to connect Azahar with the rest of the empire resurfaced as the wagon strayed farther from the forest. The trees grew scarce, giving way to virgin hills and plains speckled with the occasional cluster of trees. The routes that Charlotte had marked on the map took them through Zaphyrelia's Nine Hills. The paths made the journey longer, but it was for the best, for they could not risk being discovered by imperial guards.

As they moved stealthily through empire's lands, Dashiel couldn't help marveling at every single thing he saw, especially the mountains and the twinkling lights on the horizon, lights that belonged to towns and cities. He had only known his hometown and the forest that surrounded it. Though he'd known about the empire, he'd had no idea of Zaphyrelia's true beauty.

As the moon moved across the sky, the pair continued along the path until Sylvain stopped the cart far from the road at the foot of the second hill. Orchards of pears and apples grew with no human intervention, and the ground was covered with a fluffy layer of grass. They had to rest and prepare themselves for the days to come, which would surely be draining. Sylvain took a canvas bag from the cart. Inside was a tent big enough for a bonfire and two weary travelers. The tent's dark color made for a nighttime refuge that would avoid the prying eyes of undesirable company.

Dashiel and Sylvain settled in. While Sylvain hid the cart and his horse behind the tent, Dashiel stoked the fire, adding additional wood whenever necessary. Smoke escaped through a hole in the tent's ceiling, and the burning wood released a bittersweet aroma.

"Dashiel, I'll take first watch. You sleep," Sylvain said, grabbing his crossbow. "I'll wake you up when it's your turn."

Dashiel didn't feel tired at all. But he followed Sylvain's orders, bunching his bag of clothing into a pillow. He then began to untie his shoelaces.

"Sleep with your shoes on. At least when you are on the road," Sylvain said, grabbing a cloth from his bag. "As Cobalt Phantasms, we never know when we'll be called to action. Or have to flee."

"Good idea." Dashiel relaced his shoes.

"Also, you should sleep with your baton next to you," Sylvain said. "If we are attacked, you won't want to waste time getting it out of its case."

Dashiel set Orphée next to his makeshift pillow, then stretched out on the grass. He closed his eyes and tried to fall asleep but found it difficult. Excitement and nerves fluttered his gut, a sensation like lizards crawling up his stomach. He opened his eyes and saw Sylvain cleaning his weapon.

His companion remained a mystery. He still made Dashiel feel strange, but his presence had ceased to be unsettling. Curiosity flooded him. Who was this person in front of him? He was two or three years older than Dashiel, rather tall and well built, with a pretty-boy face and a beauty mark above his lip. But those were only trivialities. Dashiel needed to know more. What was he like inside? Could he be trusted?

"It's weird leaving Azahar," Dashiel said, propping himself up on an elbow, trying to break the ice. "It's overwhelming."

"I know how it feels . . . to leave one's hometown," Sylvain said. "I've done it many times."

Dashiel sat all the way up, his curiosity getting the better of him. "How many times?"

"If I recall correctly, six times, including this one," he answered with a dull tone.

"Tell me about your travels."

"All right." Sylvain set his crossbow on the ground beside him. "One time, I was sent away to train for the Cobalt Phantasms in Carbakiel."

"What about your first time?" Dashiel insisted.

Sylvain remained silent for a moment.

"My first time, I was very little. My parents took me with them on one of their trips. Something went wrong. I was the only one to make it back." Sylvain wore a blank expression. "It was around the time Asedia took power."

"I'm sorry," Dashiel said, stunned. "I didn't mean to intrude."

"It's fine. I don't remember them that much." Sylvain scrubbed his crossbow. "My mentors have always taken good care of me. They taught me everything I know. They're like parents to me."

"Rupert and Charlotte are amazing," Dashiel said. "You're lucky that they trained you. I can't imagine being trained by someone as strong as Rupert."

Sylvain giggled.

"Yes, guess I am. He is a great fellow, but sometimes I don't understand what he is saying with his Peskeira Islander dialect."

"You too? I thought I was the only one." The two burst into laughter. When their amusement died down, Dashiel asked, "What is it like fighting alongside them?"

"Well, Charlotte and Rupert may not always agree, but together they are one of the best squadrons in the order," Sylvain said.

Dashiel's brow crinkled at the term. "Squadron? What's that?"

"Squadrons are like teams. All official Cobalt Phantasms are divided into squadrons. There are three types: research, assistance, and combat and defense. Each squadron is named after an animal. For example, Rupert and Charlotte are part of the Bear Squadron, which belongs to the highest level of the combat category."

"What squadron are you in?" Dashiel asked.

"I haven't been assigned to one yet. There was no time."

"You think we could be assigned to the same squadron?" Dashiel asked as he lay down, crossing his arms behind his head.

"I can't really say," Sylvain answered. "But that would be . . . interesting."

The conversation paused for a minute.

"To be honest, I'm happy you came," Sylvain said, breaking the quiet. "I was never good at making friends. Before I was selected to join the order, I spent a lot of time alone. You seem like a good person to talk to, I guess. People find me odd, and they might be right. Let me tell you that you're extremely lucky to have lived a normal life."

The word *normal* cut through Dashiel like the sharp end of an icicle. There was something about his childhood, something about his present, that made his life far from normal, and he'd kept it secret for years. A secret that, if exposed, would guarantee his expulsion from the order.

He stared at his bandaged hand and pondered for a while. Was he skilled enough to avoid a cut or a slash? Would he be quick enough to hide the wound? Nothing was certain. Would people notice? Probably. He could use a little help. His father had said that Sylvain could be trusted, but could he really? Only one way to find out.

"Sylvain," Dashiel said slowly. "I'm going to tell you a secret. It's extremely personal, and you have to promise me that you won't share it with anyone."

"You really don't have to tell me."

"I know. But if I want this to work—joining the order, leaving the forest, everything—I'll need your help. Besides, my father said that I could trust you."

"He was right." Sylvain seemed a bit startled that Elias would put such faith in him. His lips lifted, but only briefly, and then his expression turned serious. "What is it that you want to tell me?"

Dashiel took a deep breath. "Well, you see, I was born with a rare blood disease called hemocarcomia."

Sylvain's eyes widened. "Hemocarcomia? The disease that makes your body eliminate your own blood?"

At his reaction, Dashiel questioned whether he had made a mistake in sharing his secret. But there was no way back now. He had to press on.

"Right. My body doesn't accept the blood that it produces, because it's made of two blood types that are total opposites. It's not contagious, but people seem to think it is."

Sylvain shrugged, puzzlement in his eyes. "I don't understand. That disease is degenerative. Kids with hemocarcomia rarely make it past childhood. And you look . . . healthy."

"The symptoms of the disease were only present when I was really young: weakness, discolored blood, unexplainable bruises and cuts. But you're right. I was lucky to outlive it."

"So, you're healed. What's the problem? The danger has passed."

"The problem is that I kinda, sort of still have it. All the symptoms disappeared except for the most obvious one: my blood is still discolored. If anyone sees me bleed, they'll know right away about the disease."

Sylvain studied him, a pensive look on his face. Dashiel's heart threatened to break as he waited for a response. Finally, Sylvian spoke. "That illness could definitely make them kick you out of the order."

Dashiel held his breath as he nodded.

"Count on me to keep your secret. I'll do whatever I can to help," Sylvain said.

"Thank you so much." Dashiel breathed a sigh of both relief and happiness. "You're my only hope."

"Your father is a great man. I would do anything for his family," Sylvain said.

All of a sudden, a single drop of blood appeared on Sylvain's neck, slowly sliding down.

"You're bleeding," Dashiel said.

"What are you talking about?"

"Your neck." He pointed at the cut. "Are you all right?"

"My neck?" Sylvain's fingers landed on the blood. "Oh. This. I must have cut myself shaving. It's nothing, really."

Dashiel took a canteen and a piece of fabric out of his bag. He wet the cloth and offered it to his companion. Sylvain looked at the cloth as if he weren't sure what to do with it.

"Clean the cut. We don't want it to get infected."

"Thanks." Sylvain reluctantly grabbed the cloth and covered the cut. "And now, it's time to rest. We need to leave before the sun rises."

"And we shall." Dashiel lay down, resting his head on his bag once more. He intended to sleep, but there was one more thing he had to say. "Sylvain?"

"Yes?"

"You aren't odd. People might not know you well." Dashiel lifted onto his elbows. "You know, you were wrong about something."

"Really? What's that?"

"You're good at making friends. Otherwise, I wouldn't be yours right now. Right?"

"Hmm." Sylvain's cheeks reddened. "Right."

"Good night." Dashiel yawned.

The anxiety that had plagued him ever since he left Azahar was gone, and peace took its place. Sylvain's willingness to help him calmed that excruciating pressure inside his stomach. He looked through the hole in the tent's ceiling. For the first time in many years, he fell asleep as he counted each star.

CHAPTER 10

LAND OF DESECRATION

ashiel and Sylvain continued their journey over the desolate hills of the empire. Good weather accompanied them all the way to the top of the ninth and final hill, where the two young men scouted the spot where the path merged with the imperial road. It was the only route to their destination. They cautiously moved toward the pathway, always on alert. Guards in uniforms the same color as their Brigadier subordinates rode ferocious black horses along the road, making sure order was kept.

Choosing his moment carefully, Sylvain merged the wagon onto the road, joining other travelers. No guard saw this happen, and no one seemed to care about it. They had been blessed by Providence, for if they had been caught evading the guards, they would have been incarcerated. They continued for miles, until they came across a fork in the road.

"Where are we going?" Dashiel asked.

"To Carbakiel. The path on the right," Sylvain responded as he steered the wagon in that direction.

Dashiel had heard that name the previous night. "Carbakiel? The place where you trained?"

"The very same."

Because most of the other travelers had split off at the fork, the path to Carbakiel was empty, and no guards were in sight. Despite the apparent tranquility, Sylvain remained vigilant.

He was a good travel companion, and Dashiel found their conversations engaging. Still, when Sylvain remained quiet and pensive for long periods, Dashiel got bored. On several occasions, he pulled out his favorite book and read to pass the time.

After two hours, the Carbakiel skyline appeared on the horizon. Dashiel couldn't wait to learn more about the town where Sylvain had trained.

"I didn't know that I'd be training in the same place as you," Dashiel said, but Sylvain was so focused on the road that he didn't respond to the comment. "Will I learn to shoot a crossbow like you do?"

"What?" Sylvain asked, confused. "You're not training in Carbakiel. You're training in St. Victoire Dowager. Also, not to brag, but no one will ever learn to shoot a crossbow like I do."

"Fine. So why are we going to Carbakiel?"

"We're catching a train there to our final destination."

"What's a . . . train?"

"You really don't know what—" Sylvain's eyes narrowed. "A train is like a longer and bigger carriage that doesn't need an animal to pull it. It can also go about fifty times faster than six horses."

Dashiel was awestruck by the thought of a machine capable of such things. "Can't wait to see it!"

He calmed his excitement by watching the countryside pass by. His gaze caught on a gray tree at the side of the road. Its bark was dried up and its limbs were almost as thin as thread. A few brown leaves hung from its branches.

"That tree is ill," Dashiel said.

"How do you know?" Sylvain asked, not taking his eyes off the road.

"I just know. An Azahar must know. Trees are important in our daily lives." Dashiel twisted his neck to get a better view of the sick tree.

He needn't have bothered. The wagon passed more trees with a similar decaying aspect.

"Look!" Dashiel pointed at the trees. "Those are sick too. Some even . . . dead."

Soon all the trees in sight were dry and gray, as was the grass surrounding them.

"How is that possible?" Dashiel mumbled.

"Look straight ahead."

Dashiel looked up to find a huge, black mountain in front of them, with the road leading directly into it. As they got closer, a thin silhouette of buildings appeared behind the now-translucent mountain—buildings that were barely visible through a thick haze of vapors. Hundreds of chimneys spouted from the structures, spewing thick, dark smoke into the sky and clouding the sun.

"This is it," Sylvain said. "The town of Carbakiel."

"Why is there so much smoke?" Dashiel asked, put off by such a horrifying image. "No wonder nature is ill."

"Those chimneys—and their smoke—are the reason why I came here to train and the reason why you *won't* train here."

"Why is that?"

"Years back, Emperor Rafael Belecrose ordered that the train, a new foreign invention, be brought to Zaphyrelia. Carbakiel was a commercially beneficial point, so a train station was constructed here," Sylvain explained, carefully guiding the wagon around a fallen tree. "When Asedia took power, he decided to build weapons factories in the same town so the trains could easily transport the products. The factories never operated under any regulations, emitting smoke that is extremely harmful."

"If there are so many problems, why did the Cobalt Phantasms set up a base here?" Dashiel asked, entranced by the withered wildflowers. Their dry petals and leaves were of an ashy color.

"For the children."

"The children?"

"Asedia ordered a great draft from all corners of the empire, so most of the men were obliged to leave the town. The sick, elderly, women, and children were left behind. The factories all decided to hire only children because they could do as much work as an adult for a third of the pay. Asedia wanted inhumanly cheap labor, and he found a way to get it by plunging Carbakiel into a vicious cycle. The adults die in battle, and the kids who manage to survive the working conditions in the factories either die from health problems or get drafted when they grow up."

"Why don't they just leave?" Dashiel's eyes returned to the city ahead.

"Because Zaphyroleans are not allowed to leave their hometowns unless they have an identification like this one." He took out the ochre booklet that Rupert had given him. "They are extremely expensive. Not everyone can afford one." Sylvain put away his booklet. "Those who try to escape are hunted down and killed—or worse, turned into Ochre Brigadiers."

A lump grew inside Dashiel's throat. Azahar had sheltered his people from the stark realities of life under Asedia's reign. They had been lucky. "How did you help the children?"

"We took care of them, protected them, fed them, and healed them. But the moment arrived when the smoke began to get to us too. The founders of the order commanded that we abort the mission." Sylvain sighed. "The kids who we took care of saw us leave, never to return. I would have stayed behind. I would have given my life for them."

"One day, we'll return here. We'll help those kids. Even if it is only you and me." Dashiel clapped his companion on the back. "I promise."

"Thanks, Dashiel."

The pair arrived at the outskirts of Carbakiel, getting a better view of the atrocious situation. The enormous factories, built of black bricks and gray cement, served as the walls of the town. The only way in or out was through a gap between two of the factories, beneath a sign of obscure metal letters that read *Carbakiel*. Four Ochre Brigadiers stood quietly inside niches built into the factory walls, and two guards were stationed on each side of the entrance. Dashiel found the Brigadiers' calm unsettling. The one time he'd encountered them, they'd been quite the opposite.

The wagon approached the entrance, and a guard stopped it.

"What is the nature of your visit?" he asked in a clipped tone.

Dashiel didn't know what to say.

Sylvain interceded. "We're going to the station, sir. We're travelers."

"Where are you going?"

"To St. Victoire Dowager in Hermesia."

Dashiel looked at his companion, confused. He hadn't known that his training would take place abroad.

"Your passports," the guard commanded.

Dashiel and Sylvain gave their ochre booklets to the guard. The guard remained silent as he rifled through the pages. A second guard walked to the rear of the wagon and rummaged through its contents. Dashiel thought of Sylvain's crossbow and his baton, both of which were in the cart. He looked nervously at Sylvain, but his companion appeared calm. Dashiel's cheeks burned as the prying eyes of the guards and Brigadiers rested on them.

A voice called from the back of the cart. "What's in this case?" If the guard had found Orphée or the crossbow, he and Sylvain were cooked.

"What's inside?" the guard demanded.

"It's nothing," Sylvain responded calmly.

The guard took the case and tossed it onto Dashiel's lap. "Open it."

"Y-y-yes, sir." Dashiel quaked. His trembling fingers landed on the case's closure and flicked it open. To his surprise, the baton wasn't inside. Instead, in the satin impression Orphée had made, there were rocks.

The guard scanned Dashiel's face. "An odd collection to have."

"Yes. They were a gift from my father, sir." Dashiel tried to smile naturally, but it came off as more of a grimace. "I love . . . rocks."

The guard returned the booklets and went back to his position beside the entrance. "You may pass."

Sylvain spurred on his horse, and they entered the town.

Dashiel exhaled heavily. "You hid my baton, right?"

"I did. And even if they'd dismantled the wagon, they never would've found it."

CHAPTER II

CARBAKIEL

ashiel and Sylvain moved slowly through the neglected streets. The factories had stripped the town of its wealth and charm, leaving behind a neglected, dark husk of sadness and death. The white brick buildings decayed under the thick layer of dirt and soot that the surrounding factories spewed.

From his perch atop the cart, Dashiel observed never-before-seen gray creatures with red scars on their bodies, barely able to walk. He flinched at the realization that these were the children Sylvain had talked about: dirty, thin, and sick, all either on their way to the factories or prowling like wraiths. Children waited in long lines to enter the factories, while malnourished women stood in lines to buy scraps of food with the minuscule earnings of their children. Soot darkened their faces, though many had thin trails of lighter skin from their eyes to their jawbones—tracks of tears they cried only during the nighttime.

The guards treated the locals as if they were animals, whacking them with weapons forged by their victims. Dashiel's stomach hardened at the sight. How was it possible for man to create so much suffering?

A painful silence enveloped the town. No one spoke; no one laughed. They stared at the visitors as they moved around. Dashiel and Sylvain parked their cart in an alley full of dusty contraptions that

Sylvain said had once helped create the white bricks. They had been reduced to mere reminders of better days.

"We'll go on foot from here," Sylvain said.

"We're leaving your cart and your horse here?" Dashiel asked incredulously, looking around the decrepit alley. "Are you sure?"

"Yes. Another Phantasm will come for the cart." Sylvain reached into his pocket and pulled out a small copper container. He showed it to Dashiel. "We won't have any problems if we use this."

"What's that?"

"Chameleon balm," Sylvain replied. "Hold it for a minute."

He gave Dashiel the container and went to the cart. He pulled out his things and placed them on the ground. He then opened a secret porthole in the cart and took out Orphée and his crossbow. After setting them next to his belongings, he grabbed the copper container.

"Although its name suggests otherwise, there's no chameleon in here," he said. "But it can give humans, animals, and things the ability to camouflage themselves. It will last long enough for an ally to come."

Sylvain opened the container; inside, there was a creamy substance. With a finger, he scooped out a small quantity of cream and slid it over the cart's boards and his horse's mane. In a matter of seconds, the cream began to disappear, and the cart and horse disappeared with it.

"That's grand!" Dashiel was shocked. "But how will they find it if it's invisible?"

"Excellent question," Sylvain said as he searched within his rucksack. He took out a piece of white chalk. "It's high time I taught you our organization's crest." He handed the chalk to Dashiel.

"Grand!"

"Please, keep it down," Sylvain whispered. "Walls have ears."

"You are probably right," Dashiel whispered back.

"I need you to draw it right there." Sylvain signaled to a nearby wall, which was dark with soot. "Draw a circle."

Dashiel drew an imperfect circle, soot raining over him as the chalk scraped against the wall.

"Draw two thick ribbons with swirling ends enveloping the upper and lower parts of the circle. Now draw one crown on each side."

Dashiel followed his companion's orders the best he could.

"Finally, draw a nine-pointed star in the middle of the circle, and add three smaller stars around it."

Dashiel took his time drawing the stars. He glanced over his shoulder at Sylvain. "Did I do it right?"

"No."

He tried again. "Better?"

"Nope."

It took multiple tries, as he had to erase his efforts with his hand. With every failed attempt, frustration pricked Dashiel's pride like a thistle. When he finished, he took a couple of steps back to admire his handwork.

"How about now?"

Sylvain was unconvinced. "It's your first time drawing our crest. You'll have time to get better. For now, use this." He handed Dashiel a piece of paper with the crest drawn on it. "Just hang it on the wall."

"Hey! Why didn't you give me this to begin with?" Dashiel shook the drawing with his dirty hands.

Sylvain laughed. "I thought it would be funny to watch you try."

"I see," Dashiel said, surprise on his face. He hadn't pegged Sylvain as a jokester. "Was it funny?"

"You have no idea."

"You do have a strange sense of humor, Sylvain Aurante." Dashiel smirked, rubbing his hands on the sides of his pants to clean his skin of soot and chalk.

Out of nowhere, a resounding, seemingly never-ending whistle filled the air.

"What's that?" Dashiel yelled to be heard over the din.

"That's the train's whistle," Sylvain explained. He took a small brass watch out of his rucksack and checked the time. "It seems that whistle belongs to the train that will take us to Hermesia. We should go to the station now."

"Incredible! It's like it was calling us." Dashiel was in awe. "I can't wait."

Belongings in tow, the pair left the alley behind. They traversed Carbakiel's grimy streets until they arrived at the plaza that housed the train station. Dashiel had never seen anything like it. Contrasting starkly with the dark and dirty town that surrounded it, the train station was in impeccable condition, built of sturdy white brick and topped with a gleaming bronze roof. A carving of the Asedia coat of arms presided over the entryway: a shield surrounded by thorns, crowned with a cuplike object. On both sides of the cup, two rams agonized, as chains imprisoned them.

To Dashiel, it was outrageous that the surrounding city fell to pieces while the imperial train station shone with splendor.

The guards circled menacingly, ensuring that everything was under control and the filthy locals were kept out of the pristine plaza. The Brigadiers remained upright in their sentinel positions.

Dashiel and Sylvain ascended the white staircase. To the side of the entryway, various ticket windows awaited. Sylvain approached one of them.

"How much for a ticket?" he asked.

"Five hundred Imperial Crests," the vendor replied.

Dashiel pulled out the bag of coins that his parents had given him and looked inside. He probably had around two hundred Imperial Crests. He couldn't afford the ticket.

After thanking the vendor, Sylvain returned to his companion. "Ready?"

Dashiel closed his eyes for a moment, inflating his reddening cheeks. He blew out a heavy breath. "I don't have enough to buy my ticket," he said quietly.

"What are you talking about?"

"I don't have five hundred Imperial Crests," Dashiel said, stressed, as he sat heavily on one of the benches outside the station.

"Not a problem, Dashiel," Sylvain said, taking a seat next to him.

Dashiel looked up. "What do you mean, 'Not a problem'?"

"It would be a problem if I didn't have your ticket right here in my hand." Sylvain took his hand out of his pocket. He held not one but two train tickets.

"I appreciate it, really, but I can't accept it. It's not fair for you to spend your money on me." Dashiel stood up. "Come on, I'll go with you, and we can get your money back."

"Dashiel, this is my welcome-to-the-order gift. I owe it to you for saving my life back in Azahar." Sylvain handed Dashiel his ticket. "Besides, didn't you say we were friends?"

Dashiel glanced at the yellow rectangle of paper in his hands. He surely needed the ticket, and he wanted with all his might to see a train. "I'll take it only if you let me pay you back when I have more money."

"Of course," Sylvain said.

"Thank you!" Dashiel shook Sylvain's hand and returned to admiring the ticket that would take him to St. Victoire Dowager, to his destiny.

Sylvain let a brief smile show. "Time to go. The train's waiting."

Carbakiel Station was even larger than it had seemed from the outside. The structure was supported by a skeleton of large metal bars. Hundreds of lamps illuminated the station's four platforms. Many people milled about, some waiting for a train and others saying goodbye to their loved ones. The white, pressurized vapor that the trains emitted descended gently and wafted between the groups of people waiting to board.

Dashiel's attention turned to the enormous metallic monster that extended from one side of the station to the other. Without taking his eyes off the train, Dashiel walked from one end of the platform to the other, drinking in every detail that this marvel of technology offered. He became entranced by the reflection in one of the windows.

"I knew you'd like it," Sylvain called out from behind him.

Dashiel snapped out of his reverie and turned around. "Like it? I love it!" He picked up his rucksack and Orphée's case. "This is our train?"

"No. Ours is at platform three."

"What are we waiting for?" Dashiel weaved his way through the crowd toward their platform.

"Wait up!" Sylvain called, hurrying after him.

Dashiel and Sylvain arrived at their platform. The passengers who were waiting to board had divided themselves into two lines: one for first-class passengers and another for people who could not afford first-class tickets. The pair walked to the back of the second line.

Dashiel watched the crowd as he waited for their train to board. Three women in expensive, brightly colored dresses, capes, and hats walked past, followed by three pages carrying their fine trunks. Dashiel guessed the women were kin, the wrinkled one leading the trio clearly the mother.

He had never seen anyone dressed so extravagantly in Azahar. They seemed ridiculous in their excessively adorned clothing and their fancy hats, pearls, and feathers. The women held themselves with impeccable posture, backs straight and chins in the air. They were so sure of their place in the world. They kept walking, ignoring the riff-raff around them as they assumed their place in the first-class line. It, too, was full of extravagance, with chairs and tables, and waiters who catered to the wealthy passengers' every whim.

Tired of waiting, Dashiel glanced at the other passengers in his line. One girl in particular caught his eye. She was wearing a marine-blue travel coat and a hat perched atop her upswept chestnut hair. Dashiel tried to be discreet, but it was difficult not to admire her looks.

"That girl's pretty good-looking, don't you think?" Sylvain elbowed Dashiel softly in his ribs, a knowing smirk on his face.

Flustered, Dashiel jerked his gaze from the girl and fixed it on the train. "What . . . what girl?"

"That girl in the blue, the one who you were gazing at a minute ago." Sylvain laughed quietly. "You should go talk to her."

"Me, talk to someone like that?" Dashiel scoffed. "She'd send me away before I could get a single word out."

Shouts rang out from the first-class line, drawing their attention away from the girl. The crowd craned their necks to try to see what had happened.

"My hat! Stop that thief!" a piercing voice cried. "That child has stolen my hat!"

A child moved stealthily past Dashiel's line. His eyes were wide, and his dirty hands clutched a violet hat adorned with feathers and pearls. He was surely one of the children who worked in the factories. Responding to the cries, three guards roamed the platforms, investigating the hat's disappearance.

"Sylvain, that kid has the hat," Dashiel said, worried.

"Let him go. Everyone in this line has seen him, and no one is going to say a word."

Indeed, several people in line had looked the other way, protecting the child.

"I don't mind that he stole it," Dashiel said, stretching his neck to keep the child in sight. "I'm worried that the guards will catch him."

"It's a shame, but we can't do anything. Let it go."

The guards got closer and closer. Surely they would notice the dirty child with the fancy hat.

"I can do something." Dashiel stepped out of line.

"Dashiel," Sylvain hissed, reaching out to grab his arm.

He evaded Sylvain's grasp and weaved between the passengers. They gave astonished gasps at his daring. He crouched next to the child, who clutched the hat as if it were the world's greatest treasure. Dashiel grabbed the hat.

"Let it go. You'll get yourself in trouble," he murmured. But the child, without understanding, shook his head defiantly. Dashiel continued pulling on the hat until the child let it slip from his grasp.

"Guards are coming," Dashiel said. "Go now."

The child walked away, and as Dashiel had predicted, the guards stopped him at the exit.

"What do you think you're doing here?" one of the guards said, grabbing the boy by the arm. "Search him!"

Another guard searched the child extensively but found nothing out of the ordinary. "You're not supposed to be here" he said. "If we see you here again, we'll beat the hell out of you. Scram!"

The guards let go of the child and went back to their positions. The boy waited for the guards to walk away before returning to Dashiel.

He looked up at the hat with large, tearful eyes. "Please, sir. I can't afford my mother's medicine. Please."

The expression on the child's face caused Dashiel's heart to shrivel. But returning the hat the boy would be a death sentence. "I can't give it to you."

Dashiel reached into his pocket, taking out the bag of money his parents had given him. He removed half the coins and placed them in the child's hand, his small fist around them.

"Never steal again. Understood?" Dashiel said with a serious face. "You won't be of any help to your family if you get caught."

"Yes, sir." The child smiled up at him in disbelief and ran back toward town as quickly as he could. He disappeared just outside the station, enveloped by the fog of the factories.

Hat in hand, Dashiel hurried back to the platform to return it to its owner. The hat had been stained with oil and ash during his tug-of-war with the child. Everyone in the economy line watched Dashiel walk to the first-class waiting area. The waiters and pages were all frantically searching for the missing hat while the other passengers sat at their tables, sipping on champagne.

The gentlemen and ladies of great distinction had revulsion written all over their faces as Dashiel searched for anyone without a hat. He found the owner: a lanky young woman with a perky, turned-up nose. It was one of the ladies who had walked past him earlier. Taking advantage of the waiters' occupied states, he slid into the first-class line a few meters from her. At the sight of him, she approached.

"Get your filthy hands off my hat," she snarled, snatching it back.

"I'm sorry, miss," Dashiel said, swallowing nervously. "I found it on the ground."

She ignored him. "Look at the state it is in. Disgusting!"

The short, stout woman beside her stood up. "Get away from him, Sister. You don't want to get infested with ticks."

The hat's owner huffed. "Sometimes common people can be so gross." She turned around and rejoined her mother, who had watched the whole exchange while sipping from her flute of champagne. Neither sister had bothered to thank Dashiel.

The rest of the first-class passengers disdainfully turned their backs on Dashiel.

One of the waiters became aware of his presence. He scanned Dashiel from head to toe, not bothering to make eye contact. In a cold voice, he said, "You can't be here. Please leave immediately."

Dashiel didn't say anything. He returned to his place beside Sylvain in the economy line. The passengers looked ahead with newfound eagerness, and Dashiel followed their eyes to the conductor, who stood between the two lines.

"All aboard!" he called in a clear, booming voice. "Please have your identifications and your tickets ready!"

"Dashiel," Sylvain said. "What you did was good in a vacuum, but you need to be more cautious. If those women had accused you of stealing their hat, nothing could have saved you from going to jail."

Sylvain took their ochre identification booklets out of his rucksack, giving one of them to Dashiel.

"Were you willing to let that child go to prison?" Dashiel asked.

Sylvain wore a reproachful expression. "You know that nobody wants to help the people of Carbakiel more than I do. But impulsive acts could have negative consequences. Remember that a Cobalt Phantasm must analyze a situation before acting. We need to stay invisible in the empire's eyes."

"Got it," Dashiel said.

The guards checked their identifications, and the pair boarded the train without any further problems. Dashiel's heart palpitated as he followed Sylvain down the narrow aisle of the train car. Even from the inside the machine was mind-boggling, a beast made of metal, wood, and vapor. Soon, it would push into motion. Soon, his training would begin. With his new friend at his side, things would surely go well.

CHAPTER 12

A BET ON DESTINY

ashiel regarded the train car with curiosity. The space was separated by small compartments, each containing a set of two varnished wooden benches. They were large enough for three passengers each and sat on opposite sides of the compartment. The upper part of each window had been opened, likely to provide better ventilation in the stuffy compartment.

The economy-class car that Dashiel had entered offered a glimpse of some first-class compartments. He glanced through a small window in the door that separated the two cars. It was draped in luxuries: The walls were adorned with candelabras, mirrors, and paintings. The seats were spacious and cushioned, upholstered with fine materials. Crystal chandeliers dangled from the ceiling, and waiters served guests exquisite delicacies and the finest drinks.

Dashiel had never seen anything so ostentatious in his life, but he did not need any of those things. He thought of himself as the luckiest person in the world just for having the opportunity to travel on a train.

He and Sylvain left their belongings in one of the baggage compartments and hunted for two free seats. They walked through the hallway until Sylvain found free spots in an otherwise full compartment.

Dashiel sat across from Sylvain and next to an uptight woman in round eyeglasses. She didn't look up from her book. This caught Dashiel's attention. He had seen countless books while working at Astor's library, but he had never seen a book like that, with its mint-green binding paste.

He was tempted to gawk but pulled his gaze from the book and glanced at the other passengers. He did a double take when he saw who was sitting next to the window.

It was the girl in blue, the one who had captured his imagination on the platform while he waited in line. She sat so close, only two seats away.

She didn't seem to notice Dashiel's presence. She only stared out the window, a faraway look in her eyes. She was a hundred times more beautiful than any of the upper-class women next door. So simple and natural. In that moment, Dashiel wished he had some of Grimley's charm with girls. If he had his best friend's skill, he could surely strike up a conversation with this girl.

The train's whistle shrieked, and the roar of the machinery broadcast their impending departure. Dashiel's thoughts wandered from the girl as the train kicked into motion. It was a delight for the senses—the vibration of the car, the aroma of the train's hot vapor and varnished seats, the sound of the machinery moving, and the vision of Carbakiel fading into the distance. Dashiel couldn't think of anything better.

Sometime after the train left Carbakiel, it slowed to a complete stop.

"We've arrived at the town of Myrtalo," announced the conductor, loud and clear.

An elderly couple next to Sylvain stood up and gathered their things. The girl in blue finally took her eyes away from the window, glancing at her traveling companions. With a small nod, she bid the older couple farewell. Next, she nodded to Sylvain. Finally, her eyes landed on Dashiel. She greeted him with a timid smile.

Startled, Dashiel displayed his teeth in what was meant to be a casual smile but ended up as an uncomfortable grimace. How he wished to have said something to her, but his mouth became as dry as his mind.

After a couple hours, the excitement of the voyage wore off, and Dashiel lost his fight against anxiety. Restlessly, he shook his right leg. Beads of perspiration formed on his palms and forehead. The bespectacled woman glanced at him, annoyed. Realizing that he was bothering her, Dashiel stopped moving. She reopened her peculiar book. Dashiel tried to read the title, but it was written in another language.

The train traveled quickly through Zaphyrelia's various provinces. But time seemed to stop whenever Dashiel stole a glance at the window and the girl in blue.

The woman beside Dashiel lowered her book and took a small basket out of her bag, extending it toward the girl in blue. It was full of spools of thread, needles, and white fabric. The girl accepted the needles and began to embroider one of the cloths. She appeared lost in concentration, unaware Dashiel was observing her every move.

The practiced movements of her thin, gloved fingers reminded Dashiel of the white flowers that bloomed on fenku branches during the summer. The sacred trees' limbs rose and fell in the breeze like gentle white waterfalls. Early in his journey, nothing else reminded Dashiel of home more.

Dashiel noticed that one of the girl's spools had fallen on the floor, rolling back and forth below the seats. He picked it up, thinking of it as an opportunity to exchange words with her.

"Ex-excuse me," Dashiel said, hoping to catch her attention.

The girl stopped her embroidery and looked at Dashiel with tender eyes.

Dashiel gulped, extending his hand with the spool. "I think . . . think . . ."

As quick as a crocodile's mouth, the girl's companion slammed her book shut, trapping Dashiel's hand. "I think not," she said with disdain.

"I just . . . I . . ." Dashiel tried to speak, not finding much success.

"Junei," the girl said, her voice as gentle as a flute and as sweet as a harp. "Let him go, please. He was trying to return the spool. Isn't that right?" She looked at Dashiel in a serene way.

Stupefied by the beauty of her voice, Dashiel nodded. The woman opened her book, begrudgingly freeing his hand.

The girl took the spool. "Thank you so much," she said, smiling, which caused Dashiel to turn red as a tomato. She turned to her companion. "Please, apologize to him."

"Me?" her companion asked, squeezing her book in her hands. "I'll do no such thing."

"Junei?" The girl gave her a tender look.

"Fine," the woman huffed. "My sincerest apologies for putting you in your place," she said, grinding her teeth with every word and refusing to look Dashiel in the eye.

"No . . . problem?" Dashiel responded, facing forward. He caught a glimpse of Sylvain, who was trying hard not to laugh.

"Sorry for the inconvenience." The girl resumed her embroidery.

The ride passed slowly as the train ran along the green fields of the empire. The girl's chaperone held her book in front of her face, but she peered at Dashiel's every movement out of the corner of her eye, boiling with anger. Dashiel gave Sylvain an uncomfortable eyebrow raise, seeking advice. His friend's expression suggested that he should stay calm.

"What in the world . . ." The chaperone lowered her book and covered her nose. "What is that ghastly smell?"

She fanned herself with the book and sniffed, trying to find the source of the unpleasant scent. She winced when her nose, like a bloodhound, pointed at Dashiel.

"Why is this not a surprise?" The chaperone quickly grabbed her bag and took out a glass perfume bottle. She spritzed Dashiel and sniffed again. "Much better."

A strong, plummy aroma took over the compartment.

The girl in blue stopped embroidering. She narrowed her eyes, as if just now understanding the reason for her companion's antics. She put her materials aside and stood up.

"I'm feeling a little motion sick," she said. "I think I'll move somewhere else." She dodged her companion's feet.

"I'll go with you," her companion said, packing her book and perfume back in the bag.

"Not necessary," the girl responded. "This young man can make sure nothing happens to me."

It took a moment for Dashiel to realize that she was talking about him. Her eyes told him to follow her.

"What? You can't be alone with this boy. You need a chaperone," her companion said, indignant.

"You're in the same train car. I'll be a few seats away. Please stay here, Junei." The girl walked to the back of the car and sat on a bench that had been vacated by passengers at the last stop.

She waited, staring at the window. Her chaperone fixed her gaze on Dashiel, mentally ordering him not to join her companion. Unable to resist any longer, Dashiel took his rucksack, stood up, and—ignoring the woman's owlish stare—walked to the back of the car. He took a seat across from the girl.

She sat gracefully, her gloved hands perched one on top of the other in her lap. Her pale skin gleamed like fine china, but her rosy cheeks emitted warmth. Her teeth were as white as snow and her chestnut hair meticulously gathered beneath a ribboned hat. It was as if a doll had come to life. Dashiel couldn't help staring at her large eyes. They weren't brown, green, blue, or black but a unique violet. Those eyes had hypnotized him the first time he saw them blink beneath her long, brilliant lashes. Her eyes shone brighter than the gemstone set into the brooch of her cape, brighter than the moon and sun.

A few seconds of silence passed. Dashiel's heart bumped mercilessly against his chest at the prospect of being so close to the girl. He had no idea what to say. *What's your name? How's your day going?*

Nothing sounded quite right. He had never been good at talking to girls. If only he had Grimley's gift of gab. He opened his mouth, but a lump in his throat prevented anything from coming out. Mortification took over, and it showed on his face, although he tried to hide it.

"My sister is a bit overprotective," the girl said, finally breaking the silence. "But she does it because she cares about me."

Dashiel nodded, still unable to speak.

"Do you have any siblings?" the girl asked.

"No...," Dashiel squeaked.

"You know, it was really brave, what you did on the platform," she said in the same sweet voice that had commanded Junei to apologize. "I don't know if I could have done something like that."

Dashiel cleared his throat. "It wasn't . . . anything . . . special," he replied, reddening a bit more.

"Are you joking?" She clapped once. "It was extremely brave."

Dashiel snickered, running his fingers up and down the dulled crimson upholstery. "It was more impulsive than brave," he said, trying not to look silly. "But thank you. People tell me I should think more before I act. But I can't . . . help it."

The girl leaned toward him.

"Sometimes the heart has better ideas than the brain. Nothing wrong with that, Mister . . .?"

Dashiel realized how rude he had been. He still hadn't introduced himself.

"Dashiel." The name practically exploded from his lips. "Dashiel Er—" He bit back the rest of his response, remembering what Charlotte had told him about being careful with his name.

The girl waited for him to finish, but Dashiel shut his mouth tight.

"I get it. In these times, you can't be too careful," she said. "Dashiel is a pretty name."

He didn't know what to say. Surely she thought he was odd. Odd, insecure, and scared to say his name. Dashiel repeatedly called himself an idiot in his head. But the girl didn't insist; maybe she had noticed how nervous he was.

"My name is Athenai Palacette," she said, extending her hand toward him. Her sweet vanilla fragrance counteracted her sister's perfume. "A pleasure."

Surprised, Dashiel fumbled for her hand and squeezed it softly. "It sure is, Miss Palacette."

"Well, since I don't know your family name, may I call you Dashiel?" she asked, returning her hand to her lap. "You can call me Athenai."

Athenai, Athenai, Athenai. The name filled Dashiel's mind. A beautiful name worthy of a beautiful girl. Any other name that Dashiel thought of sounded like a nail against glass. Raquel? No. Susana? No. Miele? No, no, and no. There was only Athenai. Saying her name was like swallowing a spoonful of honey.

"It's heartbreaking to see towns like Carbakiel," Athenai lamented, her voice almost breaking. "I heard that it was once a picturesque place. The Carbakielans were known for their white bricks, the strongest and most durable on the continent. Their famous masonry was traded throughout the continent, adding to the wealth of the little town. Everything changed when the emperor made the new factories a priority. The town stopped producing bricks and started pumping out weapons."

"Why is Asedia so cruel with them?"

"I believe they tried to rebel against him," Athenai answered. "They were faithful to the Belecrose family."

"I see . . ." Dashiel bowed his head.

"Impulsive or not, you did something truly admirable. Sadly, people have lost all valor." She softly gasped and pursed her lips. "Others never had it to begin with. Me, for example."

"You?" Dashiel said, confused.

"To tell the truth, there's a reason I wanted you to come sit with me. I was hoping to find inspiration by talking to you."

"Inspiration?"

She looked at him carefully. "I don't know you very well, but would it bother you if I shared something personal?" She tried to smile.

"No, of course not. Go ahead," Dashiel said, his eyes locked on hers. How could he say no when looking into those violet eyes? They were calming, reassuring even. In that moment, a weight lifted off his shoulders. He finally ceased fidgeting in his seat.

"My family is expecting me to take charge. They want me to lead and take care of everyone," she said with a newfound seriousness. Her eyes shone with unshed tears. "But I'm young, and I lack the experience of a leader. I fear that I'll let everyone down. I fear that I will fail."

"I've been there," Dashiel said, clenching his fingers. "But there was something that gave me inspiration, gave me bravery and strength."

He reached into his rucksack and took out his favorite book.

"The stories in this book have helped me whenever I've needed them. They fueled my dreams, made me braver, and made me give everything I have. This book is very important." He held up the weathered novel. "My favorite stories are about a king named Bruno who conquered fear and doubt to save his kingdom."

"Never heard of it."

"Perhaps I could read you something," he said.

"I'd love that."

The pair spent hours and hours drinking inspiration from fictional realms. Dashiel read every word passionately, and Athenai listened on the edge of her seat. He wished he could freeze time in that moment, for their time together seemed to slip through his fingers quickly. As they talked and read, Dashiel got to know the remarkable person in front of him. Bliss took over.

By nighttime, the train slowed down once more, coming to a stop in a larger town.

"We've arrived at Divarie Town." The conductor's voice jolted Dashiel and Athenai out of their trance. They shared a tentative smile. "Next stop, St. Victoire Dowager! Have your tickets ready."

Athenai stood up. "This is my stop."

"I wish it weren't," he said, saddened by the idea of her leaving.

"Me too." She sighed. "But I want to give you something." She rummaged in the pocket of her cape. Her hand emerged holding an egg-like object with a blue surface, golden accents, and encrusted crystals. It was a jewelry box, he realized.

Athenai held it in front of Dashiel. "This box contains something special," she said. "A seed."

"What kind of seed?" Dashiel asked.

"I can't tell for sure, but if I'm right, the seed will only grow if it's taken care of by someone strong of heart. I already tried, but it didn't work. You might be the one."

"Me?" He huffed. "How do you know?"

"I have something like a gift for knowing things like this." She handed him the box with great care. The surface was smooth against his fingertips. "Remember, one drop of water a day, and keep it close to you."

"Are you sure you want to give it to me? It seems too precious," he said, looking at the ostentatious box.

"Consider this a bet on destiny. We'll see each other again, and when that happens, you can give it back to me. Safe travels, Dashiel."

They shook hands, and she returned to her sister, who waited by the exit with their belongings. They descended onto the platform, joining the throng of people milling around the station. She was truly special, a light in the midst of a darkening land. As Dashiel watched her leave, an idea took hold of his mind. He ran toward the exit.

"Where are you going?" Sylvain asked, confused.

"I'll be right back."

He weaved through the multitude until he found Athenai and Junei. Junei recoiled at the mere sight of him.

"Dashiel? What are you doing here?" Athenai asked.

"I want to give you something too," he said, pulling out his favorite book. "I want you to have this."

"Your book?" Athenai asked. Her soft smile let Dashiel know she was moved by the gesture. "But it's so special to you."

"Let's say that I want to bet on destiny too," he said. "Two bets have a better chance of winning than one, no?"

"Right." Athenai accepted the gift and hugged it to her chest. "Thanks." Her violet eyes twinkled. "I'll take good care of it."

The train's whistle interrupted their conversation. The conductor began to shout his customary "All aboard!"

"See you soon, Athenai," Dashiel said, running back onto the train. He stared out the window as the train pulled from the station and watched as the sisters disappeared from view.

As Divarie Town faded into the background, Dashiel turned to his companion. He thanked Providence for that encounter, one he would not forget for the rest of his life.

"You know, her companion was a collaborator," Sylvain said, putting down a newspaper he must have pilfered from a long-gone passenger.

"A collaborator?" Dashiel scanned the compartment, worried about eavesdroppers, but they were alone.

"The Cobalt Phantasms have people who aren't officially part of the order helping them," Sylvain said, crossing his leg over his knee. "That girl's companion was here for a reason. She received important intel from me. She'll transmit that information to our superiors."

"How do you know that she was a collaborator?" Dashiel asked.

"All collaborators carry books with mint-green pastes," Sylvain said. "Didn't you notice?"

Dashiel remembered Junei's book. Now everything made sense.

"I wonder if Athenai knew about that," Dashiel mumbled. His thoughts began to swirl, all leading to a single question: did she know that he was a Cobalt Phantasm?

"Athenai?" Sylvain seemed surprised at his familiarity with the girl. "Well, it's possible she took you to another seat because her sister couldn't perform her task. She was too distracted by you."

He thought about it, but he knew that his companion was wrong. Maybe all she had wanted to do was get rid of her sister's distraction. Maybe she'd faked everything. But a feeling inside told him that wasn't so. Her warmth and tenderness were too genuine to be feigned. A real connection between them existed, regardless of her original intentions, and he would hold on to that idea, to that hope.

"It was more than that," Dashiel said confidently, spreading out across the bench, which he now had all to himself.

Through the train's windows, he could see that night had fallen in the distance. Sylvain wrote in his journal, and in the silence, Dashiel's mind returned to Athenai. Their short time together, their words, their emotions—it all blurred together as he began to fall asleep. He grasped the box Athenai had given and slipped into a blissful slumber.

CHAPTER 13

THE OLD SPADE
OF SPAIGNE

"Now arriving at St. Victoire Dowager." The voice of the conductor woke Dashiel.

"We're here already?" he asked, rubbing his eyes and face.

"That's right," Sylvain said joyfully.

"Two days." Dashiel yawned. "I'm not complaining or anything, but I'm starting to miss sleeping in my bed." He stretched, noticing that Sylvain was still writing in his journal. "Did you even get any sleep?"

"A couple of hours." Sylvain stood. "Come on. We have to get going."

They took their belongings and exited the train.

St. Victoire Dowager's station, which was adorned with pure marble of varied tonalities, stood five times bigger and more luxurious than the one in Carbakiel. An embellished four-faced clock hung from the structure's ceiling. There were many more trains, some of them twice the size of the one they had just disembarked, and crowds of travelers. Unfortunately, the one thing this station had in common with the one in Carbakiel was an infestation of Ochre Brigadiers and imperial soldiers.

Dashiel and Sylvain left the train platform, blending in with arriving travelers. They walked through corridors that led from the station to other large buildings. These, too, were a delight to see. Dashiel walked in awe; he had never seen buildings as elaborate as these. As they neared the doorway, they got a glimpse of the city. A massive street ran from the building to a huge edifice.

"Wow! What on earth is that?" Dashiel asked, dazzled by the structure. Its walls were yellowish, its roof a grayish silver, and its windows white with reflected sunlight.

"I think that's where the viceroy of Hermesia lives," Sylvain answered. "Listen, I need to get directions. Stay here. I'll be back in a moment."

"Yes, sir."

Sylvain walked down a side street and disappeared from view.

An hour passed, and still Sylvain was nowhere to be seen. Dashiel grew restless. What if something had happened to him? What if he needed help? He could no longer stand there, doing nothing. He clutched his belongings a bit more tightly and marched into the city.

Dashiel wandered the main street, which was bustling with all kinds of people, most of them wealthy. They walked in different directions, purchasing, selling, or taking a stroll. Dashiel looked everywhere for Sylvain, but his search was thwarted by the hundreds of distractions the city offered: the shiny windows of the shops, all of them full of wondrous items, the luxurious carriages meandering up and down the road, and the enormous mansion at the end of the street that shone beneath the sunset.

Another diversion caught Dashiel's attention. Music rang from somewhere near. He followed the sound to an alley where a swarm of people had gathered. Unable to contain his curiosity and enthusiasm, Dashiel weaved his way through the crowd until he located the source of the music. A girl stood on top of a small fountain, playing a violin. Her clothes were old. Her face was stained with dirt, and her hair threatened to tumble from the scarf that held it in place, but she played beautiful music with tremendous passion. She whirled around, increasing the tempo of the music as the spectators clapped to the rhythm of her enchanting notes.

A strong hand landed on Dashiel's shoulder. "Here you are," said a familiar voice. "I've been looking everywhere for you." Sylvain rubbed his face. He was clearly exhausted. "Don't do that again."

Dashiel turned his head to catch Sylvain's eye. "Sorry," he said, smiling and turning back to the show. "Isn't this amazing?"

"Yes, indeed. I've got the directions we needed," Sylvain said. "Come on now. Don't dawdle."

Dashiel wanted to keep watching the performance, but his duty to the Cobalt Phantasms came first.

He followed Sylvain through the streets of St. Victoire Dowager until arriving in a shabby neighborhood on the outskirts of the city. As they moved farther and farther from the city's main thoroughfare, they passed fewer and fewer people who looked rich and influential. In their place were impoverished and indigent people. Their miserable looks followed Dashiel and Sylvain, weighing on them like sacks of flour. Since he'd never been in a city before, Dashiel had been blissfully unaware of the dangers lurking in a shabby neighborhood on the outskirts of the city. Sylvain had urged vigilance.

Eventually, the two arrived at a run-down building. The base of the structure was built of grayed brick that had probably been red in better days. The wood that dressed the building seemed like it would disintegrate at a single touch, and the opaque, dirty windows dimmed the lights within.

A rusty sign above the door read, *The Spade of Spaigne Inn, Est. 1840.*

Dashiel and Sylvain walked up the building's creaking staircase and entered through a door that stuck to its frame.

Inside, the building wasn't so bad. A little old and unkempt but much cleaner than the outside. There were a few spiderwebs and a thin layer of dust on the surfaces, and the air held a musty smell, but it was quaint and comfortable. In the entryway, there was a rack that housed dozens of keys and a registration desk with a candle nearing the end of its life.

Dashiel approached the desk, noting a pile of half-organized papers and an open ledger alongside a pen and inkwell. He and Sylvain looked around, waiting for someone to attend to them, but the only person in sight was a drunkard sleeping in the inn's tavern.

"What are we doing here?" Dashiel asked.

"You'll see."

A calm voice cut through the quiet. "Good evening, gentlemen. How may I assist you?"

Dashiel turned and saw a man behind the desk. His mustache was so thick that it connected with his sideburns. He wore a discolored jacket but still seemed presentable.

"Tomas Spaigne, at your service."

"We'd like lodging, if you please," Sylvain said.

Tomas took a look at the ledger. "Very well," he said, sliding it toward them with both hands.

Sylvain approached, intent on registering. Before he could do anything, Tomas placed his hand atop the ledger.

"You should know that staying here can cause you some . . . *inconveniences*, shall we say, in this city. The viceroy has placed what amounts to a social boycott on anyone who stays even one night here."

"That's terrible. Why?" Dashiel asked.

Tomas looked away. "It's a punishment for something that happened years ago."

"Dashiel." Sylvain looked at him severely. "We're not here to ask personal questions."

"Sorry," Dashiel said, ashamed, taking a step back. "I didn't mean to intrude."

"Don't trouble your mind, young man," Tomas said amiably. "If you've already decided . . ." He removed his hand from the ledger. "Whenever you're ready."

Sylvain took the pen and grabbed one of the corners of the book. He looked Tomas directly in the eyes and firmly closed the book. The pages blew dust particles all over the place. Dashiel quickly realized that the plaster that held the book together was mint green, the same color as the book that Athenai's sister owned. Sylvain took a bluish-silver badge that bore the Cobalt Phantasm insignia out of his bag and placed it on top of the closed ledger.

Tomas wore a poker face. "I see."

He walked out from behind his desk, grabbing a key off the rack. He locked the front door and pulled the curtains across the grubby windows.

"Welcome to the Spade of Spaigne. As you must have noticed from the name, I'm the owner . . . and the guard to the entryway to the Cobalt Phantasms' base in St. Victoire Dowager," he said. "What are two young Phantasms doing here at this time of night?"

"A pleasure, Mr. Spaigne. The name is Sylvain Aurante." Sylvain put his badge back in his pocket. "We're here to train a new recruit."

Dashiel stepped forward. "Dashiel Ermitage. A pleasure," he said, imitating Sylvain's language. He placed his bag and Orphée's carrying case on the floor.

Tomas gave each of them a firm handshake. "In that case, I should leave you in the hands of the person in charge."

As if on cue, the doorknob began to rattle. The lock held firm. The three stopped talking and turned their attention to the door. After a few moments, the knob clicked and opened. A girl in ripped clothes and rolled-up sleeves appeared. She wore her messy hair tied up and held a violin and bow in her hand. Dashiel blinked in recognition; he had heard her play in town earlier that afternoon.

"Why do I even bother to attract guests if you lock the door?" Her tone was brusque, as were her mannerisms.

"Sofia, we've received a pair of special guests," Tomas said.

"Who are they?" She glared at Sylvain and Dashiel, seemingly analyzing every single detail about them. Her expression was as proud as that of a tigress on the verge of attacking its prey. Dashiel couldn't believe she was the same young woman who had played the violin so beautifully.

Tomas looked at Dashiel and Sylvian. "May I present my daughter? Her name is Sofia." He glanced at his daughter. "They are—"

"What are they doing here?" she asked.

"—a member of the order and a recruit," he continued as if Sofia hadn't interrupted. "I was about to take them to him."

"Phantasms, eh?" Sofia's eyes narrowed and her posture became rigid.

"A pleasure," Sylvain said, but Sofia ignored him, still looking at them with suspicion.

"Have they shown you a badge?" Sofia asked.

Her father nodded.

"Then I will take them. Follow me." She walked purposefully toward the left side of the entryway.

Dashiel and Sylvain remained rooted in place.

"I said, follow me!" Her brusque voice came from the other side of the entryway. Dashiel had never met anyone as irascible as Sofia.

He and Sylvain glanced at each other. They collected their belongings and followed her until they arrived at the inn's common area. It was more or less a dusty living room full of old furniture, including an ancient grandfather clock that announced the change of time with a great racket.

Sofia whisked her way through the room and into the kitchen. She headed straight for the corner of the room, where a candelabra was mounted on the wall. She grabbed its base and pushed it upward. Beneath it, the wooden floorboards split apart, revealing an underground spiral staircase.

They descended the staircase, which led to the inn's wine cellar. Various wine bottles adorned three of the room's walls. The fourth led to a tunnel.

Dozens of oil lamps illuminated the walls of the tunnel, revealing pennants painted with the Cobalt Phantasm crest. The tunnel widened as the three ventured deeper underground. A rare mixture of curiosity and anxiousness besieged Dashiel as he trod down the gloomy tunnel. As they walked, human figures began to emerge from the shadows. Other members of the order, perhaps. Despite the lamplight, their faces remained indiscernible as they discreetly greeted the trio.

They arrived at a portion of the tunnel with secret doors, rooms, practice areas, and a mess hall. The lighting was better here, humanizing the faces of the people they encountered. Sofia stopped in front of a door painted bluish gray. She knocked three times. Seconds later, a hoarse voice commanded them to enter.

"Don't say a single word unless he addresses you." Sofia opened the door, and Sylvain and Dashiel followed.

The room was full of perfectly organized things. A large desk held mountains of papers, while a chalkboard contained intricate plans and drawings. Maps of various imperial locations hung on the walls. A stocky man sat in one of the room's chairs, his round, rosy face bearing a clean beard and mustache. His hair was slicked back, and small, round lenses perched on the bridge of his nose.

"One moment, please," he said from behind a pile of papers. His gentle, hoarse voice revealed his years as a smoker. Paper in hand, he extended his index finger as he read. Once finished, he turned his eyes to Sofia.

"My dear Sofia, excellent news from our brethren in Liffle." He placed the paper on a nearby table with a smack. "The count of Hurts and Gorogoy has allowed us to establish a base on a farm in Hurts." He bellowed a loud, happy laugh. He then noticed the presence of Dashiel and Sylvain. "Oh. Who are these youths?"

"Another member and his recruit, sir," Sofia said. "I apologize. I didn't mean to disturb you." Her tone was calmer than the one she had used with Dashiel and Sylvain.

"Don't worry, Sofia," the man said, wearing a smile from ear to ear. His eyes gleamed. "For me, it's a great pleasure to meet young people who are so special." He stood up. "Sorry for the inconvenience. You are dismissed. If you see Mr. Hugont, please ask him to come."

"Of course." Sofia left the room without a second glance at Dashiel or Sylvain.

"Who do we have here?" the man asked, looking them both up and down.

Sylvain approached with astonishment on his face. "It's an honor to meet you, sir. You are an inspiration." He bowed his head as a sign of respect.

"You're too kind, young man. Your name?"

"Sylvain, sir. Sylvain Aurante." From his voice, Dashiel could tell he was moved.

Dashiel stood next to his friend and stretched his hand toward the man. "A pleasure. My name is Dashiel—"

Sylvain interrupted him, swatting his hand down. "He's Master Roderigo Regallette, the founder of the order and one of the masters of the Cobalt Phantasms. Show respect!" he barked.

"I'm sorry, sir." Dashiel lowered his head, a blush blooming across his cheeks. "What are you going to think of me?"

"Don't apologize, Son," Roderigo responded jovially, taking a seat. "How can I help you?"

"Dashiel is to begin his training here," Sylvain said.

"And I also have a letter for you, sir," Dashiel said, reverence in his words. He removed from his pocket the letter that his father had given him right before he had left Azahar.

Roderigo took the letter with his right hand, adjusting his glasses with his left in order to better see its content.

"Interesting," Roderigo said. "How do you know Elias Ermitage?"

"He's my father, sir."

Roderigo's eyes widened, growing still more luminous. "That must be why I liked you from the start, my boy. Your parents and I are old friends, although you don't look anything like your father."

"Really?" Dashiel asked, surprised.

"Your father was one of the best Cobalt Phantasms to ever defend the badge," Roderigo said. "It's wonderful that you are following in his footsteps."

"My father?" Dashiel thought there must have been some sort of mix-up. No doubt his face reflected his shock.

"You didn't know that your father was a Cobalt Phantasm?"

Dashiel shook his head. He couldn't believe that his father had belonged to the order. Ideas revolved in his head, along with several questions and answers. This must have been the reason his parents knew Rupert, Charlotte, and Sylvain. But why hadn't they told him? Was this why the elite order had chosen him? Doubt began to overtake him.

"I know what you're thinking, Son," Roderigo said. "But you were chosen for your own merits. Nepotism doesn't exist in this organization." He stowed the letter in one of his desk's drawers. "Your parents know that perfectly well."

Roderigo glanced at Sylvain. "I imagine you'll train Dashiel, right?"

"Sir, I've been told that Dashiel would be assigned a mentor at this base."

Roderigo thought for a moment. His brows rose, and he said, "I know the perfect person for the job. She's the best student I've had in years, and I know she'll mold you into the best Cobalt Phantasm you can be." Roderigo winked.

He opened a different desk drawer and took out a packet wrapped in yellow paper and brown cord. He handed it to Dashiel. "You'll need this. Go ahead and open it."

Dashiel peeled back the paper, finding a metal badge with the order's insignia, the same one Sylvain had shown Tomas. He also found a journal with a black leather cover, a pen, and two small bottles. One held ink and the other held a mysterious, shiny liquid.

"That badge will be your identification. Any base on the continent will receive you if you show it, so guard it with your life," Roderigo explained. "You'll also find it useful to write about your experiences in that journal. The mistakes you make can only help you improve if you review them."

"Thank you, sir!" He was overwhelmed with gratitude for the gifts, especially the badge, which signified that his dream was officially in the making.

"Welcome to the Cobalt Phantasms."

A knock at the door cut off Dashiel's response. "Master, it's Fineley."

Roderigo took out his pocket watch and checked the time. The small hands announced that it was already past eleven. "It'll be best for you to go to your room." He took a key out of his desk, then turned his attention to the door. "Enter!"

A middle-aged man stepped into the office. "How can I be of service, Master?"

"Fineley, thank you for coming on such short notice. We have some guests. Dashiel is a new recruit," Roderigo said. His gaze flitted to Dashiel. "Fineley Hugont is a professor here."

Fineley inclined his head in respect, and Dashiel and Sylvain did the same. "With him, we're at four recruits, Master."

"I know, and this one will do incredible things," Roderigo said. "Please take Aurante and Ermitage to their room." He handed the key to Fineley.

"Ermitage?" the professor asked, surprise written on his face.

"That's right. He's Elias's boy," Roderigo said. "Please give him one of our utility belts and explain to him the basic rules."

"Right away, Master." Fineley left the office, waiting in the tunnel while the pair to collected their belongings.

Roderigo sat down.

"It was an enormous pleasure meeting both of you. Please let me know if you need anything at all," Roderigo said. He spoke to both of them, but his gaze was directed at Dashiel. The positive and friendly glance filled him with an inexplicable sense of well-being.

He and Sylvain left the office and followed Fineley back through the tunnels beneath the inn.

"Now, a couple of things you two should know," Fineley said. "You are to use the secret passages to access the base. No one, including the guests at the inn, should see you use them. You can visit the city, but with caution and using only the tunnel's exit, which will take you to the outskirts of the city."

The three arrived at the wine cellar and walked up the spiral staircase to the kitchen.

"Food is served from six to eight in the morning and from five to seven at night."

Fineley closed the passageway, putting the candelabra back in its correct position. They left the kitchen and arrived in the common area.

"Professor Grasshop will go deeper into rules and strictures. Break the rules and you will be punished. Keep breaking them, and you shall earn permanent expulsion from the order."

They took a staircase to the inn's upper levels. Stopping outside what Dashiel presumed was their room, Fineley handed the key to Sylvain.

"Soon you both will receive further instructions, but for now, get some rest."

"Thank you," Dashiel and Sylvain said in unison.

They were finally where they were supposed to be.

CHAPTER 14

UNUSUAL MESSENGERS

Dashiel and Sylvain's room was anything but special, but there were beds, and for Dashiel that was more than enough. A window—small and opaque, thanks to a layer of sediment—offered a blurry view of the dark street. A little desk held a small lamp filled with enough oil to shine for a couple of hours. After unpacking his clothes in the room's tiny wardrobe, Dashiel put the package he had received from Roderigo on the desk.

He unwrapped the objects and placed them one by one in front of him: the journal, the badge, the quill and ink, and, finally, the little bottle of suspicious, bubbly liquid.

"What's this, Sylvain?" he asked, holding up the bottle.

Sylvain analyzed it. "These are messenger droplets."

"Messenger droplets?"

"One of the few spells the order owns. When you have to send an urgent message and you're not sure of the location of the recipient, you use these," Sylvain said, lifting the bottle. The shiny liquid caught the lamp's light. "You just have to write the name of the recipient, and the letter will be sent."

"That's grand!"

"I'll show you how to use it," Sylvain said, taking a seat on his bed. "Write whatever you want on a piece of paper. You may want to use plain ink for this."

Dashiel quickly grabbed a sheet from his journal and scribbled something on it. "Ready!" He swished the quill away from the paper, leaving a blot of ink behind.

"Now, fold it into a bird or an insect."

"I don't know how to do that," Dashiel said, discouraged.

"It's not that important, but folding it in the shape of something that flies makes it less suspicious to anyone who sees it. Let me do it." Sylvan showed Dashiel how to fold the sheet. Within minutes, it had become a pigeon.

"Can I use these now?" Dashiel tapped the bottle with his index finger.

"Not yet." Sylvain yawned. "The droplets need one more ingredient. A toenail clipping from you will do."

"A toenail clipping?" Dashiel recoiled. "Why would that be an ingredient?"

"Every single particle of yours contains all the ethereal connections you share with others, connections that constantly feed from your memories and feelings." Sylvain massaged his neck. "Blood and saliva will easily dilute because of the water; a nail clipping won't."

"You still make no sense." Dashiel shook his head. "And that is plain weird."

"Good thing you can also use other stuff." Sylvain swiftly plucked a strand of hair from Dashiel's head.

"That's . . . good?" Dashiel pressed his hand against his head, his eyes tearing up.

Sylvain yawned again, dropping the auburn hair into the bottle. "You are all set up. Write my name with the droplets."

Dashiel carefully dipped the tip of his quill into the bottle and wrote his friend's name on the pigeon's chest.

"You may want to write something about me," Sylvain instructed. "Something about my appearance or, perhaps, a characteristic of mine. Sometimes you'll need to do this to make sure that the letter gets to the right person. This spell works better when the receiver remembers you."

"All right." Dashiel dipped again and wrote *black hair*.

As the paper absorbed the messenger droplets, the pigeon began to twitch. The creature slowly awoke and took flight, circling the room before landing in Sylvain's lap.

Sylvain opened the message and smiled as he read it. "Now, it would be best if we went to sleep," he said, leaning back on his bed.

"Definitely. But first I need to do something." Dashiel's words fell on deaf ears; his friend had already fallen deeply asleep.

Dashiel removed the jewel box from his belt and placed it on top of the desk. He had no idea what kind of plant grew within or whether he would be able to help it germinate, but Athenai had seemed confident in him. He wound the box's key, and soft music began to sound. Exhaustion rendered his limbs useless, and he lay down on his bed expecting to swiftly fall asleep. But the music conjured memories of Athenai.

His memories gave way to daydreams: her soft voice, her sweet aroma, her beautiful, violet eyes. He didn't really know anything about her. She was a complete stranger, but at the same time, he felt as if he knew her well. Dashiel missed her presence and her voice.

As much as he tried, Dashiel couldn't fall asleep. Worries flooded his mind. The possibility of never seeing her again stabbed at him. An idea came to mind. An extremely crazy idea, but one that would alleviate his anxiety once and for all. An idea that would finally let him sleep.

Dashiel took a sheet out of his journal and began to write. He couldn't find the right words. He tore a new sheet out of the journal, only to discard it when he found his next attempt lacking. Finally, Dashiel managed to write something that sounded more or less decent.

The rather short letter told Athenai that he wasn't sure if he was allowed to send a letter like this, that he didn't even know if it would reach her. But he also expressed his wish to stay in contact with her. After finishing his message, Dashiel folded the sheet into another pigeon, and although it was battered from his numerous unsuccessful attempts, it seemed convincing enough to fly toward its destination. He dipped his pen in the bottle of messenger droplets and wrote, in his best handwriting, *Athenai Palacette, violet eyes.*

He waited for the letter to move, but nothing happened. The misshapen paper pigeon sat on the desk, as any ordinary piece of paper would. Disillusioned, Dashiel fisted the desk's cold surface. Maybe she had given him a fake name? If so, he couldn't blame her. He hadn't been willing to give her his full name, after all. Dashiel stared at the letter pigeon and wished with all his heart that it would come to life. When it didn't happen, he stowed his things and went back to bed.

Sylvain's snores filled the room and kept Dashiel from drifting off. Propped on his bed, Dashiel stared at the box on the desk. Its crystals glittered in the glow of a dying streetlight, as dazzling as his memories of Athenai—if that was even her real name.

Would she remember him? And if she did, would she think about him like he thought about her? Probably not.

His attention shifted to a low humming coming from somewhere in the room. Dashiel didn't give it a second thought. After all, the Spade of Spaigne was a run-down inn. For all he knew, there were insects in the room.

The humming continued until Dashiel realized that the sound was coming from the desk. He had all but accepted his failure with the messenger droplets, but a sliver of hope had him bolting upright in bed. The paper pigeon hopped across the desk, humming as it moved. When it arrived at the window, it pecked at the sill with its creased beak. Dashiel understood that the pigeon was asking to leave. Making sure that Sylvain didn't notice, Dashiel slowly opened the window.

When the opening was large enough for the pigeon to fly through, it exited hastily, disappearing into the darkness of the night.

"I guess my bet is still on," Dashiel murmured. He wound the box once more and let it sound. As he returned to his bed, he couldn't help thinking about all the possibilities that the next day could bring.

CHAPTER 15

THE PSYCHIC, THE THIEF, AND THE CHEMIST

The next morning, Dashiel and Sylvain descended the stairs for breakfast. A few people sat in the inn's common area. Since they were new, the pair found it difficult to differentiate between guests and members of the order. They slipped through the common room and into the kitchen, where they found a woman cooking. The inn's cook—plump and rosy-cheeked—moved from one side of the kitchen to the other, preparing the day's dishes as she hummed to herself.

Dashiel didn't know what to do. Maybe this woman didn't know anything about the underground base or the secret passage that led to it. He met Sylvain's gaze, and they wordlessly decided to wait until she left. Except she showed no intention of leaving. She buzzed about the room like a bumblebee, cutting vegetables, kneading three different types of dough, and tossing ingredients into a boiling pot.

"Excuse me," Dashiel called to the woman.

She stopped in the midst of her chores.

"Breakfast wull be done in a moment," she responded, wiping her hands on her apron. "Ye kin wait in th' common area." She resumed her work. The smell of freshly baked bread filled the kitchen. "By th' wey, they cull me Mrs. Marjary."

"Bloodshed and injustice justify our existence," Sylvain said, looking straight into the woman's eyes.

When the words reached her ears, she put her utensils aside. Her eyes aimed at them like loaded pistols. "Ye two mist be some o' th' Cobra Fanatics," she said, her jowls quivering.

"Cobalt Phantasms," Dashiel corrected.

"And yes, we are, ma'am," Sylvain said.

The woman placed her hands on her hips. "Weel? Shaw me yer badges." Her eyes seemed to bulge out of their sockets as they moved from Dashiel to Sylvain and back again. They scrambled to remove their crests from their pockets. At a mere glimpse of the metallic badges, she returned to the task at hand.

"Ye may pass," she said, tending to the pot.

Dashiel and Sylvain made for the hidden passageway.

"Ye know whit?" the cook said as she poured waterfalls of oil into a pot. "Ye youngbloods are insane. Ull of ye doon thare are completely 'n' undeniably demented." She waved her ladle as she spoke, spraying brown droplets across the room.

Dashiel and Sylvain hurried to the candelabra in the corner, eager to escape the line of fire.

"While ull th' years workin' fur mah insane boss—'n' ah mean *insane*," the woman continued nagging, bitter disapproval in her voice, "ah ne'er thought he'd git me heavy goin' in ull this madness."

Sylvain grabbed the candelabra that Sofia had used the night before and pushed it upward. The floor planks rumbled and moved as the woman continued her sermon, slicing and adding carrots to the boiling pot.

"They're goin' to git us ull murdered by th' Ochre, whitevur they're culled."

Dashiel couldn't wait for the floorboards to open up so that he and Sylvain could leave the kitchen.

"If Mrs. Spaigne, Providence rest her soul, hud caught win' o' this, she would've given a guid smack tae her demented husband, 'n' tae ye, ye insane youths."

When the stairway finally appeared, the two friends hurried down it. Dashiel paused to pull the lever that would close the passage.

"'N' one more thing," the woman called, getting the last word as the floor creaked shut. "Dinnae furgit tae claise that devilled passageway. Last week, they left it open. Ah fell, 'n' ah hud tae git them stitches oan mah enormous—"

The passageway shut, and silence—mercifully—returned.

"Sylvain, what was that you said up there?" Dashiel asked, holding tight to the rusty rail as he descended the spiral staircase.

"The phrase? Well, it's the most important part of our creed," Sylvain said, grabbing on to the handrail. "We use it to determine whether or not a person in front of us is loyal to our cause."

"I should learn it." Dashiel tried to remember exactly what Sylvain had said. He repeated it over and over in his mind.

"You should. Some members will put you through several tests before they trust you."

Finally, they arrived at the cellar and the tunnel that led to the base. They followed the tunnel to the mess hall. Order members of various ages sat at the wooden tables that filled the room. There was a window where large pots of food came down from the kitchen via an old pulley system. Next to it sat a table with a variety of fruits and vegetables.

They took a seat at one of the dining tables. A boy approached, filled two bowls of oatmeal from a large pot, and gave them to Dashiel and Sylvain. Dashiel thanked him, but the boy didn't say a word. He kept moving around the dining area, making sure everyone had a plate.

"Damian is a little shy, but he doesn't mean to be rude."

Dashiel looked up to find a skinny, short-haired girl, not much older than him. At her side was an unsmiling, well-built boy with intimidating eyes. He looked about Sylvain's age. The girl leaned in. "You two are new, right?"

"We arrived yesterday," Sylvain said.

"My name is Mina Halliwell," the girl said as she took a seat. She winked at her friend. "And this is Caden Slycritter."

"Arson, Mina! I prefer to be called Arson!" The boy sat next to her. Dashiel and Sylvain shook hands with both. Arson's crushing handshake hurt so much that Dashiel massaged his hand under the table.

"We're both apprentices," Mina said. "We got here a couple of days ago."

"Me too," Dashiel said, bringing a spoonful of oatmeal to his mouth.

"So . . . what's your story, partner, if I may ask?" Mina grinned.

Dashiel took a deep breath. "Where to begin?"

The foursome spent the rest of breakfast talking about how they had been selected to join the order. Arson remained silent as Mina relayed both her story and his. He had partaken in street fighting and burglary in Hermesia, catching the attention of the local Cobalt Phantasms. Mina had extraordinary abilities that her family had never allowed her to exercise because they weren't proper for a Zaphyrolean lady. The Cobalt Phantasms who discovered her disagreed.

Mina and Arson were amazed to hear about Azahar, a place that many believed was a mere legend. Dashiel and Sylvain shared the story of their battle with the Ochre Brigadiers and their travels through the empire's lands.

"So who's your mentor, Dashiel?" Mina asked.

"I don't have one yet," he responded. "Master Regallette told me that he had someone in mind, but I still don't know who it is."

"My mentor is that man over there," Mina said, gesturing to a bald man with a reddish beard.

"That's mine." Arson pointed to a woman with enormous lips and a bodybuilder's physique.

Sylvain took a bite out of an apple that he'd retrieved from the spread of fruits. "You see, your mentor depends on many factors: age, experience level, other things."

Dashiel looked at his friend. "I wish you were my mentor."

Sylvain smiled. "Me too, but your mentor will do excellent work with you. You'll see."

As the conversation continued, the dining hall emptied. With no one else to serve, the silent boy left as well. Breakfast passed peacefully—until a knife whistled past Dashiel's arm, its blade sinking halfway into the wooden table. A scarred, callused hand wrapped around the knife's hilt. He turned to find a woman with disheveled hair, a dirty face, and raggedy clothing. Sofia Spaigne.

"What was that for?" Dashiel asked, startled.

"Shut up!" Sofia bellowed, rage in her eyes. She leaned in, her face inches from his. "You think you can show up here and do whatever you feel like doing, just because you're Ermitage's son?"

"I don't know what you're talking about," Dashiel responded, trying to remain calm. His eyes moved back and forth between the blade and Sofia's face. He wasn't sure which was more unnerving.

"They forced you on me as my student, Ermitage." Her body tensed, as if it might explode at any moment. "I'm stuck with you."

Her warm breath struck his skin like a blacksmith's hammer.

He swallowed. "It's not . . . not my fault," he said, mustering his courage. "Roderigo assigned me to you, but if that bothers you, I can go ask him for a different mentor."

He pushed to his feet, but Sofia shoved him back into his chair. She leaned in even closer than before. It was as if she were about to bite him.

"You'll do no such thing." She breathed in. "I'll train you, and with blood, sweat, and tears, I'll turn you into a real man, Ermitage."

She released him and drew herself up to her full height.

"You'll rue the day I was assigned as your mentor. I promise you that," Sofia whispered, her voice ominous. She pulled the knife out of the table quickly, nearly taking Dashiel's arm with it. "You'll get a message about our first session soon. Get ready."

She walked away, knife in hand, but paused before leaving the room. "You can run away if you'd rather avoid the enormous pain you're about to feel."

Dashiel remained stock-still, breathing rapidly, his gaze fixed on the divot the knife had left in the table. When she was gone, he released a heavy breath.

"What's her problem?" Dashiel mumbled, barely overcoming the shock.

"I've never seen her so angry." Mina shook her head.

"Man, you're screwed," Arson said with his mouth full.

"Sofia Spaigne is known for being difficult, but she's in rare form today," Mina said.

"All because of me?" Dashiel said.

"Isn't it obvious? If you were in her place, you would act the same," a voice croaked from behind Dashiel and Sylvain. They turned to find a peculiar young man. His back was hunched and his skin untouched by the sun. Rosy pimples covered his face; hazel eyes hid behind large, bottle-thick glasses; and long, curly hair hung over his forehead.

"The name is Lawrence J. Octavious, a Delver apprentice." He took a moment to analyze Dashiel and his new friends, especially Sylvain.

"Hmm. Interesting." He pondered for a moment. "You must be either a Defier with high Delver tendencies or a Diviner."

"Go the hell away, Octa-pus," Arson said, leaning back in his chair, arms folded.

"I would expect nothing less from a dumb Defier," Octavious said with a cocky smirk.

Arson growled at him, pounding the table with his fist.

"Defier? Delver? Could anyone please explain?" Dashiel asked, scratching the back of his head.

"It's hilarious that you don't know something so basic." Octavious fixed his glasses and smirked. "There are three types of Cobalt Phantasm members: Defiers, Delvers, and Diviners. Defiers are those who excel in physical abilities: strength, speed, or agility. Delvers, like me, excel in mental abilities: wisdom, creativity, or grasp of science and magic. Diviners are those who possess a mixture of those two abilities. A rare kind."

Octavious took a breath. "This is a Defier base. All members here, with the exception of Master Roderigo, Professor Grasshop, and myself, are Defiers. The number of Defiers in this base is alarmingly large. I wonder how we are still alive."

"Well, you're welcome to transfer your Delver ass to another base," Arson said.

"My point proven." Octavious's croaky voice was filled with pride.

"So, what's my category?" Dashiel said.

"Hmm, let me see." Octavious scanned him from head to toe. He scratched his acne-riddled face. "Well . . ."

"What is it?" Dashiel said with a sparkle in his eyes. "Defier? Delver?"

"Nothing," Octavious said, puzzled.

"What? Hey!" Dashiel growled.

"Let me put it in a way you'll understand: no muscle density whatsoever, average height, lack of reflexes—definitely not a Defier. No extraordinary intelligence in your words or actions, lack of basic knowledge, and a dumb look—we can discard the possibility of you being a Delver. I could be wrong, but I know these things."

"Don't worry. I'm pretty sure he's mistaken." Mina gave Octavious a stern look. "Octavious, what were you saying about Sofia?"

"Oh, yes." He cleared his throat. "I heard that Spaigne's achievements had earned her the commandership of her own squadron." The pale boy lowered his head and voice, as if to prevent eavesdroppers, though the dining hall had long since emptied. "To earn a squadron, you must first train a novice, right? Well, the Founding Chapter was so impressed by her that it overlooked the fact that she had not mentored anyone—until this . . . boy came around. To tell the truth, I would be enraged, too, but I would have used hydromolaic acid instead of a knife. It leaves no trace and has no odor—my own invention."

Dashiel's discouraged eyes turned to Sylvain. "I didn't mean for that to happen. I don't want my mentor to hate me."

"Don't feel bad. It is not your fault," Sylvain said. "I'm sure she'll be mature about this whole situation, and you two will be free from each other in no time."

The conversation was interrupted by a buzz-like sound. Four scarabs flew into the dining area and landed on the table.

With a yelp of fear, Mina grabbed her plate and tried to smash the nearest bug under it. When she lifted the plate, she found only a creased piece of paper. Arson smashed the nearest beetle with his hands and unfolded the resulting paper until it was flat. Accustomed to all sorts of insects from Azahar, Dashiel extended his hand and let the beetle crawl into it. After a single chirp, the bug unfolded of its own accord. They read the messages on each of their papers.

"It's from Professor Grasshop!" Octavious screeched.

"It says that we'll have our first lesson soon," Dashiel said, lightness in his chest.

"Mine too." Mina smiled.

Octavious stood up.

"You are leaving?" Mina asked.

"Of course!" he said. "Don't you see? We have to prepare ourselves." He strode toward the exit, a hunched, hurrying form. The dining hall boy came running from the tunnels, crashing into Octavious. "Be careful, you little twit!"

The boy squeaked an apology, then walked over to the table where Dashiel and his new acquaintances were sitting. He stopped in front of Arson and held out a newspaper.

"Damian, you are a legend." Arson removed a couple Imperial Crests from his pocket. He took the newspaper and gave the coins to the kid.

The boy's eyes sparkled at the sight of the coins. He saluted Arson and walked away.

"I thought you didn't have any money," Mina said inquisitively.

"Yeah, but Octa-pus did," he said matter-of-factly. He opened the newspaper and began to read.

"This is all crap." Arson flipped through the newspaper. "'His Imperial Majesty's brave guard has done a great service to Myrtalo by hunting down the terrorist group behind the explosion of a building that took place last week,'" he read in a mocking voice. "'Terrorists are to stand trial next week.'"

"Why did you get that?" Mina snapped. "You know that it's full of lies. The people behind that trash live to flatter that son of a smartlapper."

"I know. But I needed to see the classifieds. Need some extra dough, you know." Arson took a moment to read. "Ugh, nothing good." He threw the newspaper on the table.

Curious, Dashiel glanced at the front page of the paper. He was struck by the image: a black-and-white picture of a man watching over a group of people whose backs faced the reader. He was tall, with graying black hair and dark, empty eyes. The man's penetrating stare gave Dashiel chills. He had never seen the man before, but he knew exactly who he was. The headline confirmed his hunch: "Emperor Abelon Asedia to Judge Terrorists behind Explosion."

CHAPTER 16

GRASSHOP'S RIDDLE

When the time came, Dashiel, Sylvain, Mina, and Arson made their way to the base's classroom. They stood in front of the door, excited about the endless possibilities that awaited them on the other side.

Mina took a step forward and knocked.

"Do come in," a melodious male voice rang from inside.

When the group opened the door, they were greeted by the scent of freshly cut grass and bougainvillea flowers.

Mina and Arson entered, but Dashiel stayed behind. He had noticed Sylvain standing a few meters away from the door.

"You are not coming?" Dashiel gulped, his stomach churning.

"Nope." Sylvain crossed his arms. "I've got something to do in the city. Besides, I think it will be better if there are only recruits in the first class." His eyes absorbed the gentle light of the oil lamps.

Dashiel's smile faded into an insecure wince. He had gotten used to Sylvain's company. The thought of not having his ally with him set his heart racing.

"Hey." Sylvain ruffled Dashiel's hair. "You don't need me. You've got *this*." He held up the doizemant.

"Orphée?" Dashiel clutched the baton, the metal warm between his palms. It hadn't felt cold since the moment he received it from his father.

"Trust me, you will need it." Sylvain winked before pacing deeper into the tunnel. "Good luck!"

When Sylvain was out of sight, Dashiel took a big breath. Holding tight to his baton, he stepped through the doorway.

Like the other underground rooms, the classroom had a rocky layout, but here the walls had been painted green and pink. Hung on the walls were dozens of crystal boxes, bugs crawling and hopping inside them. Butterflies, moths, and bees moved carefree through the music-filled air.

A man with a droopy nose stood in front of a podium, his eyes fixed on the contents of a thick file. His tall, slender body was concealed behind a colorful robe with puffy sleeves and a cream-colored ascot. His hair reached his sleeves, and a chaplet of silver flowers kept his sideswept bangs from completely devouring his left eye.

A soft smile appeared on the man's elongated face as he momentarily removed his gaze from the papers. "Please." He gestured at the two columns of tarnished desks, which had been dressed in crocheted table runners.

Octavious, who must have arrived earlier, sat in the first row. His desk was occupied with vials, beakers, flasks, and journals. He did not acknowledge Dashiel's arrival; he kept tinkering with his equipment.

The class began.

"My name is Professor Francis Grasshop." The man glided away from the podium, revealing a pair of gray pants and black velvet shoes. "Master Roderigo has given me the delicate task of helping you grasp the basic knowledge all Cobalt Phantasms need to succeed. With me, you will learn the order's rules and strictures, relevant history, strategy, geography and cartography, alchemy and chemistry, and my favorite, entomology."

"By the way," Grasshop said, extending his finger so a butterfly with clear wings could land on it, "this is my loyal companion, Titania. You are welcome to play with all my babies, except for her." He stroked the butterfly's wings. "I found this beauty during a trip to South America. She is my prized possession."

The professor stroked his chaplet and laughed to himself. "Oh, and my dazzling coronet as well!"

Grasshop went to his desk, placed his precious butterfly inside a doorless cage, and returned to his podium. He opened the file and took out a piece of paper. "Before we go over some basic rules, I would like to see your talents."

"Talents?" Dashiel asked, entranced by a praying mantis walking along the edge of his desk. The arrogant bug folded and unfolded its clawlike legs at him.

"You were chosen because you all possess unique and extremely useful talents. It is my duty and your mentors' to help you polish them into tools that will aid you in your missions. Please be ready to present."

It was clear to Dashiel why Sylvain had given him the baton. He could twirl it through the air and thrust it at imaginary foes. It was so simple, but doubt stirred his thoughts. What if owning a doizemant was not a talent? What if owning a doizemant gave him an unfair advantage? What talent of his would justify his place in the order if he didn't have the baton?

His fingers tapped a quick, anxious beat against the desk.

"Professor?" Octavious's hand launched into the air like a firework. "I would much appreciate it if you would allow me to present first." With his chin up, he looked around to see the reaction of his classmates.

"Oh, Lawrence," Grasshop tittered. "I am your mentor. I have already seen the perfect execution of your talent."

"Still, I think it is a good idea to enlighten my peers with my chemistry talent. I am sure they will find my demonstration rather helpful," Octavious said, maintaining intense eye contact with his mentor.

"Very well then. You may do so at the end of class if there is some time left. Now, who shall be the first?" The professor slid his finger down the list of names. "I am certainly not a fan of alphabetical order. Give me one moment."

Mina, who was sitting right in front of Dashiel, turned around. A ladybug landed on her hat's bow, and Dashiel watched it crawl down the ribbon.

"Is everything good?" she asked, slight worry in her eyes.

Dashiel flinched. "What do you mean? Why . . . why would something be not good?"

"I can hear the tapping of your fingers." She blew her hair off her face. "It is a little distracting."

"Sorry . . ." Dashiel stilled his fingers. "I am fine—ahem, I am fine," he muttered. "Just a little anxious, that's all."

"Don't worry. You'll do just fine, partner," Mina whispered, fidgeting with her hands. "I am a little nervous myself, especially with all these bugs around." She grinned.

"Ah, yes! Caden Slycritter!" Grasshop threw his hands up in the air, gaining everyone's attention. "Mr. Slycritter, could you please join me up here?"

Arson stood up from his desk. He cracked his knuckles and neck as he made his way to the front of the classroom. Whistling a tune, he leaned against Grasshop's desk to stretch his legs. He then walked around the professor, stretching his arms.

Arson finally came to a stop next to the professor.

"Whenever you are ready, please present," Grasshop growled, pursing his lips.

"I already did." Arson raised his eyebrows, both hands behind his back.

"You . . . did?" Grasshop exchanged puzzled looks with his other students.

"Ladies and gentlemen and whatever Octavious is," Arson said in a ringmaster's theatrical tone, "who can tell me what this is?" He extended one of his arms.

"An onion?" Mina's voice rang, harmonizing with the buzzing of the bees.

"Yes, an on—no! It is Professor Grasshop's coin pouch, can't you see?" Arson said, confidence in his eyes. His face flushed when he saw an onion between his fingers. "It is . . . an onion."

"That was a good try," Grasshop tittered.

"But how?" Arson murmured, scratching his head. "I saw you putting the pouch in your right pocket, right before class started."

"You do have great agility and stealth, but you underestimated the intelligence of your target. Don't worry, dearie, we shall work on that." With a flap of his hand, Grasshop gestured for his pupil to take a seat.

"Bite me," Arson said under his breath, walking back to his desk.

Grasshop clasped his hands together. "Next, we have . . . Miss Halliwell!"

Mina walked to the front and stood next to Grasshop. She took a long breath, sputtering when she almost inhaled a pair of gnats.

The professor glided to his desk and picked up one of the files. "According to your mentor's notes, you possess a certain level of telekinetic control."

"Yes, sir," Mina said, her cheeks blushing and ankles rubbing together.

Grasshop snapped his fingers. "Let's test your wonderful talent."

From one of the rocky walls, Grasshop extracted a rock as small as a marble. He placed it in front of Mina. "Whenever you are ready, dearie."

The chirping and buzzing of insects faded until the classroom was completely silent. Mina shut her eyes tight, and the rock began to levitate. Everyone gazed in silent awe as the rock danced around Mina.

"That was grand!" Dashiel shouted when she'd finished, joining everyone's applause.

"Marvelous, Miss Halliwell!" Grasshop said, holding a larger rock in his arms. "Now, how about a bigger challenge? Let's test the limits of your telekinetic talent."

Grasshop dropped the rock in front of Mina, causing the nearby bugs to bounce.

"All right . . ." Mina said, taking a deep breath and closing her eyes. "Here goes nothing." Her lips tightened, and her eyelids trembled.

The rock levitated and spun, though slower than the pebble had. Everything seemed to be fine until the rock began to shake violently. It released a sound similar to a boiling kettle's whistle. The rock moved from one side of the podium to the other, as if two ghosts were wrestling for it.

Mina had lost control over the rattling rock. Instead of moving away, Grasshop scribbled notes in his journal. He kept writing as the rock turned bloodred and burst into flames.

Beneath the rock's high-pitched scream, Dashiel heard hushed tones coming from his doizemant. The voices joined together in an adamant whisper. Dashiel could not understand the whisper's language, but he comprehended the message it conveyed. It agreed with a thought that had been growing in Dashiel's mind: an accident would take place.

Dashiel jumped between Grasshop and the rock, baton in hand. His stomach hardened, and his mouth dried up.

"Mina, you've got to stop!" Arson ran to Mina, squishing a couple of ants and beetles in the process.

"Use your brain for once, you dunce! She is in some kind of catalepsy. She cannot hear you." Octavious joined them at the front of the class. "By overheating the rock, Halliwell is causing the air and water inside it to quickly expand. The two components will eventually break the rock apart, and—"

"In Garatei, please!" Arson snapped.

"It will go kaboom and incinerate us all!" Octavious barked back.

"What can we do?" Dashiel asked, shooing the flying bugs away from the fireball with his baton.

The room turned redder, and the temperature increased. The stridulating of the crickets and the buzzing of the bees joined into a chaotic song.

Octavious grabbed two containers from his desk. "If I mix these and pour them into the rock, its temperature will go down," he explained, combining the two liquids. "We can stop it when the fire is out. It will still explode, but it will be less lethal. There is a 68 percent chance that we—"

"Do it, dammit!" Arson clenched his fists.

Octavious splashed the rock with his mixture, subduing its fire.

"TAKE COVER!" Dashiel yelled. Brandishing the doizemant, he hit the rock with all his strength.

It traveled across the classroom and exploded into smithereens just as it reached the door. Dashiel twirled his weapon with great speed, deflecting the red-hot shards that threatened to pierce his classmates. Fragments of rock knocked several of the crystal boxes and diplomas off the walls. In the wake of the explosion, the classroom slowly regained its cheerful colors.

"Argh!" Octavious roared, running to his desk. A rock had destroyed half the equipment on his desktop. "My poor journals, glassware, and tools . . . They are useless now."

Arson scoffed. "Ugh, how melodramatic." He cracked his knuckles. "Look at the bright side, Octa-pus."

"What's the bright side?" Octavious frowned.

"No one wanted to see your boring presentation anyway." Arson slapped Octavious's back and walked away.

Mina gazed at the destruction. "I'm sorry about that." She blushed, fidgeting with her hands.

The professor paced from one side of the classroom to the other. He behaved as if no accident had happened. "I don't understand what went wrong . . ."

Grasshop squinted at Mina's file. He turned the page over and read, "Halliwell needs more training. When testing her telekinetic powers, do not use anything bigger than a marble. Do not. Do not. Do not."

The professor closed the file and threw it away. "Silly me. Well, we all make mistakes. Accidents like this happen all the time."

He moved his sights from the carbonized remnants of the door to the soot-covered faces of his pupils. He placed his hand over his ascot. "Thank you for saving our lives, Mr. Octavious and Mr. Ermitage."

Dashiel's heart bumped against his chest. "You know my name?"

"Of course!" Grasshop tittered. "Your father made your family name famous. We are all expecting great things from you."

A cuckoo clock, which had been turned into a beehive, chimed the hour. Bees whirled around the dancing figurines, and golden honey ran down the chains that supported the clock's weights. Crowned with the hive's queen, the cuckoo emerged from its hiding place three times.

"My! It looks like we ran out of time, dearies," Grasshop said, gently pressing his hand to his jawbone. "That's what happens when you are having fun. Fly, fly away, lovely creatures. I'll see you tomorrow at the same time." He sat at his desk and waved as Dashiel and his classmates abandoned their seats.

"Hey, partner," Mina said, approaching the charred door. "Arson and I are going to the candy parlor. Would you like to join us?"

"Yes!" Dashiel wiped the soot off his forehead. "I just need to speak to Professor Grasshop. I'll be there in a moment."

"All right! Don't take long." Mina hesitated, her gaze flicking to Octavious, who was writing relentlessly at his desk. "Octavious? Same question."

Arson's muffled voice sounded from the tunnel. "If he's going, count me out."

"Thank you, but no thank you, Halliwell." Octavious's eyes remained fixed on the his paper. "I must rewrite this let— I have more important matters to attend to."

Arson's muffled voice came again. "Count me in!"

Mina disappeared through the scorched doorway and into the tunnel.

"Professor Grasshop, should I present now?" Dashiel walked to the professor's desk, holding his baton with both hands. "I could do it quickly."

"There is no need." The professor organized the files on his desk.

"Why not?" Dashiel lowered his baton.

"Dearie, I'm afraid there is not much I can do for you." Grasshop offered his finger to a spider. The creature climbed on timidly. "A doizemant has allowed you to become its equal, so you two can only learn from each other."

"What?"

"Do you hear voices or a whisper when you are near your doizemant?" Grasshop asked, taking the spider to a nearby spiderweb.

Dashiel's eyes rested on the baton, which shone in the light from the desk candles. "Yes . . ."

"There will come a time when no whisper will be heard. You two will truly become one. For that to happen, you must learn to communicate and listen in a whole new way." Grasshop made his way to the door, tiptoeing to avoid another insect genocide. "It's what your father told me the day he left the order. I didn't understand why"—he stood tall next to the blackened doorframe and winked—"until now."

Dashiel sighed. He'd been hoping for guidance or instructions on how to use the doizemant.

"I know nothing else about your weapon. Now, off you go!" The professor clapped at Dashiel. "We mustn't let our friends wait."

Moments later, Dashiel strode through the dark tunnels, his mind trying to solve the professor's riddle. The words fell together like a four-piece puzzle, but nothing was quite that easy when it came to his baton. Doubt rushed in, assaulting his mind. Why hadn't his father explained everything to him? Did his father think he was not wise enough to solve such a riddle?

Dashiel decided to save those thoughts for later. He wanted to enjoy his first visit to the candy parlor.

CHAPTER 17

DAGGER-SHARP WAGER

The next morning, a knock on the door interrupted Dashiel as he wrote in his journal. He scanned the hallway but found it empty. As he was retreating to his room, his eyes caught on a wrinkled piece of paper affixed to the door with a dagger—the same dagger that had nearly cut his hand off yesterday. Dashiel didn't bother to remove the knife from the door. He tore the sheet off and read it with care.

The handwriting was coarse, almost illegible. Haphazard ink stains dotted the page. The letter had unmistakably been written with rage.

Find me in the training room at nine o'clock on the dot. Don't be late. Or else.

—Sofia Spaigne

Dashiel glanced at an old clock in the hallway. There was only a half hour until the session.

"Who was it?" Sylvain asked, interrupting his meditation.

"It's from Sofia Spaigne." At the mention of his mentor's name, all excitement about the Phantasms drained from Dashiel's body. He showed the note to his friend. "It's almost time."

"Cheer up." Sylvain left his comfortable spot on his bed. He took Dashiel by the shoulders and looked him straight in the eyes. "Sofia

Spaigne will do everything in her power to scare you. She wants you to give up, to quit. Don't let her see even a glimpse of fear. Get up when you fall, and keep pushing even when you don't have any strength left. That's the only way to beat her at her own game."

Dashiel perked up, but the relief proved fleeting. "How will I keep her from seeing my blood? You've seen how she is. She loves her sharp objects."

He gestured to the door and its newest adornment.

Sylvain smiled. "I already thought of that." He removed a little container from his pocket, opened it, and took out a brown pill.

"These are dermangolin pills. They'll make your skin harder, so much so that it'll be impossible to cut."

"Where'd you get those?" Dashiel asked, amazed.

"Arson owed me a favor. But that's not important. Take it." Sylvain handed him the pill.

Seconds after Dashiel swallowed it, his skin crackled, producing hundreds of scales from head to toe. He looked like a pangolin. The scales began to fade until they disappeared.

"Did it work?" Dashiel regarded his arms and hands with awe.

"Only one way to find out." Sylvain strode purposefully to the door and grabbed the knife.

"Sylvain, wait." Dashiel backed off. "Wait!"

Sylvain didn't listen. He stabbed Dashiel's arm, but the blade slid off his skin, leaving a faint white line.

"Awesome! Sylvain, you're grand!" Dashiel said.

"I know," Sylvain replied, pride etched on his face. "Go now. And remember everything I just said."

Dashiel arrived in the training room at the designated hour. Dozens of weapons and other training objects adorned one of the walls. Nine targets spread out across the surface of another wall. Sofia Spaigne awaited him, wearing an aggressive expression, her arms firmly crossed.

"Our training is in session," she said, taking a step forward. "And when I say 'our,' I'm referring to the idea that a mentor should always be ready to learn from her students; a Cobalt Phantasm never stops learning and growing. Consider that your first lesson." She paused, assessing him with a curl of her lip. "Although I sincerely doubt that I can learn anything worthwhile from a stupid forest boy."

Sofia's presence had Dashiel's nerves on high alert. His mouth was too dry and forehead too moist. But he remembered what Sylvain had said. He needed to stand tall and hide any fear or doubt. With Orphée's case in his hand, Dashiel walked toward his mentor and stood in front of her.

"I'm ready," he said, using his deepest voice.

"We'll see about that," she said, voice heavy with sarcasm. She looked down at the suitcase he was carrying. "What's that?"

"It's my own weapon," he said, trying harden his tone. He held her gaze. "I was told I could have one."

"Really, forest boy?" Her expression was mocking. "In this session, you won't need it. Put it away."

"My name is Dashiel."

"I don't care. Do it . . . forest boy," she responded, cracking her knuckles.

Dashiel put Orphée's case in a corner and returned to his place.

"At least you know how to follow basic orders. But even a dog knows how to do that. And you know what?" she whispered in his ear. "A dog would do it better than you."

She circled him as she spoke. To intimidate him, Dashiel figured. But he refused to give in.

"There are three types of combat with which you should familiarize yourself: armed combat, long-distance combat, and hand-to-hand combat. You're dead meat if you don't master all three," she said, still circling him. "Today I'll measure your skills in each. First: long-distance combat and target practice."

Sofia selected a slingshot from among the numerous large and lethal weapons hanging from one of the walls.

"A . . . slingshot?" Dashiel asked, disappointed. He was hoping to use a pistol like Grimley's or a crossbow like Sylvain's.

"A beautiful slingshot, just for you," Sofia corrected, gritting her teeth as she placed the weapon and four stones in his hand. "Aim at any of the targets and shoot. Easy. Even you can do it."

Dashiel steadied himself and aimed at a target in the middle of the wall. When the time seemed right, he shot. The stone flew with great speed but never reached its target. The second stone met the same fate, as did the third. When he shot the fourth, it grazed the target's outermost ring.

"You failed," Sofia huffed. She returned to the wall of weapons and detached two swords and two shields, all made of wood. She threw one set of arms at Dashiel's feet.

"Second test: armed combat, defense, and strength." She shifted slowly from side to side.

This particular test reminded Dashiel of summer days in Azahar, when he and Grimley would practice with branches on the banks of the lake, dreaming of one day becoming warriors.

"Your objective is to dodge and disarm me. No time limit," she said, adopting a defensive position. "Begin whenever you wish, forest boy."

Dashiel gathered his weapons and approached Sofia. She stared him in the eyes, looking like a lioness about to tear its victim limb from limb. Dashiel began his attack, but Sofia, possessing great agility, dodged each of his thrusts. Dashiel analyzed the situation and tried striking at her hands, but she easily dodged the blow. He tried to knock her off-balance by pushing her with his shield, but she didn't give an inch. He tried and tried, but nothing seemed to work. With two simple flicks of her wrist, Dashiel was disarmed and his shield split in two.

"You failed. Not like I was expecting otherwise." Sofia walked to the middle of the room. "Finally, I'll measure your hand-to-hand combat skills, your agility, and your reflexes. I want you to knock me down. You can use any movement or technique you wish."

"I . . . I can't," Dashiel said, taking a step back.

"Why not?"

"I'm not going to knock a girl down," Dashiel tried to explain.

"Oh, I see," Sofia said. "How chivalrous of you, Ermitage." Her voice was disturbingly soft.

Dashiel didn't say anything, thinking that maybe he had found a soft spot.

Sofia walked toward him.

"Next lesson," she said, looking him in the eye. With a cheetah's speed, she swept her leg and knocked Dashiel's feet out from under him. "And it's one of the most important lessons: nothing's what it seems. Women can be as lethal or more lethal than men. Never forget that, or you'll end up with a knife in your neck."

Sofia massaged her face and sighed deeply.

"You're useless. A complete failure. Master Roderigo said you were definitely a Defier, but you're a fraud, a leech to the order."

Dashiel sprawled on the floor, trying to catch his breath. Sofia crouched beside him.

"Come on! Just admit you don't have what it takes, and all of this will be over," she said. "You're here because your father pulled some strings. Get that through your head."

"You're . . . wrong." Dashiel stood up with difficulty. "If you let me use my weapon, I'll show you."

Sofia sighed again. "Don't you get it? You're done!"

Dashiel went to the corner of the room and took Orphée from its case. When Sofia saw the weapon, her eyes widened. The fight seemed to drain out of her.

"A doizemant? Where'd you get that?" she asked in awe.

"You know what it is?"

"Of course I know. Any respectable warrior does," she said, but there was no bite to her words. She seemed only partly aware of Dashiel, her full attention fixed on the weapon.

"What do you say?" Dashiel asked, snapping her out of her trance.

"Very well," she said. "But to make things more interesting, let's make a wager. If you win, I'll accept you as one of us."

"And if I lose?"

"You'll quit this nonsense and go home."

Dashiel thought for a second. If he were to lose, he would have to give up his dream, but he had to stay true to his conviction. He wouldn't let anyone dictate what he could or could not do, not anymore. He had to believe in himself and in Orphée.

"Deal."

Sofia searched among the weapons until she selected two sharpened hooks chained together. "The doizemant can transform into twelve different weapons, but since its natural form is a baton, hooks are the best option."

Dashiel and Sofia began their combat. The hooks pecked at the baton with great speed, but Dashiel was skilled at blocking attacks with Orphée. The two continued their dance across the training room, and to the surprise of both, Dashiel managed to stay upright. When he saw a chance, he decided to use the trick that Sylvain had taught him. Backing up to give himself some space, he tapped the baton three times against the floor.

Nothing happened. Orphée didn't get any heavier.

Taking advantage of his confusion, Sofia used her hooks to snap the baton away from Dashiel's hands and immobilize him, pressing his head against the floor with a single hand.

"A true wonder, but its power level is a shame. A real shame that such a special weapon remains in such inexperienced hands," she said, letting him go. "It's a waste that you don't know anything about it. It's obvious that you're not worthy of carrying it."

Dashiel remained silent and stood up. He put Orphée back in its case and walked toward the exit.

"Where do you think you're going?" Sofia said, trying to look uninterested.

"A deal is a deal. I'm telling Roderigo I'm out," he said. His heart thundered at the mere thought of doing it.

"I meant every single word I said." She crossed her arms and sighed. "But I guess you can try to change my mind."

"Really?" Dashiel jolted.

"The lesson has concluded, Ermitage." She opened the door. "I'll see you tomorrow. Same time, same place."

"Thank you. I promise I will do my best."

"Just go," Sofia growled.

Dashiel remained in bed until sunset, gazing at his room's peeling ceiling and enjoying the warm breeze coming through the open window. His body hurt, but his pride hurt worse. He had known that joining the Cobalt Phantasms would be difficult. He knew he wasn't the strongest or the smartest. Yet he hadn't expected such humiliation in the process.

Still, he had to keep trying. He had to prove that he belonged.

An odd sound distracted him from his wallowing. He looked around and found a paper butterfly fluttering all over the room. It danced in the light of the fading sun before landing on his chest. It slowly unfolded into a letter with his name written on it in beautiful calligraphy. His heart raced as he began to read.

Dear Dashiel,

You have no idea how excited I was when I received your letter. I must admit that I thought of you often after we parted ways, and if you hadn't written to me, I would have written to you.

I am well aware of your place in the order, and even though I am not part of it, I shall keep the secret of both its existence and our correspondence.

I do apologize for the shortness of the letter. My days have been busy, but I had the urge to answer and let you know of my desire to keep in touch.

May Providence allow us to see each other again.

Cordially,

Athenai

All thoughts of his disastrous training had dissolved by the end of the letter. Extreme joy shone a light in the middle of Dashiel's uncertainty. He reached for the mysterious seed's music box, wound it, and let it play its sweet music as he reread the words of its owner and thought of what he could write about in his next letter.

CHAPTER 18

A FORESEEN DISCHARGE

Weeks passed, and springtime went away, leaving a boiling summer in its wake. Along with the heat, wagons of errant gypsies arrived in St. Victoire Dowager, as they did every year, to host their famous Knevali Festival. An exuberant energy spread throughout the city. People moved among the festival's colorful tents, marveling at trained exotic animals, dazzling dancers, daredevil jugglers, and eccentric musicians.

Dashiel didn't have time to go to the festival. He had his hands full, training with Sofia each morning and attending classes with Professor Grasshop each afternoon. Even though Sofia was still harsh in her training, her iciness was thawing little by little. Her tolerance increased, and her temper became more manageable.

At the end of each day, Dashiel collapsed onto his bed, exhausted. But every now and then, he received a secret letter from his dear Athenai, which always boosted his spirits. With every passing day, his strength and knowledge increased.

One day, Dashiel walked into the training room and found Sofia with Damian, the server from the mess hall. Dashiel had been quite surprised to learn that the mute ten-year-old was Sofia's little brother.

"I'm so sorry, Damy. I must attend to my mentoring obligations." Sofia tried to soothe the boy, who was clearly upset. "Next year we'll go to the festival, I promise. I'll make it up to you. Let's go to the candy parlor on Sunday. What do you say?" She wore a tender expression that Dashiel had never seen before.

The boy wiped his eyes and squirmed. Finally, Sofia noticed Dashiel's presence.

"I'm sorry. I didn't know you were busy," Dashiel said. "I'll go up."

The boy used Dashiel's arrival as a distraction and scurried from the room before she could say another word. "He'll understand," she murmured to herself, guilt written across her face.

"What was that about?" Dashiel asked, stretching his legs.

"None of your business, forest boy," she snapped. "Focus on your training, Ermitage. I can't wait to see the new ways that you invent to embarrass yourself today."

"What are we doing today? Please no more push-ups," he begged. "I'm still sore."

"It's your lucky day. Today you're learning how to project essence into a shield. One that you can use when you lack, well, a shield."

"I'm finally going to learn *magic*?" Dashiel gasped. "Incredible! I can't wait."

"Hold your horses," Sofia responded. "This is no cheap trick. This spell requires a lot of concentration, and we need to work on that first. Besides, not everyone can cast a shield. Let's begin."

She was right to curb his enthusiasm. The concentration exercises were tedious and boring. Dashiel imagined time as a mischievous old wizard who lengthened the hours by flipping his ancient hourglass before the last bit of sand fell. Why did Sylvain enjoy meditating so much? It was awful. Seconds turned to minutes; minutes turned to hours.

Everything went according to plan until a noise interrupted the tranquility. A man's distorted voice rang from the tunnels, interrupting Dashiel's concentration. "Sofia! Sofia!"

"Who's making that racket?" Sofia yelled, annoyed, as she walked over to the entrance of the training room. The door flew open of its own accord. A man appeared, panting as if he'd raced through the tunnels.

"Sofia, something's happened."

"Ebleck? What is it?"

"The Knevali Festival . . . something happened. Gypsies began to protest against Viceroy Fiddlestrum. The protest turned into a revolt. Imperialists came and took away those involved."

"Good thing I didn't take Damian there," she said, shoulders sagging in relief.

"Sofia, I . . . don't know how to say this."

"What do you mean, Ebleck?"

Ebleck opened his mouth, then shut it without saying a word. He fidgeted with his hands.

"Ebleck!"

"We've confirmed that Damian was at the festival when this happened," the man finally said.

Sofia looked horrified. "That's impossible. I told him not to go."

"We've also confirmed that he was taken by city guards."

Sofia became silent. Her face lost all color. She pushed the man out of her way and ran into the tunnel, leaving Dashiel alone with the distraught stranger. After a moment, Dashiel went after her.

He found Sofia and her father in the common area, locked in a devastated embrace. They were surrounded by the inn's employees and several Phantasms, including Sylvain.

"Why didn't I go with him? Why? *Why*?" Sofia fisted the couch's dusty cushion.

Tomas Spaigne sobbed along with his daughter, covering his face with his hands.

Mrs. Elain, the inn's housekeeper, cried into a handkerchief while trying to comfort her employers. "Now, now, my child. It wasn't your fault."

"Ah knew something lik' this would happen." The cook, equally distraught, sat on a couch. "He's only a bairn."

Heavy footsteps announced Roderigo, Fineley Hugont, and two other members of the order, who ducked through the inn's door and joined the group in the common room. The desolation in their faces foreshadowed bad news. Everyone circled around Roderigo, drawn by his natural gravitas and eager to hear an update.

"We've found out what happened." Roderigo sniffed. "The prisoners from the revolt have been sentenced to life service as Ochre Brigadiers."

Mrs. Elain nearly collapsed, but Sofia, whose own strength was almost gone, caught her.

"Why him? Why Damian? Why did I leave him alone?" Sofia asked, holding on to the older woman.

"It seems the gypsies did no wrong." Hugont stepped forward. "We've been informed that the viceroy ordered his men to dress as gypsies, start the revolt, and then use it as an excuse to capture more victims for the Ochre Triumphant."

The words seemed to give Sofia a shot of adrenaline. In a matter of seconds, she transformed into a warrior. "He will pay." She gritted her teeth. "I will find him. And when I do, I'll slit his throat open once and for all."

Sofia rushed to the door, ready for a fight, but Roderigo blocked her path with his arm.

"Let me go!" she screeched, stretching her arms toward the exit.

"You're not going anywhere." Roderigo's face hardened. "Security has doubled since the revolt. You would put yourself and everyone else at risk. A Cobalt Phantasm thinks before acting. We cannot be driven by blind emotion. Mister Hugont," Roderigo called.

"Yes, sir?"

"Send a message to every single Phantasm in and around this base. Missions are to be aborted immediately. Members should keep a low profile until further notice. No Phantasm is to be captured; too many things are at risk."

"He is my son! Don't hide—do something!" Tomas exploded into motion, rushing to Roderigo, grabbing him by his shirt, and winding up as if he were about to throw a punch. His eyes were red, and his tears fell to the floor. "My family has done everything for your cause. Two Spaignes have already died because of it. Where's your loyalty?"

"I'm loyal to the Spaignes, Tomas. You know of my love for Damian, but we all bear responsibility for a cause far bigger than ourselves." A tear broke free from the master's eye. "Eloise taught me that."

Tomas's grip loosened. He let go of Roderigo and walked away with a defeated slouch.

"You've heard my orders." Roderigo raised his voice and said, "Whoever disobeys will be expelled from the order."

He left the room. In a matter of seconds, the space emptied of everyone except Sofia, Dashiel, and Sylvain.

When Sofia saw Dashiel, her expression changed. Her tears subsided, and her eyebrows arched diabolically. She bolted toward him. "If I hadn't wasted my time training you, he would still be here!"

"Leave him alone." Sylvain stepped between Sofia and Dashiel. "He isn't to blame. You're using him as a scapegoat."

"Whatever," Sofia said with a huff. She pointed at Dashiel, her finger twitching with rage. "I don't want to see your face again. I don't want to know anything about you. I don't care if I'm punished. You're on your own."

She stormed away.

"Now what?" Dashiel hunched his shoulders, disheartened by the afternoon's turn of events.

"She had an obligation to you. She's failed as your mentor," Sylvain said, as upset as Dashiel had ever seen him. "We're telling Roderigo about this."

"No."

"What?"

"She might have failed me, but I won't fail her, the order, or myself. I'll prove her wrong," Dashiel said, displaying an assertiveness he'd never felt before. "I know it's against the rules, but you have to train me. Please, Sylvain." He gave his friend a pleading look. "I need you. What do you say?"

Sylvain sighed. "How can I say no to you?"

CHAPTER 19

THE EVANESCENCE OF
TIME AND WORDS

D ashiel continued training under Sylvain's watchful eye. Thinking about Roderigo's words, he decided to write in his journal every week. Even if he wasn't the most experienced or the strongest pupil, he'd at least learn from his past actions, words, and thoughts.

~

June 26, 1854

I've never woken up as early as I did today, and I don't know if I'll ever get used to it. On my first day of training with Sylvain, we ventured off into the countryside. He made me carry a heavy rock all the way to a pond. He explained that we would do this at the beginning of every session so I could build up my stamina.

After I nearly broke my back, we finally arrived at the pond, which had a huge, roaring waterfall. Its shores were decorated with countless water lilies. So beautiful. So peaceful.

Sylvain, closed-eyed, walked on the pond's surface and sat on a big rock beneath the waterfall. Not a single hair on his head got wet; he seemed to repel the water.

He explained that he was using a shield spell, the very same one Sofia had started to teach me. "A human being is composed of vital mental, emotional, and astral forces; therefore, they can be projected—with the proper training, that is," he said.

He asked me to sit next to him, but when I got close to the waterfall, its force didn't let me through. It launched me into the water like a rag doll . . .

The merciless roar of the waterfall silenced the splash caused by yet another of Dashiel's failed attempts to reach Sylvain. He swam with agility and clawed himself to the rock, but he was ultimately thrown back. With a gasp, Dashiel stopped trying. He allowed his body to float, looking up at the fading clouds. His eyelashes twitched as rogue water droplets landed on them.

The lemony smell of the water lilies faintly disguised the earthly scent of the water. With his ears submerged, he could make out the hooting of underwater creatures. They distorted the cry of the waterfall.

"You mustn't give up," Sylvain said, opening his eyes. "Not everyone is able to project a shield, but I'm confident you can. I won't stop until you do it."

Dashiel left his buoyant state, the rumble of the falls sounding louder above the water. He offered Sylvain a hand. "You promise?"

Sylvain shook Dashiel's hand. "Cross my heart."

"Good!" Taking advantage of the moment, Dashiel pulled Sylvain into the water.

Sylvain regarded Dashiel's foolery with a shaky yet serious expression. "I see you have chosen death."

His stoic facade dissolved when he punched the water, sending a wave at Dashiel. A battle of splashes began and continued until the afternoon breeze drummed on the colorful petals of the lilies.

"I believe I have won, my less-worthy opponent." Sylvain dragged himself out of the water. "All hail Sylvain, king of this nameless pond!"

"Liar!" Dashiel chuckled, throwing a lily pad at Sylvain's face. His shoulders and armpits ached from the water war, and his face was red. He tumbled down next to Sylvain.

They shared a laugh as they caught their breath.

Dashiel remained silent as he gazed at the clouds. He placed both hands on his aching abdomen. "What if something is too strong, or wise, for me to face?"

Sylvain's eyes were solemn. "Don't you worry. I shall protect you from anything or anyone that might harm you," he said, his dripping wet hair slicked over his forehead. "Am I not your friend?"

"Yes, but what if . . . what if I'm struck down? What if I never pass and prove my worth?" He extended his arm toward the sky and squinted. "Would my story never be told? Would I be forgotten?"

"I will never let that happen. You will become what you are destined to be." Sylvain finally stood up. "Let's go now. I don't want you to get a cold."

～

July 3, 1854

Sylvain gave me two days off, which was grand, as I got to sleep in.

In Professor Grasshop's class, we learned about the beginnings of the order. It seems that the Cobalt Phantasms were founded by Roderigo and a group of Diviners called the Founding Chapter, but the idea was conceived by the Belecrose family. Apparently we are called Cobalt Phantasms because the Belecroses used to have blood of that color, along with otherworldly abilities.

It amazes me how much admiration and love there is for the Belecroses, especially for the late emperor. They did so much for the people. It is sad to know that the crown prince, the last member of the dynasty, is now as wicked as Asedia.

According to Grasshop, our continent, Egadrise, is full of forces that are always around us. Other civilizations have uncovered their continents' secrets and have learned to harness their powers. In ancient times, Egadriseans knew how to harness these forces, but something happened, and the knowledge was lost. I asked what happened, and no one knew the answer.

I get the feeling that they know more than they dare to admit . . .

Unlike our scientific and religious practices, our understanding of magic is minuscule. The little knowledge that the Cobalt Phantasms have of magic was given to us by the Belecrose family.

Arson and I hung out after training again. We even took on odd jobs around town together for a little extra money. He is indeed a tough guy but seems to enjoy my company. He also enjoys pranking others, especially Octavious. He's promised to teach me a trick or two.

Sylvain's training absorbs all my energy and time. I am worn out at the end of the day. Every time I pick up a book, I fall asleep. On Thursday, Professor Grasshop gave us a surprise examination. Needless to say, I was not ready for it . . .

Mina Halliwell, like a guardian spirit, has offered to tutor me. During a tutoring session, she told me that she decided to join the order when she was denied acceptance by all the universities in Arberice.

I think it is stupid that they won't allow women to grow to their full potential. Women like Mina and my mother have a lot to give to this world.

~

July 10, 1854

Hermesia is in dire straits. Heralds woke its citizenry, announcing that taxes would increase and that anyone who did not comply would endure severe consequences.

People have started to gather. I hear them protesting in the streets. I can also hear the marching of city guards, their shouts commanding the crowds to disperse. Some of the Cobalt Phantasms are out there, trying to protect the citizens. There are not enough of us.

On my way to the base, I saw a bullet break through one of the inn's windows. Later that day, I learned that a man had been shot right in front of the inn because he wouldn't comply with the guards' orders.

We've been commanded to not leave the base.

"Keep your center, focus on the movement of each and every muscle, and feel how the energy traverses your body." I repeated Sylvain's teachings as I practiced my combat techniques. But it was hard to concentrate with the uproarious Hermesians just beyond the windows of the inn.

The protestors shout about the unfair raise in taxes, saying they cannot pay without starving their families. The rich have left the poor alone in a fight they cannot win.

Maybe it's like Sylvain and Athenai said. Asedia has started to bend their wills and twist their souls.

~

July 17, 1854

Octavious approached me after class earlier this week. He hadn't spoken much to me since the day Damian was arrested, so I was a little uneasy. He asked me to deliver a letter for him. He had to take one of Professor Grasshop's tests and could not do it himself. I advised him to use messenger droplets, but he said that doing so was strictly forbidden. Only members were permitted to use those.

I should be more careful in my correspondence with Athenai . . .

Before I left, Octavious begged me not to read the contents of the letter or ask about the message it contained. The recipient was a young painter who lives on the other side of the city. He snatched the letter out of my hands, commanded me to wait, and disappeared into his colorful hideout. The painter quickly returned, perfumed letter in hand. He instructed me to give it to "the color of my eyes."

The delivery was the first of many. At least Octavious rewards me for each.

During another delivery, I saw Sofia from afar. She was playing her violin in the usual hidden alley. Her music, though still enchanting, has become sadder. I decided to follow her after her performance. She traveled to the poorest neighborhood in the city. I was surprised by what I saw. She visited the poor, sick, and disenfranchised, gave them money and food, and played her violin for them. They enjoyed her company.

So . . . I guess she has some gentleness inside. Maybe she's not as heartless as I thought. Either way, I won't let my guard down.

Her brother is still under arrest, waiting to be transformed into a metal soldier. Tomas Spaigne is no longer tending to his inn, but I've seen him go to the city jail to visit

Damian every single day. The jolly innkeeper has become a ghost.

There was no letter from Athenai tonight, but something wonderful happened instead. When I opened the jeweled music box, I found a small, green bud popping out of the dirt.

I'm relieved, for I had started to think that it would never grow. I'll keep carrying it on my belt, hoping it blooms soon.

～

August 7, 1854

I dreamed about my parents, my friends, and Azahar. In my dream, I saw the fenku trails, the crystalline lake, and jukkes splashing in the water with their antlers and fins. Then I found myself at Gailfaur's clearing. I saw Gailfaur, the mystical divinity, surrounded by a pool of light and gazing at me.

I woke up feeling a little homesick. At times, I do miss my parents, Grimley, and Donner, and I yearn to see them. But my dreams of home inspire me. I won't let them down.

Sylvain is a great friend, but he is almost as strict as Sofia. I can still hear his barked orders: "Control your breath and your position." "Run four more miles." "Clear your mind and focus." "Watch your movement; it's sloppy." "You will carry three rocks to the lake from now on."

After training on Wednesday, I polished Orphée. To my surprise, it seemed different. Its length had increased, and strange markings now cover its surface. I can feel how its strength increases with each passing day. Papa said that we are connected. This must mean that I am changing too.

In class after a cartography lesson, Professor Grasshop tested our unique abilities again. We all did well, except for Arson. He has not been able to outsmart our teacher. Every *time he tries to steal something, he ends up with an onion in hand. The professor has started calling him Onion Boy. Grasshop said that Arson will be inducted if he manages to stealthily steal something from him. I hope he does soon . . .*

Another paper butterfly arrived from Athenai. With each letter, I get to know her a little bit better. Her sweet prose and caring words are addictive. I've gotten to know her joys and fears, and she has learned mine. I can't stop smiling . . .

How did I fall so easily for her?

As I was writing this entry, a paper owl landed on the lamp. With a shy hoot, the bird unfolded into a letter from Master Roderigo. He wants to see me in his office first thing tomorrow.

I may not be accompanied by anyone . . .

Dashiel nervously fiddled with his vest's buttons as he made his way through the tunnels to Roderigo's office. He had no idea why the master had requested his presence.

"Dashiel Ermitage," Roderigo said in his raspy voice as he opened the door. "My boy, please come inside."

Dashiel followed him into the office, which had changed since his last visit. The piles of papers were gone, and the chalkboard had notes and various drawings of a man on it. A pair of yellowish gloves that walked around the table by themselves drew Dashiel's attention. One wrote with a quill, while the other filed documents into a drawer.

Roderigo noticed Dashiel staring.

"They're quite helpful. A simple trick given by our Alferai allies," Roderigo said. "Especially if you want to avoid blisters on your hands."

"They're grand," Dashiel said, awestruck.

"They can imitate your handwriting, except for the *a*'s. Those are terribly slanted."

Roderigo sat on the edge of his desk, his expression becoming concerned. "I'm afraid this is no social meeting."

Dashiel could sense he was in for an earful.

"I know about you, Spaigne, and Aurante," Roderigo said.

"Wh-what do you mean, sir?" Sweat beaded on the back of his neck. His mind was a mess of fluttering thoughts. Did Roderigo know that Sofia wasn't training him? That Sylvain had taken her place?

"Everything's fine," Dashiel responded nervously.

Roderigo gave him a reproachful look.

Dashiel took a breath and tried for the truth this time. "Sofia isn't training me anymore. But it wasn't Sylvain's fault. I was the one who made him. If only Sofia hadn't failed me . . ."

Roderigo raised his hand. "You were wrong not to tell me, but I understand the circumstances." He cleared his throat. "She was also wrong, but please don't feel that way. Sofia can be difficult to deal with, but I know she is the right mentor for you. I know it!"

Dashiel remained silent, as he did not know what to say.

"I think you should know something about her, something that has pained her for years." Roderigo huffed, and the gloves halted their work.

"Years ago, before the order was established, a resistance organization sought to free the empire from Asedia's influence. Sofia's mother, Eloise, belonged to the resistance. The empire and its allies proved to be more powerful, and the resistance dwindled down. As a last gasp, they decided to take back Prince Markeus, as he represented the last remnant of hope and unity in the empire. During Asedia's visit to Hermesia, the resistance kidnapped the prince. Unfortunately, something went wrong. The viceroy's men seized Markeus and killed the rebels one by one."

Roderigo wiped his tiny glasses with his sleeve, then slid them on his nose. He held Dashiel's gaze, his expression grave. "Except for one. Eloise. She managed to escape. She hid for some time, until she was found by Viceroy Fiddlestrum himself."

On the edge of his seat, Dashiel asked, "What happened after?"

Roderigo's face flushed. "Eloise Fiddlestrum was murdered that night."

"Fiddlestrum? You mean Spaigne," Dashiel corrected.

"Both are correct, my boy," Roderigo said.

"You mean she was . . ."

"The viceroy's daughter." The familiar voice rang out from behind Dashiel. "He killed his own daughter, with no remorse, and allowed a bastard to turn her oldest son into a metal monster."

Sofia stepped through the open door. "Then he damned all women in the empire by creating a protocol that denied their rights. The way he sees it, women have too much time on their hands and too many thoughts in their heads."

Her expression was sinister, her back straight and tall. "Anyway, it's none of your business, idiot. It's because of you that Damian is not here."

"Sofia." Roderigo frowned. "He is not to blame. You know that very well."

"He is," Sofia hissed, her eyes welling. "My little brother is gone because of him!"

Roderigo's face hardened. "That's enough!"

"You are just defending him because he is Elias Ermitage's son!" Sofia said, earning the silence of her master. The air itself seemed to hold its breath as they waited for Roderigo to respond.

"Maybe you really have failed him," Roderigo said in a flat voice. He turned to Dashiel. "I apologize for my poor choice in terms of your mentor. I shall assign you someone else." He looked sternly at Sofia. "As for you, we shall converse on another occasion. You both can go now."

Sofia stormed out of the office. Dashiel ran after her, cutting her off before she could open the secret passageway that led to the kitchen.

"I'm deeply sorry for your loss," he said, panting from the chase.

"I couldn't care less about you or what you feel. Leave me alone!" She pushed Dashiel.

"Please! Listen." Dashiel shifted to once again block her path.

"Move away!" She threw a punch, but to her surprise, he caught it in midflight.

"Listen!" he yelled, stopping her cold. "I'm sorry for what happened to your family. No one deserves what Asedia and Fiddlestrum did. I understand you must be hurting, but I'm not here to mess around. I'm here to train, succeed, and serve my country. And I'll get there, with or without you." Dashiel leaned in, adrenaline giving him much-needed courage. "You don't intimidate me."

He released Sofia's fist, his heart beating like a drum. She remained silent. Finally, she spun on her heel and walked back down the tunnel.

Dashiel couldn't believe what he had done.

An air of freedom soothed his mind.

⁘

August 21, 1854

Sylvain was assigned to a mission to escort an ambassador safely across Hermesian territories, so I went to the pond by myself today, carrying three rocks, as Sylvain had requested. Looking at the mountain of rocks piled in front of the waterfall makes me feel stronger. I meditated for hours, just like Sylvain does. I thought about my feelings for Athenai, the anger that I released with Sofia, and my friendship with Sylvain. I thought of my home and my people and how they need to be protected.

Without even realizing it, I projected my first shield! It appeared as a pale white light surrounding my body. It lasted for a couple seconds, during which the water didn't touch me. It was a warm sensation that traveled across my body.

When I returned to my room, I was greeted by my baton's whispering. The whispering was barely audible but very adamant. I got my baton out of its case and held it with joy and pride. That's when it started to rumble. The baton broke into two and shapeshifted into two daggers. They were sharper than any sword and as light as wood.

I can't wait to tell Sylvain when he's back!

～

September 4, 1854

Yesterday morning, Sylvain was teaching me combat movements in the training room when Sofia entered. Her presence straightened my back and raised my chin. "Every time you get a pose wrong, I'll slap you. Get the swords." She took control of the lesson without a word to Sylvain.

She had come back to help me finish my training. I hid my smile as much as possible so she wouldn't realize I was pleased by her return.

She and Sylvain reached an agreement: he would train me in the mornings, and she would train me in the evenings. I am the luckiest recruit ever. I have two of the most talented members of the order showing me their ways.

I am relieved that Sofia has changed her mind.

～

September 11, 1854

Something incredible happened during our class with Professor Grasshop. Octavious has created a liquid that the others call Octa-pus ink, which coagulates the yellow substance inside the Ochre Brigadiers, immobilizing them long enough for them to be taken down. He is leaving in a couple days to be inducted as an official Cobalt Phantasm. Oddly enough, I think I'll miss him. And he will miss me—even if he won't admit it.

About me and alchemy . . . Well, I'm getting better at it. I just need a little bit of practice. I really hope my hair and Sylvain's will cease to be purple soon.

I've gotten better at firearm combat. Sofia even said that I was progressing. I'm proud of how much I've grown, but I hate how much she taunts me whenever she takes me down in close combat. She pins me to the floor and . . . expectorates in my face.

She'll see one day.

Mina was inducted into the order a few days ago, and she will join the Dolphin Squadron. Arson is still trying and failing to outsmart Professor Grasshop. Grasshop tells me that it won't be long before I finish my training here at Hermesia. I don't know what my final examination will be. I must prepare.

The little bud inside the jewel box has doubled in size. I'll read the letter Athenai sent me, listening to the box's music and imagining what could possibly bloom from the mysterious seed.

✆

September 25, 1854

Fall has arrived. The trees are crying amber tears, and this summer's merciless heat has finally started to dissolve. I look through my small window, and I'm amazed at the beauty of it all.

On Tuesday, Sofia and Sylvain administered an examination of my abilities, and I am pleased to say that . . . I passed! I hit the bull's-eye with every shot, disarmed Sylvain at sword fighting, projected my shield on command, and, most important, took down Sofia. And let her hear about it.

Sofia does seem more . . . cheerful. She even laughed at one of Sylvain's jokes. No one has ever done that.

It was an incredible day, and to top it all off, the bud inside Athenai's box looks as if it's going to bloom at any moment.

I've noticed that the base's tunnels have become almost deserted. It's a little spooky, walking alone through the dark tunnels.

The Ochre Triumphant is right around the corner. It's a huge celebration that takes place all over the empire. It might sound fun, but in reality, it is terrible. It celebrates another year of Asedia's tyranny, and it is when many victims are turned into Ochre Brigadiers as entertainment.

Poor Damian. How I wish I could go set him free.

Yesterday, I saw Sofia step into Master Roderigo's office for a fifth time. I wonder if her recent cheerfulness and the secretive visits are related . . .

~

Sofia strode into Roderigo's office.

"The plan has been revised," he said, pulling a file out of his drawer. "I have pulled some strings, and it has been approved by the Founding Chapter. I shall contact our collaborators to acquire invitations to the Ochre Triumphant."

Sofia looked at him with joy. "Thank you so much, Master." She clutched the file to her chest.

"There's just one thing I must talk to you about," Roderigo said, dampening her elation. "As you know well, a Cobalt Phantasm is not allowed to perform solo missions."

"Yes, I know," Sofia answered. "That's why the mission request specifies the need for at least two more members."

"Sofia, I'm afraid it's impossible to assign anyone else to it. A crucial task is at hand, and as you can tell, I have sent many of our people to contribute to it. Even I will be out. There's no one left."

They both took a breath.

"I was thinking maybe you could take Aurante and Ermitage."

"Dashiel Ermitage?" She snorted.

"Yes, him. You said that he was improving significantly. That he is good."

"He has improved, but he's far from ready," she said, raising her voice. "He's only going to screw things up. Aurante is good, but Ermitage?"

Roderigo's peaceful expression sharpened into a frown. "I've been lenient with you, despite the fact that you neglected your obligation to your trainee and continue to treat him with disrespect. And I have allowed you, against my better judgment, to orchestrate a mission that could bring many consequences if it fails."

He paused, allowing that ominous final word to hang in the air.

"Listen well, Sofia. Either you take Aurante *and* Ermitage, or the mission's off. That's final."

Sofia wanted to snap back, defend her case, but she knew it would be impossible to change his mind. "Fine. They both can come."

His face softened into a tender expression. "Dear, I know this mission means the world to you, and it's important to me too. But if you succeed, which I know you will, I promise to officially name Dashiel as a Phantasm and assign him to another squadron. He'll be off your back."

CHAPTER 20

INCENSE AND SHADOWS

Once the autumnal residence of the Belecrose family, the palace in the capital city of Varnaise was magnificent. Opulent wooden panels decorated the walls and ceilings of the long corridors, and twisted columns supported the mosaic-covered arches. The chandeliers and candelabras were painted black and adorned with amber-engraved crystals that reflected the candlelight.

It was a true architectural achievement, indeed, but it was most famous for two things. First, the palace rooms were rife with the aroma of incense, which grew stronger the closer one got to the emperor's wing. Second, human shadows with no owners moved through the halls, softly shrieking and moaning. This wasn't always the case. Visitors began noticing the smell and the shadows when Asedia first took possession of the palace.

The tranquility of the corridors was shattered by the fast-paced steps of a man whose medals shone as brightly as his bare head. He walked past long lines of saluting imperial guards. He stopped before a pair of doors.

"His Lordship, General Samuel Indolett, seeks an audience with His Imperial Majesty," a herald announced.

The doors opened, and the man walked into the room.

The curtains were drawn back, leaving the blue sky visible, but somehow the room remained dark. A group of musicians played in a corner, and five ministers surrounded the emperor.

"May Providence bless His Illustrious Majesty." Samuel Indolett bowed.

"Welcome to my court." Sitting proudly, Abelon Asedia greeted the general, his right hand.

The ministers moved aside and remained silent, their heads bowed.

"Your Majesty, first allow me to congratulate you on such an inspired plan," Samuel said. "Sentencing those professors to a lifetime of service as Ochre Brigadiers was a brilliant idea."

"They dared to fill their students' minds with rebellious thoughts, and that I cannot tolerate." Asedia stroked his clean-shaven chin. "Besides, we're in need of more Brigadiers."

"That will teach the others not to preach about that Belecrose scum, my lord," Samuel responded. "Whoever does shall go down in history as a vulgar terrorist who attempted insurrection and failed miserably."

There was a moment of silence before Samuel ventured a question. "How can I be of service?"

Asedia stood up and looked behind him to where a large, armored crystal showcase held a golden object similar to the cup on his imperial crest. A golden censer with the ability to manipulate the astral force. Two Ochre Brigadiers guarded it, remaining within the shadows of the room.

"The reason I called you, Samuel, is because I will be absent during Hermesia's Ochre Triumphant festivities. My son shall go in my place. You are to protect him, his entourage, and the Asedian treasures."

"With my life I shall, Your Majesty," said Samuel, a smirk of pride on his face.

"The marchioness of Pavkov and Iren!" the herald's voice interrupted.

An elaborately garbed woman came through the doors. Her dress bore a short train, her shoulders were layered with capes, and her hair was hidden underneath a heavy, opaque veil and an onyx-encrusted headdress. Her attire was as dark as ebony, her powdered face as white as milk—the customary makeup and attire of a widowed Urovenian noblewoman. She walked with her chin as high as she could raise it and moved swiftly, stopping a few meters from the emperor's desk. Some would admire her poise. Others would pity her as they would a swallow that has lost its ability to fly—its only purpose and its only bliss.

Her gray-painted lips were unsmiling, her brow puckered in a frown, and her unblinking eyes filled with bitterness.

"Your Majesty." She bowed before the emperor.

"Good morning, Marchioness," Asedia said with a macabre smirk. "How are things going in the palace?"

The woman's bitter expression didn't change. "Everything is running like clockwork, my lord."

"What about the preparations for the capital's Ochre Triumphant?"

"This year is more important than ever. No mistakes should be made," Samuel added, contempt on his face.

"Everything is going according to plan," she told the emperor without acknowledging Samuel. Her rank had given her that privilege.

"Excellent. State the reason for your presence here."

"I've come to announce the arrival of His Imperial Highness, back from his trip to Windergale," she said. "His Imperial Highness, the crown prince!" the marchioness's voice filled the room.

The doors opened again, revealing the crown prince of Zaphyrelia. Chest puffed out, he walked straight to his father without acknowledging the marchioness or the general. He bowed his head at the emperor, a sign of respect. "Your Majesty."

As regal as a prince could be, Markeus Asedia was a young man of seventeen but seemed years older. From head to toe, he was the true representation of the Asedian standard of perfection. The emperor had made sure of that. He wore his short blond hair slicked back and his ochre military uniform and sash perfectly pressed. His various medals shone as brightly as his perfectly aligned white teeth.

"Your arrival is of great convenience, Son," Asedia said. "Something urgent came up, and I won't be able to attend the Hermesian festivities. As such, you are to perform the conversion ceremony in my stead."

"The ceremony?" Markeus asked, his projected confidence displaying a small crack. "I don't think I can."

"Nonsense!" Asedia huffed. "Cancel all prior commitments and get ready. You leave at dawn."

The emperor strode to the exit, Samuel right behind him.

"Father, I don't think that's appropriate," the prince said, halting Asedia's walk. "I'm not ready."

"Appropriate?" Asedia murmured, turning his head to the prince. "I've taught you how to do it; of course you are ready."

Asedia backtracked until he was inches from his son. Markeus looked down, clenching his fists. "Please, Father . . . Don't make me."

With all his strength, Asedia slapped Markeus across the face. "How dare you contest my wishes? I am the one who says what is appropriate and what is not. Compared to me, you're nothing! You have no choice but to oblige!"

Markeus's lips trembled, and his eyes began to water. He held anger and embarrassment back, as he always had.

Asedia's expression shifted in a blink, his eyes turning tender. He placed his hand on the young prince's cheek, covering the red handprint that bloomed across his skin.

"When will you ever learn?" he said with disappointment. "I've tried to eliminate whatever is left of the cursed Belecroses, but you resist. I'm afraid you're still flawed. You still remind me of your bastard birth father."

"That coward was *not* my father, and I am *not* like him," the prince retorted, nostrils flaring. He tried to keep hold of his emotions, for the emperor detested when he showed them. "You are my true father, my only teacher and guide." Markeus's eyes widened. "Please forgive me."

"Do as I told you, and you shall earn my forgiveness," Asedia said, walking away from his son. "I know you will be a worthy monarch, but first, you must prove yourself a worthy heir."

"Yes, Father." The prince gazed at his blurry reflection in the floor.

"Hermesia has seen dark days lately, with revolts led by ungrateful subjects. Who are we to deny them a celebration?" The emperor strode to the exit, Samuel at his heels. He stepped through the door, leaving Markeus alone with the silent shadows.

The pair strolled down the amber-colored corridors and discussed matters of state, such as updates on the war against their enemies in America and Europe, their allies on the continent, and festivities in the vice-capitals.

"Samuel, any updates on our little place?" the emperor asked without breaking stride.

"My lord, I have the pleasure to announce that we have found a way to breach it." Samuel chuckled.

"Proceed." Happiness washed over the emperor, but he did not let it show.

"After receiving the intel, we sent an Ochre Command. We haven't heard from the two Brigadiers, but their commander has returned and confirmed the original reports."

The emperor stopped at an open window, which overlooked an ocean at the base of a tall cliff. Water crashed chaotically against the cliff's rocky walls, and the sea breeze ruffled Asedia's hair.

"The barrier *is* weak against extreme heat." Samuel stood next to the emperor.

"The time has come to put plan number eighty-six into motion," Asedia said, inhaling the breeze.

"I have anticipated your wishes, Your Majesty. The armory has begun its construction," Samuel said. "The foreman informed me that funds and resources are both lacking at the present. Before I cut off his tongue, he said that no substance on earth could possibly power such an invention."

"I shall correct that in due time." A shadow appeared in front of the emperor, moaned, and faded away—a reflection of one of the countless astral forces trapped inside his censer. The sight of a trapped soul etched a smile across the emperor's face. "Their days are numbered."

CHAPTER 21

OCHRE TRIUMPHANT

s the Ochre Triumphant approached, the multitudes carous-
ing in the streets during the daytime slowly dwindled. Most
Hermesians dreaded the celebration for its abhorrent nature.
The streets were highly decorated with the emperor's crest, and music
filled the air, but most people were reluctant to partake in festivities
that served no one but the ruthless sovereign.

On the day of the celebration, a chest was delivered anonymously
to the inn. Inside, it contained luxurious outfits worthy of royalty.

Everything had come together for Sofia's mission.

"Argh! This thing itches." Dashiel toyed with the colorfully embroidered ascot around his neck. "Why did I have to wear the outfit with
stockings?" He scratched his legs. "And these shoes aren't helping."

He wanted to get rid of it all.

"That one was your size." Sylvain tried not to laugh. "Besides, you
look great!"

"I'm definitely not made for these clothes."

Sylvain fixed Dashiel's ascot. "It's for one night. You look regal."
He chuckled. "Sofia, on the other hand? I can't really see her wearing
a fancy dress."

Dashiel thought for a moment. "I can't even see her using a bar of soap!" He imagined his mentor in her customary ragged dress, her greasy hair fluttering all over the place.

The pair laughed, but their amusement was short lived.

"Good evening," a voice rang out from the staircase, interrupting their antics.

Dashiel and Sylvain stared in awe at a girl wearing a beautiful peach-colored ball gown. She glided down the stairs, and the pleats in her skirt waved gracefully behind her. Her pristine face glowed, her shoulders were uncovered, and her hair was neatly styled with ribbons.

"Well." The girl—Sofia, Dashiel realized with a start—cleared her throat. "Are you ready?"

They were both still in shock. Especially Dashiel.

"What?" Sofia asked, though she clearly knew they were shocked by her appearance. She fixed them with a withering stare.

"You . . . you look pretty," Dashiel finally stammered, choking on his words.

Sofia didn't say anything, but he could tell that she was happy. Her cheeks reddened. "Thank you," she whispered, trying not to smile.

Her father entered the common area, followed by Mrs. Elain. "Oh my. You look exactly like your mother."

"This dress belonged to her," Sofia said, smiling. "Elain did an excellent job with it." She winked at the housekeeper as she fixed one of the pleats.

"Tonight is very important, and I want you to wear this." Tomas retrieved a small, velvet box from his pocket and opened it. A beautiful gold-and-pearl necklace rested inside. "I'm hoping that it will bring you luck."

Sofia gasped. "Mother's necklace?"

"Have I ever told you the story behind this?" Tomas caressed the shiny pearls, his eyes fixed on the necklace.

Sofia's grin said he had told the story a million times before but delighted in telling it. "I don't believe you have," she said, playing along.

"She was the daughter of one of Hermesia's most powerful families. I, the son of a humble locksmith and the apprentice to a jeweler. One day, the jeweler asked me to deliver a package. I didn't know what it was or who it was for. All I knew was the address of a mansion on the outskirts of St. Victoire Dowager. When I went inside to deliver the package, I learned that the necklace was a present for your mother from her father. It was then that I saw your mother for the first time. She was so beautiful and tender-hearted. Even though she had the world at her disposal, she was humble and kind to a poor locksmith's son."

"You knew she was the one," Sofia added.

With utmost care, Tomas took the necklace out of the box. "And the rest is history." He fastened the necklace around his daughter's neck. "It was her most precious possession."

Sofia ran her fingers over the pearls. "Thank you, Father. I'll take good care of it."

Tomas allowed himself a smile, something Dashiel hadn't seen him do in months. "Please promise me you'll be safe and bring Damian back."

"I will, Father," she said softly.

"Will do, sir," Sylvain and Dashiel answered.

Tomas strode to the old grandfather clock and moved its hands to nine and three, causing the floor to rumble and the inn's staircase to shift. Hidden behind it was another set of steps.

"May Providence guide you," Tomas said.

The three descended the staircase, which led to a tunnel that brought them to the outskirts of town. A coach soaked in moonlight awaited them.

"Let's go over the plan," Sofia said as the coach moved through the city. "The Brigadiers can detect weapons, so we need to be cautious. The only thing we'll have is Ermitage's doizemant, which is undetectable because it's made of kerganium."

"Yes, ma'am." Dashiel patted his jacket pockets, where he'd hidden his doizemant in its twin-dagger form.

"One more thing," Sofia added. "We need to make sure nothing and no one gets close to this dress."

"Why is that?" Dashiel asked, puzzled.

"The explosive substances that we'll use to distract the guards are sewn in under it," she replied.

"Your dress?!" Dashiel wiggled away from Sofia. "We're supposed to rescue your brother, not kill ourselves in the process!"

"How else would we smuggle explosives into the party, idiot?" Sofia bit back. "We're an explosion away from rescuing Damian."

"Everything will be fine," Sylvain said, voice calm and reassuring. He glanced out the window; they were approaching the mansion. "Now, don't forget to put on your masks."

The silver masks, which served as invitations to the party, bore the terrifying expressions of the Ochre Brigadiers. A chill went down Dashiel's spine just from looking at them.

While the streets were gloomy and silent, the grounds of the viceroy's mansion were full of life, light, and music. Lavish carriages arrived, carrying guests decked in the finest clothing, all of whom prattled about mere frivolities. The Hermesian crème de la crème had gathered to celebrate one more year of Asedia's tyrannical reign.

After passing through the extensive gardens, the trio arrived at the top of a grand set of stairs, which led to the mansion's terrace. The trio descended the staircase as the herald announced the arrival of the Grandorn siblings, their cover identities.

The patio was adorned with hundreds of eight-armed candelabras and porcelain vases with amber flowers. Couples danced gracefully to the sounds of the orchestra.

The place was infested with pike-wielding guards and Brigadiers, although they were strategically hidden to avoid ruining the party's carnivalesque atmosphere.

Proceeding to the festivities, the three did their best to act like they belonged. Sofia moved discreetly among the guests, careful to avoid any physical contact lest her skirt explode.

Sofia, Sylvain, and Dashiel met up in the most remote spot on the terrace.

Sofia raised her gaze. "There's our objective," she said under her breath, gesturing at the enormous mansion. "We're aiming for the main room on the top floor, the viceroy's office. We'll split up, and on my signal, we'll go to the mansion. The first floor is open to guests, so we'll have no problems entering. As soon as we're inside, we'll make our way to the objective."

"What's our signal?" Sylvain asked.

Sofia looked around. "I've been so busy planning the mission that I haven't spared a thought for a signal."

Dashiel listened closely to their surroundings. Hundreds of glasses clinked together as servants distributed champagne. Made of the finest crystal, the glasses produced a harmonious ring at a mere touch, a ring capable of traveling long distances.

That sound gave Dashiel an idea. He leaned to the side, picking up a discarded glass.

"What about a whistle?" Sylvain suggested.

Dashiel turned back to the pair and held up the glass. "How about this?"

"Getting drunk won't help us at all, forest boy," Sofia mocked.

"No, this." Dashiel flicked the glass with his fingernail, creating a high-pitched noise. "The signal can be four of these sounds, identical and one after the other."

"That was . . . good thinking," Sofia said, momentarily frozen with shock. She took the glass. "Asedia and Fiddlestrum are about to make their entrance. We'll slip in during the inaugural dance."

The trio parted ways and positioned themselves.

The herald called out in a clear and strong voice, "His Excellence, Viceroy Armand Fiddlestrum!"

A man with a thick, white beard and matching hair stepped onto the terrace, and all the party's guests dutifully applauded him. Dashiel glanced at Sofia. She had bitten her lip with such force that it had started to bleed. He understood; the man she hated the most in the whole world—her own grandfather, her own blood—was but a few steps away.

"His Imperial Highness, the crown prince, Markeus of Zaphyrelia!" The ovation continued in a forced manner as a young man, accompanied by two attendants, appeared at the top of the stairs. An ochre sash stretched tightly across his chest. His hair shone with the intensity of firelight.

Dashiel looked at the young prince with great curiosity. He had heard talk of the wicked and ruthless fallen Belecrose heir, but this boy was nothing like Dashiel had imagined. The prince descended the stairs, making his way to the center of the patio. Everyone, without exception and at the same time, bowed before him. He didn't say a word and took a seat on his throne.

The viceroy faced his guests. "I bid you welcome, my dear friends. Unfortunately, His Imperial Majesty will not grace us with his presence, but in his place, we welcome His Highness. The ceremony will take place after the inaugural dance."

The viceroy took a seat next to Markeus. Everybody's gaze landed on the prince. Since his father wasn't here, it was Markeus's duty to commence the ball.

"Your Highness?"

One of the prince's attendants approached him. "Your Highness, I'm afraid that there have been some complications, and Her Royal Highness, Princess Dianalucia of Windergale, couldn't attend the ball."

"What?" Markeus reacted fiercely. "Idiot. Your incompetence seemingly has no limit."

"My sincerest apologies, Sire," the attendant said, trembling and nearly choking on the words.

"Who are the other candidates, Ettore?" the prince asked, trying to remain calm in front of all the guests and failing.

From his pocket, the attendant removed a scroll with various names written on it.

"Sire, the duchesses of Handenberie and Festwiick are at your disposal."

The prince looked at his servant with disdain. "Are you serious?"

"There's also the marchioness of Gafidiel."

"Next."

"At your disposal are the daughters of the countess of Bulbaden, Lady Helga and Lady Berta," Ettore continued.

"Also at my disposal are all the pigs and mules in this entire empire, but that doesn't mean I'll dance with them," the prince replied, his brow furrowed. "Do my title and importance not guarantee me a halfway decent dance partner?"

"How about the marchioness of Olvivaten?" Samuel Indolett, the second attendant, suggested with a smile.

The prince's expression softened. "Greta of Olvivaten. Now there's the perfect candidate," he said with pleasure.

"Your Highness, the marchioness of Olvivaten is a married woman. You've already had problems with the marquess," Ettore argued, visibly nervous. "Furthermore, she's much older than Your Highness."

"Since when does that matter to me?" Markeus sipped from a cup of champagne. "Samuel, send the marchioness a request."

"With pleasure, Sire." He sprang into action.

"Sire, please, I beg you not to do this—"

The prince silenced Ettore with a single movement of his hand. He waved his empty glass in his servant's face. "Do something useful and get me . . ."

His words trailed off as he caught sight of a woman who, unlike the others Ettore had named, walked among the guests. The prince had a good eye for beautiful women, and this one was no exception.

"Samuel, wait," Markeus ordered. Samuel returned to his side. The prince studied the woman, then turned to Ettore. "Who is that in pink, the brunette?"

His attendant studied the girl but couldn't place her. He knew the names and titles of all the members of the Zaphyrolean and Hermesian nobility by heart. It was his job as the prince's secretary. According to Ettore, this particular girl didn't have a title or status. She must have come from a family with money but no political importance.

"She's no one important, Sire," Ettore said, scanning the guest list.

"I want her to join me for the inaugural dance," the prince said, arching an eyebrow.

"Your Highness, protocol dictates that the inaugural dance take place between members of the royal family or nobility—"

"Silence!" Samuel roared, cutting short Ettore's desperate plea.

"It is as good as done, Sire," said Samuel, his voice now sweet and ingratiating. "And, if I may suggest, Your Highness should visit the innermost gardens of the mansion. I believe that is a comfortable place to . . . divert yourself with her."

As quick as a falcon, he strode straight for the prince's chosen partner.

Sofia couldn't believe her good luck. She'd found the perfect moment to slip into the mansion and the perfect place to position herself so Dashiel and Sylvain would hear her signal. She raised her glass and, with a single finger, flicked it four times.

Across the patio, her partners were each making their way to the mansion. It was time for Sofia to join them. Before she could melt into the crowd, a voice stopped her in her tracks.

"His Royal Highness has bestowed upon you the honor of performing the inaugural dance with him," said none other than General Indolett.

Sofia stood frozen in place as her moment of good fortune rotted away. Why her? She couldn't dance with the prince. If she did, she'd run the risk of a fatal explosion that would end the lives of the majority of those present. Moreover, she hated the prince with every fiber of her being. Almost as much as she hated the viceroy.

She glanced around. The guests observed her, eager to learn about the young woman whom the prince had chosen for the dance. Dashiel and Sylvain stood frozen in place, shocked at the turn of events. Clearly they didn't know what to do. Neither did she.

"My sincerest apologies to His Royal Highness," Sofia finally said, "but I'm indisposed at the moment."

Sofia began to walk away, but Indolett took her by the arm.

"I'm afraid I must insist, ma'am," he said, a menacing smile shadowing his features.

Not seeing an alternative, Sofia accepted the invitation. At least her companions were aware of the hiccup in the plan. She walked to the dance floor, her face pallid, fearful for the consequences that one wrong step could bring. The prince stepped down from his throne and walked toward Sofia. His attendant brought him a mask, and he put it on.

Within seconds, Sofia and the prince stood face-to-face. Her heart beat faster than ever, and her ankles shook, but she needed to stay focused. Sofia bowed but then looked him directly in the eye. He lowered his head as a sign of respect. Then he offered her a hand. She took it, and music filled the air.

The inaugural dance had begun.

CHAPTER 22

STUMBLING WALTZ

The prince clasped Sofia's hand, while his other hand encircled her waist, bringing her even closer to him. The music began softly, and the pair moved from side to side to its rhythm. With her free hand, Sofia grabbed the skirt of her dress and moved it as far away from Markeus as possible.

"I've never seen you at these parties before," the prince finally said in a flirtatious tone, his alcohol-soaked breath filling the little space between them. "What's your name?"

"Marianna, sir," she said in a fake timid voice. "Marianna Grandorn of Barcelle. This is my first time at a party like this. I begged my Hermesian relatives to invite me. I really wanted to come."

"Of course you did," he scoffed, rolling his eyes.

His words made her pulse race. Her urge to punch him right in the gut increased, but she maintained her meek tone. "What do you mean, sir?"

"I mean, how else would you find a suitable husband, right? A prince would be quite a catch," he joked.

Her head began to burn intensely. She'd hated him before, but now she wanted to cut him open and throw rocks inside. "I'm not interested in that kind of stuff, Your Highness. I think a life as a nun would be more appealing than a life as your wife."

The prince frowned, but he kept dancing.

"You do know those words could place you in front of a firing squad, don't you?" he asked.

She sighed. She couldn't maintain the charade any longer. "Oh please, it would be more exciting than this crock."

The prince scanned her.

"What is it?" She stared with fierce eyes. "Is His Highness accustomed to girls who are seen and not heard?"

"You are certainly unconventional. Quite refreshing." His face relaxed. "Will you do me the honor of joining me for the next piece?"

"I'd rather not, Your Highness."

His frown returned. "But you are with me. You are to dance as much as I want."

"Your Highness, with all due respect, I am not a trained monkey that caters to your every whim. I have other things I would like to do."

"Marianna, I'm the future monarch of the most powerful empire in the world. I am constantly told where to go, what to eat, and who to see. I've never been given a choice. What makes you think you have one?"

"That's the thing." She was surprised to find her expression almost tender. "We all should have a choice. We should be free to decide what is good and bad for ourselves, even if others believe otherwise."

"Say that to the emperor," Markeus said with a bitter tone, his mask and medals shining bright.

The song finally reached its conclusion, and the couple was regarded with grand applause. Sofia offered Markeus a respectful curtsy.

The herald banged his cane on the ground to get everyone's attention. "The ceremony shall begin promptly. His Imperial Highness invites his honored guests to *la rivière d'ambre quadrille*."

As soon as the herald was done, murmurs filled the crowd. They were anxious to dance. As bound by the Asedian gender protocol, women stood still as the men browsed for new dance alliances. Soon, every single guest was paired up, waiting for the music to begin.

The prince surveyed his domain. Sofia caught the flash of an arrogant smirk each time his gaze landed on a lady vying for his attention.

"No one has asked for your hand. I guess you are to dance with me again." Markeus smiled maliciously. "Looks like you have no choice after all."

Sofia's dislike for the prince was written all over her face. She pinched her lips and clenched her hands. She had no other option but to oblige, again.

"Your Highness?" A man dressed in gray and wearing a silver Brigadier mask stood behind the prince. When the prince turned to him, the man bowed.

"May I?" The mysterious man spoke clearly.

The prince raised his chin; he couldn't look down on him, for the fellow was taller than he. "A different fine lady will suffice for you, sir," Markeus answered, looking away.

The man cleared his throat. "I believe that every dance and quadrille requires a change in partner."

"What if I were to ignore you?" Markeus's voice, his whole expression, was cocky.

"Then I'm afraid His Highness would be breaking the protocol set by His Majesty," the man answered in a cold tone.

Silence stretched between the pair as they fixed each other with unreadable stares. Markeus blinked first, breaking into a small smile. Only Providence knew what sadistic and repulsive things went through his mind as he looked at this new, bold contender.

The moment was interrupted when Markeus's assistant arrived. "Sire, you must prepare for the Triumphant."

The prince took Sofia's hand and kissed it. "I hope you will grant me another dance later, Marianna."

Markeus glanced at the stranger with disgust and walked away with his companion. Soon, the prince disappeared out of sight.

The orchestra proceeded, and the couples started to dance. Sofia was certain that the man in front of her had acted deliberately in order to help her out of that situation, but she recognized neither his voice nor his eyes. His touch was gentle, and his breath was fresh, unlike the prince's. She knew he couldn't be a Cobalt Phantasm because he didn't recite their creed.

She had been forced to dance with the prince, putting a halt to her mission, and now she had to dance with yet another man, fellow or foe. Her time was running short.

"Please don't take this wrong," the man said as the dance continued, "but when I asked, 'May I?' I was addressing *you*, not His Highness."

"Why would I mind?" she answered, her attention half consumed with her dress. With all the couples around her, she had to be twice as careful with the explosives. "You were supposed to ask *him*, but you would know that. I can tell you know the protocol."

"I am indeed a studied man. I know my share about that subject," he said. "But if I may say, the strictures and guidelines in this nation are, in two words, primeval and stupid."

Sofia was caught off guard. His words were so fresh, so rarely spoken.

"They are," she said, eyes wide and sparkling. Her shoulders dropped, losing the tension she'd held all night; her heart beat to the rhythm of the music. Her fingers clawed the dress away from her dancing partner. "They truly are."

"I also know that a lady is excused from a dance commitment if she were to be indisposed. I would understand if you were to suddenly have a headache." He smiled at her. "The atmosphere at these parties can be a little overwhelming."

She instantly understood what he was saying. He was offering her the chance to leave.

"Thank you." She curtsied. "Later tonight, perhaps?"

"Whenever you feel like it," the man said. "But do know that I shall think of nothing else until it happens." He looked at her, his maple-colored eyes shining like a freshly sharpened sword.

Sofia gave him a genuine smile and left the dance floor, making her way to the mansion.

A strange feeling traveled across her body. Perhaps it was the happiness of having come across someone who hadn't conformed to the standards Asedia had set. He was the opposite of Markeus. She looked back, but he was gone. It was for the best. She had to focus. She had a mission to accomplish.

Sofia, Sylvain, and Dashiel moved quickly through the rooms on the first floor of the mansion before arriving at the entrance hall. When the music came to an end, everyone, including the guards, walked to the terrace to attend the Ochre ceremony, so it was easy to move freely throughout the mansion. The trio climbed the staircase until they reached the fourth floor, where all the thick, green, velvet curtains had been closed. Sofia moved agilely through the hallways because she'd studied the mansion's floor plans for months.

She stopped in front of a closed door. She turned the knob, but it didn't open. It was locked.

"Aurante," she said, stepping away from the door, "knock it down."

"As you wish," Sylvain said. "But it'll be loud."

"We don't have time to waste," Sofia responded. "Just do it."

Sylvain nodded and prepared to knock the door down with a single kick.

"Wait," Dashiel interrupted. "Let me try."

Sofia snorted. Sylvain stepped aside and gestured to the door. *All yours.*

Dashiel pulled two small wooden picks out of his pocket. He put them in the lock and jiggled them seemingly at random until the door clicked open.

"Where did you learn to do that?" Sofia asked, trying to hide how impressed she was.

"Arson taught me a few days ago," Dashiel said, pulling the picks out of the knob.

The squadron entered the viceroy's office. The belly of the beast. The curtains were drawn shut, leaving the room in utter darkness.

Sofia approached the window. Outside, the guests had abandoned the dance floor. The prince was giving his celebratory speech. While he was talking, the guests and guards watched with rapt attention as the victims were placed in front of their respective Ochre vessels. Sofia saw her brother among the victims, and her heart responded with a quickening beat. Her brother's plight made her ill. She remembered when her older brother, Dorien, was taken away. Tears threatened to fall, but she willed them away. She had to stay strong and proceed with the mission.

While her companions lit some of the room's candles, Sofia detached the skirt from her dress. She unfastened the crinoline and placed it carefully on the floor. From between its folds, she detached several little sacks. She distributed the sacks to Sylvain and Dashiel.

"What's in here?" Dashiel asked, squeezing the bag a little. "It can't be gunpowder. The Brigadiers would have detected it."

"The bags have hetona's venom and paper-compressed calcium powder," Sylvain said, placing two bags next to a vase. "The hetona is a distant Egadrisean viper, relative of the dragon. Its venom becomes extremely flammable when it comes in contact with its teeth. That's why they can shoot fire out of their mouths, like dragons do."

Sofia went to the viceroy's highly adorned desk and placed three sacks on it, then she proceeded to look inside its drawers and through the paperwork.

"There must be something of use here," she murmured.

In one of the drawers, she found two dueling pistols. It made sense. After all, Fiddlestrum was known for his dueling and hunting skills.

"Think fast." She threw one of the pistols at Sylvain, who caught it effortlessly.

She took as many of the documents as she could and stuffed them into her bodice.

Once the bags were scattered throughout the office, Sofia picked up another bag, which contained the tool's she'd need to complete the mission: small wooden panels, gears, cranks, and two sharpened sticks, one imbued with hetona venom and the other with calcium. She set to work assembling them.

Meanwhile, Sylvain carefully peeked between the curtains. "He's still blabbing."

"Excellent," Sofia responded as she finished building something similar to a clock, one that would spark the explosion. "Time for us to go. We don't want to be near this when it explodes."

Sofia put her dress back on and hid the other dueling pistol in her waist ribbon. The trio put out the candles and left the office. They hurried through the halls until they arrived at the stairs.

Before they could dart back to the party, a voice rang out. "Stop right there!"

Chills went down her spine at the sight of two guards approaching. Sofia hadn't planned for this.

"This area is off-limits," one of the guards said coldly.

"State your purpose," the other added.

Sylvain quickly grabbed Sofia by her arm. "My sister wasn't feeling well. We were helping her find the powder room, and we got lost."

The guards studied them for a moment.

"Very well," the first guard answered. "The ladies' powder room is on the first floor. Please proceed to the Triumphant."

The trio did as they were told. Partway down the stairs, Dashiel stopped.

"What's the matter?" Sylvain paused beside him.

"Keep moving," Sofia commanded.

"Sofia, those guards are still up there," Dashiel said, his voice rising in alarm. "We have to warn them. We can't let them die."

"He's got a point, Commander," Sylvain said.

"My last lesson to you, Ermitage." Sofia's muscles tensed. "Do whatever it takes to complete your objectives."

"That's nonsense," Dashiel replied. "We shouldn't kill innocents. If we do, we won't be any different than all those people downstairs."

Sofia pondered for a second. "They're not innocent. These people would murder you without hesitation."

"Many of the imperial guards have been forced into duty." Dashiel looked at Sylvain, silently asking for backup. "They could be the fathers of those Carbakielan children."

A great applause sounded from the terrace, reaching the three Phantasms inside. The prince's speech was over, and the ceremony would take place.

"We keep moving." Sofia turned around, tensing up even more, but her squad mates didn't follow.

Sofia's face twisted in frustration. "I am your commander, and I said that we go. Those murderers are beyond salvation. They are doomed."

Sylvain gave Dashiel a defeated look and followed his commander. Before Sofia could hurry down the stairs, Dashiel grabbed her wrist. "Wait, Sofia."

She wrenched her wrist from his grasp. "Don't touch me." She clenched her teeth. "What now?"

"You once told me that mentors could learn from their apprentices. You've done a good job, but maybe it's time you learned something from me," Dashiel said. "The master of the master who previously owned my doizemant, the greatest warrior of his generation, said on his deathbed, 'Act with kindness and responsibility to protect those around us. Give your body to those who are good-natured and your heart to those who are impossible to reach.'"

An uncomfortable silence fell over the moment.

"If you don't proceed, you'll be to blame for our failure to save the victims outside and accused of treason against the order," she replied, wearing a blank expression on her face.

Dashiel bowed his head. Sofia didn't believe for one moment he was contrite. She could tell he was burning up inside. He still wanted to disobey and save those men. When he finally conceded, his voice was clipped. "Yes, *Commander.*"

The squadron continued its descent. The next few moments would determine their success.

They would either rescue Damian or suffer a terrible death.

CHAPTER 23

SPLENDOROUS BLITZ

The squad made its way back to the first floor. They remained frozen in front of the terrace doors, watching a group of four Ochre Brigadiers carry an ornate chest as if they were pallbearers. The Brigadiers lowered the box in front of the prince. He opened the chest.

Asedia's most powerful item, the astral censer, sat inside, gleaming in the candlelight. Right below the golden censer, a small glass container held a crystal that intermittently flashed maroon. The censer would steal the astral force from the victims, while the crystal would preserve their bodies by covering them with a rare kind of frozen stone.

Alarmed, Dashiel watched as the prince took both objects with the intention of dooming his victims to a lifetime of suffering. He saw Sofia impatiently nod toward the mansion's great staircase.

"What's taking so long?" she whispered, checking the foyer's clock. "The mansion should be in flames by now."

"You think the guards found the device?" Dashiel asked, sweat beading on his forehead.

"No, they would have sounded the alarm," Sylvain said. "It's possible that the igniter needed more winding."

"I'm not taking any more chances." Sofia leaned against a wall and extracted a tiny sack from the heel of her shoe.

"More explosives?" Dashiel asked, angling for a better view.

"This one contains venom and calcium." Sofia put her shoe back on.

"Enough to spark a flame," Sylvain added.

Dashiel had promised Sylvain that he wouldn't play the hero, but his mind had latched onto a thought, and time was running out. "I'll do it!"

He snatched the sack from Sofia's hand and ran toward the staircase.

"Ermitage!" Sofia raised her voice, chasing him down. "Come back here, you fool. You'll die!"

Dashiel, already halfway up the stairs, stopped in his tracks. "Your brother needs you. You have to be there for him. Besides, I would only slow you down."

Sofia sighed with desperation. Dashiel didn't wait for a response. He turned and sprinted up the stairs.

"I'm going to kill him," her angry voice rang from below.

"Commander, trust him," Sylvain said. "He's impulsive, but he knows what he's doing."

Dashiel just barely made out her response as he reached the top of the landing. "All we can do now is wait."

Many things happened over the course of the following minute. Sixty seconds were enough for Markeus to collect both of his father's treasures and position himself in front of his first victim. Those same sixty seconds were also sufficient for Dashiel to reach the office, toss the little sack inside, and run for his life, the guards in hot pursuit. During those sixty seconds, Sofia's heart beat twice as many times as it ever had in a single minute, for Damian was second in line.

"And now, I present to you the newest battalion," the prince said happily.

The censer emitted a bright violet light, which the tony guests looked upon with both awe and amusement.

Just when Sofia thought their time was up, a blinding light and deafening sound interrupted the ceremony. A heat wave caused the prince and his guests to lose their balance. The ground trembled as the mansion combusted. Wood, marble debris, and shattered glass from exploding windows rained down like meteors upon the festivities.

The mansion's uppermost level was gone, and the others were badly damaged, quickly consumed by colorful blasts of fire.

The guests, frightened and confused, ran around the patio without direction. Guards tried to extinguish the flames. The viceroy shouted for his men to find those responsible and help the guards put out the fire. An attendant instantly escorted the prince and—even more important—the Asedian treasures away from danger. Ochre Brigadiers came out of hiding and propped up the mansion's walls and pillars, preventing them from falling.

The guests kept screaming and running, trying to escape. The mission was going according to plan; the explosion had enveloped the proceedings in a smog of chaos and panic.

Sofia and Sylvain ran, dodging the meteors that were falling to the earth. Sofia rushed to her brother and freed him from his handcuffs. She removed her mask and took her brother's face in her hands.

"I need you to run like you never have before, got it? Avoid the guards and go straight to Father."

The boy nodded his assent. Slipping through the frenetic guests, he made his escape. Sylvain and Sofia worked to free the other prisoners.

As Sofia liberated the last prisoners, she wiped the sweat off her neck.

"Oh no," she whispered, breathing turning shallow. Her hand landed on her bare neck, and her eyes widened in panic. Her mother's necklace was gone. She looked around, but the necklace was nowhere to be found.

"Have you seen Dashiel?" Sylvain asked Sofia, freeing her from the tormenting thought of having lost her father's most precious possession.

"No, I was hoping he'd be back by now," she responded, looking around.

Sylvain looked panic-stricken. "But he isn't."

Sofia rolled her eyes and let out a heavy sigh. "I'll go look for him."

"I'll go with you."

"You'll do no such thing," Sofia replied, coldness in her tone. "I should've been the one to make sure the explosion happened, not him. So I'll go find him. You'll leave the party immediately. Mission accomplished."

Maybe it was the smoke that emanated from the mansion, but her eyes watered. "If something happened to him . . ." She cleared her throat and zipped up her emotions. Her face hardened. "It's my job to find him, dead or alive."

"He's alive. I know it." Sylvain's eyes shone with a modicum of pride. "He's not only my squad mate, he's my . . . best friend. I'm sorry, Commander, but I can't follow your orders. I'm coming with you."

Sofia and Sylvain made their way back to the mansion. Deep down, Sofia admired the strong friendship between the boys. That thought made her forget, for a brief moment, that Sylvain had ignored her orders.

They needed to be careful. It would be difficult to reenter the mansion with so many guards around.

Dashiel awoke with a start. His vision was blurry, and sounds seemed distant and distorted. Disoriented and weak, he pushed away a layer of debris. He tried to stand up but failed. At first he couldn't remember where he was or how he had ended up there. His head hurt, and there was an intense heat coming from above.

He scanned his surroundings. He could see, although his vision was far from crystal clear. He had ended up in one of the mansion's bedrooms, falling through a hole. Dashiel glanced up, finding flames slithering around the opening. He checked on Athenai's egg and his doizemant. They were safe and sound.

Dashiel crawled toward the guards, whom he had saved from the explosion, relieved to find them still breathing. He moved their unconscious forms away from the flames. Once again, he tried to stand up, but his shaky legs betrayed him.

An unfamiliar female voice rang out. "Is he going to be okay?"

Dashiel rubbed his eyes, but everything remained blurry. He couldn't make out anyone in the room.

"You have to leave, ma'am," he called to the woman. "It's dangerous in here."

"Must we go?"

"It's his wish. We must press on." A new voice, this time unmistakable. It was Elias.

"Papa?" Dashiel put his hands to his head. *My mind is playing tricks on me.*

Taking a deep breath, Dashiel exited the room. The hallway was empty and dark. The explosion had snuffed out all the candelabras. His adrenaline surged; Sylvain and Sofia would need his help.

A child's voice stopped Dashiel in his tracks. "Dashiel, come back. You'll hurt yourself."

Dashiel turned around. His vision was still hazy, but he could see that there was no one else in the hall. His mind was playing tricks on him once more.

"I'm not coming back!" another child's voice rang.

There was no time to lose. He had to put aside all the voices and return to his squad mates.

The viceroy's men continued to deal with the fire. Sofia and Sylvain moved as stealthily as possible, sliding across the soot-covered terrace and evading anyone who crossed their path.

A voice sounded behind them. "Well, well, well. I've been looking for you, Marianna of Barcelle. Or should I say, Sofia Spaigne?"

Sofia and Sylvain turned around to find Samuel Indolett, flanked by guards on both sides. The fire painted his eyes a demonic red.

"How clever of you, Indolett." Sofia scoffed, crossing her arms.

She and Sylvain drew the guns they had found in the viceroy's desk and pointed them at the general.

"I wouldn't do that if I were you." Indolett snapped his fingers.

Pikes bore into Sofia's and Sylvain's backs, almost piercing their skin. They were trapped.

"Drop your weapons and surrender," Indolett demanded.

Seeing no way out, Sofia and Sylvain did as they were told. Guards cuffed them.

"How curious." Indolett approached them. "I've heard about Eloise's wretched guttersnipe. Imagine my surprise when I found that dirty rascal here, masquerading as a proper lady. The lady the prince chose for the first dance." He cackled. "Truly a masquerade."

"Well, I've been unmasked, so you should take your swine mask off as well." Sofia laughed. "Oops, my mistake. That's not a mask."

The guards murmured and even chuckled.

"Silence, you imbeciles!" Indolett's face softened, but his teeth remained clenched. "You're quite the jokester, darling. Your dear mother was, too, until they spilled her guts out."

Sofia tried to wiggle out of the guards' grip. More than anything, she wanted to gouge the general's eyes out, but she couldn't move a muscle.

"Enough," Sylvain said. "Whatever you're going to do, do it now."

"Patience, young lad." Indolett turned his back on them, but his ominous words remained clear. "Soon enough, you all will get what you deserve."

The general walked back to the terrace, the guards dragging Sofia and Sylvian behind them. They were presented before the prince and the viceroy.

Markeus was taking in the destruction. The flames licking the building were almost out, but their glow remained fierce. He pulled his gaze from the rubble and looked at Sofia and Sylvain. She could tell that he was confused by the fact that the girl who had captured his attention earlier was now his prisoner. "What's the meaning of this?"

"Sire, I've found the perpetrators who caused the explosion," Indolett said. "A Spaigne and an accomplice. I believe that she caused this commotion in order to free her brother. I haven't found any other accomplices, but my men will keep searching."

"Sire, I do apologize for all of this," Viceroy Fiddlestrum interjected, nervously wringing his hands. "I shall make sure they are punished as severely as possible."

"Spaigne?" Markeus didn't take his eyes off Sofia. "Isn't she your granddaughter, Armand?"

"Sire, they are all dead to me," the viceroy answered.

"Perhaps His Highness would like to punish them personally," Indolett said.

Markeus's face softened as he walked toward Sofia. He knelt inches away from her.

"What a waste. Such a pretty face," the prince said, taking a lock of Sofia's hair in his hand. "Don't you think, Samuel?"

"Yes indeed, Sire," Indolett replied, smiling nefariously.

Nausea overtook Sofia, along with the urge to slit their throats one by one. If only she were free.

"Behead them. Their heads are to be caged and hung at the city's entrance. Their bodies are to be devoured by vultures." The prince's smile made it clear he relished the idea. "Let this be one last warning to all of Hermesia: whoever dares to act against the crown will be punished as severely . . . and *creatively* as possible."

He returned his attention to Sofia.

"Though, I could spare your life, you know, if you were willing to pay the right price." He smirked at Sofia. "The price is something that any woman would kill to pay. What I ask is . . ." He leaned in and whispered into her ear.

Sofia recoiled. "I would rather die a thousand deaths, you swine son of a smartlapper!"

"How dare you speak to His Highness in such a manner!" Indolett screeched. "You insolent wretch!"

He readied himself to hit her, but Markeus raised his hand.

"Death it is." The prince stood and accepted a saber from Indolett.

"You will be glad to know that you will be first," he said to Sofia. "Don't worry. It'll only be a slow, excruciatingly painful death."

The prince raised his sword.

The blade descended quickly and fiercely, aimed at Sofia's neck.

"Back off." Dashiel clenched his teeth. His baton blocked the path of the prince's sword before it bit into her skin.

"How dare you meddle!" The prince's hands and face reddened as he strengthened his grip on the saber. "You must have a death wish too!"

Dashiel gathered saliva, pursed his lips, and spit into the prince's eyes, distracting him for a few moments. "Don't mind me, your royal heinie."

He pulled out a pistol and with two precise shots shattered the handcuffs binding Sofia and Sylvain. For the first time since he started training with the Phantasms, Sofia gave him a proud look.

"Took you long enough," Sofia said with a smile, working along-side Sylvain to dispatch the guards who'd restrained them.

"Sorry, Commander." Dashiel smiled back. "Too many guards, and here come more."

A small army of guards and Brigadiers had gathered around them.

"This is going to be interesting," Sylvain said, picking up one of the fallen guards' pikes. "What now, Commander?"

"We need to make our way out of here, and quick." She gestured to the guards. "These are party guards; the real problem will be the imperial soldiers. It won't be long before they're here."

The trio remained back-to-back, covering each direction as their foes closed in on them.

"I want their heads," Markeus commanded Indolett's men. The attendant who stood beside him wiped a handkerchief over his face with a shaky hand. "Now, you fools!"

With a single gesture from their general, the guards began to attack the Cobalt Phantasms.

Sofia and Sylvain moved swiftly. Using martial arts, they took down multiple guards at a time. They even managed to trick an Ochre Brigadier into knocking down a few of its fellows. Sofia and Sylvain seemed unstoppable together.

For his part, Dashiel managed to fend off three guards at a time. They tried to hit him, but he disarmed them with a single flick of Orphée. As punishment for their incompetence, with three flicks of his sword, Markeus stabbed each of his men to death.

A wave of sadness washed over Dashiel when he saw the bodies on the ground, pools of blood forming around them. They'd been forced to serve Asedia to keep their families safe, and in the end, that was their undoing. Their own leader had killed them when they needed him the most.

"Useless." The prince kicked one of the bodies out of his way. He was vibrating with rage and impatience. "This has gone on long enough, peasant." Markeus turned his saber on Dashiel.

"Well, let's see what you can do." Dashiel struck a defensive pose. "Bet you're not as worthy an opponent as those men."

Angered, Markeus launched into an attack. The clash began with a loud clink of sword and baton.

The prince lived up to the rumors. He was a bloodthirsty warrior with deadly sword skills and a cheetah's quickness. A ferocious opponent indeed, but Dashiel had trained for months with the best of the order. In this, the most dangerous moment of his life, he could recall all of his arduous training. He would not back down. He was ready for this moment.

As Markeus and Dashiel clashed, it became clear that their strengths were similar. Any small thing could tip the scales.

When Dashiel had a moment, he twisted the baton with his hands. It molded to his touch as if it were mere clay, beginning its transformation into dagger form. Distracted, Markeus adopted a defensive posture, but it was no good. Dashiel had already begun his counterattack. A metallic ring filled the air. The daggers had cut clean through the steel saber, shattering it into three pieces.

"You care to surrender?" Dashiel asked, pointing the daggers at Markeus. He was trying not to pant from the exertion. Instead, he pasted on a confident smile.

"I don't think so." The prince dropped his saber's severed hilt and returned the smile as imperial soldiers and Brigadiers swarmed the patio. "Farewell, doizemant master."

Before Markeus could order his men to strike Dashiel down, a single firework rose into the sky and exploded into a huge light. A pall of white smoke fell over the patio. Blue shadows emerged from the smoke, disappearing and reappearing as they moved across the hazy patio.

Dashiel froze when a hand landed on his shoulder. When he looked around, he saw a stranger wearing a blue sash around his neck. He heard a hiss.

When the smoke was gone, Dashiel, Sylvain, and Sofia were too.

CHAPTER 24

ERMINE SQUADRON

A circle of blue candle flames surrounded Dashiel. As instructed by Sylvain, Dashiel stood in the center, naked from the waist up. Great anxiety bubbled in his belly as he waited for something—anything—to happen.

Roderigo stepped into the circle, wearing a bluish-silver sash that connected to a hooded tunic. In his hand he held a cup, its contents inscrutable in the darkness. Roderigo dipped his fingers into the cup.

"You have witnessed the horrors that have inspired our presence in this time and space." Roderigo drew a circle on Dashiel's chest.

"Scarred past, broken present, and stained future." Everyone spoke in unison, hidden by shadows.

The blue lights flickered.

Roderigo dipped his fingers in the cup again. Dashiel's skin absorbed the cold, heavy liquid. He would have felt ticklish if his mind weren't so anxious. His heart thundered in anticipation.

"You are merely a servant, yet you sustain everything around you," Roderigo continued.

"Vital servant, astral servant, emotional servant, and mental servant," everyone repeated.

"Francis." Roderigo raised his hands.

Out of the darkness, Professor Francis Grasshop, wearing the same bluish garment, entered the circle. He carried a second sash in his hands.

"This is your own ghost skin. Tonight, you are to be reborn, and this shall be your new skin, your new identity as a Cobalt Phantasm," the master said. "The ultimate gift and proof that you are one of us. Once it is on you, you shall profess our creed."

Roderigo carefully placed the sash around Dashiel's shoulders.

"I have witnessed the horrors that inspired my presence in this time and space. I am merely a servant, yet I sustain everything around me." The Cobalt Phantasm crest that Roderigo had drawn on Dashiel's chest began to shine. "Bloodshed and injustice justify my existence." He took a breath. "The stars have fallen, but my seed of honor and duty shall avenge them."

"So be it," everyone repeated three times in unison.

"I present you to a world that ignores your existence, Defier Cobalt Phantasm Dashiel Elliott Ermitage."

With that, Dashiel officially joined the order. His dream had come true. It was real, written on his skin.

The Triumphant's unexpected guests turned out to be squadrons from other bases in Hermesia, alerted and led by none other than Roderigo Regallette, who had returned from his earlier mission.

A Phantasm spy had found out about the viceroy tripling security in the city, sending his men to search for the perpetrators at the inn and ordering a mass shutdown. Roderigo decided to temporarily close the base in the capital city. Everyone was to leave as soon as possible.

"Dashiel sure seemed ecstatic when he received his ghost skin," Roderigo said, walking through the base's corridors, Sofia by his side.

"I just hope he won't misuse it," Sofia said. "It's a big responsibility."

"He deserves it." Roderigo inflated his cheeks. "Now he must join a squadron."

Sofia's expression flattened. "Oh yeah, I forgot."

"I've decided to assign him to the Fox Squadron."

There was a moment of silence from Sofia. "Well, I wish him the best."

"You'd be surprised how fast news travels. Many squadrons have heard about the explosion and his duel with Markeus. They've all asked me for him. Just as they once requested his father. They refer to him as Monarch Scourge. I will make the official announcement tonight." Roderigo's face filled with pride. He stopped. "By the way, congratulations on your own squadron. You deserve it more than anyone. I'm proud of you."

"Thank you. I won't let you down, Master."

"I know you won't." Roderigo resumed walking. "Especially if you give your brain a rest and allow your heart to speak when the time is right."

The day after the Triumphant, everyone gathered at the base's mess hall. They raised their cups as music filled the candlelit space. The crowd surrounded Roderigo as he raised his cup.

"I would like to propose a toast. To the Spaigne family, loyal friends who have always partaken in our ideals, and to our newest son, Dashiel Ermitage," Roderigo said with a big smile and flushed cheeks. "Havel!"

"Havel!" everyone responded with joy.

Tomas Spaigne stood next to Roderigo, with little Damian beside him.

"When they took Dorien, it broke me," Tomas said, tears welling in his eyes. "And when Damian was taken away, I was shattered beyond repair. But now my youngest son is back, and I owe it all to three brave heroes." He raised his mug of mead. "Sylvain, Dashiel, and Sofia, this one's for you. Havel!"

"Havel!" everyone said as they gave a round of applause.

"And now, please enjoy yourselves," Roderigo said. "You've earned it."

As the celebration kicked into high gear, Sofia went to her father. He embraced her and Damian at once, squeezing them tight. "My dear children have returned," he said.

"Not all of them. But we'll get Dorien back. I promise," Sofia said, brushing her little brother's hair with her fingers.

Dashiel and Sylvain approached the Spaigne family reunion. As soon as he saw them, Damian ran over and wrapped them in a big hug.

Sofia watched them, but her mind was elsewhere—on the mistake she'd made at the Triumphant. Her expression saddened. "I'm sorry about Mother's necklace, Father," she said. "It meant so much to you, and it's lost. It must have fallen off at the mansion during the fight."

Tomas looked troubled, but he gently patted her face. "It's fine. You and Damian being safe, that's all I care about."

Smiling, Dashiel extended his fist toward Sofia. He paused dramatically, then opened it. Hanging from his fingers, the necklace swung side to side, its pearls dancing in the light.

"Ta-da!" Dashiel said, a satisfied expression on his face.

"The necklace?" she asked, incredulous. "But how?"

"On my way out of the mansion, I saw it on the floor," he said. "All I did was pick it up. Consider it a goodbye present."

Sofia took the necklace and held it with both hands, for it was her greatest treasure. "Thank you," she finally managed.

She tried to return it to her father, but he shook his head. "It's yours now."

"I can't accept it. I almost lost it," she replied, mortified. "It's the only memento you have of her."

"That's not true." Her father smiled. "I see her every single day."

Sofia's forehead crinkled. She stared at her father in bewilderment.

"I need only look into Damian's eyes before he falls asleep or see your smile as you play the violin to remember her and feel her with me." Tomas wrapped Sofia's hand with his. "She would be very proud of you."

From the corner of her eye, Sofia saw Dashiel and Sylvain ease away from the group. Her attention was on the loving scene unfolding right before her, but an odd thought sparked inse her mind. *Ermitage wasn't such a bad person after all.* He had earned his place in the order fair and square.

Dashiel and Sylvain ventured into a cloud of compliments and celebratory remarks. Professor Grasshop, Titania on his shoulder, glided over and recited the poem "The Frogmouth and the Silver Beetle" in honor of Dashiel. Mrs. Marjary, the inn's cook, gave Dashiel a smothering hug and promised to cook him a special meal because he was too thin. The commanders of the Eel and Swan squadrons congratulated him and inquired about his squadron assignation.

"I see the Monarch Scourge is enjoying himself," Arson said before chugging down a mug.

"Nice going, partner!" Mina Halliwell said from beside her friend. "I knew you could do it." She turned to Arson, blowing her bangs off her face. "Wait a dingleberry moment. Didn't someone I know brag that he would be inducted before us?"

"A minor miscalculation." Arson smirked, bringing his hand to his jacket pocket. "I'll become an official Phantasm tonight. Grasshop will beg me to join when he sees this!"

Arson took out a chaplet made of silver flowers, its petals as sharp as knives. His smirk distorted with mischief. "Ooh, I see him now!" He strode into a wall of jovial dancers. Before he disappeared in the crowd, he glanced over his shoulder and yelled, "Congrats, Scourge!"

"There he goes . . ." Mina fixed her hat. "Well, I must get going. Mrs. Marjary asked me to move some supply crates."

"Now?" Dashiel's brow wrinkled. "Sylvain and I could give you a hand."

"I am now able to levitate five anvils at once. I can take care of a couple crates," she said with a wink. "See you guys later."

The party continued until Roderigo cleared his throat, getting everyone's attention. The mess hall instantly fell silent.

"I have an important announcement to make." Roderigo stood in the center of the room, all eyes on him. "As you know, Dashiel Elliott Ermitage has completed his training with flying colors."

The crowd burst into cheers and applause. At Roderigo's request, Dashiel joined him amid the other Phantasms. He felt warm inside. He had never been so proud in his life. It was really happening.

"Please, please," Roderigo said, waving for silence. "As is custom in our family, he is to be assigned to a squadron. Many squadrons have expressed interest in him, but I have chosen one that will surely help him achieve greatness."

Everyone held their breath. Dashiel's nerves returned.

"And that squadron is—"

"Wait!" Sofia's voice rang out from the other side of the room. She walked toward Dashiel and Roderigo, all eyes on her. "Roderigo, I believe you asked me to tell him?"

Roderigo wore a large smile on his face, even bigger than usual.

"Go ahead, Sofia." The master stepped aside, gesturing for her to take his place before the crowd.

Sofia stepped beside Dashiel. She gifted him with a heartfelt smile. "Ermitage . . . I mean, Dashiel, the Ermine Squadron cordially invites you to join it. I . . . would like to invite you."

The crowd applauded once more.

Sofia's words stunned Dashiel for a moment. "What? You want me to be in your new squadron?"

"It's entirely up to you. After what happened at the mansion, any squadron would be glad to have you." Sofia was doing her best to avoid his eyes. "The invitation extends to Sylvain as well," she added.

Dashiel looked at his friend, who raised his mug in response.

"I know I can be a handful at times, but we are a great team, the three of us . . . I think."

Sofia and Dashiel's eyes met. Silence filled the room, everyone waiting to hear his answer.

"I'm in," Dashiel said without thinking twice.

Everyone applauded with great enthusiasm.

"Tonight, we are to leave Hermesia and scatter," Roderigo said, silencing everyone once more. "I bid you farewell, my children. May Providence be with you until our paths cross again."

CHAPTER 25

LOVELY PAYOUT

The Ermine Squadron had been sent to the collaborator base in Requinn, a territory of the Alferai race. After leaving the beautiful city of St. Victoire Dowager, Dashiel, Sofia, and Sylvain experienced many highs and lows along their journey to the Ilver Mountains. Their trip was elongated because they couldn't follow the imperial roads. Fearing someone would recognize their faces from the wanted posters hanging all over the empire, they followed the hidden roadways.

"I think we're lost." Sofia scanned her map as their wagon reached the foothills of the mountain range. "What do you think, Sylvain?"

Sylvain, as usual, was silent, maintaining a seated pose with his eyes closed.

"You sure are boring," Sofia said, returning to her map.

"He's not boring," Dashiel said. "Although he sure is meditating more than before."

"I call that weird," Sofia scoffed. "He is too quiet, too reserved for his own good."

"You need to get used to his personality is all."

Sofia snorted. "Oh please. What would you know about the matter, Ermitage? You don't even have a personality."

"Hey!"

"Just saying . . ." Sofia whipped the map through the air. "Ugh, this is so confusing! For all we know, we could be on the wrong mountain."

"I think we're on the right mountain." Dashiel stroked his chin, looking at the path's gray rocks. "Let me see the map."

"No way," Sofia scoffed. "I am perfectly able to take us there."

"Come on, I just want to see it."

Dashiel tried to grab the map, but Sofia was quick to move it away.

"Last time I let you 'see the map,' we ended up lost in Wheelbeep Forest. For days," Sofia growled. "And you grew up in a damn forest. How is it even possible?"

"Yeah, I remember your whining too. You wouldn't shut your mouth."

"I am the commander. Therefore, the map is mine to have." Sofia gave Dashiel a cocky smile.

"Give me . . . the . . . map!" Dashiel screeched, finally grabbing the map by the edge. "I will find the place, not you!"

"NO!" Sofia clenched her teeth, struggling for the map. "You wouldn't be able to find the ocean, even if you were in the middle of it!"

"You wouldn't be able to find your ugly nose even if you had a mirror!" Dashiel kept pulling the map.

"My nose is not ugly, little twit!"

"All right, you two, quit it now!" Sylvain said, snapping out of his meditative state. "I only ask for five minutes without you two trying to kill each other. Just five minutes!"

Like two wolf cubs who had been scolded by their mother, Sofia and Dashiel abruptly quit arguing. Sylvain took the crumpled map off Sofia's hands and studied it.

"He started it . . ." Sofia mumbled.

"No, you started it!" Dashiel crossed his arms.

Sylvain sighed. "You kids need to learn to get along," he murmured, looking up. "We need to keep moving on this road for half a mile, then we'll take a left at the intersection."

The wagon arrived at the path to the Alferai base. As the trail was too steep, the horse didn't dare continue. The group left the wagon behind and pressed on by foot.

Dashiel pranced along the trail, his belongings dangling from his shoulder.

"What are you so happy about?" Sofia walked at a steady pace behind her companion.

"I can't wait to see the Alferai people," Dashiel responded jollily. "I read something about them in the book I gave Athenai."

Sofia grumbled. "There you go again with your Athenai."

They walked in silence for a while before reaching a narrow portion of the trail. Beside it were big, dark pits, most filled with water that had melted away from the snowy mountain peaks.

"Athenai this. Athenai that. I swear, you're obsessed," Sofia said, kicking a rock into one of the pits. The pebble made no sound, giving no indication of touching the bottom. "I can't imagine why any girl would want to be with you. She must be either ugly, desperate, or extremely demented."

"Never underestimate the power of love at first sight," Sylvain said.

"Your heart begins to race, you feel butterflies in your gut, and you feel like you're floating when that special someone touches you." Dashiel snickered. "I'm sure even you have felt it before."

"Don't be stupid," Sofia growled, her cheeks turning pink. "What an idiotic idea."

"Sofia, do you remember the Ochre Triumphant?" Sylvain interjected, smiling from ear to ear. "The music, the candlelight, and the moon joined together to create a magical atmosphere. You were there, literally ready to blow up the party. Destiny brought you into the arms of a certain someone."

Sofia thought of the man with the silver mask, the man who had saved her. He was bold, gentle, and understood her plight. A smile appeared on her face.

"I saw it all. He couldn't take his eyes off you," Sylvain added.

"Yeah, especially when he was about to behead you," Dashiel said. Sylvain snorted. "You and Markeus would make a cute couple!"

The masked man in Sofia's memories shattered. Now she could only envision Markeus. She recalled his arrogant words and actions. She even smelled his alcoholic breath for a brief moment.

"So Sofia, when is the wedding with Markeus?" Dashiel tossed over his shoulder. He quickened his pace until she was far enough out of his reach that she couldn't knee-kick him in the gut. Which was something Sofia did when Dashiel mocked her.

"That's it!" Sofia held tight to her belongings and chased after Dashiel and Sylvain. "You better run, forest boy! I'll throw you into one of these pits!"

The trio arrived at the end of the trail, where the entrance to a cavern awaited them. Exactly as Roderigo's instructions indicated, they found old oil lamps hung at the rocky entrance of the cave. Sylvain filled one of the lamps with oil. Its warm light would surely be helpful when facing the cavern's dark depths.

"Do you have what Roderigo gave us?" Sofia asked her companion.

"I do."

Sylvain took out a metal-framed crystal disk, which had been enchanted by Professor Grasshop himself, and placed it on a groove in the lamp. The light through the enchanted disk seemed no different than usual, but when Sylvain aimed it at the floor, something changed.

The ground bore a trail of encrusted gems that reflected the oil lamp's light, which, according to Roderigo, would lead them through the cave and directly to the Alferai stronghold.

They followed the gems deeper into the cavern. It was extensive, intricate, and as cold as ice, a dark maze that seemed to have no end. The ground and ceiling were covered with twisted stalactites and dark-dwelling creatures.

Sylvain turned down a short tunnel adjacent to the gem trail. Sofia and Dashiel followed the dim path to a large opening, a place where thousands of statues of ghastly creatures resided. Their faces and features bore terrorizing expressions. All were neatly positioned in countless rows.

Dashiel was on his toes. Sofia knew he was no lover of scary things.

She stopped in front of the statues. "I've heard the Alferai are hairy, one-eyed witches that suck human blood," she said, smirking at Dashiel. "They like to collect their victims' intestines and craft potions with their teeth."

"The Alferai queen lures men into her lair to become impregnated. When her unholy children are born, the father suffers a mysterious death. I also heard that they were cursed with immortality thousands of years back. They remove their own bones in diabolical rituals and then regrow them," Sylvain added. "The bones part is a nice touch."

Dashiel gulped as he trembled. "Yeah . . . nice . . . touch. How about we change the subject?"

"Hey." Sylvain gave a light pat on Dashiel's back. "Those are just rumors. Calm down. Anyway, we were playing, right, Sofia?"

"Argh! You're no fun." She sighed. "Yes . . . playing."

"They are like humans. Their queen or high priestess is the one with mystical abilities," Sylvain said. "I've heard, and now I'm *not* playing, that she can read your emotions and thoughts just by looking into your eyes. Whatever you do, don't let your guard down."

The squad came to a complete stop in front of two huge rock doors. Next to the doors, a group of people waited. The strangers identified themselves as members of the order by reciting their creed and showing their insignias. For a long while, the group waited. And then the heavy doors creaked open.

A girl of extraordinary beauty appeared in front of the group of Cobalt Phantasms. Her jeweled veils glistened in the light of the lanterns. Dashiel looked around. Almost everyone seemed hypnotized by this girl. There was something weird about her, but he couldn't pinpoint exactly what it was.

"Her Ladyship welcomes you to the Alferai palacette," she recited. "Follow me."

Everyone followed after her in a tight group. Eventually, they found themselves in the atrium of a round, white edifice built into the crust of the Ilvers. The place was huge, full of flower-covered balconies and an immense glass dome that flooded the space with celestial light. Torches bearing violet flames decorated the beautifully carved pillars. Everything was dazzling, except for the beastly gargoyles that adorned the palacette.

Alferai girls slipped out of hiding, their faces gifted with angelic beauty.

The sheer veils and flowers that wrapped their bodies fluttered as they pranced from balcony to balcony. They seemed as light as feathers, melodiously giggling and stretching their necks so they could have a better view of the foreigners. They were curious creatures but blissfully uninterested in engaging with the visitors. They seemingly could not maintain interest in any one thing for longer than a few moments.

"I am Her Ladyship's key keeper." The girl's strong voice caught Dashiel off guard. "Before you proceed, it is imperative that I mention our rules. Listen well, humans. My sisters are off-limits. You are not to approach them without their consent, unless having a broken neck is what you are looking for during your stay here. Our protectors do not take kindly to strangers who break that rule."

As the key keeper spoke, Dashiel took in his surroundings. From afar, he saw a familiar face walking among the prancing Alferai. His pulse raced, and his hands began to sweat.

When the timing was right, Dashiel slithered away from the group without anyone noticing. He chased after the group of Alferai as they moved through the corridors of the palacette. Seeing his opportunity, he reached for the familiar girl and grabbed her hand.

The girl turned around, confirming Dashiel's suspicions. It was the girl from the train who'd held his attention in her tender grasp.

It was the girl who took his breath away with every letter she sent. It was Athenai.

"Hello, Dashiel," a familiar melodious voice sounded. "I told you that we would see each other again."

Dashiel's heart pounded with joy.

"Hi there," he said with a smile that traveled from ear to ear.

Out of the blue, the floor evaporated beneath Dashiel. Something grabbed him by the leg and pulled with force. In a matter of seconds, he was floating upside down. He slowly turned until he saw a horrible gray face with bright violet eyes, giant fangs, and a grotesque snout. It was one of the gargoyles of the palacette, the caretakers of the Alferai. The guardian roared, ejecting shards of stone into his face.

Dashiel screamed. "Please, put me down!"

"Mika, stop this very instant!" Athenai commanded.

At the sound of her voice, the gargoyle ceased roaring and rattling Dashiel like a rag doll. Sylvain and Sofia came running as fast as they could.

"What the hell? What did you do now, Dashiel?" Sofia drew her pistol.

The gargoyle roared at the newcomers.

"I didn't do anything!" Dashiel protested, blood rushing to his head.

"What is going on here?" asked the Alferai who had welcomed them earlier. She drew close enough to identify Dashiel, even red-faced and wrong side up. She frowned, clenching her fists. "Good heavens! You again?"

It did not take Dashiel long to recognize the owner of that frown. He now understood why he had gotten that strange feeling earlier. This was Junei, Athenai's sister and chaperone, looking different from that uptight woman on the train.

"Mika, put him down." Athenai raised her tone. "Now!"

The gargoyle let go of Dashiel, and he came crashing down to the ground.

"Are you all right?" Junei rushed to Athenai. "Did that rascal do anything to you?"

"I'm fine," Athenai said. "Dashiel, on the other hand . . ."

Sylvain helped Dashiel up. "You all right there?"

Dashiel nodded, his eyes rolling around like marbles in a ceramic bowl. His gaze finally settled on his arm. The gargoyle had mangled it. Fortunately, the dermangolin pills had worked as planned, preventing any bleeding that would've exposed him as a hemocarcomist.

"I'm so sorry about this," Athenai said, walking toward Dashiel. The gargoyle emitted steam from its nose. "It's all right," she said to the guardian in a tender voice, petting its enormous paw. "I believe Caprisei and Ralei were looking for you. Go find them."

The gargoyle left the corridor, growling and dragging its heavy stone paws.

Sylvain and Sofia helped Dashiel to the wall.

"Dashiel!" Athenai knelt next to him. "Junei, please go get some water with a few drops of amengebeaux juice."

"Me? I'll do no such thing." Junei crossed her arms. "Let him die. He's a human. There are millions like him."

Athenai gave her a serious look.

"All right, all right. I'll go," Junei grumbled, stomping her feet and mumbling as she followed her sister's orders.

Athenai turned to Dashiel. "You'll be all right. I'll make sure of it."

"I'm fine, really," Dashiel said softly. "Are you . . . you . . . ?"

"Shush." She put a finger to his mouth. "Don't waste your energy."

Dashiel closed his eyes.

"Don't worry. He's going to be fine," Sofia kicked his leg. "He has a stone-hard head. He's taken worse. He'll survive."

"Oh my!" Athenai said, finally noticing Dashiel's companions. "And you are?"

"The name's Sofia Spaigne," she said, leaning against the wall. She waited for Sylvain to say something, but he remained silent. "And he's Sylvain Aurante. We're his squad mates."

"It's lovely to make your acquaintances." Athenai offered a sweet grin to Sylvain. "I recognize you from the train."

Sylvain nodded, seemingly uninterested.

"My name's Athenai."

"Athenai?" Sofia gasped. "You're not . . . ugly," she mumbled.

"Pardon me?" Athenai said sweetly.

"Nothing!" Sofia said. "Nice to meet you."

Dashiel opened his eyes. "I can't believe this. What are you doing here?"

"Well . . ." She gave him a timid look. "I kind of live here."

"Wait a moment." Dashiel sat up straight with much difficulty. "Does that mean you're an . . .?"

"An Alferai?" She nodded. "Yes, the high priestess of the Alferai race, in fact."

"The priestess . . ." He trembled.

"Please forgive me." Athenai shook her head. "I wanted to tell you, but it was dangerous to reveal my identity in a letter. The Alferai community have to appear neutral, otherwise Asedia would have a reason to attack us. I hope you're not mad at me," she finished, eyes downcast.

"I guess we should start all over, correctly," Dashiel answered. "Hello! My name is Dashiel Ermitage from Azahar Forest." He offered Athenai a formal handshake.

Athenai found the notion funny. "Athenai, of the Alferai race."

And this time as they got to know each other's true selves, they did so hand in hand.

Sylvain and Sofia left Dashiel and Athenai to their reunion.

"Look at them. So . . . clingy." Sofia shuddered.

"What letters is she talking about?" Sylvain grumbled at Sofia, concern arching his eyebrows.

"The letters that Athenai and Dashiel exchanged during your stay in Hermesia," she replied. "With the messenger droplets."

"They did what?!"

"You didn't know?" She looked away, laughing to herself.

"No," he answered, gazing at his friend. "Sending messenger droplet letters to non-Phantasms is strictly forbidden. And you didn't say anything?"

"I intercepted and read a couple of them. They were good for a laugh, all those corny phrases and cloying shit." Sofia chuckled at the memory. "They were harmless."

"This is not . . ." Sylvain stared at Athenai with great suspicion. "It's not how it's meant to be."

Junei returned with a crystal goblet filled with pink water. Athenai took the goblet and helped Dashiel drink from it. The amengebeaux drops instantly reinvigorated Dashiel. He was able to stand without a hitch.

"As much fun as it is spending time with these mortals, you have to tend to your obligations," Junei said reproachfully to her sister, avoiding eye contact with the humans she disliked so much. "Those documents won't write and sign themselves."

"They might have to do it on this occasion. Let our glove spell do the job. Would you please guide them, Junei?" Athenai smiled at Dashiel. "I would like to show Dashiel and his friends around." She stood up. "Then we shall host a feast tonight."

CHAPTER 26

THE BIRTH OF AMORE

The palacette concealed many more secrets than sentient limestone creatures and a battalion of immortal maidens skilled in all the arts and sciences known to man. The biggest secret was the oath fire, a rare light that gleamed insistently. Hidden in the palacette, it connected to the priestess and provided for the Alferai. Athenai's oath fire was something beyond the reach of the palacette's inhabitants but, at the same time, right in front of their noses. It was contained within each of the bricks, crystals, and metals that surrounded them.

One night, Sylvain awoke to the sound of rattling. Dashiel's nightstand was shaking.

Dashiel might've been able to sleep through the tremors, but Sylvain was easily roused, always ready for any circumstance. He stretched his hand toward a crystal lamp that was embedded in the wall. At his touch, a purple light spread throughout the room, building into a warm yellow glow.

Sylvain looked at his companion's nightstand, investigating the origin of the sound that had awoken him. Listening carefully, he pinpointed Dashiel's jewel box as the source of the noise. It shook and rattled across the nightstand.

Sylvain didn't know what to do. The egg had never acted like that before.

"Dashiel, your egg is doing weird things," Sylvain said from his bed, covering his head with his pillow, but Dashiel didn't wake up.

"Dashiel, the egg," Sylvain said more firmly. Nothing. The rattling and shaking continued, getting stronger and stronger. Sylvain left his bed and walked over to Dashiel's.

He shook his friend. "Dashiel, wake up!"

Dashiel finally complied. "What is it?" he said, barely able to open an eye.

"Something's happening to your egg."

Dashiel looked at his jewel box. At this point, it was quivering around the nightstand, moving like crazy.

"Did you touch it? Did you do something to it?" He quickly grabbed the egg, wrapping it in his hands.

"No. It woke me up." Sylvain yawned.

Dashiel tried to open it, but it wouldn't budge. It vibrated with greater force. "This isn't normal," he said, walking toward the door.

"Where are you going?" Sylvain asked.

"To the person who knows how this thing works."

Dashiel left the room and ran as fast as he could through the empty palacette. In contrast to the rooms, which the oath fire kept at an agreeable temperature, the rest of the palacette was freezing. He shivered against the chill until exertion warmed him.

Daylight was hours away, but lamps and moonlight provided some respite from the darkness of the night. As he ran past a seemingly interminable line of doors and rooms, Dashiel could see his breath, frosty in the morning air.

Finally, he arrived at Athenai's chambers. He asked the gargoyles guarding the doors for permission to enter, but they were still asleep, curled up comfortably with their giant clubs. Dashiel asked for permission again, but the gargoyles didn't stir. Amid snores, one of the gargoyles opened a single violet eye and—without paying attention to Dashiel—quickly shut it once more. The egg hadn't stopped trembling in Dashiel's hands. He didn't see any other option. He needed to speak with Athenai.

Quietly, Dashiel opened the doors and tiptoed into her office.

The room was two floors of baroque architecture adorned with various pieces of art. The roof had been painted to represent the night sky, and the painted stars descended from the fresco and fluttered throughout the entire space. One of the walls contained a giant book-case filled with books, most of them held together by mint-colored spines—the books given to all Phantasm collaborators. The tall windows were shut tight, and a majestic balcony provided a perfect view of the entire palacette.

"Athenai! Something is happening to the egg!" Dashiel called, but there was no response. The cavernous room echoed his words back to him. "Athenai?"

Maybe it was too early for her to begin her high-priestess duties. Dashiel set the egg down on her desk.

"Don't worry. I'll get you out of there soon," he whispered to what-ever grew within the egg.

A chill ran down Dashiel's spine. The office was as cold as the hall-ways. Dashiel touched the jewel box. It was freezing against his skin. He brought the egg to his chest and hugged it tightly. "I promise," he whispered, trembling along with it.

The cold began to soothe Dashiel, and within minutes, he was asleep at the foot of the desk.

When he woke, the egg was no longer shaking or rattling. Dawn illuminated the entire office. Dashiel didn't know whether to be relieved or worried that he'd slept for so long. He didn't give it much thought; his attention was drawn to the small box in his hands.

The egg suddenly hatched with the speed of a heartbeat. Inside, the bud opened, giving way to a beautiful flower. Each red-tipped petal blended into a vivid blue at the base. It was similar to a rose in appearance but smaller in size and more beautiful than any flower Dashiel had ever seen in his life. *A flower worthy of Athenai*, he thought. He would give it to her as soon as she arrived. Surely this would make her extremely happy.

Everything seemed normal until the flower began to move. Its stem stretched until it touched Dashiel's skin. It wrapped itself around his fingers and then his hands. Dashiel tried to shake it off, but it was useless. The stem held on tightly, growing and wrapping around his arm. He clawed at it, but the stem grew thorns to defend itself. When the flower arrived at his elbow, it stopped moving. Dashiel remained motionless, not knowing what to do.

What the hell did you give me, Athenai? Dashiel wondered.

Two of the flower's petals lowered to the height of its sepal, allowing Dashiel to see two brilliant blue points: its eyes. The flower emitted a sigh.

Fear zipped down Dashiel's spine. He hurled the jewel box to the other side of the office. The stems let go of him as the egg flew through the air. It landed on the cold, hard ground.

Finally freed, Dashiel took a few steps back, ultimately tripping over his feet and landing on his backside.

At that precise moment, the doors of the office creaked open. Athenai appeared behind them.

"What are you doing here?" she asked, worried by the sight of Dashiel on the floor.

"The egg started to do weird things, and I came here—"

"Your skin is totally white!" Athenai touched his face. "You're frozen!" She went to a coat hanger and grabbed a fur cape.

"I thought something had happened to the bud." He looked at the jewel box on the floor. It had slammed shut. "But it frightened me."

Athenai didn't seem to hear him. "Why did you run through the palacette dressed like this?" She motioned to his pajamas.

He looked at himself. His mother had sewn these pajamas for him. He was still barefoot. No wonder he couldn't bear the cold. Athenai laid the cape around his shoulders. She walked over to a glass cabinet and took out a bronze sun sculpture. She petted it, and sunlight streamed out of it, positioning itself in the center of the room and emitting warmth throughout. She tapped her foot against the ground, and a warm, lit hearth emerged from it. Athenai took Dashiel by the hand and led him to the fireplace.

"What happened with the bud? Where's the egg?" The two took a seat in front of the hearth. Dashiel's cheeks began to recover their color.

"The bud opened, and it attacked me!"

Athenai looked at him with a wrinkle between her brows. "What?"

"It did this to my arm." Dashiel rolled up his sleeve, baring the little marks left by the flower's thorns.

Athenai tried—unsuccessfully—to cover up a snicker.

"It's not funny," Dashiel said seriously. "What type of plant attacks you while looking at you with its creepy eyes?"

"Dashiel, it was just showing you its affection."

He didn't know how to respond. "Affection? I don't understand."

"Well, the seed in the jewel box belongs to an extremely rare species of flower called scarlet vanity," she replied, standing up. "Along with their mothers, they grow together in a group called a bouquet. The mother communicates to them how beautiful and strong they are, and they feed off that positive energy."

She searched throughout the room until she found the jewel box on the floor.

"Months ago, during one of my trips to Windergale, I visited the ruins of Gormuall. While I was there, I witnessed something truly horrific. Zaphyrolean soldiers vandalized the ruins, dropping a huge rock onto a bouquet of scarlet vanities that grew there. All the flowers were crushed, except for a single seed."

She picked up the box from the floor.

"Without the mother, it's almost impossible for a seed to germinate through other means. I tried for months, with no apparent success. As soon as I met you, I thought that you could make this seed grow."

Jewel box in hand, Athenai sat down once more in front of the hearth.

Dashiel tried to smile. "Well, looks like it worked out." He put his hand on the egg and looked at Athenai. "Well, here, it's yours."

"There's no way I could accept this," she said.

"Why not?" He'd been so sure she would appreciate what he had grown for her that her response left him flustered. "Don't you like it?"

"I-I do. It's not that." Athenai petted the jewel box. "For months, it's been fed by your positive energy, your emotions, your dreams, your thoughts. It's practically a part of you. You deserve each other."

Dashiel furrowed his brow. "I don't think I'd know how to take care of something like this."

"Give it a chance." Athenai's violet eyes shone with the dawn light. "It's alone in the world."

Dashiel couldn't possibly say no to that face.

"Also, scarlet vanities are adorable!"

Dashiel rubbed his chin. "Fine," he responded, not seeing an alternative. "I'll take care of it."

"Splendid!" Athenai said. "Come out, little seed. Don't be afraid," she whispered to the egg in a sweet voice.

The upper part of the egg began to open, and from its edge, two little leaves peeked out.

"I'm not sure if I'll be a good owner." The flower looked at Dashiel timidly. "But I'll try, so please bear with me."

At his words, the flower flew out of the egg like a slingshot and clung to him with its little stem once more, apparently demonstrating its love by rubbing against Dashiel's face. It was so happy that a few thorns ejected off its stem, causing Dashiel to flinch.

Athenai placed the jewel box on the floor. "Now, aren't you going to give it a name?"

The flower unwound itself from Dashiel and returned to the egg. It seemed anxious, switching its gaze from Athenai to Dashiel.

"Yeah, you're right." Dashiel thought for a moment. "How about Bruno? Like the monarch from my book. My favorite character."

Athenai laughed. "That would work, if it weren't a female."

"How do you know for sure? It looks like a Bruno to me."

"If she were male, her stem would be opaque, the pattern of her petals would be reversed, and her eyes would be green."

"That's a little tougher." Dashiel thought for another moment. "I don't really know what name would fit her."

"Let's think," she said. "What about Amálaba?"

Dashiel shook his head, feeling a great dislike for that name.

"Sine?"

Nope.

"Lena?"

"None of these names really fit her, do they?" He looked at his flower, her petals shining in the firelight. She stared at him with admiration. "How about Amore?"

Athenai considered the name. "It will do perfectly."

"What do you think, Amore?" he asked the scarlet vanity.

The flower shook her little leaves while bouncing from side to side. She obviously loved her new name.

"It's decided. Amore it is!"

Amore left the jewel box and attached herself to Dashiel once more.

"In time, you'll see that the scarlet vanity can be very useful once it matures," Athenai said. "You'll have to teach her some tricks."

Dashiel smiled nervously. "We'll start with controlling her thorns."

A comfortable silence descended on the bedchambers, but Dashiel's wandering mind didn't take long to unsettle him.

"Athenai?" he asked apprehensively. "Have you ever read my mind?"

Surprised, Athenai sat up straight.

He hurried to clarify. He didn't want to offend her, but he had to ask. "I was told that you were capable of reading a person's thoughts and emotions by looking into their eyes."

She remained silent for a moment. "I do have an ability similar to what you're describing. As the leader of my people, I have to make sure no one will hurt them. But no, I've never read yours."

His moment of relief was quickly outshone by doubt. "Why didn't you? How did you know I was the one to help Amore grow?"

"I don't know for sure. I guess I was impressed by the way you saved that child in the train station. The way you behaved and spoke was not ordinary. With every action, you shared kindness; with every word, you overflowed with an enthusiasm for life. Your thoughts and emotions were so strong and full of conviction, so palpable, that I took the chance."

"Athenai, I would give you my entire mind if you were to ask for it." He touched her cheek. "But can it be that? Mine? Can you promise that we are going to discover each other day by day? I want to earn your trust the right way."

"I believe we are far beyond trust."

"I know, but . . ." He choked on his words.

"It's still important to you," she said, finishing his sentence. She turned to him and grabbed his hands. "By all that I hold dear, I promise."

Their morning passed together in front of the hearth, all thanks to that special flower. Their lives did not allow them much time together, but they had finally found a moment to themselves. What more could Dashiel ask for? Athenai by his side and Amore in his pocket.

Everything was bliss.

CHAPTER 27

CHANGE OF HEART

On the cold morning of the nineteenth day of December, Dashiel bundled up in his warmest clothing and went for a walk by himself. Sylvain, in customary fashion, had already slipped out of the room. He had been acting rather strange lately.

The Alferai were hard at work decorating the palacette with glistening Christmas ornaments, which they had crafted, and singing carols in their angelic voices. The gargoyles, adorned with ribbons and festive spheres, harmonized with their own rough and out-of-tune voices. Meanwhile, the visitors admired the fruits of their hosts' labors. Christmas was mere days away, and the preparations made Dashiel feel warm inside.

Walking through the halls, he realized that the number of guests at the palacette had grown significantly. It was not hard to identify who they were, as they all wore blue Phantasm sashes.

In the center of the palacette's courtyard stood an immense pine tree covered in ornaments and decorations. Hundreds of copper suns floated around its highest point. Junei directed an army of Alferai, giving orders left and right. Dashiel looked throughout the courtyard, but neither Athenai nor his friends were present.

The doors of the palacette opened, and from the caverns a cloaked figure emerged. Junei received the visitor personally, inviting him further into the palacette. The young man removed his cloak, revealing brown curly hair and dark eyes. His manners were elegant and his speech eloquent. In his hands he held a book bound together with a mint-colored paste. The same kind of book the Cobalt Phantasms gave to their collaborators.

"They await your presence in the Autumn Room," Junei said with her customary bitter tone. "Follow me."

The pair wandered out of sight, and Dashiel fixed his gaze back on the beautiful crystal decorations adorning the Christmas tree.

Amore, who had been hiding in the warmth of his vest pocket, climbed up his arm and rubbed her petals on his face. In the weeks since her bloom, she wouldn't leave him for even an instant.

"Want to know a secret?" he asked, glancing at his flower.

Amore indicated her interest by giving a chirping sound.

"Today's my birthday," he spoke softly. "No one knows, so please keep my secret."

The flower chirped and wrapped itself around a hole in his jacket's collar.

Dashiel had never liked his birthday. He tried to blame it on his solitary years as a child, but he'd never been able to place his resentment for this particular day. He shoved those thoughts into the back of his mind and hoped that his secret would last until the end of the day.

Dashiel didn't know how to feel about the enormous tree in front of him. As an Azahar, he could easily tell that the tree was dead and withering away with every passing second. The thought pinched his chest, and yet he liked all the shiny and colorful decorations on and around the tree. He stared in awe as the Alferai levitated the warming copper suns to the ceiling, where they kept the atrium warm and melted the snow that collected on the outside of the glass dome. The carols of Alferai girls and gargoyles made the courtyard festive and cozy.

"That tree!" Sofia's voice sounded next to him. "Every December, my parents, my brothers, and I used to get a Christmas tree for the inn." Her eyes glowed at the recollection. "I would be in charge of the ornaments. There wasn't a single inch of the inn left undecorated."

"My Christmases weren't as special, I guess." Dashiel chuckled, keeping his eyes on the tree. "Pine trees were limited in Azahar, so cutting one down was out of the question, but my mother would read stories, and we would eat berry honey cake surrounded by old candles. The barrier blocked most of the snow from the outside, so I've never seen anything like this."

There was a brief moment of silence.

"So . . . what do you need, Sofia?" Dashiel turned to his commander.

"Me?" she scoffed. "I don't need anything."

"Well, you usually aren't this open with me unless you want something."

Sofia's teeth grated. "Maybe a quick favor."

"I knew it."

"Do you still know how to, you know . . .?" She fidgeted her hands, aping the lock picking he'd done at the viceroy's mansion.

"Pick a lock? Yes. You know I can. Why?"

"Did you see all those Phantasms who just arrived?"

"Yes."

"Well, they're here for a gathering of the Founding Chapter. Apparently they are gathering to discuss a matter of great importance. I definitely want to know what's going on. There's a locked balcony in the room where they'll meet. We can listen from there."

"Sorry, I can't." His eyes returned to the tree.

"Why not?" Sofia growled, placing herself between Dashiel and his festive view.

"Because I promised Sylvain I wouldn't do it again. He called it a vicious skill."

"Well, you can call it a virtuous skill when it helps me."

"I don't know, Sofia. I did promise Sylvain that I wouldn't. Besides, he took away my tools."

"Please, Dashiel." Sofia leaned forward, her lower lip protruding in a supplicating pout and her honey-colored eyes glowing like a pile of leaves on an autumnal afternoon. "When have I ever let you down?"

"Well, the time I fell down that well, the time those rabid dogs chased me, the time when—"

"Fine, fine! I get it." Sofia swatted at the air. "But please, I need to know what's going on in there. Aren't you even a little curious?"

Dashiel gave it a thought. Being discovered would bring great consequences, but the meeting was something of great interest. He tried to think of picking the lock and eavesdropping on his superiors as following the order of his squad commander. Besides, it would take his thoughts away from his birthday.

"OK. Fine. I'll do it," Dashiel answered.

"Great!" Sofia squealed, her hands clasped together.

"I believe I have a pin we could use," he said, patting one of his utility belt's bags. "Now, I need anything that will create enough tension."

From her pocket, Sofia took out a flatheaded screwdriver. "Will this do?"

"Perfect!" Dashiel took the tool, a question brewing in his mind. "Why were you carrying a screwdriver with you?"

"Oh, for nothing." Sofia giggled, looking up at the glass ceiling. "Tried to unhinge the door. Didn't work."

A soft sigh rose from Dashiel's collar. He glanced down to find Amore waking from a brief slumber. She wriggled in the jacket's hole, startling Sofia.

"That's amazing!" She peered closer, marveling at the sleep-groggy flower. "What is it?" She stretched out her hand, ready to pet the petals.

"Sofia, I would advise you not to do that," Dashiel said in a rush. "She doesn't take too kindly when girls get too—"

Amore swiftly spawned a thorn, sharp enough to prick Sofia's hand. Though high pitched, the sound that followed was definitely a growl.

"—close to me," Dashiel finished belatedly.

"Ouch!" Sofia rubbed her hand. "You little . . . Ouch!"

Amore chirped, seemingly laughing at Sofia's distress.

"We better go," Dashiel said, trying to defuse the situation.

"Let's go." With a sideways look at the flower, she grumbled, "If you're not careful, I might remove all your pretty petals, you tiny piece of . . . Argh!"

Dashiel and Sofia traversed the festive corridors of the fifth floor until they arrived in front of a tapestry. She swept the hanging aside, unveiling a small, wooden door.

"This is it," Sofia said. "Work your magic."

Dashiel took his makeshift lockpicking tools from his utility belt and played with them until the creaky door opened.

It led to a balcony powdered in dust and dirt, unlike everything else in the palacette. Silently, Sofia and Dashiel crawled to the edge of the balcony and took a peek at the room. The chamber was made entirely of wood, its walls partially covered by long tapestries with varied images. Except for chairs set in a semicircle and a podium, the room was unfurnished. Low voices rose from below.

"I can't believe it," Sofia whispered. "They're all here."

"Who are they supposed to be?" Dashiel squinted, trying to get a better view of the group.

"Didn't you learn anything from Professor Grasshop? The Founding Chapter of the Cobalt Phantasms, the council of the order, the real brains and brawn."

Sofia pointed at one of the members, a kind-looking lady accompanied by her dog. "There's Dr. Normandine, the most renowned Egadrisean inventor and engineer. She designs the weapons and tools we use."

Sofia moved her finger to another person. He was a young man with rich, tanned skin and reddish-brown eyes.

"That's Oleiro. The youngest member to command a squadron and become a council member. He is the strongest Defier there is. He's taken down fifty Ochre Brigadiers by himself."

She pointed at a broad-shouldered man who glowered at the inventor's dog, which had started to drool on his shoes. He wore fine clothing and had a meticulously shaven face.

"And that's Colonel Harry Garrafal, the most talented strategist on the continent. He's the one who approves or rejects every mission pitched by the squadrons."

Dashiel looked at his friend, realizing that she was mesmerized. He'd never seen her like this. It was as if she were fulfilling a long-held dream.

The doors opened, revealing Roderigo and the man Dashiel had seen in the courtyard.

Roderigo stopped in front of everyone.

"Bloodshed and injustice justify our existence," Roderigo said, loud and clear. The echo repeated his words in an almost ominous way.

Everyone stood up.

"The stars have fallen, but our seeds of honor and duty shall avenge them," they answered.

"Welcome to our collaborator base." Roderigo remained standing. "Before we start, let me introduce you to Sebastian Calabel, son of the Libercian president and future head ambassador of his country, collaborator and interpreter, and honorary Cobalt Phantasm."

Roderigo took the podium. "Let's begin with some unsettling news. The Lizard Squadron is nowhere to be found. They went on a data retrieval mission in northern Zaphyrelia. We lost contact with them a few days ago. I've sent the Goat and Bull squadrons to find them.

"Asedia has ordered the construction of some weird mechanism outside Base 1296. The Bear Squadron has moved into the base and will keep us posted."

As Roderigo continued down the list of topics to discuss, the man who accompanied him looked up. His gaze went directly to the balcony.

Dashiel's heart pounded. Strangely enough, the man gave them a quick smirk and returned his attention to the meeting.

"We shall continue with news about the Urovenian war front." Roderigo took a seat and signaled to his companion. "Sebastian?"

The man stood before the chapter, looking distinguished. "I've spoken to King Dimetrius's ministers. His generals have noticed that, over the course of the past few months, the number of Ochre Brigadiers has increased alarmingly." As the man spoke, he was clever with the placement of each word. "They fear that if things continue like this, Asedia will conquer the southern Urovenian territories."

"That's why that son of a bitch raised the number of Ochre Triumphant tributes," Garrafal interjected.

Normandine petted her beloved dog. "No one is safe these days. Hundreds have been charged unjustly in order to turn them. Some of them were my colleagues . . ."

"And there's more." Roderigo took out a wrinkled document and passed it around. "During mission number 6,791, a squadron was able to retrieve some documents from the possession of Armand Fiddlestrum."

Colonel Garrafal scoffed. "Oh, you mean the mission that risked many lives for one little brat? The mission I don't recall approving?"

"In these letters," Roderigo continued, disregarding the comment, "Asedia tells the viceroy to supervise the transportation of two hundred units of Ochre Brigadiers from the Carmine Kingdom through Hermesian lands, with Balkian soldiers escorting them."

The rest of the members began to murmur.

"How is this relevant?" another member asked. "This might as well be another of the many Brigadier relocations."

"Why did you gather us here today, Roderigo?" Garrafal asked, crossing his legs. "We have plenty of work to tend to at our bases. Asedia and his allies have become a larger pain in the ass."

"That is why you should listen to my words." Roderigo wiped sweat from his brow. "This relocation in particular could give us an advantage. I have formulated a plan to help us deal with the Brigadiers. If we succeed, we won't have to worry about them, at least not as we currently are."

"Another sweet plan of yours?" Garrafal scoffed.

"We're listening," Normandine said. "Please, proceed."

"We must aid and abet the overthrow of Beckel Swannagger, ally of Asedia and pyrone of the Carmines, producers of the Ochre carcasses."

The council went wild with murmurs and groans.

"Has old age dulled your mind?" Garrafal demanded.

"Calm down and listen!" Roderigo stood up and stomped. "With this relocation, the Carmine Kingdom is left with almost no Brigadier forces. Five of the seven Carmine lords are readying to strike Swannagger down. Their people are willing to fight. It's a matter of sparking the fuse. If we help them, we'll stop the largest producer of Brigadiers on the continent. Please, think about that."

"It would certainly help both countries," Normandine added.

"Our spies have also confirmed that the Carmine pyrone possesses a spherite, a treasure given to the pyrone's firstborn."

The room filled with murmurs once again.

"If Beckel Swannagger is taken care of and we can befriend the new pyrone and acquire the spherite, our work here will be much easier," Roderigo said.

"Yes, yes, that sounds delightful." Garrafal clapped. "Must I remind you of what happened last time a monarch was dethroned without an indisputable ruler?" Garrafal pointed at Sebastian. "You should know very well, as it's part of your country's history. The Libercian Revolution, the horrors of which are comparable to those of the Reign of Terror. The Carmines are giant brutes. They will destroy one another over the power, and destruction and chaos will take over."

In response, Roderigo dusted the top rail of his chair. "There's an heir."

The murmuring ceased. The members leaned forward, consumed by curiosity.

"Who might that be?" someone asked. "Some impostor picked up from the streets? I've seen those before."

Sebastian took a step forward. "We have located Prince Audric, the pyrone's younger brother."

"That's impossible," a feminine voice said.

"He died years ago," agreed another member. "Beckel killed him in a duel."

"He did not!" Roderigo pounded the chair. "He did fight with Beckel, and he did lose, but he was *not* killed. Defeated and blinded, he was sent to Tortoise Husk Prison, but a great fire ravaged the prison, and he managed to escape, adopting the identity of a hermit."

"How do you know it's really him and not some impostor? Allow me to remind you of the man who claimed to be Emperor Rafael Belecrose's brother."

"He's not an impostor," Roderigo said. "Among the spells the Belecrose gave us, we found one, though incomplete and ineffective, that could determine the lineage of a person. Our Delvers found some clues in America and Asia, worked day and night, and successfully completed the spell."

"The man we have is none other than Audric Swannagger, second prince of the Carmines," Sebastian added.

Garrafal uncrossed his arms. "Then by all means, bring him here!"

"Yes," the members agreed as one.

"At the moment, that is impossible." Roderigo lowered his eyes. "He seems to be a tad unstable. Indisposed, if I may say. He tends to show aggression when people are around him, so I had to lock him in one of these rooms."

"Lock him up?" Garrafal stood up. "The Carmines are stubborn by nature. Their trust is hard to earn, and you lock him up?" He paced throughout the room. "I am not risking our Phantasms, nor am I compromising the stability of both countries, for an insane, stubborn man. We made an oath to the Belecrose. We are to remain in the shadows, nothing but a breeze for those in need. I say we dismiss this case."

Murmurs buzzed around the room like bees. Some members seemed to agree with Garrafal, others with Roderigo.

Oleiro walked to the front of the room. "Let's take a vote. Those who are in favor of Roderigo's plan?"

Several hands raised.

"Those who are in favor of Colonel Garrafal's dismissal?"

By a couple of votes, Roderigo's plan was overruled. Those who objected cited the unwillingness of the prince. Decision made, the plan was doomed to be forgotten in the archives.

The meeting moved on to less-exciting topics.

"We better go," Sofia whispered, wiggling away from the balcony. She and Dashiel exited the room and closed the door with the utmost care.

"Aren't you glad you listened to me?" Sofia elbowed Dashiel.

A trio of Alferai pranced in front of them, singing festive carols and waving long ribbons.

"Fine, you were right," Dashiel said with a low voice.

"Very interesting, don't you think?" The voice came from beside the door. Sofia turned to find the man who'd stood next to Roderigo in the meeting.

"We . . . we were just . . . exploring the palacette. That's all." She brushed dirt and dust off her clothes. She stood tall, her eyes signaling Dashiel to keep his mouth shut.

"Don't worry. I won't tell anyone," the man said, smiling mostly at Sofia. "Unfortunately, that meeting was a waste of time."

Sofia scanned the man in front of her. "And you are?"

"I guess we haven't properly been acquainted, but our paths have crossed before. I would never forget such fiery eyes."

Sofia blushed. "Is that so?"

"It was at the Ochre Triumphant, if I'm not mistaken."

Sofia's offered him a dazed look. That voice. Those eyes, which had peered out from behind a silver mask. This man had helped her carry out her mission when Prince Markeus tried to detain her.

"My, where are my manners?" He stretched out his hand. "Sebastian Calabel of Libercia, at your service."

Sofia shook hands with him. "Sofia Spaigne, squadron commander."

"What a pretty name, Miss Spaigne," he said.

"Do call me Sofia."

Their hands remained clasped longer than a usual handshake would last.

"And, impressively, you're pretty strong," he said, a smile playing at the corners of his mouth.

"I guess I am." She tightened her grip.

Sebastian responded by tightening his even more. "I like it."

"Hi!" Dashiel, sensing a lull, finally spoke. "My name is Dashiel Ermitage. Nice to meet you."

The charged atmosphere shattered.

"*The* Dashiel Ermitage?" Sebastian offered his hand. "Athenai and I go way back. I've heard so much about you."

Dashiel blushed, shaking his hand. "All good things, I hope."

"Of course," Sebastian said, taking out a pocket watch and peeking at its face. "I'm afraid I must get going. A snowstorm is about to hit the mountains, and wanries will come down the mountain peaks. If I don't go now, I might be stuck here for the holiday festivities."

"That would be unfortunate." Sofia smiled. "I mean, not being home. Not being able to go home for the festivities. There's plenty of space here for one more . . . Not that I'm saying that you should . . ."

Sofia's face was as red as a tomato.

"I would love to stay, but I promised my family I would be there. I . . ." Sebastian floundered for words, finally settling on, "Farewell."

He was about to walk off when he appeared to find the courage to say what he had held back earlier. "Sofia?"

"Yes?"

"As an honorary member of the order, I was awarded a flask of messenger droplets." The Libercian man blushed. "What I'm trying to say is . . . may I write to you?"

Sofia remained calm, smiling at the idea. "I guess you can, if you happen to remember something about me."

"You can rest assured that I will. I would rather forget my own name than forget any single detail about you." He tipped his hat at them. "I really hope our paths cross again, Sofia." He turned to Dashiel. "Mr. Ermitage."

Sebastian whisked his way through the hallways.

"I think he likes you!" Dashiel taunted Sofia with a mischievous smirk. "And you like him back!"

"Oh, shut up." She punched him in the chest. "Sylvain wanted to meet for a training session. What do you say?"

"Sounds great," Dashiel said.

They began their journey across the immense edifice. Even after months in the palacette, they still got lost sometimes. At first they followed the path to the training room, but with a wrong turn, the path changed. They soon found themselves in front of Athenai's quarters.

"Sofia? This isn't the way to the training room." He stopped. "Let's head back."

"Move it, forest boy." Sofia pulled him by the hand. "We're late."

"Late for what?" Dashiel asked, avoiding a pillar.

"Late for the party." She gave another tug at his hand.

"Party?" Dashiel flinched. Sofia bit her lower lip and clenched her fist. She hadn't meant to give the surprise away. "Whose party?"

Sofia sighed. "Yours."

Dashiel dug in his heels, stopping their progression. "Sofia, I appreciate you and the others, but I don't do birthday celebrations."

"Well, you better go in there and enjoy yourself, and you better act surprised . . . or you'll wake up tied to a wanri nest."

Sofia pushed Dashiel through the doors and into Athenai's pitch-dark office.

Dashiel turned around. "Sofia, please, I don't—"

Multicolored sparks flew through the room, following a sonorous bang. The room illuminated.

With a loud and melodic "Surprise!" people jumped out from their hiding places. They all looked jubilant as they approached him, Sylvain leading. Dashiel couldn't understand the feeling he was experiencing. He was ready to be disgusted by the celebration, but oddly, he felt nothing of the sort.

His cheeks regained their color when the group parted and revealed Athenai. She held a small cake with a single blue, sparkling, star-shaped candle on top. For the first time since he could remember, he felt happy on his birthday.

"Happy birthday, Dashiel." Athenai stretched the cake toward him. "Make a wish."

Everyone got closer, and he snuffed out the candle.

"What did you wish for, Dashy boy?" Sofia asked.

"Nothing," Dashiel answered, a smile taking over his face. "I think I already have everything I ever wanted."

He'd spoken the truth. He had his love and his friends, and he was living out his dream of adventure. He was whole.

Everyone rushed to embrace Dashiel. Amore crawled up his shoulder and rubbed her petals against his face.

"Happy birthday, Eli," said Sylvain, hugging Dashiel tightly.

How did Sylvain know about his pet name? Dashiel only allowed his family and Grimley to call him by that name, but he really didn't mind that Sylvain had done it. After all, they had become inseparable. He was thankful for their steadfast friendship.

Sofia pushed Sylvain out of the way and hugged Dashiel.

"Happy birthday, Dashiel," she said, smiling. "Don't get used to this." She winked.

"Never," he said, playfully shoving his commander away. "But how did you know it was my birthday?"

"Sylvain told us!" Mina Halliwell said, appearing from the crowd. "He sure knows you well, partner."

"You talk in your sleep," Sylvain admitted.

"We've been planning everything for weeks," Athenai said.

"You really made it hard to keep it a secret!" Sofia stuffed her mouth with food. "You really are nosy."

"Well," Athenai said, clasping her hands together in delight, "please enjoy yourselves!"

"Fine by me." Sofia took out her violin and began to play one of her own songs, while Athenai's sisters played the tambourine, the flute, and the harp. The Alferai musicians soon abandoned their instruments, which continued to play alongside Sofia as they floated all over the room. Athenai's sisters danced to the tune, and the festivity went on until nightfall.

When the party was at its peak, Dashiel and Athenai found the right moment to tiptoe away. They stepped outside the palacette, sitting in a stone gazebo. The snow on the mountains shone with the northern lights. They sat together for a while in comfortable silence.

"Dashiel, I need you to close your eyes," Athenai said, hands behind her back. "I have something to give you."

"Oh, you shouldn't have . . ." Dashiel said with a light voice. "What is it?"

"No, no. It's a surprise."

"Maybe a hint?" He stretched his neck to see what hid behind Athenai.

"Well, if you aren't going to close your eyes, I might give it to you as a Christmas present."

"No, it's fine!" Dashiel tightly shut his eyes. He felt something land in his outstretched hands.

"Open them!"

Dashiel looked down to find a book. At first he did not recognize it, but then it came to him. This was his favorite book in the whole world, all fixed up. The pages had been cleaned, and a spine and an embossed cover had been added to it.

"This is my book?"

Athenai nodded with satisfaction and joy.

"Thank you so much!" Dashiel scanned the book, absorbing every detail. "You're absolutely grand!"

"You're welcome."

"Also, thank you for the party, Athenai," Dashiel said, his cheeks reddening in the cold. "You and Sylvain shouldn't have bothered."

"It's the least I can do for the person I care about the most," she answered, leaning her head against his shoulder.

His heart pounded against his chest. Happiness and adrenaline rushed through his body.

"I . . . I feel the same way about you." His cheeks warmed, and he struggled to remain calm as he felt butterflies in his stomach. "If I share something really personal with you, will you promise not to laugh?"

"I promise," she said, her hand on his chest.

"It might seem funny, or insane, but before today, I always dreaded my birthday. Even today, I cursed it," he continued, gaining courage as he looked into her eyes. "There was no need to hate it, but there was no real reason to celebrate it either. I felt sad and angry all day, but when I looked at you, that changed. You've changed everything."

The words were flowing, and he didn't think he could stop them. He didn't want to stop them. "Because of hemocarcomia, I was bedridden, a prisoner in my own room, a castaway in my own house. I was always exhausted and weak. I would wake up with scars and bruises I couldn't explain. My body was in constant pain, and the worst part was the loneliness. Needless to say, my childhood sucked."

The lights kept on dancing through the dark.

"That's when you got the book?" she asked, truly invested in his story.

"Yes, the book is the only thing that kept me sane," Dashiel said. "I used to have the most horrific nightmares, almost every night."

"Nightmares about what?" she asked.

"I don't remember." He squinted and tried to recall, but nothing came to mind. "All I can remember is waking up screaming and feeling pain."

"I'm so sorry, Dashiel." Athenai put her hand on his knee. "It must have been hard."

"You know what? Not everything was terrible," he said, smiling as he remembered. "My parents loved me and always tried to make me feel better. My mother was a character, and my father was . . . happy." His lips trembled. "At least for a while. Then he became cold and distant, though I've never known why."

"Parents are like that sometimes," Athenai said. "My mother was very strict with me and my sisters, but she loved me very much. I bet your father loves you too."

Dashiel allowed his eyes to feast on her lovely features. She was a vision.

"Sometimes I would go outside, sit on the roof of my house, and look at the stars. I don't know why, but the stars were ten times brighter when observed from my rooftop than anywhere else. They comforted me and helped me deal with the pain I felt in my body and mind. I still look at them when I lose my way."

"That sounds beautiful," Athenai said, inching closer.

"I noticed that the stars can't be seen from here, but you know what? I don't need them." He caressed her cheek. Her violet eyes shone. "No wonder I couldn't stop staring at you that day, in Carbakiel. Your eyes emit a similar light."

Dashiel couldn't take his eyes off her porcelain face. He touched her arm. It was so smooth, so soft. He could find no difference between her skin and her silky dress. Her subtle vanilla aroma enchanted his nose. His senses begged him for more.

Euphoria overpowered them both. The moment felt right. They got closer and closer. They didn't try to stop it; it was the right time and place. His heart pounded mercilessly, and his head reeled. They shared their first kiss under that night sky, wrapped in prancing lights.

CHAPTER 28

A BITTER COLD LAMENT

The clocks in the palacette struck three in the morning. Everything was silent; everything was at peace. Everything except the palacette's kitchen.

"I really should stop eating these," Dashiel said to Amore as he gobbled another marzipan macaron, one of Athenai's many culinary specialties.

Amore chirped in response, swinging from cabinet to cabinet.

"If Sofia finds out I've gained weight," Dashiel said before gulping a glass of milk, "she'll make me run a thousand miles." He wiped his chin with his sleeve. "But I can't help it. They're so good!"

He stashed some pink macarons in his jacket pocket and then placed the rest back in the pantry.

"Let's go," Dashiel called.

Amore wrapped herself around his neck, and they tiptoed out of the kitchen.

Once they put enough distance between themselves and the kitchen, Dashiel slowed his pace. The freezing temperature had compelled him to put on as many layers of clothing as possible. He liked strolling the decked halls because he could let his thoughts wander. He imagined what his next adventure with his friends would be.

The Outerland was so expansive, nothing like Azahar. There were so many possibilities.

His mind and heart urged him to find a way to prove he was worth more than anyone had bargained for.

His thoughts were interrupted by a loud clink and clank. He looked around, but nothing seemed to be out of order. He kept walking until he came across a man standing in the middle of the corridor. He was almost as tall as the ceiling and held a wooden staff.

"Hey," Dashiel said as he approached. "It's a cold night, don't you think?"

The man did not answer.

"Are you all right? Are you lost?" Dashiel asked.

The man did not respond.

Dashiel peered around the man. The door was unhinged and chipped, the white walls dappled with blood.

"What happened here?" Though his mind told him to walk away, Dashiel slowly moved toward the man.

When the man turned to him, Dashiel caught a glimpse of two unconscious guards lying on the floor. The giant man looked up, startling Dashiel with his milky eyes. They held no trace of pupils or irises.

He stepped back. Could this be the man Roderigo had spoken about?

"Who are you?" Dashiel asked, reaching for the baton on his back.

Something snapped within the man, and he rushed toward Dashiel in a rage. Dashiel moved fast and avoided the attack, but the man charged like a bull in a ring.

"Calm down!" Dashiel shouted as he avoided another assault.

The man growled and then jumped off a nearby balcony, landing a few feet from the adorned pine tree. He managed to open the palacette's heavy stone doors without a hitch and made his way into the caverns.

"Wait!" Dashiel yelled, setting off in hot pursuit. "It's not safe out there!"

"Dashiel, what's the matter?" Sylvain, who must have heard the ruckus, asked from a higher balcony.

"I saw a blind man going into the caverns," Dashiel said, buttoning his coat. "The storm is raging outside. He could die! I think he's the man Roderigo spoke about. Alert the others."

"Wait!" Sylvain yelled. "You can't go alone. It's dangerous!"

Amore chirped as she braided herself to Dashiel's arm.

"No," Dashiel said firmly, unraveling Amore from his arm and placing her on a column. "Go to Athenai. Stay here."

Dashiel followed the stranger through the caverns and to the exit. Outside, the wind howled, and snow descended with force, landing on the already heavy blanket of snow on the ground. The cold was merciless and penetrated any vestige of warmth. Dashiel followed the stranger, stomping through the thick snow. Wind hit him in the face, and his fingers and toes grew numb.

"Co-come back!" Dashiel yelled at the blurry silhouette of the man. "It's not safe out here."

The man stopped at the sound of Dashiel's voice. Dashiel walked with his arm protecting his face, pausing a few steps away from the man.

"We . . . need to . . . to . . . to go back," Dashiel said, his teeth chattering and limbs becoming number by the minute.

The man didn't respond. He stood tall, crooked staff in hand. His long hair thrashed in the merciless wind, and his ragged clothes were covered with snowflakes. He seemed unaffected by the cold.

"You wouldn't dare make me," the man said. "You have no idea how much I've been through. You do not have a say in my life."

"I'm not here to tell you what to do," Dashiel said. "I just want to take you to safety."

"I don't need your help." The man swung his stick, which whistled through the space between them and caused Dashiel to take a step back. His milky eyes were wide and full of rage. "I don't need your help. Let me be!"

Dashiel gathered his strength and took two steps forward.

"It's dangerous." The freezing wind half blinded him, and he covered his face once again. "Don't be so stubborn. Let me help you."

"Stay away from me!" The man moved onward.

Dashiel followed him down the mountain trail, which was nearly unrecognizable in the blizzard. He was aware of the danger; after all, the pits were hidden beneath layers of ice and snow.

Dashiel managed to grab the man by his arm. Finally fed up, the man roared, threw away his walking stick, and attacked Dashiel. They wrestled in the cloud-white snow. The man was strong and did not take long to pin Dashiel to the ground.

A screech sounded from afar, stopping the fight. The sound grew louder and louder. The snowstorm made everything hard to see, but someone—or some*thing*—was clearly there.

A huge, white mass landed on the ground, making everything tremble. From the blob, two massive wings spread. A long neck appeared, and on its end emerged a large head with eyes glowing red and a scythe-shaped beak. Long, sharp, and heavy feathers grew from its beak and tail. They danced in the strong winds.

Dashiel had never seen a bird that doubled his own height. "What the hell is that?" he asked, breathing heavily and holding his baton in a defensive position.

"I can feel the presence of a bird, and its aura is enormous," the man responded. "Must be a snow vulture."

Otherwise known as a wanri, one of the most dangerous creatures on the Egadrisean continent. Dashiel adjusted his grip on his doizemant.

The great bird tilted its head, locking its eyes on Dashiel and his companion. It exhaled a screech. The bird's breath was even colder than the harsh winds surrounding them.

"Listen," the man spoke gently, slowly reaching for his stick. "We have to run."

"Run?"

"Wanries can't stomach their prey unless it's frozen solid," the man whispered in Dashiel's ear. "As long as its breath doesn't get you, you'll be fine. But it'll try to freeze us at all costs. On the count of three, we run as fast as possible. There must be a hiding place around here."

"All right" Dashiel answered, slowly drawing his baton out.

"One," the man began. "Two . . . three!"

They bolted as fast as they could, and the bird gave chase, screeching and spraying its frozen breath. When they managed to put some distance between themselves and the creature, it spread its wings and took flight. The wanri nose-dived, narrowly missing them.

But they were not in the clear. The man slipped and fell into the snow. The wanri screeched as it landed, trapping his body under its claws. The bird opened its beak, preparing to freeze him solid.

Dashiel didn't hesitate. He rushed down the trail to stop the wanri from murdering its prey.

"You had it coming!" Gathering all his strength, he whacked the bird as hard as he could with the baton. It was surprisingly fun. No wonder Old Astor had enjoyed caning him so much back in Azahar.

The bird screeched louder than it had all morning, letting go of the man. Dashiel helped him up, but there was nowhere to run. They found themselves surrounded by a dozen wanries, each of which had heard its friend's call.

The pack began to close in on them.

"Any ideas?" Dashiel asked, swinging Orphée to fend off an advancing wanri.

"None," the man answered, hitting another wanri and breaking his walking stick in the process.

Dashiel retreated a few steps, slipping along the icy trail. An idea struck, and he crouched to the ground. He brushed aside some snow, uncovering one of the trail's bottomless pits. It had been sealed off by accumulating ice.

The baton's whispering joined the wind's discordant melody as the wanries began their attack.

Dashiel tried to break the ice with the baton, but the weapon lacked heft, and after spending so much time in the extreme cold, he lacked the strength. Then it came to him: he needed *a lot* of weight.

"I have an idea." Dashiel pummeled a wanri's beak. "It better work, or else we're bird food!"

He pounded the baton three times against the icy ground. "Please, Orphée," Dashiel whispered.

The ice did not break, but the baton emitted a dull light. The whispering ceased as it began to change shape. In a matter of seconds, the baton had turned into a mallet, relieving Dashiel enormously. He had earned another doizemant form.

He lifted the mallet and threw it down as hard as possible. The ice cracked and, in seconds, shattered. He, the man, and Orphée fell through the hole, escaping the hungry predators.

Dashiel and the man waited halfway down the hole for hours, sitting on a ledge of ice and snow, surrounded by razor-sharp stalactites. The gusts were gone, but the temperature continued to drop.

He shivered as he tried to absorb the heat of one of the matches he had on him.

"It's re-re-really cold down here." Dashiel offered the man a match.

"I'm fine," the man said with a rusty voice.

"Good . . ."

"You risked your life to save me, and in return, I attacked you." He was restless, tearing the two halves of his walking stick into smaller pieces. "I would like to offer you an apology."

The man offered him a reverent nod.

"No big deal. It was exciting in a way, almost getting frozen and eaten." Dashiel threw the burnt match into the pit. "And that fight in the snow." He rubbed his neck. "Man, you are savage."

The man gave him a tiny smirk. "I guess living all by myself for so long has made me forget my manners."

Dashiel rubbed his hands together. "Who cares about manners with that strength? You are a great warrior."

"You are too," the man replied, his voice sounding more human.

A silence hung in the air for a few moments.

"I heard . . . That is, someone me-me-mentioned Audric Swannagger was a guest at the palacette. You're the prince, aren't you?" Dashiel asked, trying to keep his mind away from the sheer cold that pierced through his skin.

"Locked in a room against my own will." The man scoffed, "Your people have an odd understanding of what a guest is."

"I knew it. You are the prince they were talking about." Dashiel said, his mind filling up with questions. He had never been in the presence of a royal. At least, not one who wanted him dead. "What happened to you? Why are you so reluctant to return to your home?"

"Stop asking questions." The man ceased shredding his walking stick. "We aren't having this conversation."

"We might die of frostbite soon." Dashiel chuckled through a wave of shivers. "We might as well, right? If you will be the last person I e-e-ever meet, I would like to get to know you better."

"I *was* a prince." He shook his head. "A long, long time ago . . ."

"What was your family like?" Dashiel kept on shivering. His shoes, pants, and jacket had become stiff and frosted.

"My mother died in childbirth; it was only me, my brother, and our father. My father was never around, so Beckel looked after me."

A short-lived warmth traversed his chest. The idea of their brotherly bond made him happy and gave him peace.

"Beckel and I were inseparable, or at least we were until our father passed and Beckel became king." Audric choked on his words.

"What ha-ha-happened to him?" Dashiel asked.

Audric crushed one of the pieces of his cane. "In our folklore, the king is considered a fire divinity. A foolish fairy tale. My brother believed it to be truth. He saw his unnatural beauty and strength as a sign of his perfect existence. That is when his mind became deranged.

He hid in his palaces and castles and concealed his face with masks, as he thought no one was worthy of beholding his face."

Audric doodled on the frozen ground with a piece of his walking stick.

"As I lost all contact with my brother, I fell in love with the daughter of a Peskeiran duke. Tullie and I, we fell madly in love. Little did I know that my brother had plans to marry her and cement an alliance with the duchy."

Freezing tears rolled down Audric's cheeks. It was clear that his memories were painful.

"Everything worsened when Asedia arrived, promising Beckel eternal youth in the form of an elixir from a flower he possessed and power in the form of metal soldiers. At the peak of his madness, my brother committed abhorrent acts. I couldn't bear to watch him destroy our home, Tullie, and himself, so I challenged him to a duel for the crown. He defeated me and sent me to the terrible Tortoise Husk to rot. After my departure, he forced Tullie to marry him. When I managed to escape, I learned that Tullie had been exiled."

The ice ledge shook and began to crack. Ice shards fell down the bottomless pit. Neither of them moved. There was no climbing out of this pit; there was nothing to do but wait to either freeze or fall.

"I was young and stupid, and when I tried to stand up to him, I failed, and I paid the price." Audric placed his fingers under his eyes. "My kingdom is in ruins, my love is lost, and I am full of shame." He threw the pieces of his walking stick into the pit. "That is why I cannot go back."

Dashiel bowed his head. "I'm so-or-rry you had to go through all that."

"Don't be . . ." Audric closed his iris-less eyes and leaned his head against the frozen wall. "I don't expect you to understand my pain, my shame. Fortunately for you, you were born to be your own ruler, owing nothing to anyone but yourself."

Silence overcame the moment, for Dashiel didn't know what else to say. He was starting to feel oddly sleepy, and it became harder to keep his eyes fully open. His heart shriveled at what the fellow next to him had been through. Audric had lost everything in life. Even himself, to fear.

"Fear is as real as a rrrr-re-eflection, but the actions moved by it are as real as the pa-palm of your hand." Dashiel yawned loudly as it became harder for him to keep his eyes open. "You must not let your fear dictate what you're capable of."

"Where did you get that?"

"My mother," Dashiel answered, wiping his nose with his sleeve.

"I wish it were that easy. I already tried, and I failed."

"You should have kept on trying. You should keep on trying." Dashiel smirked. "There's nothing to lose."

"It's no use . . . Tullie might be dead now."

"You're wrong," Dashiel insisted. "We don't know what happened to Tullie, and I sure hope she's safe, but there are still many that need you. You owe it to them."

"No."

"Keep on trying." Dashiel gathered his energy to raise his voice. "Try again!"

Audric pounded the ice wall. "I already said no!"

"Why not?" Dashiel clenched his fingers. "You have a chance to make things right for your country. Don't waste it. If I had it in my hands to change the fate of Zaphyrelia, I would jump into it without a thought, and I'm not even the damn prince."

"I can't be reckless anymore!" Audric howled. "It took one reckless decision for my life to end."

"Don't be so hard on yourself. You were a child when you faced your bro-brother. You've grown. You're not the sa-ssssame." Dashiel wrapped his arms around himself.

Silence took over once more. The merciless wind that howled above the pit was barely audible.

Dashiel's mind began to wander. He wondered if Sylvain and Sofia were looking for him. He imagined a worried Sylvain, searching through the walls of gray snow. His mind switched to an aggressive Sofia, hellfire in her eyes. If he ever saw her again, she'd strangle him and yell at him for being such a reckless idiot.

Dashiel laughed.

"How can you be l-laughing?" Audric said through chattering teeth, for even he had begun to shiver.

"I . . . I was thinking of all the sticky situations I've g-gotten mmm-my-myself into. You say that it takes one reckless decision for one's life to end. Well, I must be the luckiest fool."

Audric chuckled for a brief moment.

"One would think that I'd have learned my lesson. I guess I haven't," Dashiel said, teeth chattering, memories fluttering inside his head. "Maybe I am immature and reckless, but I know I can always count on Sylvain and Sofia to get me out of trouble."

"Who?"

"My . . . my . . . my friends," Dashiel responded. His lips were numb, and he imagined they'd turned the same gray as Audric's. "They must be looking for me right now . . . Well, I sure hope they are; otherwise, we're screwed."

Audric gave off a hearty laugh. "Must be nice to have friends like that."

"Friends like what?"

"Friends who are with you no matter what," Audric said, building a timid smile. "Friends who support you, teach you, or . . ."

"Save you frrrr-from huge, bloodthirsty birrrds?" Dashiel asked.

Audric snickered. "Yeah, tha-that too."

"Audric, whateverrr you de-de-decide, I'll be you-your friend," Dashiel said. "I promise that I'll help you. If you wa-want to escape, I will help you esss-cape."

"You mean that?"

"Ye-yes, if we e-ever get out of . . . of here." Dashiel leaned against the wall and closed his eyes. "I feel exhausted."

"Dashiel?" Audric said a short time later, but Dashiel didn't have the energy to answer. He heard Audric carefully pushing himself closer, but he didn't bother opening his eyes.

"That . . . tha . . ." Dashiel tried to speak, losing the world around him. One by one, his senses started to leave him. He could hear Audric calling for him, but he was too tired. He had to rest his eyes for a while.

"No, no, no!" Audric shook Dashiel's shoulder. "You . . . you can't fall asleep! Wake up. You have to wake up!"

A tiny part of Dashiel was aware that Audric took off his own jacket and wrapped Dashiel within it. Audric rubbed his hands together and placed them on Dashiel's pale face. The storm above raged on, and the temperature kept on dropping. Only time would tell if they were to survive.

Dashiel woke up inside the mountain's jewel cavern. He was lying on a blanket of snow, covered by Audric's ragged jacket, Orphée by his side. In front of him were Sylvain and Sofia, their faces full of concern.

"Thank Providence that you woke up," Sylvain panted, his eyes welling with tears.

"What happened?" Dashiel asked, his vision still blurry.

"Sylvain and I searched everywhere for you. When we found you, you had been unconscious for hours," Sofia said. "This man kept you alive."

Dashiel turned to his right to find Audric standing over him. His expression told Dashiel he was greatly relieved to hear he was still alive.

"What about the wanries?" Dashiel asked.

"You don't have to worry about them." She gave him one of her mischievous expressions. "By the way, we'll finally have some decent meat at dinner."

Dashiel turned to Audric. "Thank you for saving me."

"I couldn't let my only friend die." Audric crossed his arms. His face was emotionless, probably because of the others' presence.

With Sylvain's help, Dashiel stood. "Well, we better get you away from here."

"All Phantasms are looking for him," Sylvain said. "You might get caught."

"I'll be fine," Dashiel said, picking Orphée up. "Let's go."

"No," Audric said.

"Wha-what? Why?" Dashiel stammered.

"I can't believe I'm saying this . . ." Audric took a big breath. "Do you think the Carmine people would want me to lead them? Of course not. Who would ever listen to the command of a blind man? Aura reading is useful, but it has its limitations."

"Let me be your eyes!" Dashiel blurted. "Have faith in me and my fellow Phantasms, and we shall take you there."

"What if I can't find Tullie?"

"We'll find her t-together," Dashiel said. "You must do it for her, and for all the people who depend on you."

Audric paused for a moment. Dashiel knew that gears were turning in his new friend's mind.

"If you really mean that, Dashiel Ermitage, then it will be an honor to fight by your side," Audric said. "I shall return my nation to the light, find Tullie, and face Beckel once and for all."

"That's what I'm talking about!" Dashiel struggled to sit up straight. "By the way, what is your name?"

"You already know that. Audric."

Dashiel shook his head. "Wrong answer! Who the heck are you?"

The man pondered for a moment. For years, Audric had tried to suppress and forget. But if he was going to face Beckel, he had to be his true self. He had to relive the memories, however difficult they were, and embrace them.

"I am Audric Johann Swannagger," Audric said, "son of Helmuth III, prince of all Carmines. And soon, liberator of his oppressed people."

"Sofia, we need to see Roderigo," Dashiel said. "All of us. Now."

Back at the palacette, the Founding Chapter had been reunited in the same room as before. Audric spoke to the members, and after a vote, the Founding Chapter decided to aid the prince in his quest. They spent most of Christmas Day inside that room, discussing terms and planning the next steps.

"I'll ask once more, Your Highness." Garrafal crossed his arms and raised his upper lip. "Are you sure you want to proceed? You are fully aware of the consequences?"

"Yes," Audric answered firmly. "My brother has caused enough pain."

"That's extraordinary news!" Roderigo said with his customary joviality.

"But there are some conditions," Audric said.

"Conditions?" Garrafal gasped. "You are in no—"

Normandine shushed him, allowing the prince to speak.

"When the time comes, I want Dashiel Ermitage and the Ermine Squadron to be my escorts," Audric said.

"My . . ." Roderigo's face flushed. "They are talented, Your Highness, but perhaps a more-experienced squadron would be more suitable to aid you."

Audric shook his head, scattering droplets of water on the floor. Melting snow continued dripping down his hair. "With all due respect, sir, I still do not trust you, nor do I trust whatever organization you have going on here. My trust lies only in Dashiel and his companions."

"Very well. We shall fulfill our end of the bargain, but you must fulfill yours." Garrafal crossed his arms.

"You have my word," Audric answered. "Help me save my kingdom, and in return, I will stop the production of Brigadier carcasses and grant you the Carmine gift, my brother's spherite."

CHAPTER 29

YN REKUS LIOUS

As the snow slowly melted under the warm spring sun, the Cobalt Phantasms moved stealthily across the nation, stoking the people's anger toward the Carmine king. It was easy for the Carmine people to believe the stories of illness and poverty that the Phantasms spread, because those stories reflected their everyday lives. People went hungry as their pyrone stuffed himself with the continent's finest delicacies and threw lavish parties with his court. To make things worse, Beckel had allowed Asedia to strip the country of its natural resources to benefit his reign.

The Phantasms protected the furious citizens, gathering followers and clearing the way for the ever-growing crowd as it marched toward the capital.

The embodiment of a freedom flag, Audric traveled across the land, gaining strength as he went. One by one, the Carmine lords swore loyalty to the prince and united their power and influence. Soon enough, the prince led his allies to Minka, where the king had isolated himself.

Thousands stormed the town and its castle. As days passed under the siege, the overwhelmed castle guards began to desert. Some ran. Others joined the blind prince.

Soon the crowds took down the gates, and Audric, Dashiel, and the prince's other companions entered. The castle in Minka, the final remnant of Beckel's power, had been conquered.

The pyrone's residence was adorned with crimson lanterns and dragon-shaped pillars. Thousands of planters hung from the dragons' snouts. The infrasol flowers inside the planters had black petals and ochre anthers. The castle halls were decorated with banners bearing the royal family's coat of arms.

Beautifully crafted mirrors hung from the walls. They were crowned with gold flying serpents and reflected the return of their long-lost son. Audric and his escorts marched through each room in search of his brother and the love of his life.

One of the Carmine lords appeared before the prince. He clicked his heels together and saluted. "Sire, your brother has been found and secured. He is in the dining room in the east wing."

"Good. What about the former queen?" Audric clenched his fingers and raised his eyebrows in anticipation.

"She is nowhere to be found, Sire."

"Keep looking." Audric stepped away from the lord, a disheartened look crossing his face. Black petals showered from the planters, emitting a strong, bitter smell. "Leave not a single stone unturned, understood?"

"As you wish, Your Highness." The lord clicked his heels and saluted before walking off.

"What did he say?" Dashiel approached the prince, who leaned against a credenza.

"She's not here!" Audric howled, swiping two vases off the highly embellished piece of furniture. The shattering of porcelain echoed down the hall, and more petals fell from above. "She must be six feet underground."

"No! You mustn't give up." Dashiel placed his hand on Audric's shoulder. Dashiel met Audric's fogged-up eyes. "You've come so far. Let's not lose hope, all right?"

"You might be right. I believe there is one thing to be done," Audric said. "It's time my brother and I met face-to-face."

"Are you ready?"

"My head hurts, and I'm about to throw up," Audric said, leaning against a wall. "Ready as I'll ever be."

Audric and his escorts made their way to the room where his brother had been found. Two guards moved out of the way, allowing Audric to enter.

The dining room remained set from that morning, a memory of the hours before all the servants fled to either join Audric or escape certain defeat. The once-exquisite food remained on the table, now swarmed by flies. Beside it were countless bottles of the finest vintage. Half the candles in the grand chandelier had burned out, and most of the room's dimmed light came from the candelabras that lined the wall and a row of tall windows. The chamber's remaining inhabitant was a cloaked figure who watched sadly as plebeian filth infested his castle and infrasol gardens.

When Audric entered, the man turned around. He wore an iron mask with the face of a dragon—an important symbol to the Swannaggers. It was believed that they were descendants of dragons.

"Welcome home, Brother." Beckel strode gracefully toward the table and sat in a golden chair. "I really hope there are no hard feelings between us. After all, a pyrone does what a pyrone must do."

"Where's Tullie, Beckel? What have you done with her?"

The man removed his mask. His fresh, symmetrical face; his large, brightly colored eyes; his sensual lips—his good looks could take an angel's breath away. He dressed in the finest silks and satins, and the ends of his slim fingers bore ten perfect, razor-sharp nails.

"Our ancestors' home, invaded by peasants," Beckel mumbled as he sipped from his cup. "Disgraceful."

"Audric," Dashiel called, "this man cannot be your older brother. He seems way younger than you."

Audric closed his eyes and focused. "His dark aura doesn't lie. This is my brother," he answered. "It's what's inside his cup that keeps him young. The infrasol flower."

Audric approached the table.

"I won't ask again. Where is Tullie?" He fisted the ebony table, knocking down some of the glasses.

Beckel raised his cup and drained its contents. "It's a shame that you never appreciated the pleasures of the life I offered you. The taste of this elixir, for one." He filled his cup, uninterested in his brother's words.

The imprisoned king was not going to confess. He was a lost cause.

"Beckel, I stand before you as the pyrone that the people have chosen," Audric said, holding tight to his wooden staff. "By the charges of treason and murder, you are under arrest."

"The peasants?" He scoffed. "You are pyrone in the eyes of scum. Me, on the other hand, I am pyrone in the eyes of Providence." He slammed his cup down onto the table. "Fool."

"It's over, Beckel. The people deserve better." Audric hit the marble floor with his staff. "Guards!"

Guards entered the room to take Beckel into custody.

"No, it's not over." Beckel laughed as he stood up. "Not if I call upon the protection of Yn Rekus Lious."

"Yn Rekus Lious?" Dashiel took a step forward.

"It is part of an ancient oath that all Egadrisean royal houses abide by," Sylvain explained. "If a king is to fall to the pride of his own blood, by Providence's command, he shall be given the chance to dismiss destiny by his own hand."

"You are a man of honor, Audric," Beckel continued, slurring his words slightly and twirling a lock of hair with his finger. "You have no choice but to respect the laws of Yn Rekus Lious."

"He has no obligation to you," Dashiel said.

"Your forces are depleted. Your fate is in his hands," Sylvain added.

Dashiel placed his hand on the prince's shoulder. "You won already. You don't have to do this."

The prince's face told a different story. He was in deep conflict.

"But," Beckel interjected, "if honor is not strong enough as motivation, maybe you'll be interested in knowing the fate of dear Tullie, and in this . . ."

Held in his long nails was a spherical object with strange silver markings, and it was glowing a hot red. It was a spherite, an item that could create a limitless amount of any fire known to man. An object powerful enough to counteract Asedia's earth spherite.

"A treasure given to every firstborn in our lineage. A right distinct from the right to rule." Beckel laid his hand on the table, still clutching the spherite. "Not even a crown guarantees you such a legendary treasure."

Audric grabbed Dashiel's hand. "My loyal friend, you've seen the man behind these blind eyes," Audric whispered. "Do you trust him?"

No words were needed for Dashiel to understand Audric's dilemma. On one hand, he could defeat his brother, avenge his honor, and acquire an object that could help his allies win back their freedom. On the other hand, he could lose the throne and his own life, not to mention the opportunity to find Tullie.

"Always," Dashiel whispered back, concern etched on his face.

"Beckel! I accept your claim of Yn Rekus Lious." Audric positioned himself in front of his brother.

"An honorable man." Beckel stood up and let his cloak slide down to the floor. "But not a wise one."

Beckel and Audric positioned themselves on each side of the dining room while the people gathered to witness the duel. A servant brought forth a case that contained two unusual daggers.

"These daggers were forged to serve Yn Rekus Lious," Audric explained to Dashiel and Sylvain as the servant handed a weapon to each combatant. "We shall duel with nothing but our bodies, our wits, and these daggers. Victory goes to whoever stains his dagger with his opponent's blood."

"Or to whoever claims the life of his adversary." Beckel smirked.

It had been a year of heavy rains in the kingdom, but while Dashiel, Audric, and the others traversed Carmine, it had seemed as though the sky had cried itself dry. The gray clouds had nothing left to give. But they stormed now. Thunder witnessed two brothers fighting to the death. Lightning witnessed Beckel pushing his brother against the dining table, flipping it over, and spilling bottles of wine and infrasol elixir over the cold floor.

When the lightning was as blinding as the sun and the thunder as strong as an earthquake, the proceedings reached a crescendo. Beckel grabbed his brother by the arm and immobilized him. The king forced his brother to the room's long line of tall windows, which offered a view of gardens full of infrasol hedges. Hundreds of Carmines watched, horror written on their faces.

"This brings back so many memories." Beckel burst into laughter as he pushed his brother against one of the windows, cracking it. "Oh, how I enjoyed the last time I defeated you. Your screams of agony when I stole the light from your eyes. Tullie's tears falling to the floor."

He pushed once more, widening the cracks in the glass.

"You're still a stupid child, Audric. You are ruled by emotion, a slave to love. You never learn. And now you'll pay for that mistake once more."

Dashiel couldn't take it anymore. He wanted to help his friend, but he was quickly detained by Sylvain.

"If you interfere, he will lose by default."

Dashiel had no choice but to watch Beckel as he continued smashing Audric into the icy window. Beckel paused right when the slightest touch could break the window, relishing his victory.

"As I am a reasonable man, I will tell you about Tullie's fate before killing you." Though his words were a whisper in his brother's ear, Dashiel heard them clearly in the silent room. "For years, she lived in despair, as her womb would not bear an heir. She became a farce, the laughingstock of her court. I saw her pain and sadness every day. Her expression became a grimace of endless suffering, like the one she wore when I got rid of you all those years ago. She became a nuisance. She had to go. I'm sure you understand, Brother."

Audric seemed to be gathering his strength, trying to set himself free, but his brother was still too strong.

"That fool! If she had only known that I wasn't planning on passing on my crown," Beckel said. "The infrasol made me an eternal king, but also a barren one. I was the reason the Carmine Kingdom remained without an heir. Not her."

Beckel's lips curled into a savage grin.

"But she certainly made a convenient scapegoat, don't you think, dear Brother?"

Audric vibrated with anger and adrenaline. He finally managed to break free from his brother's grasp, pushing him to the floor. The brawl continued, and the tables turned when Audric placed his dagger to his brother's throat. The knife pierced his royal skin, and a yellowish blood bathed its blade.

"You . . ." Beckel was barely able to articulate a word. "Won."

"Where's Tullie?" Audric clenched his teeth.

Beckel chuckled as if he were a child playing a game.

Audric became enraged, pushing the knife farther into the skin, causing more corrupted blood to emerge.

"Where is she?!"

Beckel gasped. "In Zaphyrelia."

"Where, exactly?" Audric tightened his grip on the knife.

"I don't know," the deposed king said with much difficulty. "Asedia's men took her away. I was never told where."

Audric pressed the knife deeper into his brother's flesh. With a mere flick of his wrist, he could end the man who had destroyed his life. But he did not do it. Perhaps Audric had realized that taking his brother's life would not change anything. It would stain his hands and his soul forever.

"Beckel Hanndersel Swannagger." Audric removed the knife from his brother's neck. "You are to be exiled from the Carmine Kingdom and live a life of confinement. You will never harm anyone else again."

A lord's voice proclaimed his victory. "LONG LIVE PYRONE AUDRIC!"

Everyone began to celebrate. The fight had been dangerous, but it had been fruitful; there was no doubt Audric deserved to rule. The Carmine Kingdom was finally free. Celebration rang from the corridors of the castle to the outskirts of the town.

Dashiel knew that the future was uncertain for his friend. Audric might never be a perfect king, but he would be the king whom the Carmines deserved. And for that night, he had earned the chance to try for greatness.

As Audric walked to address his people, a roar rang out from behind. "Stupid!"

"Aah!" Audric screamed, startling everyone.

Beckel had slashed his back with his sharp claws, which had ripped cloth and bored into his skin. Beckel took advantage of his brother's pain to land some hits and bring him down with a quick knee to the ribs.

The celebration outside the room ceased as everyone watched, terrorized.

Beckel lifted his brother, throwing him toward the windows.

"I am the one true lord of this kingdom!" Beckel roared. He ran to the dining table and soaked his neck with the infrasol elixir. His wound immediately vanished.

"I am a divinity! You cannot defeat me!" Beckel took out the spherite. "I am perfect. My body and mind are without flaws. You are imperfect," he raged, knocking over plates of food and spilling elixir everywhere. "Let these flames wash away your imperfect existence!"

With the spherite in hand, he cast a flame that set his whole arm on fire.

"That's it." Sylvain took out his crossbow and aimed at Beckel.

"One more step and you die!" Sofia shouted, pointing her pistol at the deposed king.

"Go on." Beckel raised his flaming claws. "Shoot, and I will burn the castle to the ground."

"Lower your weapons!" Sylvain commanded everyone. "The spherite has enough power to bring down this place."

"But Audric . . ." Dashiel's frightened eyes turned to Sylvain. "He needs our help. Beckel cheated."

"Eli." Sylvain's hardened expression softened for a brief moment. "We cannot afford to risk the consequences."

Dashiel lowered his doizemant, praying for the kingdom's true ruler to pick himself back up.

Audric tried to recuperate, barely able to rise to his elbows and knees. He coughed up blood, which blended with the unholy infrasol elixir.

"I didn't get here by letting anyone get the best of me." Beckel raced toward his brother, his flaming, clawed hand resembling the head of a demonic dragon. "Gods don't follow rules. They make them! Goodbye, little brother."

Audric closed his eyes, and mouthed the name of his lost lover in his final moments. A wave of sadness washed over Dashiel as he watched the mad king race forward, blinded by greed and pride.

It was this single-minded focus that proved to be the king's undoing. For just as he was about to incinerate his brother, Beckel slipped in a puddle of elixir that he and his brother had spilled during the duel. He stumbled, unable to control his limbs. He tripped over his brother, who remained hunched in front of the cracked window. Beckel crashed through the window, meeting the fate to which he had thought to doom Audric.

His fall was accompanied by a screech, one that turned beastly when the spherite's fire started to burn the bush of infrasol he had landed on. The screams continued as the flames blazed and the infrasol gardens—and the deposed ruler, trapped inside a bush—became nothing but ash.

The duel had ended, and not a soul present could deny its victor. Audric Swannagger had earned the opportunity to rule the proud Carmines.

CHAPTER 30

THE FINAL STROKE

Asedia strode into the Varnasian great armory, where hundreds of mindless workers constructed his fleet of Brigadiers. He passed battalions of lifeless vessels before stopping in front of a particular set of Ochre Brigadiers. Looking at them, he felt great pride, for these Brigadiers were of a superior design, twice as fast and deadly as the old models. He had gathered some of the brightest minds on the continent to create them, before taking their lives so they wouldn't share the vessels' weaknesses.

After contemplating his newest creations, Asedia paid a visit to the general's quarters, where Samuel was busy interrogating a prisoner. It was not the duty of an imperial general, but he enjoyed it. Wearing brass knuckles, Samuel pounded away at the prisoner, who dripped blood as if he were a piece of raw meat.

"Maybe you're ready to talk now?" Samuel asked, whaling away with his knuckles. "Tell us what this is."

The general took out a blue sash embroidered with circles and stars and held it aloft with both hands.

The man, whose eyes could barely open, remained silent. He held his chin up at his torturer. His hands stayed tied behind his back.

Infuriated by the lack of a response, Samuel punched the man in the gut.

"If you talk, we'll let you live. If you swear loyalty to His Imperial Majesty, we will offer you a place in our army." Samuel used his snake-charmer voice. "Who are you loyal to?"

The man looked up. "You and your bastard emperor can go to hell!" He spat blood at Asedia's feet.

Samuel proceeded with the torture, breaking the prisoner's leg. Having seen enough, Asedia intervened. He raised his censer at the man. It emitted a bright light and a shriek. The astral force of the man abandoned his body and entered the object. An empty vessel, his body slammed against the floor. Asedia then took out his spherite and covered the body with freezing stone. Soon, the body was a distorted statue, forever frozen in an expression of terror.

Silence ensued.

"Your Majesty," Samuel finally spoke. His bloodied hands twitched. "He was about to give in."

"He was not," Asedia said, placing his censer on a table. Tools, bolts, scraps of metal, and blueprints were illuminated by the glow of the astral force. "Like they didn't." He gestured at a pile of corpses wearing similar red-stained sashes. Asedia slid his fingers down the blue sash that Samuel had held up in front of the prisoner.

"Azahar silk . . . imbued with magic."

"Magic? I thought our Windergalese allies had annihilated all threatening magic within the empire." Samuel rubbed blood off his bare head. "What does it mean, Your Majesty?"

"It means that the time has come to strike." Asedia tied the sash around the statue's distorted neck. "The town might be insignificant, but I fear that an enemy might be taking advantage of its protection."

"My lord?"

"What is the status of plan eighty-six?" He thought once more of his monstrous metal soldiers and the new levels of harm they could reach.

"It was successfully finished a few days ago," Samuel answered. "But as I said before, we lack the power to make it work."

"And as I told you then, I have the solution." From the folds of his cloak, Asedia took out a spherical object, the fire spherite that used to belong to King Beckel.

"Another one?" Samuel gasped. "How did Your Majesty acquire it?"

"An old friend of mine." He grinned. "With this in our possession, we will have all the power we need."

"If I may ask," Samuel said, "does Your Majesty believe that what you've been looking for all these years is there in the forest?"

"Remember that the best place to hide something is right under a person's nose."

Samuel brought his hand to his chest. "Then I shall not rest until Your Majesty possesses what you most desire."

Back in the palace, the emperor sat on his throne in silence. The palace's outer walls were bathed in the amber light of twilight, while its inside was filled with beautiful melodies and ghastly astral apparitions. The whole household remained in complete silence. Not a single soul dared to move or make a noise. Anyone who dared to disrupt the atmosphere was gravely punished.

Asedia looked upon his court. Markeus was behind the piano. He was a true virtuoso, as he ought to be—Asedia had brought the greatest pianists from all over the world to tutor him. His fingers moved like hummingbirds across the keys, every note filled with passion.

The emperor enjoyed the soothing sound of the piano. What memories those songs brought back to him! Memories both happy and sad. Memories of love and treason. Listening to his son play always put him in a generous mood.

When the music ended, everyone applauded lightly, careful not to overshadow Asedia's loud applause.

"Markeus, come to me," Asedia finally called to his son.

Markeus left the piano and stood before the emperor. "Yes, Father?"

"You begged for a chance to prove your worth," Asedia said. "Here's your opportunity." He stood up. "What would you be willing to do for me and Zaphyrelia?"

"I would lie, steal, and kill. I would travel to the end of the world and back," Markeus responded without a moment's hesitation. "Name your wish and consider it done, Father."

Asedia's face was distorted by a twisted grin.

"I shall give you a task. A test, we'll call it. If you succeed, you will finally validate your claim to my throne. If you fail, you will face grave consequences."

"I am ready," answered the prince. "I won't let you down."

"What do you know of a place called Azahar?"

"It's an insignificant town inside a forest filled with traitors and cowards," Markeus recited. "It was never conquered, so you made sure it was forgotten."

"Indeed," Asedia said. "Why was it never conquered?"

"Some sort of sorcery made it impossible."

"Yes, a barrier, one I have long sought to shatter. The wait is finally over. I need you to conquer Azahar, with General Indolett by your side. Take as many men as you need; burn the town to ashes; assassinate every man, woman, and child; and bring me whatever treasures you can find and the head of their precious deity."

"I will." Markeus knelt, bringing his fist to his chest.

"My son, always remember that you are an Asedia. All those years of arduous training and sacrifice have led you to this, your final examination." He went to his son. "You were born a flawed Belecrose, yes, but I have given you strength and greatness. If you use them as you should, you will then be victorious and reborn as the man I know you can be."

"Yes, Father," Markeus answered solemnly.

"And to make sure you succeed," Asedia continued, gesturing to the marchioness of Pavkov and Iren, "I present to you a gift. The final stroke of this masterpiece of mine."

The marchioness, looking like a disgraced swallow in her countenance, held up a chest.

Asedia opened it and, with a soft touch, took out a rusty object.

"Is that a . . . ?"

"Yes," Asedia said. "With this, you shall be the most powerful weapon ever created. Make me proud."

CHAPTER 31

ENLIGHTENED

Fanfare and the shouts of adoring multitudes filled the air as the Carmine archbishop dressed the prince in a tunic made from the finest gold threads. Drums played and cups clinked as Audric knelt on a purple cushion, his court watching his every move. Cannonballs flew through the air and sabers rose when the archbishop painted Audric's face with holy oils and handed him his scepter and orb.

The archbishop lifted the crown from its resting place, purifying it in sunrays filtered through stained glass. The archbishop placed the crown, heavy with the weight of the metal it was made from and the duty it represented, upon the head of the prince. When the rites had been chanted, the archbishop spoke.

"To the citizens of the Carmine lands, I present the shining light, the providential strength and wisdom. His Royal Majesty, Pyrone Audric Johann II!"

Time stilled for a moment. Audric stood before his people as a father.

"From this moment onward, I swear, as Providence is my witness, that I shall live for my people and the ideals that have made our nation what it is. I beg Providence for wisdom, and to you who bestow your faith upon me, there will be no time, day or night, when I do not think about your well-being."

The court burst into applause.

"My first royal decree," Audric said, "will be to break all ties to Asedia's Zaphyrelia. Asedia will no longer lurk in our shadows and steal our peace. Therefore, the production of Ochre Brigadiers has been forever banned."

The court cheered. Bells chimed, and the whole country began to celebrate. Joy and laughter took over the throne room.

The day of the coronation, Dashiel was called in for an audience with the king.

"My king?" Dashiel waved his hand, trying to keep a solemn expression. "You called for me?"

"My men and I have searched everywhere, but my brother and the spherite are nowhere to be found." Audric's concern shone through.

Dashiel went cold. "He's alive?"

"I'm afraid so," Audric said. "We'll keep looking. My brother must pay for his crimes, and the spherite must aid the Cobalt Phantasms."

"Have you found out anything about Tullie?" Dashiel asked, eager to talk about something other than the grim possibility of the spherite falling into the wrong hands. His gaze landed on a painting of a past Carmine pyrone.

Audric shook his head. "Not a single clue. I have decided that, once my country is back on its feet, I will search for her myself and bring her home with me, where she belongs."

"I wish you the best of luck, Audric." Dashiel bowed his head. "I am to leave soon. I will never forget you."

"You're leaving?" Audric held his breath. The palace lanterns projected various shades of red onto his face. "So soon?"

"I must." Dashiel's shoulders drooped. "There is so much to be done. Zaphyrelia is still poisoned by Asedia and his sympathizers.

People are still suffering. Also, I'd like to think that everything I do for the Cobalt Phantasms keeps Azahar safe."

Many good things had taken place—Audric had even knighted Dashiel—but he was still tormented by doubt. The fear of not living up to his family name lurked in the back of his head. He constantly told himself to stop worrying, but he still wondered what quest or action would finally prove his worth.

"Your heart is too pure for this world, my friend." Audric chuckled. "What is Ermine Squadron's next move?"

"I asked Master Roderigo to reopen Carbakiel's base and assign my squadron to it. He accepted, as he was very pleased with our performance here," Dashiel said, wandering around the audience chamber.

"Why there?" the king asked with a stern look.

"I made a promise to a close friend," Dashiel said, hope ringing with every word. "I'll tell him the good news when we return to the palacette."

"I understand . . . I will never forget you or your service, my brave knight. Without you, none of this would have happened," Audric said. "My kingdom and I are in great debt to you. The doors will always be open, and if there is anything that my crown can grant you, any wish, please tell me, and it shall be yours."

Audric had done so much for him already. Dashiel did not want to take advantage of his friend, but there was something that stole his peace of mind.

"As it just so happens, maybe there's one thing you can do for me."

Dashiel whispered his request, so nobody outside the chamber could hear.

"Say no more." Audric clapped contentedly. "To the treasure chamber."

At the Founding Chapter's request, all Cobalt Phantasms were to return to their bases in Zaphyrelia. Dashiel and the others exchanged goodbyes with the new Carmine king and allies, and the loaded wagons departed. Within a few days, the Carmine pine trees receded from view, and the landscape was reduced to magnificent, flowery Zaphyrolean plains.

One night before arriving at the Ilver Mountains, Dashiel stayed up late, watching the stars above. His hand rested in his vest's pocket, protecting what Audric had granted him. He scooted beneath the roof of his wagon, where his companions rested. Sofia snored as she slept on top of the supply baskets. Amore hung from one of the wooden boards overhead, rocking herself to sleep.

Dashiel turned to Sylvain, who had positioned himself in a meditative pose. He worried when Sylvain started to mumble strange things and shake his head. Concerned, Dashiel crawled to his friend. "Sylvain?"

His friend opened his eyes and gasped, startling Dashiel. Sylvain's green irises shone brightly in the moonlight.

"Are you all right?" Dashiel asked. "You must've fallen asleep."

"Yes, yes, I'm fine." Sylvain was quick to calm himself. "That must be it." He stretched and lit an oil lamp. "Just a nightmare."

Dashiel sat next to his friend. He tried to fall asleep but couldn't manage to do so. He gave the inside of the wagon another look. Sylvain's bandaged hand caught his attention.

"What happened to your hand?" Dashiel asked.

Sylvain reached for one of his books. "I hurt it when I cleaned my crossbow this morning." He glued his eyes to the darkened pages.

"Nightmares? Hurting yourself with your crossbow?" Dashiel chuckled. "You're acting weird."

"I'm really tired." Sylvain slid his hand down his face. "You should get some sleep too. You look terrible when you don't."

He meant it as a joke, but his words fell flat. He wouldn't even make eye contact with Dashiel.

"I can't sleep. I'm too anxious," Dashiel said, his leg shaking. "Too restless."

"Why? We helped Audric and saved his country. I thought you'd be happy." Sylvain finally lowered his book.

"I am, but I can't wait to get back to the palacette." Dashiel rubbed his arm with his hand, shivering. "Back to Athenai."

"Oh," Sylvain said coldly. "Her."

Dashiel sat up straight. "Do you have something you want to say?" he asked, raising his voice slightly. "It's kind of obvious you don't like her."

"I never said I didn't like her," Sylvain answered. "I don't care that much about her."

"I wish you did."

"Why is that so important to you?" Sylvain was as annoyed as Dashiel had ever seen him.

Dashiel rummaged inside his pocket. He pulled out a silver ring with a center stone as small as a raindrop. "Because I want you to be my best man."

"Wait, what?" Sylvain was unable to hide his dislike and exasperation.

Dashiel's face fell. "I imagined your reaction a little differently."

"How did you expect me to react to this?"

"I thought you'd be a bit happier? I found the girl I want to spend the rest of my life with." He held the ring up. When a moonbeam caressed the tiny stone, specks of light appeared all over the wagon.

"Don't you think you're taking things too fast? You're still a boy."

"My father married my mother at a young age." Dashiel wore a dreamy expression. "Athenai will never lack for a heart full of love, Sylvain. I just know the time is right. When I'm with her, I don't feel like a boy. I feel like I could do or be anything I want."

"Dashiel, you can't provide for her and her family, let alone protect them, with a loving heart. A commitment of such proportions requires a lot more than that." Sylvain held his book with one hand and patted it repeatedly with the other.

"I might not have a cent to my name or an army at my disposal, but I'll work hard. I will never stop until her wants and desires are fulfilled."

Sylvain put his book aside.

"You aren't thinking things through." Sylvain huffed. "Are you aware that your children will inevitably be born Alferai? They will not be human."

Dashiel's eyes twinkled. "I don't mind."

"Have you thought about the Alferai curse?"

"The Alferai curse?"

"The lover of an Alferai dies when an heir enters the world. Are you really willing to lose your life for an Alferai child?"

"That's an old wives' tale," Dashiel said. "But if my fate is to die, then so be it, as long as I am next to Athenai."

Sylvain shook his head in disbelief. "Are you mad?!" He raised his voice, almost waking Sofia. "You can't marry her. She isn't right for you."

Annoyance besieged Dashiel, hardening his voice. "What do you know about who's right for me? You're supposed to be my friend. Why won't you support my decision?"

"Because I know things, Dashiel. I know things that you don't."

"What things?" Dashiel put his ring away, vanishing the light that had showered the wagon's walls.

"Dashiel, I'm not . . ."

"What things?" he insisted. "If you really are my friend, you'll tell me."

Sylvain gave a resigned sigh.

"Sylvain?" Dashiel prompted.

"She's been unfaithful to you," he finally said. "Athenai has been lying to you."

Dashiel shook his head. "Is this one of your jokes? Because you are *not* funny. You're acting like a real jerk."

"No joke," Sylvain said, dead serious. "She's not who you think she is."

He opened his rucksack and rummaged inside until he found two letters. One was folded into a butterfly, the other into a crane.

"I didn't know how to tell you. I wanted to save you the suffering." He handed the letters to Dashiel. "But things have become worse than I expected."

Dashiel's hands trembled as he received the letters, recognizing the stationery, handwriting, and scent. "Where did you get these?"

"After I found out that you had been exchanging letters with her, I became suspicious. It seemed possible that she could be an Asedian spy. Before leaving for the Carmine Kingdom, I took a peek at her desk and came across these."

"You did what?! She's no spy!"

"I'm sorry for not telling you before. You're my only friend." Sylvain looked away. "I didn't want you to get hurt."

Still in disbelief, Dashiel began to read the first letter.

By the end of the missive, Dashiel's throat had slammed shut, and the world had seemingly turned black.

CHAPTER 32

COLD STREAK

ashiel hadn't been able to sleep at all for days. He didn't dare close his eyes for longer than a couple seconds. When he did, all he could see were the poisonous words written in those letters. He felt as if his body were controlled by a puppeteer. His feet and hands moved, but they were clumsy and failed to perform even the most basic tasks.

The letter's words echoed in his head as the stone doors of the palacette opened before him.

My Dear Love . . .

The palacette's courtyard was full of ghosts. Their faces were blurry, their dialogue incomprehensible. They stared at him and mocked him. He could only walk past them, wishing that they would stop tormenting him.

How I crave your presence . . . I yearn to delight my senses with you . . .

The sounds around him disappeared for a moment, as if the world had come to an end. His heartbeat and breathing synced to a slow, mournful beat. He had received, read, and reread countless letters from Athenai, all full of her mystical prose and precious calligraphy.

But none of the letters addressed to him, which he had held as proof of their connection, had ever exuded such passion.

That idiot remains clueless about us . . . He truly believes I have feelings for him. He has nothing on you . . .

He reached the staircase and began to climb.

I know you don't like me speaking of him, but you are going to laugh at this. He's a hemocarcomist that pretends to be a Cobalt Phantasm. He told me that he dreaded his birthday. What kind of fool dreads his own birthday?

One of the ghosts approached him and stood in his way. Dashiel didn't care to recognize who it was. He could hear its annoying mumbling.

Dashiel is leaving for Carmine Kingdom soon, and this spring is to be the most beautiful yet. I'll be waiting for you in my chambers every afternoon until his return . . .

Dashiel became more and more annoyed as the ghost failed to budge.

"Get out of my way!" Dashiel roared. He made to push the ghost aside, but it took the hint. It moved out of the way, and he rushed up the final flight of stairs.

Forever Yours,

Athenai

Dashiel's heart pounded against his chest with the force of a locomotive. He felt as if his body did not belong to him anymore. His knees threatened to buckle with every step. He had entered delirium. Moments earlier, he had clung to a faint hope that this was all a misunderstanding. But that hope dissipated as he reached the top of the stairs and turned down the final hallway to Athenai's chambers.

During his journey back to the Ilver Mountains, Dashiel had sent a letter to Athenai stating that he would arrive the following day. He had asked his companions to speed up their voyage to reach the palacette a day in advance. To finally unveil the truth.

The gargoyles who watched the doors to Athenai's chambers had been instructed to always allow Dashiel's entry, so they merely stood by as he approached. Eager to know the truth once and for all, he shoved the doors open.

As he entered, he faced in real life an image that he had conjured constantly in his head since reading the letters. Athenai was there, and next to her was the man whom his heart had cursed over and over during sleepless nights.

It was Sebastian Calabel, a man he had met months before.

"Dashiel!" Athenai exclaimed happily, without a trace of shame. "You've returned early!" She ran to embrace him, but he stepped aside.

"What's going on?" She gave him a baffled look.

"Who would've thought?" Sebastian's voice rang out from the other side of the room. "A pleasure to see you again, Mr. Ermitage."

Sebastian walked toward Dashiel, but his approach was quickly halted by the point of a doizemant.

"You!" Dashiel swung his baton at the ambassador, nearly hitting him.

"Dashiel!" Athenai screeched.

Sebastian was quick to grab a coffee table to shield himself. "What are you on about, Ermitage?"

"Shut up!" Dashiel kept attacking him.

"Dashiel, please stop!" Athenai's pained cries nearly caused Dashiel to lower his weapon.

He could not recognize his own behavior. Whatever had possessed him to act this way was beyond his understanding. He had to obey his pain.

Seeing that he wouldn't stop, Athenai snapped her fingers, creating a violet light that wrapped around Dashiel's doizemant and froze it in midair.

"Sebastian, please leave us." Athenai's tone was authoritative.

"Forget that," Sebastian told her. "I'm not leaving you alone with him. He's gone mad."

"It's fine. I'll be fine," she responded, doing her best to affect a calm voice. "Please, Sebastian. It appears Dashiel and I have matters to discuss."

Sebastian sighed. "I'll respect your wishes. But please, Ermitage, think about what you're doing." He slowly made his way to the exit and closed the door behind him, his eyes never leaving Dashiel's doizemant.

"You're so affectionate with each other," Dashiel mocked. "Makes me want to vomit."

"What is going on with you?" Athenai asked, voice laced with irritation. "Seriously, what's your problem?"

"You two are my problem! I came back hoping that it was all a lie, but I've seen it with my own eyes. It's all true. Every single word."

"Sebastian and I? He's a friend of mine."

"Don't lie! You two have been making a fool of me." He remembered the letters that Sylvain had given him, word for word. "Why aren't you brave enough to tell me the truth? Don't you owe me at least that much?"

"He is very important to me, but not the way you imagine," she explained. "Sebastian and I have been friends since we were children. Two years ago, when my mother passed away, I found great solace in him. We care deeply for each other, but we are only good friends. He only came to deliver an important message."

"Liar," Dashiel repeated.

"But it's the truth!" she said. "If there were a way to make you understand . . ."

Fueled by pain and sadness, Dashiel grabbed Athenai by the arms. "Tell me the truth!"

"Let go of me!" Athenai wiggled in his grip. "You're hurting me!"

In that moment, their eyes met. Dashiel's heart and mind pulled him in two directions. There had never been a time in which confusion and pain entwined with such perfection. His arms lost all strength. He let go of her.

"I never wanted to hurt you. Just tell me the truth." His knees stopped obeying his command and bent to the floor. "Please, Athenai."

Her breath was shallow. Her eyes were wide.

"Dashiel," she cried. "You have to believe me. I never wrote such an indecorous letter, and neither did Sebastian!"

A chill ran down his spine.

"I never said anything about the letters," Dashiel whispered. He pulled himself to his feet.

Athenai seemed to realize what had happened at the same time as he did. "I'm sorry . . ." Her eyes didn't dare to meet his. "I didn't mean to . . ."

"You went inside my mind?"

"You . . . you weren't yourself," she stammered. "You seemed like you'd gone mad. I was frightened!"

She slowly approached him. When she got too close, he sprang backward.

"Don't come near me," Dashiel yelled. "And stay the hell out of my head!"

"But I never . . ."

"You promised you would never do that to me." He inched away from her. "Who knows how many other lies I've fallen for."

"What? It was an accident! It was just a reflex, Dashiel. A defense mechanism. You scared me."

"I won't fall for your lies, not anymore." Dashiel screamed, fueled by desperation. "You have no honor!"

"You're being hurtful now," she said, tears in her eyes.

"*I'm* the one who's hurtful?" he scoffed. "Tell me, what was I? A puppet for your shameful desires? What does he have that I don't?"

"Stop it!"

"I gave you all of myself. I told you everything about me, but you were laughing at me this whole time. Maybe you should read my mind right now. That'll save time. You'll find out how much I detest you."

Athenai's tear-stained face turned to exasperation. "Dashiel, there's no reason for you to act like this. You're acting like a child."

"I guess that's what love does to you!" He clenched his fists. "But I wouldn't expect a wicked witch like you to understand that."

Athenai slapped him across the face. He imagined a red handprint blooming on his cheek as it began to warm.

"Leave me," Athenai whispered. "You are an imbecile. I thought you were intelligent, but you've shown me that you're just a small-minded child. You know nothing, Dashiel Ermitage, and you will live to regret those words."

Dashiel stared at her. He wanted to believe her, but nothing made sense. The only thing he could be certain of was that she had betrayed his trust. He wanted to embrace her and never let go, but he feared he would fall for her deceit again. He wanted to declare his love for her, but his memories of those words were no longer sweet but sour. They had gone beyond the point of no return. Both sides had shot words in this duel, and—just like bullets—there was no way to take them back.

"Get out. NOW!"

As if spurred by her shout, the bricks of the floor began to rise. They formed a wall, which pushed Dashiel out of the bedchambers. The doors shut tight, and both guardian gargoyles blocked them.

"I don't want to see you ever again!" Athenai shouted from the other side of the door.

"Fine by me," he whispered, a single tear trickling down his face like a shooting star.

A part of him was shattered by what he had done, but the other part was relieved that it was over and that he had exposed a lie that would have otherwise killed him with sadness. His heart ached with regret and longing, but the evidence spoke for itself, and that helped him cope with his emotions. He felt a strange peace. But was it really peace? He told himself that it was, and if it wasn't, it felt good enough to keep him on track. He walked away and did not look back. He let go of everything. His heart had been crushed to dust, but at the very least, he had defended his dignity.

Dashiel spent the rest of the day lying on his bed. Exhaustion had petrified him. He could scarcely move. In his mind, he relived the fight with Athenai. Still livid, he convinced his mind, over and over again, that it was for the best. His memories of their confrontation had become so muddled that time had started to tamper with them. Every time he thought about the fight, a different version would appear for him to contemplate.

His rest was interrupted by a firm knock on the door. Dashiel took his time to open it, and when he did, his rucksack and Orphée's case flew inside, landing on the floor. Sofia appeared, holding Amore's egg in her hands.

"Why would you leave your junk in the wagon? I had to carry all this!" Sofia let herself into the room and placed the jewel box on the nightstand. "Next time, I'll throw your stuff into the pits."

"By all means, Sofia, make yourself at home."

"You should leave sarcasm to someone who can handle it, forest boy." She took a seat on Sylvain's bed.

She waited for him to say something, but Dashiel remained in sullen silence, staring at the ceiling.

"What's the matter?"

"It seems Athenai was cheating on me. I confronted her," Dashiel said, his eyes moving from one side to the other. "It did *not* go well."

"You can't be stupid enough to believe that." Sofia gestured desperately with her hands. "I don't know her well, but it's obvious she is extremely fond of you. Why must you ruin everything?"

"Well, see for yourself." He handed her the letters Sylvain had given him. "It seems they've been exchanging letters for some time. Athenai and Sebastian Calabel," he explained. "It's her handwriting. I recognize it."

Sofia read Athenai's letter, and then she read Sebastian's.

"How fake," she growled.

"I know. I didn't see through the game she was playing."

"No, you fool. The letter supposedly written by Sebastian is fake."

"What?" Dashiel sprang up. "It can't be."

"It can be," Sofia answered, scanning the letters for a second time.

"How do you know?"

Sofia became silent.

"I-I . . ." She looked away. "I've been getting letters from Sebastian lately."

"He sent you letters?"

"None of your business." Her cheeks turned apple red. She studied him for a moment and then, with a sigh, removed a paper crane from her pocket. "I got this one today."

Dashiel took the letter and, ignoring its contents, studied the handwriting. He returned to the other one. They didn't match.

"It *is* a fake . . ." he declared.

"Who gave it to you?" Sofia snatched the fake letter from Dashiel's trembling hands.

"Sylvain. He said he found them on her desk."

"It seems like he fell into someone's trap." Sofia crushed the paper. "Come on, Aurante. I thought you were smarter than this."

By now, he knew Athenai's handwriting like the palm of his hand, but he was desperate to know the truth. He took out one of the letters he had received from her and set it beside the one he was given. As much as he tried, he couldn't find an anomaly. It was more than obvious that they matched. The urge to tear both letters to pieces and proceed with his life seduced him. He decided to give them one last look.

The size of the letters, the length of the loops, and the pressure of the strokes were identical. Even the commas and the dots were the same.

He recalled the pain of their separation. It was time to give up.

His gaze wandered to the bottom of the letter, and he ran his finger over Athenai's name, a final goodbye. Something caught his attention. The first letter of her name, the *a*, was slanted. He blinked to clear his sight. Athenai's *a* was indeed slanted. Sebastian's *a* was slanted. All of the *a*'s on the sheet were slanted.

It was then that it hit him.

The words of Master Roderigo echoed.

"They're quite helpful. A simple trick given by our Alferai allies . . . They can imitate your handwriting, except for the a's. Those are terribly slanted."

The words of Junei.

"Those documents won't write and sign themselves."

The words of Athenai.

"Let our glove spell do the job. Would you please guide them, Junei?"

"This is also a fake!" Dashiel said, starting to hyperventilate.

"Oh, Dashiel." Sofia's eyes were full of pity. "You're so dumb."

"The biggest imbecile in the world," he said, the remains of his broken world collapsing.

"Who would do such a thing?" Sofia asked. But Dashiel was already slipping out the door.

Dashiel stormed through the entire palacette until he found the cold beauty that had brought so much pain to his existence.

"Junei!" Filled with rage, Dashiel's voice caused a nearby vase to shake.

Junei walked up a flight of stairs and smiled at the sight of Dashiel.

"Good evening, Mr. Ermitage. Is there anything I can assist you with?"

His nostrils flared. "Did you write these letters?" He flapped the letters in front of her face.

"Yes, I did." Her expression exuded pride as she batted the letters aside. "And they worked like a charm."

"Why?"

"I've spent my whole life protecting my sister from insects like you." Junei grabbed her skirt and climbed up two steps.

"Like me?"

"What can you offer her? A shack in a stinking forest?" she scoffed. "You are of no use to her. You are a penniless joke. Now that she's free, she'll find someone of high birth, someone who will provide wealth and protection for her and her family."

"Why would you ever hurt your sister like that?"

"Siblings do whatever it takes to protect their kin."

"But you—"

"Stop blaming me!" Junei cawed, interrupting Dashiel. "I only showed her the truth behind this cute facade. I wrote the letters and arranged Sebastian's visit. You did the rest. Let's say I made a bet on destiny, too, and I won." She smirked. "If you're looking for someone to blame, look in the mirror. You were the one who rose to the bait. You were the one who yelled things you can't take back. If I were you, I would be more careful. Words have proven themselves deadlier than the edge of an arrow."

Dashiel grabbed her arm. "You're coming with me. You've got some explaining to do."

"I'll do nothing of the sort." She freed herself of his grip.

"I'll make you."

"Don't you even try," Junei said. "My gargoyles are not like my sister's. They'll shred you into pieces if you dare to touch me again."

True to her word, Junei's protectors began to growl in the shadows of the high ceilings.

"You must be the lowest and wickedest being in the world." Dashiel clenched his teeth. "You will *not* get away with this."

"Oh, but I already have. And you helped me!" She winked and walked away. Before she could get too far, she turned back to him. "One final thing. Please thank Sylvain for the marvelous idea. He is a genius."

Junei kept walking with an air of satisfaction as Dashiel's head caught fire. He didn't want to believe her words, but the pieces fit so perfectly together. He had learned a bitter lesson and a painful truth.

CHAPTER 33

BREAKING POINT

ashiel tried, and he failed; he tried, and he failed. During every attempt he made to reach Athenai's chambers, the gargoyles sent him flying away. He called her name a thousand times, and a thousand times he was ignored. Without a doubt, he had messed things up this time. He had let his jealousy get the best of him. Would she ever forgive him? He asked himself that question every time he tried to talk to her, but with every failure, the answer was clearly no.

His thoughts tormented him.

He leaned against one of the balcony pillars, looking out on the palacette below. In his mind's eye, he imagined Athenai crying, suffering because of him. He saw Junei mocking him for falling into her trap. He saw Sylvain looking at him with his kind eyes. His stupid, traitorous eyes. Dashiel punched the marble handrail many times. If it hadn't been for the dermangolin pills, his hands would have been bathed in blood, and his secret would have been revealed.

Dashiel then remembered that the pills had almost ran out but asking the traitor for more was out of the question.

He cursed his "friend" in every possible way as he hunted him down. He searched all day, but Sylvain was nowhere to be found.

Finally, at sunset, he saw Sylvain in the courtyard. On the verge of madness, Dashiel made his way down to confront his former friend. He pushed people out of his way. He jumped down flights of stairs. He raced through the long corridors.

He finally arrived at the courtyard and stood face-to-face with Sylvain.

Sylvain moved slowly, meditating as usual. He held his bandaged hands together and chanted to himself. He noticed Dashiel, but he ignored him.

Dashiel grabbed him by the shoulder, seething with rage. He barely had control over his body. "How could you do that to me? You knew she was everything to me. Why?"

He punched Sylvain in the face.

Sylvain didn't flinch. He stood tall. He seemed to absorb Dashiel's attack, which made Dashiel angrier.

"Dashiel, please, not now." Sylvain tried to avoid Dashiel. "We can talk later."

"Now, you son of a smartlapper!" Dashiel yelled, drawing the attention of those around them. "Did you really think I was so stupid that I'd never find out?"

He tried to kick his friend, but Sylvain reached out a hand and blocked the blow.

"Please, listen to me." His heavy breathing made Dashiel's hair flutter. "We can talk this out, I promise you. But not right now."

"Are you scared of me? Is that it?" Dashiel pushed Sylvain's shoulder with force.

"Enough."

Dashiel punched Sylvain again. "Are you not man enough to defend yourself?"

"I said, *enough*!" Sylvain's muscles tensed, and hundreds of veins appeared all over his body. His pupils contracted until they were barely visible.

Dashiel flinched at Sylvain's transformation, but he couldn't back down. There was still so much anger within him. He adopted an offensive position. "Fight, you coward!"

A crowd of Alferai girls and humans gathered around them, obstructing any escape.

Dashiel landed another punch.

"You want a fight?" Sylvain growled. His fingers twitched. His pupils had disappeared for good. "You'll get one."

In a fraction of a second, one of Sylvain's fists traveled past Dashiel's head, creating a gust of wind that made the palacette torchlights flicker. If it had hit Dashiel, he would have died.

"That was just a warning." Sylvain's distorted voice rang loud. As he stepped forward, the floor cracked, as if his weight had increased tenfold. "Yield, Dashiel, or I will cause some serious damage."

"Don't hold back, then," Dashiel said, running toward Sylvain.

He punched his friend in the gut several times, but it didn't seem to affect Sylvain at all. With a single movement of his arm, Sylvain sent Dashiel flying to the edge of the circle of spectators. Dashiel stood up and waited for the right moment to attack again. He had never seen such force.

Dashiel and Sylvain began to exchange blows.

"Dashiel! Sylvain!" Sofia made her way through the people. "Stop it this very instant! You're Cobalt Phantasms—you're squad mates. Fighting among us is forbidden!" she yelled, but both Dashiel and Sylvain ignored her words. They continued battling. "You idiots have to stop!"

"I'm not afraid of you, Sylvain," Dashiel said. "I'll avenge my honor, even if it's the last thing I do."

"IT WILL BE THE LAST THING YOU DO." Sylvain's voice was demonic.

The sound of the fight and the roar of the audience filled the palacette.

Sylvain was so fast that the mere suggestion of an attack made Dashiel stumble.

When she found an opportunity, Sofia entered the fray. She tried to separate the two, but the brush of Sylvain's arm launched her to the floor.

Distracted by Sofia's fall, Dashiel didn't notice Sylvain's attack until it was too late. His friend's hand locked around his neck. Dashiel could hardly breathe, but he kept fighting. Sylvain lifted him and tightened his grip. Dashiel's eyes widened in fear. At first he thought that the Sylvain he knew was forever gone, but it crossed his mind that maybe Sylvain had always been like this, a monster.

"Sylvain, no!" Sofia cried, still on the ground.

Dashiel couldn't breathe anymore. The world around him began to turn dark. His throat tingled, crushed little by little. An agonizing ringing in his ears announced his defeat. "Maybe . . . this is for the best," he whispered. Dashiel's arms and feet stopped moving, hanging from his body like abandoned puppets.

A voice rang through the crowd. "Out of the way! Out of the way!" Through the haze that was darkening his vision, Dashiel saw Roderigo, followed by Professor Grasshop and Hugont. Roderigo gasped as he took in the horrific scene.

"Sylvain," he said softly, not wanting to enrage the being in front of him. "Sylvain, listen to me. Please put him down. Let him go." The master spoke calmly and gently.

Sylvain's strength seemed to keep increasing. He looked at Roderigo with a beastly expression. His nostrils flared.

"Please, Sylvain. You are going to kill him."

Sylvain reacted to these words.

You are going to kill him. You are going to kill him.

His irises grew back, and his protruding veins blended into his skin once more. He quickly let go of Dashiel, who fell to the ground.

Sofia rushed to his side. She checked his pulse. "I can barely feel a thing."

His mentor's muffled voice was the last thing Dashiel heard before he lost consciousness.

✿

Sylvain stared at his hand. Its veins had deflated. He couldn't remember what had happened. He was traumatized to find Dashiel lying on the floor, his neck covered with a red handprint. His own handprint.

"Dashiel?" Sylvain said, dizzily backing away.

"He needs help. *Right now!*" Sofia's alarmed voice filled the courtyard.

Roderigo took charge. "Professor Grasshop, please help Ermitage up to the infirmary. Sofia, go with him."

Sylvain watched with disbelief as Dashiel was carried away. "What have I done?" he mumbled.

"You tell me," Roderigo demanded, anger in his voice. "Do you realize what you could have done?"

Sylvain did not answer. He quickly took the bandage off his hand and stared at it frightfully.

"No, no, no . . ." he mumbled. He closed his eyes and tried to calm down, but it was no use.

"THERE IS NOTHING TO SEE HERE. DISPERSE!" Professor Grasshop shouted to the people around them. "Fly away, fly away!"

Roderigo turned to Sylvain.

"Come with me immediately. You two are in serious trouble."

CHAPTER 34

IRREVERSIBLE

When he recovered from his injuries, Dashiel met with Roderigo in the same room where the Founding Chapter had gathered. He was accused of disturbing the peace of a host base, fighting another Phantasm, and utterly disobeying the orders of a commander. Sofia tried to argue in his favor, but she was ordered not to interfere. When Roderigo asked if he had something to say in his defense, Dashiel remained silent. With heavy disappointment in his eyes, the founder of the Cobalt Phantasms informed Dashiel that he had been forever expelled from the order. He was to return home at dawn.

After his expulsion, Dashiel locked himself in his room so no unwanted visitors could barge in. He angrily threw his things into his rucksack as Amore watched, confused by his behavior. He placed his baton in its case, and it too went into his bag.

As he emptied the drawer of his nightstand, he came across the crystal bottle that, until the start of that week, had held his derman-golin pills. Only one remained now. He had meant to ask Sylvain for more pills, but things had happened—things neither of them could take back. In the end, it didn't matter if he was exposed as a hemocarc-omist; there was no reason to hide his secret anymore.

Dashiel looked at the bottle, and reflected back were memories of the traitor he had once considered his best friend. Filled with rage, he spiked the bottle on the floor. It shattered into countless pieces. He returned to the nightstand and began to pack the rest of his things. He turned to the jewel box. Amore quickly shut herself inside the egg.

"Amore, we are leaving." Dashiel knocked on the lid. The scarlet vanity refused to open it.

"Come on, we need to leave. Now!" he urged, but to no avail.

He knelt down and softly tried to force the egg open.

"I'm sorry, all right? I didn't mean for any of this to happen," he said. "Please come out."

The flower reached out one of her thorny vines and pricked his hand. She knew about his fight with Athenai, and her behavior toward her owner had become rather erratic.

"Fine!" Dashiel stood up, annoyed by her shenanigans. "Never come out. I don't care . . ." Dashiel dropped the box inside his rucksack. "But you're coming with me."

Soon, all his belongings were packed, except for the sash, the journal, and the badge, Cobalt Phantasm mementos that he was instructed to leave behind.

He left his room and made his way to the courtyard. All eyes darted his way. Everyone had witnessed the fight, and while the event was a blur to Dashiel, they perfectly remembered the scandal he had caused.

As the palacette doors opened, he looked back. His eyes naturally landed on Athenai's balcony. He wished with all his might that Athenai would come out, that she would let him explain his stupidity. There weren't enough words in the world to earn her forgiveness. She was right. He would always regret what he had said to her.

His insides squeezed as he walked into the cavern and the doors behind him shut tight. His loneliness made the cavern darker and colder. Clutching his belongings, he stepped onto the dark and hopeless trail.

"Dashiel!" Sylvain's voice called from behind him. His footsteps sounded on the hard ground. "Dashiel, wait!"

"Leave me alone." Dashiel kept walking. "You're the last person I want to see."

Sylvain pulled up alongside him. He scrubbed a hand over his face. "I'm sorry, all right? I shouldn't have done that to you." He winced.

Dashiel wanted to put on a mad face, but his disappointment and shame were too strong. Sylvain's expression seemed genuine, but Dashiel was not going to fall for it again.

"A little too late for that." Dashiel kept walking. His hand could barely hold on to the strap of his rucksack. "Go back."

"If it makes you feel any better, I was also expelled from the order."

Dashiel halted. "Thanks, Sylvain! That really doesn't make me feel any better."

Sylvain's trembling eyes welled up. "I was the worst friend in the world."

"That's an understatement."

Sylvain flinched. His eyes were filled with hurt and resignation. "You trusted me, and I failed you. I understand how you must feel."

"No, you don't. You don't know what it's like to be alone in the dark for years, to be weak, scarred, and scared. To spend every single night wishing for your life to change. You don't know the fear of ending your days sweeping dust off old shelves, pretending every day that you aren't a disappointment to your father." Dashiel tried to stand tall, tried to keep his knees from buckling. "For one moment, I had everything that ill and weak boy ever wanted. But now, everything's turned to dust."

"I feel terrible." Sylvain drew near. "It was never my intention to hurt you."

"Then why did you do it?" Dashiel waited for Sylvain to give an answer, but the truth seemed to have gotten stuck between his lips. With a sigh, he said, "It doesn't matter anymore."

"Wait!" Sylvain grabbed Dashiel by the arm. "We can go back. I can convince them to take you back! I'll tell Athenai the truth. Let me make it up to you."

"Don't you get it?" Dashiel's mind filled with painful memories, and adrenaline took over. "It's over!"

Powered by renewed rage, Dashiel punched Sylvain in the face.

A painful silence reigned in the caverns.

"Do you feel better now?" Sylvain's lip bled.

"No. I'd feel better if I hadn't dishonored the cause I believed in, if I could spare Athenai the pain of my words, and if I could forget you ever came into my life."

Dashiel walked away.

"You can still go back."

"It's fine, Sylvain. Maybe I never should've left Azahar in the first place. All of this was a mistake from the beginning. It was a mistake to think I could do great things, that I was more than a weak, dumb Azahar boy."

Dashiel had lost his guiding star when his dearest friend betrayed him. He had no idea how to move on. He had never felt so lonely and lost in his life. Exhausted and finished with Sylvain's games, Dashiel ignored his stammering and resumed his dishonored walk.

"But you are . . ." Sylvain whispered.

"Oh, I forgot something." Dashiel stopped. He reached for his belt and unraveled the bag of coins his mother had given him. He tossed the little bag to Sylvain. "My debt is paid."

Sylvain opened the bag, which was full of gold coins, enough for a morning train ticket to Hermesia. From the tomb of coins, a humble silver ring with a tiny raindrop stone gleamed.

The sight pinched Dashiel's chest, and he fled. Sylvain's hurried footsteps sounded from behind, but they stopped abruptly. The echo of flesh and metal slamming against the cold surface caught Dashiel's attention. He turned around and found Sylvain convulsing on the ground, surrounded by spilled coins.

"Sylvain?"

At first Dashiel thought that Sylvain was trying to fool him, but he quickly realized that something serious was happening. He went to his friend's side and tried to help him, without much success. He struggled to remain calm. The sight of Sylvain in peril had erased his hatred and replaced it with pure fear.

"Help!" Dashiel screamed his lungs out. "Someone, please help!"

Footsteps thundered from the other side of the cavern.

"What happened?" Doctor Normandine and her dog came running.

"We were arguing, and then he dropped to the ground," Dashiel responded, fear in his eyes.

"We need to take him inside. Help me." She placed Sylvain's arm around her shoulder and helped Dashiel get the other arm.

Dashiel and Normandine took Sylvain to the palacette's courtyard, and there they set him down on the floor.

Sylvain's body writhed in agony.

"Hazelnut," Normandine called to her dog. "Go get Roderigo, fast!"

The dog barked and ran up the courtyard staircase.

"Dashiel!" Sofia's voice rang from the second floor. "What happened to him? What did you do?" She raced to their side.

"I didn't do anything," Dashiel responded. "He just passed out."

Sylvain was still shaking without control. A violent tremor tossed something out of his shirt, an object that hung around his neck. Dashiel was hypnotized by the colorful, translucent object.

When Sylvain's seizure calmed, Dashiel gripped the object between his fingers. He immediately recognized it. It was a chunk of crystallized fenku sap. How did Sylvain come across such a jewel? Fenku sap was extremely rare, and those not from Azahar were forbidden to acquire it.

There was something oddly familiar about the nugget of sap. Dashiel felt strange holding it.

Roderigo, followed by Athenai, arrived in the courtyard.

"What happened, Normandine?" Roderigo knelt beside Sylvain.

"Please, help him!" Dashiel begged, his lips trembling and eyes welling.

"Aurante, Aurante." Roderigo patted Sylvain's face. "Wake up."

Sylvain didn't respond. Roderigo proceeded to inspect Sylvain.

He took Sylvain's bandaged hand. "What happened to his hands?"

"I don't know," Dashiel answered, dizzy with confusion. "They were like that when we returned from Carmine Kingdom. He said he was fine."

"Let's check . . ."

With care, Roderigo unwound the bandages, revealing plump, reddish-brown spots all over Sylvain's hands.

"Burn marks," Roderigo declared.

He ripped Sylvain's sleeve open, revealing a clump of black blisters and charred skin all the way up to his shoulder. With a mere touch, the blisters exploded, ejecting brown pus.

Sylvain responded with an agonized shriek.

"It's expanding," Roderigo whispered with a concerned tone. "Azahar. We need to go to Azahar!"

"It would take weeks, Roderigo," Normandine said. "He won't make it."

"Not by normal means." Roderigo turned to Athenai. "We need your help, Miss Athenai."

Her name gave Dashiel chills. Her presence made him nervous. He longed to reunite with her, but the situation was far from ideal.

"Please, take us to Azahar," Roderigo begged. "His life depends on it."

"Of course," she responded instantly.

To Dashiel, her words felt like a blast of freezing water.

Athenai put two fingers in her mouth and whistled. In no time, a gargoyle, larger than the rest, dropped from the ledge.

"Mika," she called to the limestone creature, "please get one of the carriages."

The gargoyle obeyed and wandered into one of the corridors.

Athenai removed her diadem, which held a glistening crystal amulet. Dashiel recognized it from the brooch on her traveling cape, the pendant on her necklaces, and the stone on her headwear. She had always carried it with her.

"What is that?" Sofia asked.

"This is a spatial splicer. It has allowed my ancestors to easily travel through space." She removed the amulet from her diadem. "It will take us there, but in order for my amulet to work, I need something from Azahar."

Everyone turned to Dashiel.

"I left my stuff in the cavern," Dashiel said, worried. "The only thing I have is my baton's case."

"Is the case made of Azahar wood?" Roderigo asked.

Dashiel shook his head. "Father gave it to me in Azahar, but the doizemant isn't from there."

Sylvain shrieked again, and oddly, that gave Dashiel an idea.

"But Sylvain's necklace is." Dashiel grabbed the colorful pendant and raised it for everyone to see. He untied the necklace and offered it to Athenai. "This is made out of fenku sap."

Athenai did not address him. She took the necklace from his hands and held the crystallized sap to the light. Its bright colors absorbed the morning sun, which was shining through the dome.

"This might work."

Athenai scraped the sap with her finger until she collected enough dust. She held the amulet firmly, removing its silver cover. She poured the dust inside the amulet and closed it once more. The dust began to whirl within the amulet, emitting a warm light.

The gargoyle returned with Athenai's order. The crumbly carriage was made of a dark wood and gilded with copper carvings and statuettes. The creature placed it in the middle of the courtyard.

"Thank you." Athenai petted the gargoyle's rough arm. "We can only take up to ten passengers, Roderigo."

Everyone began to move. Roderigo lifted Sylvain into his arms.

"Master, why Azahar?" Dashiel asked. "What is going on?"

"Lucan, Ting, Boe." Roderigo picked from the available Phantasms. "You are coming with us." He turned to Dashiel. "Ermitage, no time for questions. Get inside the carriage. Now."

Still confused, Dashiel did as he was ordered.

Roderigo looked around. "Oblea, Wallace, and Spaigne, you too."

The chosen members boarded, Roderigo following with Sylvain in arms.

Soon the carriage was at its maximum capacity.

"Master Normandine, I leave you in charge," Roderigo called through one of the windows. "Please inform Professor Grasshop of the situation."

"Count on us," Normandine responded. "May Providence guide you."

As Athenai climbed into the carriage, she felt a gentle tug on her dress. When she turned around, she found the gargoyle. It was hard to decipher the creature's expression, but Athenai had practice. It did not like her leaving.

"I must go."

The gargoyle pouted.

"I'm sorry, but I cannot take you with me." She hugged him. "Do know that I love you. Please take care of Junei and the others."

The gargoyle stood straight, acknowledging his mistress's orders.

Athenai hopped into the carriage. She focused and touched the roof of the carriage as the amulet on her diadem shone with increasing intensity. The carriage began to shake and rumble.

"Getting through Gailfaur's barrier might cause some instability," Athenai shouted so her voice could be heard over the noise. "Everyone hang on tight!"

The amulet chimed, and the carriage and its occupants turned to sparks.

CHAPTER 35

GANGRENOUS HOMECOMING

The carriage materialized, and as Athenai had predicted, it quickly became unstable, sparking in and out of existence. Bits of copper fell off the carriage as it rapidly taxied through the trees. After the long, thrilling ride, the carriage's rampage finally came to an end, knocking down torches at the end of the trail.

As soon as Dashiel descended from the carriage, he realized that something had gone terribly wrong in Azahar. The sky was tinted bloodred, filtered through dark, thick clouds. The air—once pure and clean—boiled, and gray particles rained down on the forest, covering all surfaces like ghostly snow.

"Is this the right place?" Sofia jumped out of the broken-down carriage. "Wrong turn, I guess?"

As they unloaded the carriage, everyone wore an uneasy expression, for the beauty that they'd heard so much about was nowhere to be found.

"This is Pistil Plaza," Dashiel responded, feeling a punch in the gut. His lungs burned with every breath. "This is Azahar."

A painful silence had stricken the town, stripping it of its life. The bustling market had been replaced by the ominous rustling of dried leaves and Sylvain's screams. The fresh smell of the wild had been replaced by a hot, putrid odor, and the beautiful colors created by the sun's rays had been drained. For Dashiel, the worst part was the complete lack of life in the main plaza. Not a soul to be found. The windows of the buildings were broken, their walls riddled with bullets.

"They were attacked." Dashiel's eyes watered from the pungent smell. "This is wrong. This is terribly wrong."

"Hello?" Roderigo yelled. "Is anybody there? We need help!"

Not a single answer returned to him.

Sofia and the others ran through the town in search of its citizens. They knocked on doors and called as loud as they could, all to no effect. Dashiel ran to the town hall and pounded on the doors as hard as he could. Receiving no response, he tried to open them, but they were locked.

Out of the blue, a loud drumming rang out. The ground shook and cracked open, swallowing part of the main plaza's stone fountain and knocking over some of the trees.

"Dashiel, no one is here. We must get to your house right away. Which way?" Roderigo called, carrying Sylvain—still convulsing—in his arms.

Dashiel looked around but couldn't find the path he was looking for. Part of the forest hid behind a thick cloud of velvety smoke, which came from shrouder brew. The order used the brew to produce a large amount of smoke that, if inhaled, was capable of petrifying anyone without a cobalt sash.

"The path we need is over there." Dashiel signaled toward the smoke, wondering why it was not affecting anyone.

Before they could continue, bullets flew in their direction, missing them narrowly. One of them burrowed into the door of Athenai's carriage.

"An ambush!" Sofia shielded herself behind the carriage. "They're hidden inside the buildings!"

Four of the Phantasms who had accompanied Roderigo took up defensive positions. The exchange of shots reached a crescendo.

"Keep going!" Sofia shouted. "We'll keep them busy."

"Understood." Roderigo held tightly to Sylvain. "Ermitage, Boe, Athenai, come!"

The master and the others vanished into the smoke, all but Dashiel.

"I won't leave you alone. You can't fight all of them by yourself!" Dashiel took cover next to Sofia.

"Don't be stupid!" Sofia drew her pistol. "Who will guide them?" she said, shooting in the direction of the town's chapel. "That's an order. Go—*now!*"

Dashiel scampered away in the direction of the path, joining the others and vanishing into the smoke.

After a while, the smoke dissipated, revealing the footpaths and red-painted woods. The color of the forest wasn't the only strange thing ahead. The fenku, the lively caretakers of the Azahar people, were immobile, their bark peeling off and their branches and dried leaves scattered throughout the path.

The group waded farther into the botanical graveyard until a distant howling filled the air.

Boe, who had been leading the group along with Dashiel, stopped everyone. "What is that?"

"It's just a howl." Dashiel's heart continued its chaotic palpitation. "The sisyphus wolves must be confused because of the smoke."

Boe aimed his pistol at everything that seemed suspicious. "You live with wolves around you?"

"They usually stay off the trails." Dashiel kept walking. "Don't worry, they're docile creatures."

The group went farther until they came across a creature whose milky-white, spiky fur was covered in a thick layer of dirt. Its snout was as long as a crocodile's, and its pink, translucent claws were long enough to excavate and roll rocks out of its way. Its paws toyed with a blob of meat.

Dashiel gasped when he realized what the wolf had in front of it. A human body, the half-eaten body of an Azahar townsman. He couldn't believe his eyes. An Azahar had never been attacked by a wolf before. Sisyphus wolves had always protected them. Something terrible must have happened for the wolves to behave in this way.

When the wolf noticed their presence, it looked up, tearing flesh away with its sharp fangs. The wolf snarled, baring rows of red-dyed fangs.

"Doesn't seem docile to me." Boe placed himself in front of the group and aimed at the murderous animal. "Stay behind, and don't move a muscle."

The wolf kept snarling, adopting an attacking position. Before the animal had the chance to kill them, Sylvain began to scream and twist in pain.

At the sound, the wolf pulled its ears back and whined. Then it sprinted into the woods.

The path had been cleared.

"I don't understand," Dashiel mumbled, unable to recognize the blob of meat in front of them. "They've never attacked an Azahar."

Dashiel guided his party to Stamen Plaza, where most of the Azahar houses, including his own, had been built centuries before. Not a single person could be seen; not a single sound could be heard. The sky turned redder with every passing moment. The air was still unbearable to breathe.

"That's my house." Dashiel signaled to one of the humblest houses in the plaza.

The group hurried through the vegetable garden, up the stone steps, and onto the rustic porch. Dashiel opened the door.

In the blink of an eye, a musket was aimed at his face. "Stop right there!" a woman's voice commanded. "Or I'll shoot your brains out!"

Dashiel couldn't speak.

"Miss Malanks!" Roderigo called. "If you want to avoid a tragedy, I'd advise you to lower your weapon this instant."

Recognizing the name, Dashiel looked up to a familiar face. A tall, lanky woman with a nose that was long enough to serve as a bird's perch. It was Charlotte Malanks, her face partially darkened by soot.

"Dashiel? Master Roderigo?" She put away her musket and saluted. "Master Regallette, please forgive me. You have no idea the days we've been through."

Charlotte looked down and gasped at the mere sight of Sylvain. "He looks terrible."

"Worse by the minute." Roderigo gifted Sylvain a tender glimpse.

"Please, come inside."

The lanky woman moved aside, and the party entered.

The Ermitage house was as small as it had always been, but it felt even smaller so full of occupants. Along with the Phantasms, familiar faces crowded his home. Some bore injuries and disfigurations from head to toe. Others, like Mrs. Begonia, tended to the injured. To protect against stray bullets, the windows had been shut and boarded, raising the temperature and making the house even hotter than the inferno outside.

"Where's Elias?" Roderigo avoided the agonized people lying on the floor.

"Elias and Rupert are leading the Olivine Berets across the forest, taking care of the remaining imperials; they will take long. We are not enough."

"My apprentices are taking care of them too. Miss Malanks, we lost communication with you months ago. What happened?"

"The empire built a huge contraption that travels along the edge of the barrier, a siege engine. The siege began days ago, ramming and throwing flames at the barrier day and night. Late last night, the barrier faltered, and a wave of imperials managed to slip in. We fought them off, but things got worse when the barrier failed once again this morning and the animals went berserk, attacking indiscriminately."

"How are our current defenses?" Roderigo asked.

"The barrier is turning to dust, the fenku are unresponsive, and the luciums have faded away. In other words, we are screwed. We threw our last shrouder brew vials into the rivers, hoping that the smoke would disorient the attackers. We had to dilute them, so they will not petrify our enemies."

"What about the Azahar people? The town's council?"

"The people managed to escape during the first attack. Most of them went to the mines. Some of us opted to stay here and tend to the injured. The town's council had to be moved to Sepal Plaza. They don't know what to do."

As the conversation between Roderigo and Charlotte continued, Dashiel was hypnotized by a horrendous sight: a human-shaped figure wrapped tightly in a red-stained cloth. Azahar was a small place. Twenty-seven families lived there, and it had been like that for decades. Even though he had spent most of his life sheltered inside that house, he had become familiar with every single soul in town. He dreaded the idea that the wretched person concealed under the sheet was someone he knew. His thoughts bounced between the unrecognizable bloodied body on the trail and the mummy in front of him. They both had families that loved them. They both had duties, dull and repetitive at times but carried out with enthusiasm. His head gonged as he hoped that his friends were safe.

"Dashiel?" A familiar voice woke him from his trance.

His mother embraced him. "Thank Providence you're safe!"

Dashiel's mother had always been known as a docent of pristine appearance, but her skirt and apron were stained in a variety of colors, red predominantly, and her glasses had fogged over. Her frizzy braids, barely holding up, swung from side to side like a mule's tail.

"I am, Mama, but Sylvain . . ." He gestured helplessly to the shuddering boy in Roderigo's arms.

She hurried to Sylvain's side, holding her hand to her mouth. Her eyes watered, and her head trembled as she caressed his ebony hair.

"Emily," Roderigo said gently, "he needs urgent help."

She wiped her tears off her face. "Of course. Quick, take him upstairs. The room to the right."

Roderigo did as told and rushed upstairs.

Emily wiped the sweat off her forehead and rolled up her sleeves. "We don't have enough hands," she mumbled.

"Please, Mrs. Ermitage. Allow me to help." Athenai's sweet voice rang out from a corner. "I'm an Alferai. My people's medicinal knowledge might be of service."

"My goodness, how fortunate we are to have you here, dear." Emily approached her. "I'd greatly appreciate your help."

Dashiel felt awkward having the girl he was no longer with and his mother in the same room, talking to each other. Getting along.

Dashiel observed, mesmerized, as Athenai made her way up the stairs.

"Mama," Dashiel said before his mother followed. "What is going on here? What's the problem with Sylvain?"

"Not now, honey." She followed Athenai. "No time to explain."

"But I want to help. Is he going to be fine?" Dashiel said, his temples throbbing.

"Not now . . ."

Dreading the atmosphere of blood and death, Dashiel followed his mother to his room, where the treatments were being prepared.

Sylvain was on the bed, the brown pus oozing from him staining the ivory sheets.

A familiar croaky voice spoke. "Here are the things you require, Mrs. Ermitage."

Lawrence Octavious came into the room carrying a bag that rattled with the slightest movement. Unlike everyone else's, Octavious's appearance was untouched, a clear sign that he had not bothered to help much.

"Thank you, Octavious. Lakandula oil, please." Emily cleaned the pus off.

Like a rat, Octavious scavenged inside the bag. When his gaze rose, he quickly noticed Dashiel.

"If it isn't Dashiel!" Octavious smirked as he handed a flask to Emily. "The Monarch Scourge."

"How did you up end here?" Dashiel whispered.

Emily poured the oil into a mortar. "Aloe and mogapie root too!"

"After my induction," Octavious whispered back, "I was sent away to test my Brigadier coagulant on some specimens that the order possessed." Octavious fixed his glasses. "Little did I know that the carcasses I would be testing on were here. I was stranded when the siege engine was built. Your mother offered to teach me some of her unsophisticated medicinal remedies."

"Octavious, the ingredients," Emily insisted.

"Yes, ma'am." Octavious's voice cracked.

"Mrs. Ermitage, may I suggest using this amengebeaux fruit?" Athenai removed a scaly, pink, heart-shaped fruit from her pocket. "Its pulp can numb the senses and reduce pain."

"Thank you, dear."

Emily took the fruit and minced it so fast that it was fortunate she didn't chop off a finger.

"Please tell me." Dashiel got closer to Octavious. "Do you know what the problem with Sylvain is?"

"Well, if my theory is correct, I would say that Sylvain is—"

"Octavious!" Emily roared, interrupting him.

"Yes, ma'am," he said to Emily. "I'm sorry, Ermitage." He grabbed the ingredients and walked away.

In the middle of the chaos, Sylvain's lips began to tremble. "I . . . I . . ."

"Shush." Emily placed her hand on his head. "Don't waste your energy."

"I'm . . . so . . . sorry I failed you, mu—"

Sylvain convulsed as violently as ever. He let go of the most terrifying screams Dashiel had ever heard. The brown blisters multiplied, and the black burn marks spread all over his body. Things got worse when Emily tried to apply her medicinal concoction to Sylvain's charred skin, as it caused the blisters to explode.

"Quickly! We need to strap him in place!" Emily said. "He's hurting himself."

With much difficulty, Sylvain was strapped to the bed, but the screams did not stop. Stricken by pain, he tried to set himself free, causing the bed to creak.

"We need to try something else!" Octavious yelled over Sylvain's howling.

"Don't you have sisyphus wolf saliva?" Athenai asked. "I've been told that it can cure most anything."

"My dear, we don't have any left," Emily replied, saddened. "It's impossible to get any at this time."

Her words hit Dashiel like an arrow. He'd used the remaining sisyphus saliva to help his friend the year before.

Sylvain kept screeching.

"We need to try something else!" Emily yelled.

"I know another recipe!" Athenai focused on the supplies before her. "Let's try tamanu oil, hazel leaves, and rafflesia essence."

"There's no rafflesia essence," Octavious said, wiping pus off his glasses.

The noise, the voices, and the screams were too much for Dashiel. Distressed, he held his head in his hands and let out a scream of his own, stopping everyone cold.

"WHAT IS GOING ON?!" Dashiel roared.

There was no answer. Everyone stared at him.

He was on the verge of once again demanding an answer when his father walked through the door. His custodian tunic was in rags, and wounds covered his body and face.

"Dashiel," Elias called amid Sylvain's screams. "Come with me."

Dashiel shook his head. "Papa, I can't leave him like this."

"He's going to be fine." Elias turned and walked back out of the room. "Come now."

Dashiel stood there, staring at Sylvain, who convulsed as Emily hurried to prepare another remedy.

"Stop behaving like a child and obey!" Elias's voice thundered from downstairs.

He understood that as much as it hurt seeing his friend suffering, there was nothing he could do.

Dashiel went after his father.

CHAPTER 36

FORCED OBLIVION

"**W**hat is going on?" Dashiel snarled as he left the house, his father right behind him. "The fenku trees are dying, and the luciums are gone. I saw a sisyphus wolf shred an Azahar to pieces! Why is Gailfaur allowing this? Has he forsaken us?"

Elias massaged his temples. "Dashiel—"

"I am done with all this secrecy," he said, stepping into the family's vegetable patch. "Tell me what is happening."

"Dashiel, let me—"

"Why is Gailfaur not protecting us?" Dashiel continued, accidentally squashing the greens.

"Dashiel—"

"WHY?"

"Because Gailfaur is dead, damn it!" Elias blurted out. "He's no longer here!"

Dashiel felt as if he had been smacked in the back of his head. "Wha-what? Dead? That . . . that's impossible."

"He's been dead for many years, Dashiel."

"It . . . can't be. We have the barrier and the lucium spirits. I even saw the centaur with my own eyes when I left to train."

"Yes, all those things drew their energy from a deity, but not the one you think."

Dashiel gasped. "I'm lost. I don't understand anything. I don't understand how this is happening. Why am I here and not up there with Sylvain?"

"Be quiet and listen." Elias thought for a moment. "Try to open your mind. Many years ago, when I served in the imperial army, your grandfather Elliott Ermitage, who was Gailfaur's custodian at the time, learned that Gailfaur had become ill in his old age. He tried everything, but Gailfaur's energy kept dwindling. My father, worried that Gailfaur would be too weak to cast a shield over Azahar during Asedia's invasion, prayed to the deity for an answer. Gailfaur told him that Providence had arranged for a new vessel to carry on with his purpose, a vessel born in a town far from the forest."

The loud drumming started again, shaking the ground and tumbling down trees and edifices.

"He traveled to a little town called Carbakiel and found the vessel, who happened to be a child. My father told the child's parents about the forest, Gailfaur, and the child's destiny. He begged them to move to Azahar, but they refused. He told them about the reign of oppression that Asedia would bring, yet they refused to believe. Their confidence in the Belecroses blinded them. Some time passed, and Carbakiel fell to Asedia."

In his mind, Dashiel could picture the enslaved children that dwelled in those factories. The children who had never known any better.

"The child's parents tried to escape to the haven that the old man had promised them, but they were followed. When they arrived at the Azahar border, soldiers killed them. My father was able to save the child. He took the child to the sacred terrains as Gailfaur expired, and Gailfaur's essence fused with that of the child. The child then became the reincarnation of Gailfaur."

"What happened to the child?"

"My father trained him to use his powers. Most important, he learned to project his divine vital force to create a barrier, a shield to protect us all. Unfortunately, my father passed away, and the child was all by himself once more."

Elias wiped his sweat with his sleeve.

"Your mother and I . . . We were not able to conceive a child, so we decided to adopt him."

"You mean, I have a brother?"

Elias pursed his lips.

"I do? Who?" Dashiel's mind began to spin. "Sylvain?"

"The boy who was promised, the child from Carbakiel, the reincarnation of Gailfaur, and your brother . . ." Elias seemed to almost choke on his words. "He is none other than Sylvain Aurante. Sylvain is an Ermitage."

"That can't be." Dashiel trembled. "He can't be Gailfaur . . . He can't be my brother."

"Dashiel, think about it. Superhuman strength and speed, divine aim, and mastery over the ability of force projection. He tones his power down when he's around people, but the signs have always been there."

"But I met Sylvain last year. I would remember if he were my brother."

"No, you wouldn't." Elias's face saddened. "No one would."

Dashiel frowned. "That makes no sense."

"When you were a child, your mother and I decided that you were healthy enough to finally live a more normal life. We promised you that, on your birthday, we would allow you to leave the house. You were so happy. Then, days before your birthday, you suffered a relapse. We decided that it was best for you to delay the plan."

The land shook. The houses creaked, and their windows shattered.

"You were upset and ran away from home. We looked everywhere for you, but it was Sylvain who found and saved you. In the process, a terrible accident exposed him for what he truly is. He didn't have the power to manipulate memories, so he forced everyone under the shield to forget the incident. His goal was to protect himself and his family, but he ended up being entirely erased from their minds. If not for the flute, your mother and I would have forgotten him too.

"By overstepping his powers, he lost control of them. He became a danger to everyone and everything." Elias's voice was mournful. "At first, he found it to be difficult. So we secluded him in the sacred terrains, where he practiced his control until he was old enough to join the Cobalt Phantasms as my apprentice. He found a way to command the luciums, project the decoy centaur, and maintain harmony among Azahar's creatures by meditating and focusing."

"Why did I forget about him?"

"Your health worsened when he left. You missed him so much and blamed yourself for his departure. We had to erase your memories too. We did so on your birthday. Otherwise, you would have died."

By the end of the story, Dashiel's eyes were brimming with tears. It all made sense: Why Sylvain spent ridiculous amounts of time meditating. His beastly reaction during the fight at the palacette. Dashiel's inexplicable hatred toward his own birthday. Everything fit perfectly together.

"He went through that for me? He is the one who deserves to be remembered, not me."

Elias couldn't meet his eyes. "It wasn't your fault."

"This morning, I wished to forget him . . ."

Elias grabbed Dashiel's face. "Deep down, you love him. He knows that. The best thing you can do is pull yourself together and fight for him."

Dashiel regained his composure and took a big breath. "I've made so many mistakes . . . It's time to make things right."

"We must go." Elias began to walk toward the woods.

"Where are we going?"

"We need to hurry," Elias said, severity in his eyes. "The barrier is a projection of Sylvain's vital force. If the barrier is destroyed, Sylvain dies. Your mother and her assistants are doing all they can to keep the fire from spreading, but that won't be enough."

"He must withdraw it, then."

"Exactly. He can always recast it when he is better, but for now, we need to be prepared to fend off Markeus and his forces."

Elias continued walking, but Dashiel stayed behind, thinking about the truth his father had shared.

"Papa, if the barrier is withdrawn, will we all remember Sylvain?"

Elias turned around. "I don't know. Anything could happen. Let's hope that at least things will return to normal."

A terrible tremble shook the earth. Trees fell to the ground, darkened dust fell off the decaying barrier, and bewildered animals ran in all directions.

"We need to hurry," Elias said. "Time is running out."

He ran into the woods, Dashiel hot on his heels.

CHAPTER 37

BACK TO A BROKEN BEGINNING

D ashiel and Elias journeyed through the unknown dangers of the besieged Azahar. They traveled through the woods, avoiding the wolf-infested trails, until they arrived at Petal Plaza. The plaza was intact because, according to his father, the Olivine Berets had pushed back the imperial soldiers before they could reach it. Elias led the way through the abandoned organic buildings, stopping in front of a place that Dashiel knew well.

Old Astor's library.

"What are we doing here, Papa?" Dashiel asked.

"Old Astor officiates the heirloom ceremony," Elias said. "If we want a chance to defeat the empire's army, we will need your heirloom."

The library's door opened with the chime of the rusty bell.

The building had lost the battle against seas of dust, a battle that Dashiel used to fight every day. Some books had fallen to the floor because of the trembling, something Old Astor would never allow in less-precarious circumstances.

"Ah, there you are!" Astor emerged from the back, holding a towering pile of damaged books. "You can start by dusting the whole place."

The old man dropped the books on his desk. "Go on. What are you waiting for?" He snapped his bony, hairy fingers as he sat on his desk.

Dashiel didn't know what to say.

"Astor, Dashiel . . ." Elias stepped on a book.

"WATCH YOUR STEP, ERMITAGE!" the old man yelled.

Elias brushed the book aside, causing the bookkeeper to growl. "Dashiel's not here to help you."

"I know," Astor said in an odd, calm tone, "but he can at least be useful, now that he's failed to protect Gailfaur."

"Protect Gailfaur?" Dashiel turned to his father. "What does he mean?"

Elias shut his eyes with annoyance and took a deep breath. "Keeping up the barrier for so long had an exhausting effect on Sylvain. Because of his human nature, his power drained him three times as fast, making him weak and, at times, defenseless. So we decided to assign a Cobalt Phantasm as his Outerland protector. I couldn't go, because I had to keep up appearances, and I couldn't entrust Sylvain to anyone else. You, an aspiring Phantasm and his brother, were the obvious option."

"And you failed miserably!" Old Astor cackled.

Dashiel, disheartened, looked away. "I see . . ."

Another rumble shook the forest, causing some of the books and dust to fall off the shelves. Astor let out an irritated screech.

"We aren't discussing that with you," Elias told Astor, annoyance in his tone.

"Then why are you here?" The old man's voice held the same tone Dashiel had come to recognize as a warning. A smack from his cane always followed. "I don't believe I can interest you in a novel."

Elias unfolded a document and began to read.

"The council of Azahar has revoked the punishment administered to Dashiel Ermitage on April 2, 1854, and calls for the master of ceremonies to complete the Ermitage heirloom ceremony immediately."

Astor gave them a brusque smirk. "Your little paper doesn't impress me!" he cackled. "Where are all the signatures of the council?"

"Signed by all members." Elias slammed the paper onto the old man's desk. Dust particles flew all over the room. "You are to comply at once."

Astor grumbled as he read the paper with care. "All right, but I require at least one week."

"Two days, max." Elias countered.

"Impossible." Astor folded his hands, an evil smirk inching across his face. "Goodbye, Ermitages."

Elias looked around. "What a shame. All these books burned to ashes." He picked up a book from the dusty floor. "I guess you won't mind if I do *this!*" Elias ripped the book in half.

"STOP IT, YOU IDIOT!" the old man squealed like a warthog.

"Two days." Elias approached Astor fearlessly, placing two of his fingers at a dangerous distance from the old man's face.

"How I hate when you get away with this kind of stuff, Ermitage," Astor said. "Wait a moment." The old man abandoned his desk and took his cane. "Come with me."

He tottered to a corner shelf and took out his rusty key. Dashiel knew that shelf as a home for uncatalogued books. It was one of the many things Astor had forbidden him to touch beyond light dusting.

He removed a book from the shelf, revealing a keyhole. With a turn of the key, the bookcase dropped into the ground, raising a cloud of dust and unveiling an opening.

Astor signaled to Dashiel as he went through the opening, and Dashiel followed. They soon found themselves inside a mechanism that seemed centuries old. Its moldy wood was rotting away, its ropes were worn, and its cranks and gears were rusty.

"You, the lever." The old man signaled to a rotten stick.

Dashiel grasped the lever and began to spin it, causing the mechanism to descend.

"Do as he says. There's no time to lose. The heirloom holds the power to protect Azahar, to protect Sylvain," Dashiel's father said before he and the small library disappeared from sight.

Another rumble shook the forest, and two of the books from the uncatalogued shelf fell into the mechanism.

"Faster, you useless boy!" the old man screeched.

The mechanism took them to an ancient brick room filled from floor to ceiling with towers of books. Though he wasn't sure how, Dashiel knew these tomes were unlike any in the library above.

He followed Astor through the labyrinth of books. Curious, he approached one of the towers and touched the spines, trying to read their inscrutable titles.

"These books were entrusted to me by the Belecrose family." The old man limped along, his cane clicking against the floor. "DON'T TOUCH THEM!"

Dashiel kept walking until they arrived at a vast underground chamber.

Astor raised his hands. "Feast your unworthy eyes upon the roots of the first fenku tree."

The chamber walls and ceiling were covered in gigantic, tangled roots with boxes tied to their ends. Glowing minerals that grew from the ground and walls illuminated the room.

Right under the roots, there was a pedestal with a cushion in the center.

"They're enormous," Dashiel said, overwhelmed by the size of the roots.

"The first fenku was a gift from Gailfaur to humanity, but he had too much faith in the stupid people. As soon as the humans got the chance, they chopped down the tree, leaving only its roots. The roots hold the heirlooms of all Azahar families, twenty-seven in total."

Old Astor growled as he hobbled closer.

"In order to receive yours, you must become one with your lineage. Many have failed. Based on what I know about you, Ermitage, it's eminently possible that you'll fail too. Sit," Astor ordered. "And close your eyes."

Dashiel sat on the cushion.

"The ceremony shall be a success when you experience an epiphany. The fenku will help you piece together who you are, connecting and bonding you to your lineage. Always remember that blood not only keeps you alive but also makes you one with those who share it." The old man leaned on his cane. "Clear your mind. In order to complete yourself, you must first let go of unnecessary pieces."

Dashiel closed his eyes and brushed his thoughts away. His past anger and present uncertainty vanished. His mind was clear, but nothing happened.

"It's not working." Dashiel opened one eye.

"Of course it's not working. We haven't started yet, you idiot." Astor stood in front of Dashiel. "Keep your head empty. Shouldn't be hard for you." Astor cackled despite the gravity of the situation.

The old man waved his cane in the air. "*Saoma ol meenus Kiarbect!*"

Astor's body and cane moved harmoniously.

"Repeat after me!" Astor groaned. "*Saoma ol meenus Kiarbect.*"

Dashiel did as told and chanted with the old man.

"*Saoma ol meenus Kiarbect.*"

"*Saoma ol meenus Kiarbect.*"

"*SAOMA OL MEENUS KIARBECT!*"

CHAPTER 38

THE OCHRE BADGE OF DECISIVENESS

Sepal Plaza had always served as Azahar's main source of food and wood supplies. On its fertile grounds, the Azahar tended their farms and domestic animals and stored wood in sheds. But for the first time in many years, the townspeople had abandoned their duties. During the imperial siege, one of the barns was repurposed into a meeting place for the town's council, and a carpentry shed into a Cobalt Phantasm base.

Inside that shed, the sweet aroma of wood hid the stench of the burning barrier, and endless amounts of sawdust covered the wooden floors. The walls were adorned with tools and creations made by the town's carpenters before they took shelter. Roderigo himself had boarded all the windows.

The hands of a cuckoo clock suggested that the sun shone brightly in the sky, but many candles had been set on the working tables, as morning, day, and night had been concealed by a deathly crimson mask.

Roderigo stood in front of his fellow Phantasms. Charlotte Malanks, Rupert Golk, Sofia Spaigne, and the other members whom Roderigo had chosen at the palacette waited for him to speak.

"My children, you know that Azahar is of great importance to our cause. Losing this territory could mean the end. We're not many, but we must not let it fall; that is out of the question. I know you are not with your squadrons. You're exhausted and worried, I understand, but we must remain strong for those who need us. We've always helped in the shadows, but this is the time to fight in the light. If Azahar is destroyed, so is our purpose."

Everyone's eyes burned with motivation.

"Wallace, Ting, and Oblea, the lumberjack's patriarch has ordered the lumberjacks and carpenters to build barricades on the forest's edge. I must ask you to assist them; they need as many hands as possible."

"Yes, sir!" the three Phantasms said in unison. They hurried out of the shed to fulfill their task.

"Malanks and Boe, the townspeople are forming a militia. I need you to make sure the assembly goes without a hitch. Keep the morale high and assist them. Worry not about the lack of weaponry; that shall be fixed in due time."

"Right away, Master." Malanks and Boe both stood straight.

"One more thing. The council has ordered the miners to join the militia. The current mining patriarch, Omilier Deguiser, is a rather difficult individual, so keep an eye on him."

Roderigo was about to assign the next task when the shed's door opened. One of the Phantasms aimed his musket at the door and prepared to shoot.

The butt of a musket pointed at Athenai's face. The Phantasm who held the gun blinked once and then quickly lowered his weapon.

"Roderigo? You called for me?" Athenai stepped into the candlelight.

"Ah yes, Miss Athenai, please come forward." Roderigo wiped the sweat off his forehead, brushing aside a lock of graying hair that hung from his receding hairline. "First of all, I'm sorry for involving you in this mess."

"You once risked your life for my mother. You have my eternal gratitude."

Roderigo walked to a sawdust-infested working table. He moved aside the carpentry tools and gadgets and placed a worn briefcase in front of him. "How's Sylvain?"

"We've managed to slow down the burns, but I'm afraid we don't have the right resources to heal him. Mrs. Ermitage's remedies are not working, and neither are mine."

The land shook, causing the shed to tremble and creak.

"Have you tried the saliva of the local wolves? It possesses extraordinary healing properties." Roderigo's face filled with hope.

"We ran out, and finding more is out of the question."

The land shook with greater force. The shed's smoky windows began to crack, and a ladder came crashing down, splitting in two.

"We have no choice . . ." Roderigo snapped the briefcase open, revealing documents bearing the order's crest. "The barrier will have to be withdrawn sooner than expected."

"Lower the barrier?" The room erupted with worried protests.

"We won't stand a chance," Sofia said.

"We lack weaponry, resources, and manpower," one of the remaining chosen added. "We'll be crushed!"

"The council has already decided on it." Roderigo took out a variety of papers, journals, and artifacts, all containing the order's top-secret data. "But there won't be bloodshed if Miss Athenai agrees to help us one last time."

"Me?"

"I know you've done far more than you should," Roderigo said, pinching his glabella, "but I must beg you to take on a crucial task, one that could tip the balance in our favor."

Athenai remained silent.

Roderigo handed her a scroll. "You will find all the base locations in there, with names and other details as well. I need you to travel to every base in your carriage and bring all the available Cobalt Phantasms to Azahar."

Athenai thought of the dangers she was entangling herself in. She thought of her sisters, who needed her alive. If Junei were there, she would tell her not to do it, but there was nothing that could stop her. Her amulet could travel to most of the places on the list; she had made sure of that.

She then thought of Dashiel, the ingrate who had broken a heart that still beat for him in spite of everything. She put her feelings aside and thought about what she had learned of him. He was greatly impulsive, putting himself in danger for complete strangers in the past. He was selfless, a trait she admired. If she wanted to be a good leader to her people, she had to be willing to sacrifice her life for causes that mattered.

"I'll do it, Roderigo."

"Excellent!" Roderigo's sweaty cheeks deflated with relief. "I don't know how we'll ever repay you."

"Oh my, I forgot." Athenai placed her finger on her rosy cheek. "The carriage won't last long. It's falling to pieces."

"Then your first stop should be the palacette. Doctor Normandine will be more than happy to fix it. She's always been intrigued by your amulet and its space-travel capabilities."

"I'll go with her," Sofia offered. "The way to the main plaza is full of dangers."

"No." Roderigo stopped her. "I need you to deliver an urgent message to Elias and Dashiel. Mr. Golk will accompany her."

"Me!" A brusque voice came from a corner, followed by a loud laugh. "Bring on!"

A man—twice as tall as Athenai and three times the size of Roderigo—stepped forward. His hair had been pulled back in a tiny bun, and his muscular body dripped with sweat. He smelled like a combination of armpit and wet dog.

"Miss Athenai, Rupert is one of our strongest Phantasms. You can rest assured no harm will come to you."

The tanned giant grinned, revealing corn-yellow teeth. "*Mil pleeser, lettei misee.*"

"A pleasure . . ." Athenai tried to smile at the intimidating man.

"I have arranged for a local to guide you." Roderigo turned to Rupert. "Not that I mistrust your knowledge of these areas, Rupert, but the diluted shrouder veil will disorient anyone who hasn't lived here long enough."

"We off," Rupert said in his thick Peskeiran accent. "Order *brootha* and *sisteree* await."

"One last thing." Roderigo held his closed hand in front of Athenai. "You'd better take this with you. One glimpse, and everyone will follow you without question."

Roderigo opened his hand to reveal a Cobalt Phantasm badge, but this particular insignia was different from all others.

"It's ochre!" Sofia gasped. "Roderigo, I didn't know the situation was that critical."

Night had fallen, but the sky glowed under the intensity of the fire used to destroy the barrier.

The guide who Roderigo had hired for Athenai and her escort was a young Azahar shepherd. Short and skinny, he wore his blond hair in an old-fashioned bowl cut. He was shy and feared everything, even his own shadow. An odd choice for a guide, but she supposed he was chosen because everyone else was busy, or maybe because he and Athenai had something in common. They both knew Dashiel well.

Before leaving the makeshift base, Rupert had asked them both to remain silent, for they could draw the attention of an imperial soldier or a wild animal. So Athenai lowered her voice to a whisper. "Donner."

"Yes, Miss Palacette?" The fellow's bony shoulders shook. "W-we . . . shouldn't be talking."

"You're an Azahar, so you must know something about the sisyphus wolf."

"The basics, like they're terrifying creatures that live underground." His eyes moved from side to side like a lamb's.

"Do you know how to get some of their saliva?" Athenai asked in an even lower tone.

"When approached correctly, wolves allow the Azahar to collect some." Donner looked around in fright, like he was expecting a wolf. "But it is impossible now that they've gone nuts."

"There must be a way," she insisted.

Donner pondered. "Well, sisyphus cubs drool a lot, and their fangs and claws aren't as sharp."

"Great!" Athenai toned her enthusiasm down so she wouldn't be heard. "Where can I find a cub?"

"*Great*? You shouldn't get close to those things. They're dreadful creatures, even under control."

"I must if we want a chance at victory." Athenai's eyes shone with confidence. "Where?"

"I'm sorry." Donner clenched his fists and looked straight ahead. "I can't let you put yourself at risk."

He bit his lips closed, as if physically restraining himself from telling her what he knew. He paced ahead, putting greater distance between himself and her pleading eyes.

Athenai did not know what to say or do. She needed the healing ingredient, but it would be impossible to get without Donner's help. An idea bloomed in her head. She recalled something that Dashiel had told her. Donner was scared of the Ochre Brigadiers, even more so after one had dropped a tree on top of him.

She had to act quickly. "You might be right, Donner . . ."

"I am?"

"Yes." Athenai faked a contrite expression. "We might have a better chance against the Brigadiers."

Donner's face paled. His teeth chattered. "Bri-Brigadiers?"

"I've never faced one before, but I guess they aren't as bad as those terrible wolves, right?"

"Rrrr-right . . ."

She had planted the seed in his mind and stirred his thoughts. It was time to put her idea into action.

"Argh!" She let go of a tiny scream and dropped to the ground.

Rupert and Donner were quick to notice.

"Wot is problem?" the giant asked.

"I must have slipped on a fenku branch." She turned to Donner. "Could you please help me up?"

Donner nodded and offered her his trembling hand. Athenai took it, and in one swift motion she sprang up from the floor and wrapped her arm around his neck. Her irises met his.

She went inside his mind.

Donner's mind was not complex at all. His intentions, which happened to be the most superficial layer of his mind, were of a sincere nature.

She had to dive deeper.

As Donner was an emotionally driven being, his fears, or at least the one she had planted moments earlier, helped her gain access to the next layer of his subconscious: his thoughts.

"*What am I doing? Stupid, stupid, stupid!*"

No.

"*What was that? Oh wait, a rabbit . . . faster, faster, faster . . . Hopefully it didn't notice me . . .*"

No.

"*Oh no, now she's talking to me . . .*"

No.

"*Cubs! Those little beasts sometimes wander off from their mothers and play at the clearings, but I will never tell her . . .*"

Voilà!

"Much appreciated." Athenai let go of Donner. "Please proceed. I'll be fine." She brushed a strand of her hair behind her ear.

Athenai had the information she needed. All she had to do was accomplish Roderigo's mission and then go find that saliva.

CHAPTER 39

PARADOXICAL MEMORIES

I am the wind that travels across the sky.

What is that? So shiny, so pure . . .

I see a massive city from afar. Beautiful, like no other place on earth.

As I get closer to the city, I feel heavier. As the weight increases, I lose altitude. I fall from the sky into the city. My body breaks through the roof of a towering building and then through the floor, collecting the shattered bricks and mortar. I am a stone that sinks into the warm layers of the earth's crust. The roots of the trees try to grab me, but they cannot hold me. Their trunks snap. The roots cover my body, and leaves sprout from them. I am now a leafy creature that can scarcely control the movement of its fingers and toes. A light brighter than the sun surrounds my chaotic body, removing me from existence.

I am in a familiar setting, an Azahar trail. It is morning, but the trail torches are lit. The sun is harsh, but the fenku are not sheltering me from it. I walk, prance, and run, but my speed remains constant. With every step, the trail changes.

One step, then the trail perfectly straightens. Two steps, and the trees perfectly align. Three steps, and the sunlight causes the leaves to fall off. As they fall, the leaves become transparent. As they float down, the transparent leaves piece together, crafting glistening crystal walls. The sunlight dims, and the sky turns black; the stars fall from the skies and come together. The clusters of stars emit a cold light. The trees, the mossy ground, and the sky have turned gold.

As I walk, I can see nothing but an endless corridor of dulled crystal walls. I run, but the corridor seems to have no end, no exit. I try to find my reflection in any of the walls, but it is impossible. I can't justify my existence. I am, but there is nothing I can be made of.

How do I know what the crystal walls reflect? Well, they reflect the shadows that pass by me. They reflect a lullaby and the soft touch of an eagle.

I doubt without having a mind, I despair without having a heart, and I leave fingerprints on the walls without having flesh. My finger-prints are turning to spiderwebs, which turn to cracks.

What is that warmth? It must come from my fingertips. A green light encompasses my silhouette.

Wait a moment! The light is me, and I am the light. My reflection is blurry, but at least I am visible now.

I walk down the corridor, but I can't continue; there is no floor. I look down, up, left, and right and see nothing. I can't go back. I can't go forward.

Is that . . . my book? I see it leaning against a shattered wall.

Book is a funny word . . . What is a book? Is it really mine? Mine is an amusing word. It sounds like nine, fine, time . . . TIME IS RUNNING SHORT . . . Short . . . short . . . shush.

I reach for the book, but when I finally touch it, the blank pages fly away from the binding and spin in the air. I feel like singing, but I don't know how to sing. I don't even own a mouth . . .

Books have pages. I am the blank pages. I jump into nothingness, but a page comes to my rescue. I jump from the page, but another one saves me. Why do I do this? Because it is amusing and repetitive.

Repetition is addictive.

The pages have all been used, but the corridor is back, in front of me, behind me, next to me. Should I continue or jump down to nothingness?

JUMP TO NOTHINGNESS, OF COURSE!

Wonder if a page will catch me . . .

Wait a moment! I hear something. I hear the blood rush inside my . . . my . . . What was it? It doesn't matter. All that matters is that I have these two children in front of me. A boy and a girl standing in front of a dead end, an enormous crystal window that leads to a garden.

Same age? Maybe . . . siblings? Maybe . . . maybe, maybe, maybe . . . I AM LOST!

All I know is that I like their freckles and golden hair. I like their home, if this is their home. I like that they are speaking in an incomprehensible tongue.

I don't own a tongue, don't own a mouth.

She is holding a doll; he's holding a . . . he's holding a . . . what is that called? Whatever! He's holding something. Good for him. I like him already. I'll call him Source.

What about her? Should I really name her? Oh, well, from this day on, she shall be known as Reason. She is adorable. Not as much as Source, though.

Maybe, just maybe, I'm being biased.

They want to play . . . or kill me . . . or be me . . . SIN, PUNISHMENT, FORGIVENESS.

What? Reason is fading away. I want to fade away too . . . too . . . tooo.

Don't go away, Rea . . . Reas . . . Re . . . You! Come back.

She is no longer there, but her doll is still here, lying on the floor.

The doll is broken . . . I AM NOT BROKEN! I AM LOST!

How am I lost? I know where, when, how, what I am . . .

WHO . . . ?

How interesting the broken doll is . . . I hate it! I feel superior to it. I want to love it; I need to feel something.

Source has reached for my face. His little hand feels warm on my nonexistent cheek. He smiles at me. His freckles shine like the stars.

His smile has twisted into a smirk.

His hand feels rough. It is no longer warm but boiling hot. Burning ochre sands emanate from the boy's hand.

Sand is coming from everywhere I look. It is taking over the corridor. The sand reaches my knees, and the doll is engulfed by it.

The boy is now a sand statue. His eyes cry tears of crystal-clear blood. As the blood droplets touch the sand, the sand increases in volume. The smile comes off his face and lands in the sand.

I sink as the boy disintegrates before my eyes. I try to swim to the surface, but something pulls me down.

If I had a mouth, I would yell. Help! Help! LEAVE ME BE! HELP!

Who am I?

Years have passed like mere seconds. I'm burning like a candle, but how am I still here?

Dust, cold dust, has wrapped me . . . DUST . . . DUST . . . DUST . . . I am a dust ball surrounded by an ocean of boiling sand.

Where is the dust coming from? From the little girl's doll, of course.

I hear a sound . . .

Hello? *I call.*

Who are you? *I hear.*

I AM . . .

Dashiel gasped out of the epiphany, shaking and sweating. He looked around and found everything unchanged. He was still in the dark, sitting under the roots of the first fenku tree.

"Finally, you're back," Sofia said, crouching by his side.

"How long was I gone for?" Dashiel rubbed his eyes and stretched his arms.

"Three days."

"Three days?!" Dashiel sprang up. "How's Sylvain? What's happening with the invasion?"

"Athenai has brought every member of the order to Azahar, and now they are getting ready to fight off Markeus. As for Sylvain, he's barely holding up, just like the barrier. Your mother is doing her best to conserve his energy."

"I was supposed to be gone for a day, maybe two." He dizzily moved around. "What are you doing here? Where's my father?"

He looked around the empty chamber. "And where is Astor?"

"Your father is helping set the barricades. The old man told me to stay here and give you something." Sofia patted the brown leather satchel she carried on her.

Dashiel's attention traveled to the trees. He walked in circles, staring straight up into the tangled fresco. "No, no, no!"

"What the hell are you looking at?"

Hopelessness weighed his shoulders. "It didn't work?"

"What?"

"I was supposed to receive my heirloom, an object that could help save Azahar."

"Relax. I'm sure it will come down at any moment."

The chamber began to shake, and the roots slithered like serpents.

"Like I said . . ." Sofia gestured up.

One root untwined from the tangle, holding something. It stretched toward Dashiel and presented him with a gilded square box.

The first fenku's chamber shook again; the siege engine was the reason this time. The mineral's light dimmed, and some of the gigantic roots untwined and slammed against the ground.

"We'd better get back," Sofia said. "I don't want to be here when things fall apart!"

"Me neither."

Another root fell from the ceiling, nearly crushing Sofia. "Ugh, I'm starting to hate this place . . ."

She and Dashiel ran for it, evading the crushing roots and the tumbling book towers.

Back at Astor's library, Dashiel placed the box on the desk. With trembling fingers, he opened it and found a rather unusual item.

It was a golden cylinder a bit larger than a bullet.

Sofia grabbed the heirloom. She huffed. "All that trouble for this useless, cheap knickknack?"

"No, it has to be more than that. Remember what you once said to me?" Dashiel took the cylinder and enveloped it with his fingers. He thought of his epiphany and whispered, "Nothing is what it seems."

The cylinder lengthened, transforming into a rod. Intricate ornamentation and crystal pearls appeared on its surface, and its tips transfigured into golden flowers, petals unfolding regally.

"Why must you get all the cool stuff?" Sofia complained.

The mere sight of the heirloom filled Dashiel's mind with puzzlement. Usually the Azahar heirlooms represented the history of their respective families, but the object he held did not convey anything about the Ermitage family.

"What does it do?"

"I don't know." Dashiel moved his wrist to better see the rod. "Didn't you say Astor had given you something?"

"Yes, a book." Sofia took a book with a dull red paste out of the satchel. "He told me to read it once you were awake."

Dashiel recognized the book from when he used to work for the old man, back when he had first begun the job. It was a work in progress, and Dashiel, tempted by his curiosity, had leafed through it, earning a reprimand from crazy Old Astor.

Sofia moved through the pages. "He said page . . . one hundred and twelve!" Sofia found the right page.

"'The Cardinal Scepter, or the Key of Cardinalius, grants the bearer complete and total manipulation over the Cardinal Xielum.'" Sofia lowered the paper. "Cardinal Xielum? What the heck is a Cardinal Xielum?"

"I know. I read about it in the book that Sylvain gave me!" Dashiel snapped his fingers. "Xielum is an Egadrisean term for the mythological elements."

"The four mythological elements are air, fire, earth, and . . ."

"Water!" Dashiel shouted. "That's how we'll prevent the fire from destroying the forest, and I know the place to start. Let's go!"

Sofia did not move, her eyes glued to the book. "Wait!"

"What?"

"There's more." Sofia held the book closer to the candlelight. "'Beware of indiscriminate use of the Key of Cardinalius, as the price in blood might lead the bearer to death.'"

Sofia looked at Dashiel, silently asking him with her eyes if this was worth it.

He didn't need to consider. "There's no other way."

At the lake, the once-crystalline water rippled as the forest trembled. The crimson sky began to turn black, dangerous amounts of cinder filled the space, and the air was unbreathable. The only aspects of the landscape that remained unchanged were the waterfalls, which no longer cried of happiness but in dismay for their homeland.

"All right." Dashiel held tight to the scepter. "This is it! I hope this gives us an advantage."

"Fingers crossed," Sofia said. "And how do we lower the barrier?"

Dashiel frowned. "I didn't think about that."

"What? That's the most important part of the plan!"

"I know . . ." Dashiel assessed their options. "If only we had messenger droplets. I would send a message to my dad, asking him to lower the barrier with his flute, but I left mine at the palacette."

"Flute?"

"Yeah, it's connected to Gailfaur's powers. It can control the barrier."

Sofia rummaged inside her satchel until she found something. She took out a marble-crafted pan flute encrusted with precious stones. "You mean this?"

Dashiel was amazed to see Gailfaur's Flute in Sofia's hands. His father never allowed anyone who was not part of the Ermitage clan to touch it, let alone hold it.

"Where did you get that?"

"Your father gave it to me." Sofia offered him the instrument. "He said it could come in handy. Seems he was right."

Dashiel gently put his hand on the flute and pushed it back to her.

"I need you to do it." His hands trembled. "I don't know what the scepter might do, or if I am to survive after using it. The barrier has to be withdrawn at the right time, not a second too early nor a second too late."

He paused, the word *survive* repeating in his mind. "Sofia, promise me that no matter what happens to me, you will protect Sylvain and Athenai."

Sofia studied the flute for a moment, then studied Dashiel. He knew what she saw in his decisive stare: the expression he wore in that moment was the same one he'd had when he confronted her back in Hermesia. It was warm and compelling. "Count on me."

"Thank you. I want you to know that I couldn't have asked for a better teacher."

"Hey!" Sofia pointed at him. Her eyes glowed like two ardent torches. "You'll survive, Ermitage. I don't know how you do it, but you always do. We can talk about how great I am once this shit is done, all right?"

"Deal." Dashiel offered his hand, but Sofia hugged him instead.

"Hey, don't mention it. That's what friends are for." She gently punched his shoulder. "Because, like it or not, we are friends."

Dashiel nodded and turned to the cinder-covered lake. He held tightly to the scepter and walked to the water's edge. The mossy ground of the forest turned into uneven sand strewn with countless pebbles. He was afraid.

But he couldn't back down. Everyone he cared about was in danger. Sylvain had sacrificed so much for him. It was time for Dashiel to repay the debt.

He stepped into the warm lake. He walked until the water reached his knees, ashes from the burning barrier clinging to his clothes.

He raised the scepter and, in his mind, commanded the water to obey him. The scepter and Orphée bore certain similarities. Both of them seemed to be living entities. The difference was that while his doizemant's power level and disposition were closely bound to his, the scepter felt intrinsically powerful and was, with no doubt, more servient.

The water began to ripple. The ripples grew in intensity as the scepter began to change. Crystal materialized, forming gleaming tridents on both its tips. The water surrounded him, helixing upward. The pressure of the water increased. Something told him that it was going to get worse, and if that was so, it could throw him off-balance and end everything.

"Sofia!" he called, barely hearing his own voice. "Get ready!"

"What are you going to do?" she asked as the strong magic moved the water. "Are you sure you can control it?"

"All I can think of is rain," Dashiel said, planting his feet as hard as he could in the sand. "A single splash might extinguish the fire, but rain will prevent it from spreading."

The pressure of the water became unbearable. He could feel his body slowly tipping over, but he knew how to stay in place. He focused his thoughts and emotions, and in a matter of seconds, his force projection surrounded him, shielding him from the monstrous current.

A hurricane of water swirled into the sky, spreading over the forest.

"NOW!" He hoped his distorted voice could be heard from inside the water.

It seemed that Sofia blew the flute as loudly as her lungs allowed her, and its sound traveled to all corners of the forest. The burnt barrier began to disintegrate.

And then, for the first time in sixteen years, the barrier was no more.

By Dashiel's command, the water began to pour with triple the force, speed, and size of normal rain. When the droplets reached the ground, they slowly made their way back to the source to fall once again. The paradoxical rain, as Dashiel called it in his mind, would do the trick.

Before he could rejoin Sophia, a long-lost memory of a stormy night years ago overtook Dashiel's mind.

He lay on his bed, frightened as never before, thinking that the thunderclaps were the screams of ghosts. Sylvain sat on his bed and told Dashiel he was braver than he thought. His brother then read his favorite book in the whole world, a book of brave and wise kings, sorcerers, and warriors. He read to Dashiel until he fell asleep.

"Dashiel, Markeus's army is coming, and the barricades won't last long." Sofia approached the empty void, where the crystalline lake once was. "We need to help everyone."

Dashiel did not move. He stood there, holding the glowing scepter.

"Are you all right?"

He snapped out of his silent state. "I guess I am."

A tear rolled down his cheek.

"You're crying . . ."

Dashiel swiped the tear away. It was warm, unlike the cold rainwater. The warmth traveled across his body.

"I'm sorry. I was reminiscing." Dashiel walked dizzily toward Sofia. "I feel strange, but I'll be fine. It's time to go. Sylvain needs our help."

He placed the scepter in its holster and held Orphée with both hands.

"One more thing." Sofia opened her hand to reveal a silky sash.

"My sash? I mean, the one that used to be mine?"

"It *is* yours. Once a Phantasm, always a Phantasm. I don't give a damn what others say." Sofia placed the sash around his neck and tied it with a knot. "You are one of us."

Dashiel stood straight and saluted her. "Commander, waiting for an order."

Sofia tied her sash around her ponytail. "Let's show them the Ermine Squadron's true might."

"FOR SYLVAIN!"

The hill where the imperial military camp had been built had a privileged view of Azahar. The imperial battalions gazed in astonishment as the monstrous water swirl dominated the sky. The roaring flames that afflicted the edge of the forest were rapidly extinguished.

Oddly enough, the melodies that came from the prince's tent perfectly narrated the unfolding events.

General Indolett strode to the prince's luxurious tent, where Ettore, Markeus's lifelong assistant, guarded his master's solitude.

"I request an audience with His Highness," Indolett told Ettore.

Ettore went inside and nervously approached the lavish piano on which the prince fabricated intricate melodies. When behind the instrument, the prince resembled a siren, a radiant angel who was not afraid to send its victims to Charon.

"Sire?"

"What?" The prince did not take his attention off the keys. The music became more violent as the tempo quickened. "What do you want?"

"Sire, General Indolett is here to report."

The prince disregarded his attendant, continuing his cadenza.

"Sire, the report," Ettore insisted.

"*Sire, the report,*" Markeus mocked, caressing the keys into the end of the music. "Ettore, be useful and let him in."

Ettore did as he was told. The assistant and the general addressed Markeus's finale with a solemn applause.

"I'll see you tonight, my dear friend," he said to the piano, closing the fallboard. "You know that I am very good at celebrating."

Markeus left the instrument behind and stood before the general. "General?"

"I apologize for the interruption, Sire." Indolett bowed.

"No, no, it's fine. Inspiration had gone sour hours ago." Markeus allowed his assistant to button his shirt. "The report?"

"Your Highness, their barrier has been lowered, but that unholy rain is putting out the siege engine's fire. I have also been informed that they have built barricades. I commanded our cannon Brigadiers to position themselves in front of the aforementioned."

"Don't make it too easy, Indolett. I like challenges," Markeus said. "Those cowards better give it their best. Otherwise, it won't be as fun."

"What are your orders, Sire?"

"Bring me Swannagger's spherite." The prince put on a silk vest. "The siege engine has fulfilled its purpose."

"It shall be done, Sire. What about the attack?"

"It is time." Markeus's shaven features turned sullen. "General, tonight there will be no mercy. I want all their heads."

"As you wish." A macabre smirk grew on Indolett's scarred face.

Ettore slid Markeus's ochre jacket over his shoulders. The prince and the general made their way to the tent's exit. Moments later, they mounted their purebred horses and rode to the front of the imperial battalions.

"IT IS BY PROVIDENCE'S DECREE THAT WE GIVE THEM HELL!" the general roared to the countless rows of soldiers and metallic Brigadiers.

The men roared, and the bloodthirsty Brigadiers clanked their weaponry.

Markeus gave the signal.

"CHARGE!" Indolett's voice rang with the might of a hundred storms.

CHAPTER 40

THE BALLAD OF THE UNSUNG HEROES

Battalions of imperial soldiers and Ochre Brigadiers marched toward the forest. The Cobalt Phantasms braced themselves behind the barricades, and the Olivine Berets, hidden in the trees, prepared to rain their spear-long arrows down upon the incoming army.

"DRAW!" Elias shouted. "LOOSE!"

The Olivine Berets took deep breaths and shot their arrows into the oncoming threat. The arrows struck the enemies with the force of meteorites, impaling the soldiers. But they could do nothing against the Brigadiers, which used cannons and swords to destroy the barricades.

"Olivine Berets, retreat into the woods!" Elias ordered his men. "Regroup with the rest and take your positions!"

Elias went into the woods, leaving Roderigo and Oleiro, his fellow Phantasm master, to deal with the first wave of soldiers.

"Delvers, be swift!" Roderigo shouted as he ignited a firework rocket fuse.

Oleiro swung his mace, the spiked ball whizzing through the air. "Defiers, don't let your guard down!"

With a great whistling, the firework flew into the rainy sky and exploded in a blinding blue light. The defenders began to spill big cauldrons full of shrouder brew. Its smoke traveled quickly and concealed the forest's edge.

The barricades started to give in. In a matter of distressing minutes, they were breached, and the imperial forces entered the forest.

The Cobalt Phantasms followed their masters' commands. The Delvers used their ghost sashes to turn invisible and pricked the soldiers with venomous and somniferous needles, while the Defiers fenced off the enemies and threw hetona-venom bombs toward the Brigadiers.

The forest defense proved to be well-organized, but that did not stop the prince's forces from pushing deeper and deeper into the trees.

The battle for Azahar had begun.

Dashiel ran across the forest, aiding whoever seemed in need of help. Everywhere he turned, there was a battle going on.

On his way to Pistil Plaza, a Brigadier stood in his path. The metallic monster swung its flaming sword at him, but it missed, destroying the trail's torches.

Dashiel fended off the Brigadier's blows.

"Dashiel, behind you!" Someone dashed from the woods and sliced the Brigadier that had been creeping up behind Dashiel. The machine broke in two.

Dashiel was shocked when he realized who had saved him.

"Grimley!" He ran to his childhood friend.

"So happy to see you, Dashiel," Grimley said, smiling. "I missed you."

"I missed you, too, my friend." Dashiel lowered his head. "I'm so sorry about what happened. I never wanted you to go to the mines."

Grimley pushed his chin up.

"Hey, it wasn't your fault," Grimley said. "Look at us now. I've worked my way up to head of the miners, and you're on your way to becoming a custodian. I don't regret it, so neither should you."

Dashiel heart dropped at his friend's words. How was he to tell him about what had happened? About him breaking their promise, a promise that had made their friendship so special.

"You know, about that . . ."

From the woods, a new-model Brigadier charged them at high speed. The metallic foe began its attack.

"Don't worry, Dashiel," Grimley said. "I'll take care of this junk-head. Take cover."

With great agility, Grimley fought the Brigadier.

"Are you sure you don't need help?" Dashiel asked, hiding his baton from view.

"Nah." Grimley carved up the Brigadier with two pickaxes. He'd always been talented at single combat. In spite of the crisis that had come to Azahar, some things hadn't changed. "Enjoy the show!"

It was obvious that Grimley had trained hard, for his fighting technique was now flawless as he decapitated the Brigadier.

Two Brigadiers came to aid their fallen friend. Grimley tried his best to take them down, but they proved to be too much. The new models could repair themselves.

Grimley landed on one knee. "These things are getting stronger," he panted.

Dashiel couldn't take it any longer. He took Orphée out of hiding. He pounded the doizemant against the ground three times to turn into a mallet. He smashed it against the chest of the first Brigadier, causing it to fall. With his mallet, he destroyed its legs and arms beyond repair. Carrying all those rocks to the waterfall in Hermesia had increased strength. He could carry Orphée with no problem, something he could not do before his journey started.

He twisted Orphée, causing it to change into its dagger form. Dashiel moved with agility, as Sofia had taught him, climbing up the second Brigadier and stabbing his daggers into its chest. He chopped off the head, and the Brigadier came crashing to the ground.

"Wow!" Grimley's mouth was wide open. "Where did you learn that?"

"Well, I . . ."

"Can't believe the things a custodian learns. It's almost as if you—"

Dashiel couldn't answer. He stood there with Brigadier oils dripping from his hair, weapon, and sash.

"Oh." Grimley's face saddened. "I understand."

Dashiel's heart dropped. Did his friend know about him training in the Outerland? Or did he suspect nothing? Was Grimley hurt by Dashiel's broken promise, or was his pride wounded by Dashiel saving him once more?

"Dashiel." Grimley grabbed up his pickaxes. "I'm happy to see you again. Let's get them the hell out of our home."

Grimley kicked off into the woods.

"Wait," Dashiel called, but Grimley had already disappeared from view. "I need to tell you something!"

Dashiel was devoured by remorse. Grimley deserved to become a Cobalt Phantasm as much as he had, perhaps even more. He did have some explaining to do, but Azahar needed to be saved first.

The magical rain poured as the blazes of war spread to the uncultivated fields of Sepal Plaza, where Elias and his men fought off hundreds of imperial soldiers at a time.

Charlotte Malanks shielded herself with her musket. "Elias! They're too many!" she whined, shooting an oncoming soldier right in the gut.

"Reinforcements are on their way." Elias clashed his saber against an enemy weapon.

"HELP IS NEEDER, BROOTHA!" Rupert roared as he grabbed two soldiers, crashed their bodies together, and used them as nunchucks.

"Let me try something!" Elias said.

He whistled a tune and waited, but nothing happened. He evaded an attack and whistled again. This time, Elias's single whistle was joined by hundreds of different sounds coming from the woods.

As soldiers marched across Azahar, they would find themselves in awe of the natural orchestra. They would not expect that an army of lion-tailed elves, gnomes, and other creatures would come out of hiding and join the Azahar forces. Most of the mystical creatures in Azahar were peaceful and tried not to leave the sacred terrains, but— like the humans—they had come together to fight off the menace.

Azahar's creatures played all kinds of tricks. They deafened the soldiers by banging their metal pans and flutes and tripped the marching army with fenku branches, stealing their weapons in the process.

Their intervention gave the Azahar some relief, but waves of soldiers and Brigadiers kept on coming. The Brigadiers shot their cannonballs at the town's buildings, destroying them.

"Well, well." Samuel Indolett approached Elias. "If it isn't the Belecroses' most loyal general."

Indolett gave Elias a grisly smile.

"Samuel Indolett. What an absolutely disgusting surprise."

"A surprise indeed. I thought we had gotten rid of all the Belecrose generals years ago." Indolett's lips twisted in delight. "I'm truly surprised that Rafael Belecrose's lapdog was hiding here all along."

"You would know something about that, wouldn't you, Indolett? You're still sitting on Asedia's lap."

Both men drew their sabers. The metal clashed and clanged.

"Oh, you've really let yourself go," Indolett said, laughing.

"And you've gone bald."

Dashiel found himself surrounded by dozens of imperial soldiers. He fought off as many as he could, but they kept coming. Dashiel twirled his baton, shielding himself from countless bullets. Everyone else had their hands full. He was on his own and in trouble.

Suddenly, a howling rang out, and it was as loud as a train whistle. From the rainy, dark depths of the woods, a creature slowly approached. A sisyphus wolf. Its claws and snout were longer than they should have been, and it was twice as big as usual. Its formerly white coat had been covered in dirt and dyed red.

They were in the presence of the sisyphus alpha male.

Dashiel and the imperial soldiers froze in place as they witnessed something terrifying. From between the trees, more wolves joined their leader in a howling chorus.

To Dashiel's surprise, the wolves went straight for the forest's enemies, leaving him intact—an undeniable sign that Sylvain's health was improving.

The wolves that did not shred the soldiers with their needle-sharp fangs burrowed into the ground. When the soldiers least expected it, the wolves punched through the forest floor with their translucent claws and pulled the soldiers belowground with them.

With the help of the sisyphus wolves, Dashiel did not take long to knock down the remaining soldiers. When the last foe fell, the wolves howled and took off into the forest. The alpha, however, remained.

The enormous creature stared at Dashiel with its red-hot eyes. Something about those eyes baffled him.

Another memory came to him.

Many years ago, Sylvain brought an orphaned sisyphus cub to the house. The cub was injured and weak, so his brother convinced their parents to let him stay, at least until he was well enough to get by. Dashiel remembered how Sylvain took care of the cub, which stuck by his side. Sylvain had the ability to make those around him feel safe.

Dashiel finally understood that the wolf in front of him was the same injured cub Sylvain had rescued.

"He is going to be fine. We'll protect him." Dashiel spoke to the wolf as if it were a long-lost friend. "Together."

The alpha barked at him, then opened its enormous snout and began to drool.

"You want me to take some of your saliva to Sylvain?"

The wolf huffed, the viscous saliva falling to the ground. Dashiel quickly unclasped a bags from his utility belt and filled it with the saliva.

Once Dashiel had collected enough, the wolf barked and sprinted off.

"Thank you!"

On the southern slopes of the forest, Azahar of all backgrounds worked together to keep the enemy away from Petal Plaza. Crazy Old Astor, Sofia, and her brethren all fought side by side.

Sofia used her hooks to grab the enemies and send them to Astor, who crushed their skulls with his cane. Arson punched soldiers to the ground, and Mina used her powers to wrap them with the fenku branches.

As Azahar improved, some of the fenku began to raise their branches off the ground and whip the invaders. The imperial soldiers tried to attack the trees, which threw them out of the forest.

Seeing the trees as potential enemies, the Brigadiers chopped and blasted them with their ardent swords and cannons.

A Brigadier prepared to shoot a tree down, but Sofia was quick to insert a hetona venom bomb inside its muzzle. The metal soldier exploded, tumbling on top of imperial soldiers.

Everyone turned their efforts toward protecting the fenku.

The lumberjacks fenced off incoming soldiers, while the miners, using their pickaxes, distracted the metallic monsters long enough for the Phantasms to climb up their necks and inject them with Octa-pus ink, coagulating their oils and leaving them useless.

The energized fenku dismembered the immobilized Ochre Brigadiers and shot their pieces at other soldiers and Brigadiers.

Dashiel arrived at one of the trails where some Azahar guards were fighting off an advancing wave of soldiers. They had the help of a vexed herd of jukkes, Azahar's aquatic deer, which rampaged up and down the trail. The jukkes' tails and fins swept the soldiers off their feet, and their razor-sharp antlers impaled them.

As the fourth wave of soldiers was defeated, an Olivine Beret came running down the trail. "Sepal Plaza is falling! We have to go there right away."

"Impossible," the leader of the guards said. "The enemy is advancing to the clearings. We must stay and defend this trail so they cannot enter the sacred terrains."

"Go." Dashiel placed himself in front of the Olivine Berets. "They need as much help as they can get. I'll take care of these." He gestured to the enemies.

The guards stared at Dashiel in disbelief. Like everyone else in Azahar, they had always considered him one of the weakest members of their town.

"Are you sure, Ermitage?" one of them asked. "You don't stand a chance by yourself."

"If the council falls, we are all doomed." Dashiel spoke with confidence. "Leave this to me."

"All right," the leader of the guards said. "Attention! We march to Sepal Plaza. *Now!*"

The Olivine Berets marched into the woods.

"Good luck, young Ermitage," the guard said. "You'll need it."

Dashiel held tight to Orphée and made his way north, where the clearings and sacred terrains awaited.

CHAPTER 41

WHAT MAKES A DOIZEMASTER

The forest clearings were the entrance to the sacred terrains. Known as the most dangerous part of the forest, the northern woods were the densest and the darkest, containing the largest concentration of fenku, whose entwined branches prevented light from seeping in. This darkness used to serve as the hallowed ground's first line of defense, but no more; the vast majority of the fenku were still unresponsive. The hurricane that Dashiel had summoned blocked the sun, but that did not stop its dying rays from slipping into the forest and bathing Azahar in a short-lived, grayish light.

Even though the clearings were visible, they overflowed with a different kind of eeriness. The constant rain had altered all colors and softened the ground to mud. Dashiel remained on his toes, watchful of any change or movement.

"Me and my big mouth," he muttered to himself.

The Olivine Beret had told him that imperial forces were on their way to the clearings, but there was not a single person or machine in sight. The battle for Azahar was taking place everywhere else except for this area.

He had to go back.

Dashiel was about to leave the clearing when a mirage appeared before him. Athenai. Her wet hair was messy, and her once-white clothes were stained with the blood of others, but her beauty remained intact.

Her serene face frowned at the mere sight of him.

"What are you doing here?" he asked in a soft tone. "It's dangerous."

"I can take care of myself, thank you." She passed by him, searching for something on the ground. Her vanilla fragrance had almost disappeared.

Dashiel felt like he'd received a punch in the gut. For a brief moment, the adamant rain pricked his skin mercilessly.

"How's Sylvain?" He inched closer, leaving a trail of mud behind.

Obviously she did not want to talk to him, but she was not so cold-hearted as to leave him worried.

"He's woken up. His burns are no longer spreading, but they are still a danger to his life." Athenai's cold tone gave him chills. "I decided to come find an ingredient that could help him."

"Well, I managed to find some sisyphus wolf saliva," Dashiel said timidly.

"You did?"

"Yes." He offered the bag viscous fluid to her.

"Thank you." Athenai took the bag. Her eyes avoided his. "Well, I'd better go back . . ."

Athenai walked away.

"You were right!" Dashiel's throat began closing on him. "I-I will always live to regret my words."

Athenai stopped. "I have nothing else to say."

"But I do."

She stared at him, pain in her eyes.

"Athenai, please forgive me," Dashiel began. "I was an idiot. I was a fool for not trusting you. If I could travel back in time, I would beat myself over and over. Our relationship was the most wonderful thing that had ever happened in my life, and I blew it, like the stupid child I am."

Beneath the pounding rain, the clearing was silent.

"Please believe me. Please, you have to—"

Athenai's fingers landed on his lips. "Sylvain told me everything."

"Everything?"

"Yes," she whispered. "About his plan, about the letters, about . . ." She adopted a bitter expression. "Junei."

Dashiel closed his eyes and let go of all the air stored in his chest.

"But even though it was Sylvain and Junei's scheme to break us apart, I expected you to act differently." She placed her hand over her chest.

"I know . . . I was a complete imbecile," he whispered.

Their eyes finally met. Dashiel felt as if it had been an eternity since she had looked at him. Her eyes no longer reflected pain and anger, but exhaustion.

"Now is not the time. We'll talk later," she said, giving a hint of a smile. "We must hurry. Sylvain is healing, and the invaders must be out before he can cast another barrier."

"Am I interrupting a tender moment?" The cold voice echoed from all directions.

"Who's there?!" Dashiel called.

"I see that the Alferai are helping the empire's enemies," the voice said. "Such treason will be paid for in blood."

"Show yourself!" Dashiel walked around Athenai, guarding her from any incoming danger.

"But all in due time . . ." From the darkness of the woods, a beastly silhouette appeared. As it stepped out from the darkness, it took the form of a man. "First, I have to deal with the vermin."

Markeus Asedia stepped into the clearing, his uniform drenched from the rain.

"You!" Dashiel gasped as he pointed Orphée at his foe. "You and your army, leave the forest!"

"No can do, peasant. As picturesque as this forest may be, the empire has plans for it."

The prince gestured toward Dashiel's weapon. "So, you are the doizemant master I faced back in Hermesia. How fortuitous."

He came closer.

"You aren't as impressive without the mask. Those freckles! I can't even take you seriously." Markeus cackled.

Dashiel took Athenai's hand and placed the Cardinal Scepter in it.

"Go on and take this." He closed her porcelain hand around the staff. "Please protect it. Go now."

Athenai tried to run into the forest, but guards fenced her in.

"I'm afraid I cannot let you leave." With a snap of Markeus's fingers, soldiers closed in on Athenai. "Hand over that scepter, and I'll forget your trespass and relieve the palacette from any blame."

The guards drew their weapons.

"You have me mistaken, sir." Athenai's hand gathered violet light, and with a twist of her wrist, a ball of light cleared two of the soldiers out of her way. She sprinted down the muddy path.

"Follow her!" Markeus roared.

One of the soldiers stayed behind. "But, sir—"

"I gave you an order!" Markeus huffed. "Get me that scepter, idiot!"

The guards ran into the woods, leaving the two rivals alone.

There they were once again: facing each other, surrounded by chaos. Markeus's eyes shone with hatred and rage, while Dashiel's eyes undoubtedly reflected his innermost desire to protect what was precious to him.

"Tonight, you will die by my hand," Markeus said as he and Dashiel circled each other. "Then I shall eliminate your precious Alferai, this forest, and the vermin that live in it."

He took out his pistol and aimed it at Dashiel.

"What? You're going to shoot me?" Dashiel scoffed. "How honorable of you."

"What do you know of honor? You are just peasant scum who has taken advantage of the cowardly protection of this nauseating place."

"I'd rather be peasant scum than sell my life away to a tyrant."

Markeus gave a grim smirk as he threw his pistol into the mud, losing it forever. "For you, I have a more appropriate weapon."

With a snap of his fingers, a scrap of rusty metal appeared in his hand.

Dashiel was shocked by the sight of an object he knew very well. How had Markeus ever managed to acquire such a virtuous item?

"A doizemant?"

"Right," the prince answered. "But unlike yours, this one is dead, harmless. My father ripped its wielder's heart out, killing her and the doizemant at the same time."

Markeus took the weapon and cut his hand. From his palm, a bluish-silver fluid emerged. His blood dripped over the rusty surface. Drops of the blue blood landed on the ground, and at first contact, the grass grew three times its size. The prince smeared his face, shoulder, and arm with his blood.

Dashiel couldn't believe his eyes. His mind went berserk. "Is that . . . Belecrose blood?" It was the all-powerful sign of the fallen dynasty he had heard so much about. He had to be cautious.

The doizemant began to rumble. Its rust disappeared and darkened as it morphed. The metal melted and took over everything that the mystical blood bathed. Part of the prince's face disappeared behind a demonic black mask. His shoulder and arm were replaced by a long, twisted blade. Most of his body was under the protection of kerganium armor. The rarest weapon and the rarest blood had forged the most powerful warrior in the world.

With a slash of his doizemant, Markeus chopped down a tree that a hundred saws would not have been able to cut through.

"Or maybe it's not quite dead." Markeus took an offensive pose. "Behold a true doizemaster! I am the most powerful weapon ever created! By the end of the night, you'll die, and Azahar will finally belong to the empire."

The two doizemants clashed with force. Dashiel had managed to fight off this rival before, but Markeus's new weapon made him stronger. He knew it was a matter of time before his doizemant gave in to the ungodly power it faced.

As they battled, Dashiel's mind grew restless, trying to figure out a way to defeat such power. He thought of using his Phantasm sash to turn himself invisible, but his doizemant, which could not disappear, and the mud would give him away. His only option was to attack directly and hope for the best.

Dashiel tried both his mallet and daggers, but Markeus counteracted them.

With a kick of Markeus's boot, Dashiel was thrown to the ground, losing his baton in the mud puddles.

"Not so strong without your baton, eh, peasant?"

Dashiel searched around him, but his doizemant was nowhere to be found. Markeus kicked him in the face, plunging him into the mud. The prince raised the sword over his head. "If you will not bow before a monarch, you will die before a god!"

Dashiel tried to project his shield, but to no avail. His sight was blurry, and his bewildered thoughts twisted reality.

The sword began its deadly journey, ending with a sonorous thump.

Dashiel's mind went blank, and sparks of color appeared—his memories of the people in his life. Sylvain reading his favorite book before bedtime. His parents sitting with him on the rooftop, watching the starry night. Athenai's warm lips touching his.

Dashiel opened his eyes, ready to see his battered body lying on the ground, his soul finally resting in afterlife bliss. He looked up into his paradoxical rain. He took a moment to probe his surroundings. His body slowly sank into the cold mud. The humid grass tickled his right hand, and the smoky smell of his clothes taunted his nose. He opened his gasping mouth. The water that landed on his lips had a bitter taste.

Life had not abandoned him, but how?

When he angled his head, he noticed his arm in front of him, a defense reflex. A slithering vine had wrapped around his forearm and part of Markeus's blade. The prince was trying to set his weapon free, but it held.

The vine was thick yet mostly smooth, its cutting thorns skimming Dashiel's skin. It slithered until a bud came into view. The bud opened, showing its brilliant scarlet petals and shiny blue eyes.

"Amore!" Dashiel exclaimed. "You've saved me."

The flower chirped at him, shaking water droplets off her petals.

"What is the meaning of this?" The prince tugged at his sword with all his strength. "Release it at once!"

"It's too dangerous," Dashiel said to his savior, trying to convince her to go to safety, but she did not listen. She held on tight to his arm and chirped.

The flower unwrapped the dark doizemant, setting the prince free to continue his attack. "Very well . . . It's you and me now."

The duel proceeded.

Since he didn't have his baton, Dashiel used his sash to turn himself and Amore invisible. As he had thought, the mud gave him away, but at least he had enough time to avoid the attacks.

One by one, the clearing's fenku came back to life and wrapped the prince in their elastic branches. The trees gave Dashiel time to catch his breath as Markeus chopped himself free.

Dashiel barely avoided a slash that would have chopped off his head. And still his doizemant was nowhere to be found. By now, it was likely buried deep within a puddle of mud. Dashiel used all the defensive techniques he had learned from his mentors, but he had to find his baton if he wanted a chance to survive.

Enraged, Markeus went after Dashiel at full speed and force.

With a slash, the enemy doizemant struck down another tree. Dashiel's options were running out. He would need to find his weapon, or he would be next to taste the edge of that sword.

The prince slashed more trees, which fell to the ground. One of them landed in the mud, revealing a part of Dashiel's doizemant.

Dashiel rolled away from another attack and aimed his vine-wrapped arm at the weapon. "Amore?" The flower stretched her vine and grappled with the doizemant, bringing it back to him in time to parry another strike from the prince.

The doizemants clashed with painful clanks. The rain came and went, losing strength as the magical hurricane shrank.

The duel moved from clearing to clearing. Before they knew it, they were in Gailfaur's clearing, the entrance to the sacred terrains.

Dashiel found himself retreating until his back hit a hard surface. A rock. He stood in the same place his journey had begun.

"Can't you comprehend? I am absolute!" Seeing his opportunity, Markeus charged, but Dashiel was quick to react, sending Amore to seize a fenku tree. Dashiel moved out of the way, and Markeus's doizemant pierced the rock.

The prince tried to free his weapon from the rock, but it didn't budge. Seeing his chance, Dashiel bounced from the fenku. Little did he know that, on his way down, his baton would transform into a sword. Dashiel slammed Markeus's doizemant with the newly formed sword, the weapons emitting an ear-splitting sound that traversed the forest.

In the aftermath of the clash, silence filled the battleground, and the paradoxical rain seemed to freeze.

Markeus used his strength to free his weapon, smashing the rock to smithereens. The godly weapon had resisted the final hit Dashiel could offer. Markeus stared at Dashiel with demonic eyes. One last slash, and his nemesis would be no more.

The prince's expression changed when his doizemant-fused arm refused to obey his commands. He tried to swing his sword, but it merely fell to the ground.

"Work, you stupid thing!"

Markeus's doizemaster armor and weapon began to rust and crack. Piece by piece, the kerganium abandoned his body. Soon enough, the most powerful weapon on earth and the prince's victory were reduced to dust.

"Care to surrender?" Dashiel pointed his sword at the prince.

"How?" Markeus asked, kneeling, splashing mud with his fist. "It was supposed to be indestructible. I was supposed to be a god! How did your puny little baton manage to defeat me?" He barely managed to stand up.

"To wield a doizemant, one must learn an important lesson, Your Highness." Dashiel kept his weapon pointed at his rival. "It doesn't matter if you are small or weak. As long as you dwell on kindness, justice, and your bonds with others, your doizemant can defeat even a god. Nothing is what it seems."

"Spare me the lecture," Markeus replied, holding his wounded arm. "Keep fighting. Don't stop. Finish me now, if you're man enough!"

"No."

"No?" The prince clenched his fists. "I damaged your home beyond repair. I killed many who you care about. You must feel anger, hatred toward me."

"You are the most talented warrior I've ever dueled against, but you are just like an Ochre Brigadier. An empty, cold, and unfeeling pawn to Asedia's hatred."

Surprisingly, Dashiel's heart empathized with the prince.

"I don't hate you. I pity you and the loneliness you've been plunged into." Dashiel took a step forward. "No one has ever truly loved you. Am I wrong?"

Dashiel's words pierced through the prince's mind and soul.

"I've never been lonely in my life, because I don't need anyone but myself." Markeus spat as he stood up. "I hate you!"

He took out King Beckel's fire spherite, creating a raging barrier of fire with it.

"We shall meet again, doizemant bearer," he called through the burning wall, his voice echoing ominously. "And I swear upon this cursed land that next time, your blood will run down my blade!"

As the divine rain extinguished the final flames from the forest, Dashiel found that the prince had escaped.

CHAPTER 42

VENOUS REVELATION

An imperial drum line called Asedia's soldiers back. Whether marching, running, or thrown out by the fenku, they left the forest with the taste of defeat in their mouths.

Azahar, aided by the Cobalt Phantasms, finally tasted victory.

A wave of green light, emitted from the Ermitage household, traveled at a great velocity. It froze at the edge of the forest and expanded, once again shielding the forest from its enemies.

The paradoxical rain had stopped, and the sunrays shone with renewed beauty. The battle had been tough, but it was over.

The air was warm and humid. Dashiel lay on the ground in the clearing, his hair gliding over a pool of mud, oil, and flowers. He heard the singing of birds, the rustling of leaves, and the sighing sounds of Amore as she rested, curled on his arm and leaning against his neck.

The reenergized fenku trees entwined their branches once more, filtering light that landed on the ground like shattered glass. One shard of light landed on Dashiel's face. He recalled the copper doorknob that guarded his father's den, which had become as green as the moss growing in the windowsills. Fading memories resurrected once more. A lonely child grappled with the greening doorknob, wishing with all his might for friends, strength, and adventure. The memories faded as quickly as they came. Only three words remained inside his head: *friends, strength*, and *adventure*.

The first word faded into an image of all his friends. Grimley and Donner had taught him to dream beyond barriers. Audric Swannagger had taught him to be true to himself. His fellow Cobalt Phantasms had taught him to persevere. Sofia Spaigne, who had become one of his truest friends, had taught him to never give up on anyone.

Dashiel gathered his remaining strength and stood.

The second fading word helped him realized that leaving the forest and joining the Cobalt Phantasms had not made him any stronger. He'd found strength when he humbled himself before his doizemant. He'd found strength when he guarded a tiny sprout from the whole world, and he'd found strength when he shared a kiss with Athenai on a cold winter's night.

Dashiel panted as he wandered onto the trail in front of him.

The last word faded from his mind for good. Dashiel had explored, battled ferocious enemies, and gained glory, but those things did not matter.

Sylvain, his brother, was the greatest adventure in his heart.

Dashiel limped down the slippery trail, stepping over slashed torches and rusting sabers and pistols. The fight with Markeus and the use of the Key of Cardinalius had left him sore and exhausted. He wanted to go back home and rejoin his friends and family. He wanted to see his brother. He wanted to talk to Athenai. There were so many things he ought to do, but all he could do was walk, hoping his feet would carry him.

Dried mud and machine oil hardened his face and body. Sweat rolled down his forehead.

He savored his surroundings: The braided fenku overhead. The rejuvenated lucium spirits that were healing the damaged flora and fauna. The breathtaking Azahar spring afternoon. For the first time in forever, Dashiel smiled at the mere thought of being part of such routine beauty.

As he approached the end of the trail, Dashiel heard singing and laughing. The Azahar and the Cobalt Phantasms rejoiced. They had earned it, for they had accomplished the impossible.

Dashiel arrived at the main plaza. Unable to hold himself up, he collapsed to his knees.

"Dashiel!" Sofia's voice stood out from the crowd. She put his arm around her shoulders and lifted him up. "It's over. We did it!"

"Thank you, Commander," he said, smiling, trying to hide how painful it was to be awake in that moment. "How's Sylvain?"

"He's much better. He's resting, and so should you, soldier."

From the crowd, a red-cheeked Roderigo emerged. He stopped before them.

"Master, are there any more threats?" Dashiel asked.

"Not anymore, my boy." Roderigo saluted him, pride in his eyes. "You made it possible, Son. We all did."

The founding master raised his hands, triggering a vigorous cheer.

"Very well," Dashiel responded. He would've collapsed if it hadn't been for his friend's support.

From the crowd, Athenai came forward, holding the scepter. She didn't say a word. She smiled at him, clearly relieved to see him there in front of her.

Dashiel tried to stand up as straight as he could. He wanted to tell her how much he loved her. But it wasn't possible. He'd spent the last of his energy on the walk to town.

Athenai's face, like everyone else's, went pale. The scepter escaped from her hands and thumped the dew-covered, mossy ground.

The townspeople murmured. They stepped forward and then retreated backward.

"Dashiel?" Athenai whispered.

Confused, he turned his head to Sofia. What had changed? Why was everyone behaving so strangely?

"You're bleeding . . ." Sofia looked not at his eyes but at his forehead. Her body trembled.

What he'd thought was sweat from the hot, humid day was blood. Blood from a wound that Markeus had inflicted during their fight. It was no mystery what had happened. He'd stopped taking the pills that Sylvain had given him some time ago, and their effect had worn off. His skin, no longer as strong as armor, bled like everyone else's.

"I can explain," he said with much difficulty, but no one listened. "If I had told you about my hemocarcomia, I wouldn't have been able to join you. Please forgive me . . ."

"Oh, child," Roderigo said, "the blood of a hemocarcomist is dull gray."

Roderigo's voice was barely above a whisper. He brushed off some of Dashiel's blood with his fingers. His shook as his fingers caught the sunlight.

"Your blood is blue, Dashiel. Cobalt blue."

ABOUT THE AUTHOR

TONY M. QUINTANA may be a new face on the scene, but he's been a longtime fan of fantasy stories. Now, he creates fresh and unique tales featuring original plots, immersive dialogue, and relatable characters that anyone can enjoy, inspired by his lifelong interest in the history of European monarchies. The result is innovative work in the fantasy genre, which he hopes will promote the values of kindness, service, and self-worth and the importance of environmental preservation. Born in Cancun, Mexico, Tony earned his bachelor's degree in Texas. When he's not writing, he loves to travel around the world and explore new cultures from which he then draws inspiration.